Trick or Treats

Trick or Treats

EDITED BY
LORI PERKINS

BLACK
LACE

1 3 5 7 9 10 8 6 4 2

First published in the US by Ravenous Romance as *Famgbangers* (2010) and
Slave to Love (2013)

First published in the United Kingdom in 2013 by Black Lace Books,
an imprint of Ebury Publishing
A Random House Group Company
Copyright © Ravenous Romance

The authors have asserted their right under the Copyright, Designs and
Patents Act 1988 to be identified as the authors of this work.

These stories are works of fiction. Names and characters are the
product of the authors' imaginations and any resemblance to actual persons,
living or dead, is entirely coincidental

All rights reserved. No part of this publication may be reproduced, stored in
a retrieval system, or transmitted in any form or by any means, electronic,
mechanical, photocopying, recording or otherwise, without the prior
permission of the copyright owner
The Random House Group Limited Reg. No. 954009

Addresses for companies within the Random House Group can be found at
www.randomhouse.co.uk

A CIP catalogue record for this book is available from the British Library

The Random House Group Limited supports the Forest Stewardship
Council® (FSC®), the leading international forest-certification organisation.
Our books carrying the FSC label are printed on FSC®-certified paper.
FSC is the only forest-certification scheme supported by the leading
environmental organisations, including Greenpeace.
Our paper procurement policy can be found at:
www.randomhouse.co.uk/environment

Printed and bound by CPI Group (UK) Ltd, Croydon, CR0 4YY

ISBN: 9780352346858
To buy books by your favourite authors and register for offers, visit:
www.blacklace.co.uk

Contents

Forbidden Pleasures

By Rebecca Leigh

Even from the great distance between them, Marcus Valiant could smell her blood.

The wind whipped wildly around his body. His long blond hair thrashed against his face and shoulders and his black trench coat beat violently against his legs. Despite the ferocity of the passing storm, Marcus stood motionless, stalwart against the tempest. There was no doubt he could withstand the forces of Mother Nature. But Marcus was doubtful he could withstand the allure of Juliet Jackson much longer. The scent of her blood was the most enticing aroma he'd encountered in over seven hundred years. Her blood called to him; it enslaved him.

From his vantage point at the summit of the mountain, he could see her. She stalked the night, like him, a predator seeking her prey. She moved with erotic grace through the thick overgrowth of the forest below him, weaving in and out of the trees, silent and agile.

Like the rest of her kind, Juliet only hunted at night. Choosing to feed under the cloak of the protective darkness. Marcus had come here to find sanctuary on this lonely cliff, unaware that tonight this would be her chosen hunting ground.

Damn the coincidence.

He watched as she hid behind an outcropping of rock on the side of the mountain, concealed from the view, invisible to her prey. But she was not invisible to Marcus. He could always see her, always find her. Her scent was too powerful for him to ignore.

He felt himself lurch forward as she stalked her prey, following the wild boar deeper into the cover of the jungle. She closed in on the creature quickly, making no sound, even when her paws contacted with the dried leaves and twigs of the underbrush. Marcus watched as she pounced and sank her teeth ruthlessly into the animal's neck. He tensed when the creature squirmed and weakened under Juliet's grip. He moaned when she bit the boar's throat, tearing at the meat, blood pouring freely into her mouth.

The frenzied spectacle nearly brought Marcus to orgasm. He felt his cock pulse inside his skin-tight jeans. He threw his head back and growled.

He wanted to taste Juliet. He needed to drink from her. But he also craved more than her blood. Much more. Marcus longed to thrust his cock deep inside her; hear her scream in delight as he massaged her clit and made her come. Marcus needed to possess her, to take her as his mate.

Her kill complete, Juliet moved once again through the dark forest. Marcus continued his vigil. Each time she would pass from beneath the tangled canopy, her silver hair would catch the light of the full moon and shine in the dark night. Her beauty was unsurpassed. Her power inescapable. Her appeal undeniable.

Marcus could think of nothing more tempting than a female silver panther, hot and wet from her most recent slaughter.

The moon's glow reflected in his dark eyes, signaling his hunger. His passion. At the mere sight of her, his mouth watered and his loins pulsed.

Forbidden.

Juliet was forbidden to him. Centuries of law stood between him and the only woman he'd ever wanted with this much intensity. The elder vampires did not take kindly to disobedience, especially defiance of one of their most sacred laws: Never mate with a shifter. If any of his kind was found to have violated the law, the punishment was immediate. Execution. He'd known others that had suffered the fate of being strung out upon a cross and left alone to face the rising sun.

But even the fear of death could not compete with the passion welling inside Marcus as he watched Juliet disappear into the distance.

He breathed deeply, one last smell of her forbidden fragrance before taking flight. He could no longer deny his desire. He would have Juliet as his lover, law be damned.

He knew where she would go after her kill. Juliet had a predictable routine, one he'd memorized in his obsession to learn everything about the woman who had ensnared his every thought. Even before he realized she was a shifter, before he knew she was forbidden, he'd been unable to get enough of her. He'd kept an eye on her, learned her every move.

Tonight was Friday. So Juliet, the woman, was on her way to the Overstreet Bar. It was the only pub open to non-humans in this small town nestled at the foot of the Rockies.

Panthers rarely traveled in their shifted form, so Marcus was able to get to the bar much more quickly than Juliet. He found a table in the darkest corner of the tavern, sat, and waited.

Wanted.

When Juliet finally arrived, she wore a tight top cut low enough that Marcus could see the swell of her voluptuous breasts peeking above the black lace. The shirt's hem stopped just above her ribcage, leaving her midriff completely exposed. Her short black leather skirt hugged her thighs. And her spiked heels accentuated her long, powerful legs. All Marcus could think about was ripping off her clothes and ravaging her.

Even in her human form, Juliet moved like a cat, sleek and confident, to the bar. She stood with her back against the smooth wood, resting on her forearms. She ordered a drink and turned her attention to the dance floor. She was hunting again, not for nourishment this time but for excitement.

Marcus decided to give it to her.

He moved to the bar. When he stood next to her, he pushed his arm roughly against her shoulder as he picked up his beer, knocking her off balance.

"Excuse you," he said, his voice brusque. He knew he

was taking a chance with this approach, but he also knew that the panther in Juliet would be hard-pressed to ignore the impression of dominance in his discourteous behavior.

"Excuse *me*?" She swung around and glared at him. "Excuse you, asshole."

She turned back toward the dance floor, but didn't move away. In fact, he felt a slight shift in the air when she curved ever so slightly closer to him.

"Have you been stood up?" This time he made sure that his voice was husky, lustful.

"Hardly," she laughed. "I'm on the prowl."

"Indeed." He moved his lips so that his breath spread across her face and neck, seducing her with a single word.

"Perhaps my hunt has come to an end," she purred and inched even closer to him.

He felt her nipple, hard and taut, brush against his arm through the thin laced material of her top and lost all self-control. He grabbed her and swung her around so that they faced one another, their lips barely an inch apart.

"You're a naughty little kitty, aren't you?"

Juliet didn't say a word. She stood up. Marcus stared at her with a fiery intensity, awaiting her next move.

His cock nearly jumped out of his jeans when Juliet began to slither in a seductive dance in front of him. He could feel his penis thicken and pulse with each provocative curve of her luscious form. His shaft pushed painfully against the inside of his zipper. He reached his hand down to calm the aching.

Marcus rubbed himself through the taut fabric. Juliet's eyes skated down his body and watched Marcus touch himself. She licked her lips and slid her hands up her sides to her breasts, giving them each a sensual squeeze.

Her breasts looked like they were going to spill from the skimpy top. Marcus's heart thundered. His arousal was mounting to a near uncontrollable level. His breath hitched and his fangs extended.

"You're a vamp?" Most shifters failed to develop their ability to sense other non-human creatures, so her question didn't surprise him. What did surprise Marcus was that the way she said the word *vamp* was full of lust. Marcus found himself excited even more that she didn't care he was not one of her own kind.

He tried to answer, but the only sound he could make was a strangled growl. His eyes glowed red when she hitched up her skirt and glided her own hand between her legs.

Her already magnetic scent was heightened by the smell of her arousal as she caressed herself. Inside him, all hell broke lose when she pulled her hand back up and let him smell her fingers.

"Good kitty," he hissed, grabbing her by the waist and pulling her savagely to him. Her body molded to his and she continued her sinuous dance.

Up and down the length of his body, she moved. Her breasts smoothed over his taut chest and abs. Her hands glided down his thighs. To finally feel her body against his caused a violent tremor to spread down Marcus's spine. He threw his head back and let loose a low, feral growl. Every cell inside him screamed for her.

"Are you a good vamp?" she asked, then grabbed his cock and squeezed. "Or a bad vamp?"

"If I'm bad, will you punish me, kitty?"

"Oh yes," she said and slid her hand over his jean-clad shaft.

"Let's get out of here." Marcus meant it as a command rather than a question. The alternative would be throwing Juliet down on the dance floor, ripping off her clothes, and fucking her in front of the human crowd. Not that he'd mind an audience, but the spectacle wouldn't be an average sex scene. After all, they both had fangs. And Marcus intended to use his.

Juliet purred in response, a deep throaty sound that made Marcus's blood boil. He hitched her lithe frame onto his hips and carried her from the bar. She clung to him, her face nuzzled against his neck. Her sex grinded against his waist and her nails dug into his back when he took flight.

She licked his ear and whispered, "Where are we going?"

"My lair."

He flew through the open window of his apartment and sprawled her onto his bed as they landed.

"That was exhilarating!" she said, her dark hair wind blown and falling enticingly over her shoulders.

"Wait until you feel this." Marcus unzipped his jeans and yanked them down to his feet. His cock, unhindered by underwear, popped from its confinement and jutted toward her lips. Juliet was only inches away and her breath spread over his crown like a warm summer wind.

"Looks tasty." Juliet reached over the short distance between them and grabbed the base of Marcus's shaft.

"Oh, that does feel good," she said as she pulled her hand up with a hard, swift movement.

She repeated the action again, from base to tip. Marcus's foreskin skated between her fingertips and he grunted in ecstasy. When she slipped her hot mouth over the crown, his entire body shuddered. She laved the juices that trailed from his slit and moaned. He thrust his hips forward and she took his entire cock into her mouth, nipping and licking every inch of him. With each thrust, the scent of her arousal grew stronger. It mixed with the smell of his own musk, further stimulating his reaction to her.

In all his centuries, many women had pleasured Marcus. But he'd never felt anything as electrifying as Juliet's mouth on his cock. He'd wanted her for so long, imagined this scenario night after night. She pumped and purred, provoking a ravenous flame in him to ignite.

"Oh, shit!" He growled. His legs tightened and his balls constricted as he shot into her mouth. She gulped down each spurt, refusing to let go of his shaft.

"Naughty vamp." Juliet said when she finally moved her mouth from him, licking her lips. She rose from the bed and slapped him on the ass. "Lay down face first. It's time for your punishment."

Her voice was commanding and laced with a growl. Marcus ripped off the rest of his clothes and did as she ordered. With his face buried in the satin sheets, he heard her unzip her top. The next sensation he felt was her naked body straddling his back. Her pussy was hot and damp, her juices spread across his skin as she humped his neck.

Juliet slid her cunt to his ass cheeks and slapped him

again. It was sharp and painful, but made his cock fill with blood. He groaned when she slapped him again, with more intensity.

"Punish me," he managed between breathless pants.

"Silence. I'll tell you when to talk," she commanded. Then, Marcus felt the belt she'd been wearing slip under one of his wrists. Juliet used the thin strip of leather to bring his hand behind his back, where she fastened both of his wrists together.

"Now roll over."

He did, his hands now not only secured together, but locked behind his back. He could have broken free if he'd wanted to, but he didn't. Juliet's domination over him was far too titillating.

He was fully aroused once again and his cock stood straight in the air. With a sensual moan, Juliet lowered herself onto his shaft, pressing his cock into her until his balls nestled against her ass.

She rode him slowly at first, rising and falling in long, luxurious strokes. Her hands fisted his pecks until she pinched his nipples. A painful but rousing spark jolted down Marcus's spine.

With each thrust, she moved harder and quicker. Their bodies slapped together in a violent frenzy. He was so aroused that his fangs jutted from his half-opened mouth.

"Yes," she said and lowered her neck to his lips. She knew what his body wanted—needed—and she offered it to him willingly.

Marcus accepted the invitation and sank his teeth deep into her skin. His eyes rolled back into his head and his eyelids closed. Her blood flowed hot and wet into his mouth. She tasted like she smelled, a combination of sweet wine and forest. He relished every ounce of her titillating nectar. It pulsed through his veins in rhythm with the thrusts of his cock in her pussy.

As he drank, he felt her hands tighten around his chest. A sharp pain ripped through his muscles. Juliet had partially shifted and her claws punctured his skin. Marcus opened his eyes to see that her hair, jet black in her human form, had transformed into a long sheet of white. It fell over his face like a wave.

With a savage rip, he undid the belt that bound his hands, reached around his body, and gripped her butt. He used the strength of his forearms to push her onto his shaft faster and harder. Her growls joined his own, piercing the serenity of the dark, quiet room.

Another stab of her claws into his chest and he felt her climax, her warm juices flowing over his cock. He took one last deep drink of her blood, thrust his hips up as hard as he could, and shot his come deep into her body.

They both heaved as she collapsed on top of him. Her hair returned to its human shade and her claws subsided. He licked her neck, closing the wound where he'd bitten her, then let his own fangs recede.

"That was the best fuck I've ever had." Juliet said through breathy huffs.

"No fucking kidding." Marcus wrapped his arms around her and moved her so that they lay face to face. Juliet was much better than he'd ever imagined. He knew he would never get enough of her. "You are a good kitty."

"What now?" She asked, moving her fingers in a line down the taut muscles of his chest and over his still-throbbing cock.

"I've always wanted a pet. I don't think my landlord requires a deposit."

She smiled and looked into his eyes. "Better get a leash."

Juliet grabbed his shaft and stroked him until he was hard and thick. He responded by engulfing her mouth in his with a searing, passionate kiss. It was the first time they had kissed. But as he explored her mouth, tasted her, smelled her, Marcus knew it would not be their last.

The Creatures from Craigslist

By Jeremy Wagner

Nancy Monday always thought the great thing about Craigslist was how she could blow into any town in the United States and pretty much get laid or get off with someone, somehow.

She found fishing through the postings a lame excursion. Lots of spam and fake ads. Also, she screened a lot of men and women—she went both ways and was happy to scream it—and found most pictures to be disappointing. She wanted hot bodies to play with, and just as important, she felt sex with strangers should be lustful and fun and fast and with partners who were toned, ripped, or otherwise drop-dead gorgeous.

Personalities, in her book, were overrated. Nancy didn't deny being shallow or slutty, she embraced it and figured it was her business and anyone who frowned upon it could fuck off.

She landed at Chicago's O'Hare Airport early in the morning and went straight to a trade-show. She managed the marketing department for a large cookware company and worked the company trade booth. Her career, she felt, was beyond boring and the trade-show was torture. Maybe she did it as a subconscious form of masochism. She was down with S&M stuff, but granted, there wasn't anything she found sexy about promoting pots and pans, no matter how shiny the stainless steel might be.

Nancy politely forgoes the numerous evening parties to do what she wants in her own little world. In her suite at the hotel she's checked into downtown, she readies herself for a night already booked with the promise of fornicating adventures.

A few days earlier, before she flew out of Boston, Nancy had browsed the new postings in Chicago for a sex-laden rendezvous. On Craigslist, she clicked her way down the following thread: *Chicago craigslist > city of Chicago > personals > casual encounters*. Then, she entered the following search: *mm4w*. "Male male for woman" was her sole fantasy to be lived out in Chicago.

Nancy remembered previous threesomes, enacted in every imaginable combo. Now, she felt the bug to revisit a three-way. She hungered for two men to take her . . . two muscular, well-endowed bastards who could treat her like the whore she knows she is while she's in the Windy City.

One man, by himself, hasn't cut it in the last decade. This is why she's been single for the last seven years. Nancy cheated on her fiancé back then. She felt it was necessary since her libido was too strong and her fiancé wouldn't bring anyone else into the bedroom—even other beautiful women with Nancy's blessing. Her ex was too much of a prude and, she realized a year into their engagement, she was a late-bloomer with her insatiable sexual desire.

She knew she should've just broken up with her fiancé first before she started going to the swinger's parties alone, or before hooking up with the football players, or the female rock singer, or her old boss, but . . . *c'est la vie*.

C'est la vie. She figured the relationship was doomed and it ended the obvious way when he found out. Just as well. She never thought a marriage should be open to the public anyway.

Nancy thought of the Chicago ads she browsed under *mm4w* days ago. She remembered finding an ad for two guys who wanted blowjobs in a parking lot from a chick before they went to the Blackhawks game, an ad from a couple of boneheads said they wanted to double-team a Polish girl with red hair, while other mm4w ads didn't yield much of anything. She thought most of those guys—if they were even real—sounded a little too gay in their explanations as to why they both wanted to mix boy-butter and do a woman together.

Nancy's eyes had opened wide when she found a heading halfway down the page. The screen displayed the following ad: 2 Brothers—mm4w. She read: 2 good-looking, super-athletic brothers looking for a hot and sexy woman to live out our fantasy. Come, be the center of our attention and the object of our desire. Let's have some fucking fun.

"Sounds good to me." She spoke the words to her laptop as she replied to the ad from the comfort of her home office.

In less than twenty-four hours, the two men from the ad replied to her initial response and soon an intense and sex-filled dialogue started.

Nancy learned the brothers were twins in their mid-twenties and of Italian descent. They called themselves Romulus and Remus and she was surprised to read how well written their erotic and sensuous words were. Moreover, if the pictures were real, the hard-body twins with their olive-oil skin, striking blue eyes, long black hair, and girthy cocks gave Nancy's forty-year-old genitalia a blast of heat and blood like she'd never known before.

She in turn emailed photos of herself, showing off her own shapely build and ample breasts and porn-blonde hair.

By the time her departure to Chicago drew near, Nancy had locked in a date with Romulus and Remus and planned for them to be at her suite at nine the first night she was in town.

Now in her suite, Nancy waits, fresh from a bath and in a sheer pink negligee and high heels. Her attire consisted of nothing more and she glides a finger over her shaven vulva in lubricated anticipation of the twin's arrival.

She touches herself in an absent-minded way as her thoughts drift to her last email swap with the guys. They showed her much and told her much, but now, as she reflected on their correspondence, they also revealed nothing. She found their names odd. In addition, Nancy didn't know where they hailed from. In between the erotic messages and nude photos there was nothing mentioned regarding trivial things such as city or suburban residences or what they did for a living.

Not that any of it mattered when fucking was the primary focus for them all. Yet, Nancy feels something akin to a mixture of mystery and lust tempered with unease when she thinks more about the two potential lovers.

The pinch of apprehension excites her as does any form of danger in a sexual arena. She'd had some close calls before but she always protected herself with self-defense moves and the powerful mace disguised as hairspray she put in her checked bag on every trip. Risk made her wet, but whatever this feeling is—woman's intuition or other —it was giving her gooseflesh.

Perhaps it was the animal-like look the pair wore on their faces and in their eyes. Or, maybe it was the tone and underlying meaning of their words when the twins wrote something about the promise of the life-altering, orgasmic heights Nancy would reach once the brothers "shed their skins" and revealed to her the sexual potency from their lupine loins.

Were these fuckers for real? She stops touching herself as she thinks about it. And what about that word she forgot to look up. *Lupine? What the hell's that mean?* All thoughts of who the twins were and what the definitions of their nutty terminology meant evaporate as a heavy knocking comes from the front door of her suite. The sudden knock startles her, but Nancy is pleased as a wall clock in the room shows nine p.m.

Right on time, boys.

Nancy dusts herself one quick and last time with her fragrance of choice—Hanae Mori Butterfly—before going to the door to greet her visitors. She pauses and peeks through the keyhole. Even though the men look distorted and odd through the fish-eye lens of the peephole, the twins look yummy. She holds her breath and turns the knob, opening the door.

"Hello, Nancy." The men speak to her with simultaneous voices uttering the two words in perfect time and both in the same deep and sexy timbre.

Just the sound of their voices is enough to almost make her lose it and come with spontaneous abandon. What is it about these guys that does this to her? Aside from their sensual vocal tone, the men are hotter than Chicago in August. They're identical in every way. From their long, curly, and black hair, vibrant blue eyes and stubble-covered Roman faces, brown skin, and brilliant smiles to their six-foot heights, athletic builds, and matching outfits of tight black muscle shirts, even tighter blue jeans and leather boots, these boys ooze sex and have *fuck-machine* written all over them.

Nancy responds with a soft voice. "Hi guys. C'mon in."

The twins enter Nancy's suite and give a quick glance around before turning their gaze upon her. Their stares are intense and ravenous in their power. Their eyes alone visually violate her and it arouses her on a new level.

"I'm Romulus." The first stud says, smiling huge and white and never breaking eye contact with Nancy.

"I'm Remus." The other brother speaks and like Romulus, Remus holds her with a relentless stare she is both too stimulated and too startled to turn from.

Nancy sees how these two men were created in almost

perfect and identical physical forms, save for the star-shaped scar on Remus' left brow. The scar splits apart his left eyebrow like a teeny-tiny impact crater left behind by a small meteor impact on the tiny forest of thick and delicate hairs there.

"Introductions done. May we get down to business?" Romulus speaks, not seeming to wait for an answer as he begins removing his clothes. His shirt and boots go first and then the pants. Nancy notes the twins are both undressing in unison as if this were planned and choreographed beforehand. The men both have short, black hair covering their bodies from their ankles to their collarbones. She'd dated Italian men before who were hairy like these two, and she didn't mind it as long as they kept it groomed like these manscaped brothers did.

As her eyes roam, she soon notices they both didn't sport underwear.

"Uh, yeah. No need for small-talk, boys, I . . ." Nancy's words peter out as she finds herself unable to form another syllable at the sight of their thick and indistinguishable cocks.

The men are uncircumcised, and as she watches with fascinated eyes, both penises swell with blood, rise rigid and erect, and push the twin glandes up and past their foreskin sheaths like the fat heads of snakes emerging from flesh tunnels. And like snakes, the vertical cocks sway, like separate, involuntary organs with minds of their own, moving with the sensual motion of cobras.

Nancy isn't sure what she's looking at. Like some of the other ways these unique and hot men move, their hard and slithering sexes point and stir with synched and choreographed motions. She wonders what they're going to feel like once they penetrate her.

God help me.

Mesmerized by the dancing genitalia, Nancy's trance is broken as the twins approach her. Romulus puts his arms out and yanks her negligee down and off before embracing her. Remus glides behind her and she can feel his hot breath on the back of her neck. He's panting like a dog and she feels sensuous chills throughout her body.

For a second, Nancy swims into Romulus' luminous blue eyes before he shuts them and gives her a deep, apolaustic kiss. It makes her feel faint. His tongue, like his cock, is an undulating creature unto itself and she finds it large and lengthy. He drives it into her mouth and tickles the back of her throat. He kisses her like no man ever has.

Before Nancy loses the strength in her legs, Romulus breaks the kiss and steps back for a moment, releasing Nancy so she can catch her breath.

"That . . . kiss." She inhales and sees dots before her eyes. She feels intoxicated and tries grasping the real world. "Your tongue. It's so . . . so . . . so—"

"Large and sexy?" Romulus speaks in his dreamy, baritone voice which sounds to Nancy like audible sex. "Yes. The better to lick you with, my dear."

"How 'bout this meat pipe, huh?" Remus whispers to Nancy from behind while his substantial hardness presses into the small of her back. "The better to fuck you with, aye?"

Before Nancy can answer, her breath is once again

taken away as Romulus lays another asphyxiating and mind-blowing kiss on her.

As she becomes lost in the power of Romulus' dominating tongue, Nancy feels Remus drop down behind her, his sultry breath traveling from the base of her neck to her tailbone. She almost inhales Romulus' tongue as she feels Remus burying his face into her gluteal cleft.

Is this fucker gonna toss my salad? The thought makes Nancy wetter than she already is and she thinks she's found three-way heaven with these two. In anticipation of some oncoming anilingus, she tries to relax her sphincter while struggling to tongue-wrestle Romulus. However, instead of Remus's own tongue doing any back-door explorations, he only sniffs her. She feels Remus' staccato inhalations and exhalations as he sniffs away at her ass like some sexy cur.

"Nice. You smell delicious." Remus speaks and rises to his feet and cups Nancy's capacious breasts from behind. He plants his nose on the nape of her neck. "Mmmm. Hanae, right? Mori Butterfly?"

Nancy stops kissing Romulus. She opens her eyes and looks into Romulus' already open orbs. She breaks her lip-lock with Romulus and turns to Remus. She's impressed by his knowledgeable nose. "Yes. You're correct on that one."

"Thought so. Warm and spicy with vanilla. A woody Oriental fragrance hard to miss." Remus states this observation and begins kissing her neck.

"With that schnozz in her ass, you already know what she had for lunch, brother." Romulus lets out a guttural laugh at this and Remus joins him in laughter. Romulus stifles his laugh and still smiling, he stares serious at Nancy. "We both have an uncanny sense of smell."

Nancy smiles back at Romulus with a thousand different ideas in her head. She feels a mixture of nervousness and exhilaration. These men are odd and fucking sexy as hell. She's curious about them and also, she's feeling something else. *Trepidation?*

Before she can put a mental finger on her exact state of mind, a spontaneous moan escapes her as she feels Romulus' mouth on her breasts and nipples while Remus places his hand between her legs from behind and eases a pair of wriggling fingers into her lubricated slit.

Romulus sucks and nibbles away hard on Nancy's right nipple, his crazy tongue flicking upon it inside his mouth. She almost gives in to the intensity of it. Then, Romulus pulls his full lips away and looking past Nancy, he mutters to Remus. "Look, brother. Does this remind you of anything?"

Remus continues fingering Nancy while he looks over her right shoulder. He chuckles in her ear. "Yes. *Lupa*. The she-wolf. Giver of sustenance."

Again she remembers the earlier word, *lupine*, and now, *Lupa*. Nancy doesn't know what the fuck these guys are talking about and she's too caught up in the foreplay to ask. Remus withdraws his digits from Nancy and moves around to her front. He joins his brother and places his mouth upon her left breast and applies relentless, oral suction to her left nipple.

Nancy looks down at the twins. Their long, curly black

hair hangs down in their faces as they grip her limbs with strong hands while they suckle and make strange noises. She clears her throat. "You fuckers are wild."

Remus stops his sucking and looks into her face. His mouth moist and his cupid lips bright red. "Wild? Yes, love. You might say that."

"Feral's more like it." Romulus speaks through lips looking bruised and full. He laughs to himself as if this were some inside joke he was acknowledging.

"Well, I'll take it. The wilder the better." Nancy grips the twins, a throbbing penis in each hand. Each member feels like some searing, vein-burdened, high-tension wire she now strokes while wondering if perhaps she is in over her sweet blonde head this time.

"The wilder the better, aye?" Romulus stands and stares into her. He tempers his words with a tone that implies the twins will deliver something untamed. This, Nancy doesn't doubt.

Remus stands straight and looks at his brother and nods. "Shall we?"

Romulus nods without a reply and walks his naked and muscle-bound body to the large bay windows in the suite. He pulls open the heavy red and brown curtains and reveals the Gold Coast of Chicago.

Below the hotel window is the winding and lighted Lake Shore Drive and reflective, nighttime water of Lake Michigan beyond. Nancy walks toward the window and takes in the beautiful night sky and the enormous, full, and orange-colored moon hanging overhead.

She is startled when, at the sight of the moon, the twins

throw their heads back and howl in unison at the ceiling like a banshee duo.

An angry stomping from the room above tells Nancy other people in the hotel have heard these two nutballs. "Quiet it down guys. You're getting a little too loud."

The twins stop baying and turn to focus their attention on her. She notices with alarm that their eyes no longer retain the once vivacious blue. The original color has been replaced by bright yellow spheres with pupils darker than space. There's an intent in those four eyes, and it strikes Nancy as one part predatory, one part lustful, and one-hundred percent unnatural *animalia*.

"You want wild?" Romulus sounds out of breath, as if he just jogged around the suite.

"So now you got wild, bella." Remus also sounds winded as he speaks and winces with sudden flash of pain on his face.

"You guys all right?" Nancy speaks and recognizes the panic in her delivery. She sees the twins both doubling over, as if their nude bodies were seized with massive stomach and muscle cramps.

Romulus gasps and fights to speak as he holds himself. "Do you remember the email? When we mentioned we would shed our skins?"

Nancy nods. She recalls the mention of the twins' promise to bring her to life-altering, orgasmic heights. Something else about sexual potency, but her mind has trouble recalling it all. The scene in front of her steals all of her attention.

"Well." Remus speaks now with a voice filled with pain

and confidence. "We're going to show just what we mean."

On Remus' last word, Nancy steps back and watches with bewildered and shocked eyes as the twins begin a simultaneous transformation. They go from doubling over to snapping straight up. They spread their muscular arms and legs raise their faces to the ceiling and howl again, louder this time.

Nancy imagines the other guests in adjoining rooms are either irritated or jealous by the rowdy howling sounds. *If they only knew.* She thinks this thought to herself as she continues watching Romulus and Remus.

Their howls diminish while their changing continues. The twins bask in the moonlight pouring into the suite through the large window. Nancy hears the unmistakable sounds of cracking. She sees what appears to be their hands and feet and limbs and spines growing longer. With that, their individual heights increase until their beautiful manes almost touch the ceiling. Their hair grows longer from the tops of their heads and the hair across their ripped bodies grows thicker and wilder from every fiber of their flesh until they bear thick coats of shiny fur.

Nancy is too flabbergasted to run or scream or pass out at the outlandish scene. She stands still, slack mouth open and eyes bulging like a deer caught in the high-beams of a tractor-trailer.

The overall transmutation is mere minutes in duration, but for Nancy, it seems like she's been subject to hours watching a bad horror movie. Impossible as she thinks it is, she sees their ears grow into large, hairy, and pointy things while their lower jaws and noses burst forward and stretch out into long, canine-like snouts stuffed with dangerous-looking teeth.

Nancy's eyes glance down. Between the twin's new legs, and sprouting from thick, jungle-like masses of runaway pubic hair, she spies the erect penile snakes there. They look much bigger and intimidating now. They continue moving on their own, swaying to some unheard music. The shafts of each are a blood-red color and below them are the hairiest balls Nancy's ever seen in her vocation as a self-proclaimed slut.

The noisy limb- and hair-popping sight quiets down. The ongoing physical modifications the twins have endured ends with the pair of monster men purging themselves of corporeal waste on the hotel room floor.

I didn't sign up for this shit. Nancy looks on, thinking how she's done just about everything and loved it all, but this particular situation is beginning to tread too close to bestiality and scat territory. She knows, even with her low morals, there are lines she refuses to ever cross.

Nancy doesn't care that she's naked when she decides to blaze out of the room and get to the hotel foyer. She finds the power to move and begins turning away to run, but the fierce glares from the fiendish twins stops her dead in her first step. She can't tell the twins apart, they look the same: huge and hairy and ferocious. They're now more beast than man. Only when she spots the eyebrow scar does she identify Remus from Romulus.

The twins snap their large, drooling jaws at her. Their

long and lolling tongues hang off their lower mandibles before lashing out and swiping their wet snouts. They growl at her and their muzzles crinkle back to display and flash their glistening black gums and the numerous and menacing sharp fangs imbedded therein.

"Oh my god." Nancy eyeballs their scary canine teeth and feels weak. "Are you guys like, furry vampires or something?"

"Fuck vampires." Romulus speaks in a new, unerotic voice. The words come out snarling and animalistic, created on a different tongue. "They're so pale and cold."

"Yeah." Remus speaks in a low, cracking, and growling voice. "We're hot-blooded, babe. Furry and ferocious. We'll fuck the living shit out of anything that moves. Vampires got nothing on us."

"We're were-fucking-wolves." Romulus advances with his massive clawed hands reaching out for Nancy. "And we're gonna fuck you like you've never known."

Nancy feels the iron grip of Romulus' claws—or paws? she wonders—before being lifted into the air. She squeals as Romulus tosses her over to Remus. Remus catches her and she doesn't touch the ground as the werewolf brothers pass her around the room like a blonde basketball.

Dizzy from the rough play, Nancy feels disoriented and doesn't realize Romulus has pulled her to the ground with him until she feels her hands on his hairy chest and finds herself looking down into his werewolf face, just inches away from her own countenance.

Romulus' carrion breath blasts her in the nose and it's

an instant turn-off. But the sudden touch of a gentle nail on her clit and the lapping of the flat and wide wolf tongue across her nipples turns her on again with increased ardor. She whimpers with pleasure.

"We will take you now." Romulus growls his statement.

Nancy is unable to protest. She's confused by her feelings of fear and unbidden lust. She straddles Romulus, the wolf-man, and feels his free-roaming cock jabbing and squirming towards her vagina. She doesn't pause. She raises herself up a couple inches to guide him inside of her. She grips his cock and it feels like she's holding a hot and shaggy monster dildo.

As she feels Romulus penetrating, Nancy realizes how much she loathes pubic hair on men and wishes she had shaved these two brutes. Though, she knows, she'd need a weed-whacker to tame, trim, and shave the heavy-duty coarse and wild pubes down there.

"Don't leave me out." Remus's growl of a sentence comes on hot breath Nancy feels upon her left ear.

Remus speaks from behind her while she's astride Romulus and gyrating up and down on him. She abandons all restraint, taking great pleasure in the coitus. She feels Remus' large claws flat on her back and then feels a sudden warm and wet discharge on her ass. Before she can utter the words, *wait*, or *lube, please*, Remus is working his hard creature-penis into her asshole.

Either by pure, uncut arousal or desensitized by the unexplainable events related to this entire pornographic and paranormal scene, Nancy is surprised to find her ass accommodating Remus with ease.

Nancy cries out in pure ecstasy as the pleasure from the werewolves' double-penetration is overwhelming, causing her to climax three times in quick succession.

"Do you know what this is, love?" Romulus poses the question through his mess of jagged teeth.

Nancy's response is a high-pitched squeal. She can't speak as carnal gratification owns her. Moreover, she doesn't want to hear words right now. She's enjoying the sensation of the wolf-men inside her, their dual infiltration separated only by a thin wall of flesh inside her. She feels each explosive and binary stroke. The sensation is too good and too wrong to bear. She wishes the guys would be quiet as chit-chat threatens to ruin her concentration while she takes her pistoning lovers deep inside.

Romulus snaps his jaws. "Tell her then, brother."

Remus leans in from behind while sodomizing Nancy with his slow and deliberate fucking. All of their faces almost touch. He licks his muzzle. "We're just two young wolves fucking a cougar."

This makes Nancy stop. She tightens her muscles and prevents the well-endowed creatures from any lubricated movement. She exhales, frustrated, and catches her breath before saying, "Shut the fuck up and just fuck me, 'kay?"

The twins release low, guttural growls and then renew their simultaneous double-penetration with even more aggression.

The kinky three-way sex with the werewolf brothers continued through the night and Nancy came countless times and was screwed raw.

Nancy didn't remember passing out but she awoke late the next day, sore and with visions of numerous sex acts rolling through her head. Her body was covered in scratches. She felt dehydrated and her crotch felt like it was t-boned by a garbage truck.

She noticed shed hair covering everything in the suite, not to mention strands between her teeth and in the black hair-ball she hacked up on the carpet like a cat.

Nancy realized she missed the end of the trade-show and also missed her flight home. No worries, she figured. It was Friday night and she'd stay an extra day in Chicago and get back to Boston over the weekend.

After booking her suite again and making apologetic phone-calls to her boss, Nancy took a long and satisfying shower. Afterward, she wrapped a terrycloth robe around herself and played on her laptop. She hit Craigslist again.

Just for fun, she tells herself. *Just for fun.*

Thinking back to the night before, and still feeling the sensation of the long-gone twins inside her, Nancy wasn't sure if she'd ever top anything this erotic, crazy, and downright weird ever again.

But then she perused *casual encounters > m4f* and finds an ad reading: *Like graveyards and coffins and s-e-x? Hot and older Romanian gentleman looking to exchange fluids—the redder, the better.*

Nancy clicked REPLY.

Shattered Resistance

By Lucy Felthouse

Suzy drew her jacket collar up more snugly around her neck. It was damn cold; an icy wind blew through the park, stirring up the fallen leaves and muffling the silence. Not that it made any difference. She'd never have heard him coming anyway—he would appear from nowhere, swiftly and silently. Just like always.

Dane was great at creeping up on people. He was also a vampire, which naturally gave him the advantage. But Suzy only cared about the fact that Dane was dangerous, sexy, and immortal. Some girls use guys for their cars, their houses, their money, or even for sex. Not Suzy. She wanted Dane for what he was. All-powerful, lightning fast, indestructible. Well, almost indestructible. She'd take her chances—it was still better than being human. No illness, no aging and a drastically reduced chance of dying. What's not to like? Dane was everything Suzy aspired to be. And unfortunately for Dane, Suzy was determined to make her aspiration reality.

Now, what Suzy wanted, she usually got. The fact that

Suzy was extremely attracted to Dane didn't help matters. So she not only wanted to be *like* him, she wanted to be *with* him. Which is why she was lurking in the deserted park at such a late hour. That and the fact she knew he'd be walking back to his dorm room this way. She'd known him long enough to have memorized his every move. He may have been a supernatural being, but not much got past Suzy, much less the man that was going to make her immortal. Oh, he was. He just didn't know it yet.

Soon she felt the hair on the back of her neck stand up. By that point, of course, it was already too late. Had he wanted to kill her, she'd already be dead. The mere thought turned her on. Knowing that he could take her life within seconds and nobody would ever know what happened got her juices flowing. His strength and beauty rocked her to her very core.

She turned to look at him, her pussy already responding to what she knew she'd see before her eyes registered the image. He stood there, tall, thin, and gorgeous. His dark hair was chin-length and looked as though he'd been dragged backwards through a bush. His eyes, normally a deep and startling shade of blue, were impossible to make out in the darkness. But she knew without being able to see properly that his facial expression was currently one of amusement.

"What are you doing out here, Suzy?" His tone was exasperated rather than surprised, the result of many similar meetings with Suzy in a variety of places.

"Waiting for you."

His full lips curved in a sensual smile. "Isn't it supposed

to be the other way round? Doesn't the vampire normally lurk in the dark waiting for his prey to come along, then sink his teeth into their neck and *drink zer blood?*"

He mocked the old vampire characters and legends readily, since he was proof that not all the age-old rumours were true. He could do mirrors, garlic, fire, and daylight, though only small amounts of direct sunlight. As a student, though, that wasn't really an issue. Since the majority dragged themselves out of bed late morning, spent the day in lectures and then partied the nights away, Dane wasn't exposed to much sunlight. Nobody knew there was anything amiss. Until Suzy, that is.

"I'm saving you the trouble of hunting down your prey. I'm right here for the taking. Drink my blood, give me some of yours, I'll turn, everybody's happy."

"Not this old chestnut again. I fail to see how turning you could make me happy. What would I get out of it?"

"I'd be forever in your debt," Suzy replied, sidling closer and smiling coyly up at him. "I'd do anything you wanted."

"There's nothing you can offer me that you couldn't offer as a human being."

"I beg to differ. According to legend, if I'm human, you can have sex with me. If you manage to have sex with me without killing me, it'll be great, but the pleasure can be surpassed. However, if I'm a vampire, you can make love to me. You can connect with me, mind and body and have the most mind-blowing orgasm of your life. I don't want to be screwed and thrown away like old rubbish. I want to fuck you like there's no tomorrow, and then do it all over again. I want you Dane, you know that. But I also want to be with you. You know there's something between us, and that we could be great together."

"I'm sorry, Suzy, I just can't do it. I'm not willing to take your life away in order to have great sex."

"It's not just about sex, and you know it. We can't be together if I'm human, it'd never work. But if I was a vampire . . ."

"Suzy, forget it. Just leave me alone, please."

And he was gone as suddenly as he had appeared. Suzy wasn't too concerned. He'd turned her down before, she could handle it. It was only a matter of time before he gave in. But then again, he was immortal and had so much more time. She'd better up her game.

Suzy decided she'd have to play dirty. She didn't really want to, but she didn't see that she had any other choice. He wasn't responding to her pleas, so she'd force his hand. It wouldn't be pretty, but it'd be so worth it.

Later that night Suzy crept into Dane's room, hoping desperately that she'd left it late enough and he was asleep. Another couple of bullshit rumors dispelled, she thought— vampires DO sleep, and they don't sleep in coffins. Well, they can, but it's not necessary for survival. Besides, how could someone living in student accommodation sleep in a coffin without somebody noticing? Surely even Goths have never done that!

Dane was in bed, and he appeared to be asleep. Perfect. Suzy crept over as silently as possible. Her heart was pounding in her chest—she knew she was taking a risk, but she had no other choice. He *would* turn her. She loved him deeply, and just knew they'd be perfect together. Slinking closer, she cringed at every minute sound, knowing that if something sounded quiet to her, with Dane's super-sensitive hearing it would be magnified tenfold. In fact, she was surprised she hadn't woken him already.

As she stood by the side of the bed looking down on Dane, Suzy's nerve almost gave way. He was so handsome, and yet so dangerous. Yet here she was, slinking into his room in the dead of the night to make sure she got her way. She must be nuts. Still, no backing out now. She was lucky he hadn't heard her up until now; trying to get back out of the room undetected she might not be so lucky.

Suzy took a deep breath, knowing she had to act fast to put her plan into action before Dane awoke. She grabbed the duvet that covered him, wondering what he wore for bed, if anything. She didn't have to wonder for long. She pulled, and revealed his body in all its naked glory. As he was lying on his back, nothing was left to the imagination. Suzy was pleased to note than even in its flaccid state, Dane's penis was still an impressive size. Not that she'd expected anything less—vampires were superior in every other way—it just wouldn't make sense for him to have a small cock.

Time to make it bigger, she thought. Discarding the duvet, Suzy sat gingerly on the edge of the bed, reached for Dane's cock and began to stroke it. As she did, she maneuvred herself so she could reach it with her mouth. His prick began to grow tumescent beneath her fingers and she leant down and closed her lips around the tip.

Continuing to caress him with her hand, she began to lick and suck at the head of his rapidly swelling shaft. She'd always enjoyed giving head and considered herself to be pretty good at it—but giving oral sex to a vampire was on a whole other level.

Dane's breathing started to become somewhat labored, and Suzy was unsure if he was going to wake, or whether he thought he was just having a particularly realistic dream. She felt sure her luck would run out soon and that he'd regain consciousness and discover what was really going on. As his cock became more rigid as a result of her ministrations, she sensed he was going to come soon and smiled inwardly. Soon he'd be hers, and she'd be his. Her plan was coming together perfectly.

Dane's cock began to pulse, a sign of his impending orgasm. She looked up at his face and was shocked to see his eyes wide open and watching her. Their eyes met, and he smiled; his incisors white, strong—and elongated. Suzy had been so intent on the job at hand that she hadn't realized quite how turned on she'd become, until more pussy juices began to seep out and onto the already-soaked material of her panties. Surely he couldn't turn her down now. He clearly wasn't going to stop her at this point in time—and who knew how long he'd been awake and aware of what she was doing?

Moving her hand off his shaft, Suzy deep-throated Dane's cock, despite its now extremely impressive size. Dane moaned loudly, no longer able to stave off his orgasm, and gasped as he shot load after load of white hot come down Suzy's throat.

"Fucking hell, Suzy. You don't give up, do you?" Dane said when he recovered the power of speech.

Suzy shook her head, simultaneously swallowing his spunk and wiping her lips on her sleeve. She grinned wickedly at him, and enquired,

"Care to return the favor?"

"After a blow job like that, what do you think?"

Suzy stood and stripped naked within seconds, then rejoined him on the bed. Now there was no resistance. Dane's hands were all over Suzy's skin, making her feel as though she was being set alight everywhere he touched. Her pussy was molten, the juices trickling in a steady stream down her inner thighs. They kissed deeply; Dane's teeth having retracted in the afterglow of his orgasm. His fingers caressed her pussy lips and her clit, then delved gently deeper, finding her red-hot core. He pushed two fingers inside, smiling as she moaned into his mouth. He bent his fingers, searching out her sweet spot and knowing instantly when he hit it as Suzy's back arched, crushing her breasts against him, and seconds later, covering his hand with a sudden gush of wetness.

Her body trembled as she ejaculated, and Dane marvelled at the strength of her inner muscles as they clenched tightly around his fingers. It also had the effect of fully rejuvenating his semi-erect cock, making it ready for action once more. In one fluid motion, Dane pushed Suzy onto her back, and entered her.

Both of them moaned deeply at the blissful sensation of penetration. Suzy's cunt stretched to accommodate Dane's length and girth, and she relished the feeling of being filled so completely by the man she loved and desired so much.

Dane felt like he'd come home. He'd wanted Suzy for so long, but had been resisting the temptation, as he was unwilling to end her human life, despite her being so desperate to throw it away. He still wasn't sure he was capable of doing what she wanted, though he knew he'd be breaking both their hearts if he refused.

He'd been turned unwillingly—a female vampire had taken a fancy to him and turned him so she would have companionship. It hadn't worked out; Dane's feelings had never been mutual, so the moment her back was turned, he left. After the initial novelty of immortality had worn off, he understood why the female had done what she'd done.

It was possible to maintain relationships with humans, but inevitably they would grow old and die, leaving the vampire alone once more. There was no way Dane would be able to handle having this happen over and over. It would be soul-destroying to have to keep watching people you cared about wither and pass away. And yet, he still didn't give in to the temptation to turn someone as a constant companion. Even if he did, there was no guarantee she'd stay with him for good. There was nothing to stop her leaving, the way he had all those years ago.

However, he'd come to realize that Suzy was different. He'd gone to the university for something to do, and besides, a little more knowledge never hurt anybody. As soon as he met Suzy he knew that she was streetwise. More than streetwise, actually. She was incredibly smart and quick off the mark, and they'd established a friendship. Soon enough, though, Suzy began to ask uncomfortable questions and Dane thought she knew more than she was letting on. Despite telling himself it was impossible, he thought Suzy suspected his true nature.

Then one night, he knew for sure. They'd been hanging out, Dane as always maintaining a distance so as to stop their relationship developing beyond the platonic. And she'd just come out with it.

"So, come on then. Show me your fangs."

From then on, under Suzy's relentless and informed questioning, everything had come out. The whole sorry story.

Back in the present, Dane was close to coming again. He normally had more stamina than this, being supernatural and all. But the combination of Suzy's red-hot, impossibly tight pussy around his cock, her ample tits mashing against his chest, her thrashing and moaning, clamping her legs around him and digging her nails into his back was driving him wild. It also helped that she wasn't scared of him.

"Dane . . ." Suzy wailed, "Please fuck me harder, I'm close and I want us to come together."

Dane didn't need to be told twice. He began to pound harder into Suzy, his hips pumping rapidly back and forth. Dane knew he couldn't hold back much longer, and judging by the sweet agony on Suzy's face, nor could she. He slipped a hand between their bodies and pinched Suzy's clit—hard.

With a gasp, Suzy's body went momentarily rigid, then

the contractions started, her pussy rhythmically clamping his cock, setting off his own orgasm. As she came, Suzy whispered,

"Bite me . . ."

At the very moment of his climax, all Dane's fight left him. All he could concentrate on was his release, so, hardly thinking, he lowered his lips to Suzy's neck, and did as she asked.

He felt her warmth flowing through his veins, her thoughts, her feelings, her orgasm. He could see with absolute certainty that being a vampire, and as a result, being with him, forever, was what Suzy wanted. In that moment he was certain. He knew if he turned her, she would never leave him. For she loved him. Mind, body, and soul.

He drew back, gently cradling her head as his spent penis slipped out of her. Then he ran his sharpest fingernail across his throat and pulled her mouth to him.

When it was over, they fucked like there was no tomorrow. And did it until it was tomorrow. Eventually, they were satiated, albeit temporarily. As Suzy lay in Dane's arms, she smiled, thinking how hard he had resisted her many advances.

He may have been a supernatural being, she thought, but I am a woman. And now I am both.

Mate Run

By Isabo Kelly

She felt him behind her, closing in, and her adrenaline spiked, sending another burst of speed through her muscles. Heart pounding, blood singing in her veins, the dark shapes of thick trunks blurred as she ran. She didn't dare risk a glance over her shoulder, but she knew where he was, could smell him in the air.

He wasn't the one she wanted to catch her.

She dodged over obstacles littering the forest floor until she reached the river. The water was deep and cold this early in the summer, but she was a good swimmer. Without pausing, she leapt into the dark swirling liquid and let the current carry her.

Only when the river turned, and the current slowed to a lazy roll, did she return to the shore. She paused, crouching on the bank, and sniffed the air. No scent. She'd lost the young one. For now.

But her ruse wouldn't fool him for long. Nor would it distract the others. They'd played this game before.

Irina spun to her feet and took off again, letting the

warm night air dry her naked flesh. The night sang to her, pulsing in her blood. Her nerves tingled and her body swelled with the rising of her estrus. The scent of her excitement called to them, all of them. And the thrill of their hunger drove her faster through the trees.

Breathing hard, she laughed and paused to scent the air again.

She caught his scent a split second before a hand closed over her mouth.

"Shhh," he murmured against her ear. "If you struggle, you'll attract the others."

She flicked her tongue out, tasting the palm covering her mouth, smiling when she heard his sharp intake of breath. And because she knew it would excite them both, she did struggle against his grip. He had to use both arms, wrapped tightly around her upper body, to hold her against his chest.

"Enough," he snarled. "Or I will let that young one find you."

Chuckling, she sank against his heat, grinding her naked ass against his already erect cock. "No, you won't, Max," she whispered.

"Don't be so sure, woman." His lips brushed her ear lobe. "He's near. Your little river trick barely slowed him down."

"Gregory's grown clever over the last few months. But you still won't let him have me."

"And why do you assume that? I think I might enjoy letting him catch you for a change. Letting him fuck you until you scream. Watching as he finally tastes you."

She laughed, a low, throaty sound she knew made him

crazy. "I know you too well, love. You've never liked to share."

He cupped her breast in one hand, squeezing firmly enough to make her gasp. She knew he could be a gentle lover. But tonight, this night, neither of them would be happy with gentle. He pinched her nipple until she rose on her toes and bit her lip to keep from crying out.

The brush of his laugh across her neck made her thighs clench.

"I'm not the only one who doesn't like to share," he murmured.

That was true enough. But until she conceived, she couldn't take a permanent mate. Which meant he wasn't bound to her any more than she was bound to him, though they'd danced this dance for many seasons.

His hand slipped down across her stomach, pausing just above her hair, resting in that sensitive spot on her lower abdomen, the spot he knew drove her wild. The heat and pressure of his strong fingers, so close to her, had moisture dripping down her inner thigh. Panting in anticipation, she reached back and gripped his straining cock. Then his body stiffened and his head snapped up. She caught the smell in the next instant. "He's found you. He's almost here."

"Will you allow him to have me tonight?" Her heartbeat sped at the thought that this time he might follow through on his threat.

"Never." He didn't even hesitate. Taking her hand from his cock, he took a single step away from her. "Come. We'll outrun him."

"Like this?" She glanced down at her naked body, enjoying the feel of his gaze drinking her in.

Then he glanced at the forest behind her and shook his head. "Shift. We'll be faster."

With a laugh she knew was too loud, she moved a few feet from him and let the change take her. At this time of the month, when her cycle was at its peak, she shifted to her animal form in moments. When the change was complete, she blinked and with her heightened eyesight sharpening the view, savored the handsome form of the male tiger standing a few feet away.

They ran side by side for an hour, slipping through the forest on silent paws, changing course, crossing the river three times in three places, taking to the tree limbs to confuse their pursuer further. Finally, finally, Gregory gave up the chase as the rest had much earlier in the night.

He wouldn't have her this time. She belonged to her chosen tonight.

Leaping onto a White Oak tree limb, she crouched on her feline tummy and stared at the male below. He paced beneath her, his dark eyes intent on her. Licking her lips, she growled softly, then changed. Their only chance of conception was in human form. Sensitive human skin rubbed against rough silvery bark when she was finished. Wrapping her legs around the branch, she squeezed, overwhelmed by need and lust. She wasn't so far gone as to rub her sensitive clitoris against the bark, she didn't enjoy that level of pain, but her body pushed her to find a release for all this pent up desire.

A moment later, Max was on the branch too, near the trunk, once again in human form. She let her gaze travel across his golden skin, over the tightening muscles of his abdomen to the thick length of his erection. Licking her human lips this time, she rose on hands and knees and crawled toward him, balancing effortlessly on the thick limb. He reached back to hold the large trunk, a move that thrust his cock toward her. She smiled and rose before him, taking his hard thickness into her mouth.

He didn't touch her, which was her preference, as she licked and sucked the length of his cock, swirling her tongue around the head and dipping the tip just beneath his foreskin. She heard the bark crunch under his grip and growled in pleasure. Even the precariousness of their position in the tree turned her on. And he knew it.

"Do you want me to fuck you up here?" His voice was low and rough in the quiet night.

She didn't answer immediately, instead sliding down his cock to the base before pulling back until only the very tip of his erection remained between her lips. Staring up at him, she smiled. And when he hissed and bucked his hips toward her, she swallowed the full length of him again.

Without mercy, she released him and sat back, grinning. His rapid breathing, the intensity of his gaze, the obviously straining muscles of his arms, all attested to his desperation. She loved seeing him like this. "We might fall," she warned. The branch was thick enough to accommodate their bodies but their lovemaking had never been tame.

"The ground is soft here."

"Did you arrange that? Did you have this spot picked out?"

His eyes gleamed in the darkness. "You mean, did I assume I would catch you again?"

"You knew you would." Her smile dropped as she rose to her feet before him. "I don't want any other male."

"Good." He let go of the tree to take her into his arms. "Because you're mine. And I will kill to keep you."

The truth of his words shivered through her. But until she conceived . . .

Rather than face the future, she embraced the moment. He'd caught her tonight. He'd won. She was his. And he was hers. A fact she intended to take advantage of.

Rising on her toes, she pressed her mouth against his. His grip tightened, his lips parted and their tongues tangled as desperation rose.

She'd fallen in love with Maxim Rudikov two years ago, during her very first run, her first receptive estrous cycle. When he'd caught her, when he'd kissed her, she knew she'd accept no other male. But she had to continue running, every season, until she conceived. Females were rare. The run was the only way for their kind, the only way to prevent disaster.

Wrapping one leg around his hip, she leaned into him, fusing every part of her she could to his body. In that moment, as with every cycle, she didn't care about the future, conception, even the other tiger males somewhere out in the woods. Right now, all she wanted, all she needed was Max. Loud, hard, and fast.

This time.

Maybe next time they'd go slow. They had three days, and she meant to savor every moment.

Lifting her off her feet with one had around her waist, he carefully, expertly turned so her back was to the trunk. She gave over completely to him, trusting him not to drop her. When her feet touched the thickest part of the branch, he lifted his mouth.

"Turn around."

She smiled and obeyed, bracing her hands against the trunk as he pulled her hips closer to his. When he was sure of her balance, he slid his hand over her ass, caressing gently. The tension in his touch thrilled her. He smacked her cheek once, a short sharp move that stung for an instant before he soothed the area with another soft caress. She arched her back and her head snapped up at the pleasure coursing through her.

He slid his hand between her cheeks, gliding under her to finger her dripping entrance. "I love you," he murmured. "You're mine."

"Yes."

He rubbed her clit softly, circling the sensitive flesh, knowing exactly what it took to bring her the most pleasure. When she moaned and rocked against his hand, her forehead pressed against the tree trunk, he replaced his hand with his cock. The friction of his entrance tightened her muscles until he was buried fully. Then she relaxed and breathed.

"Only you," she sighed. "Only you."

His rhythm was slow, steady, relentless. The hair on his groin rubbed against her ass cheeks, his skin slapped erotically against her, sweat dripped between her small breasts, the scent of his heightened potency wrapped around her. Her musk and his mingled to form a spicy, sweaty smell unique to them, to their joining. She loved that scent.

Every jolt of his thrusts, every squeeze of his hands on her hips, made her tingle and groan. The warm night air brushed across her peaked nipples, sending an extra wave of pleasure through her body. He never increased his pace, and never slowed. The steady, constant strokes pushed her relentlessly toward climax, but she held back, biting her lip and resisting the urge to finger her clitoris. She wanted to come with him this first time. He so rarely let her. Not for her first climax anyway. But this time, she wanted their first orgasms to be as one. After, she'd let him pleasure her as much as her body could stand. And she'd return the favor. But just this once . . . just this once . . .

When he leaned forward and bit her shoulder, she knew she'd won. He finally pumped harder and his hand came around her hips to circle her clit firmly. The combination of his teeth and his fingers pushed her over the edge, sending her screaming into the kind of climax that only happened with a slow build. His roar of release echoed in the trees, blending with her voice in a kind of music that made her blood hum.

After a moment of simply holding her, he turned her in his arms and kissed her on the mouth. "I've missed you this month. I was actually counting the days until your cycle started."

She grinned and cupped his cheek in one hand. "I missed you too. But we have three days."

"It's not enough. I want you all the time."

"It'll happen. Eventually."

"Not eventually. Now. After this cycle. Move in with me. Marry me."

"You know I can't."

"Why not? You won't let another male catch you anyway. And I won't allow another male to have you. Child or not, we're mated. The run is nothing more than a formality now."

She sighed. He was right. But . . . "If we go against convention, so will others. What will that do for our society?"

"Bring it into the modern era," he snapped. "This run is ridiculous. Our males should be able to control themselves better."

"Said by the male who's found his mate. What of the ones that never find a tiger partner? The ones that have to do with human lovers and no children. There's a reason for the run. Those without an option for a tiger mate turned violent in the past, going so far as to kill females. What makes you think that's changed? Modern times haven't altered our natures a wit."

His growl vibrated through his chest and across her breasts as he glanced away. She understood his frustration. But there was a reason the elders had established the rules of their society. And to go against them risked much.

"Then I'll just have to get you pregnant this time," he snapped, facing her again.

She raised a brow. "You think you can?"

His eyes narrowed and a rumble like a suppressed roar filled the air between them. Before she could blink or laugh at his reaction, he kissed her, hard and deep, then lifted her off her feet. In a move that stole her breath, he stepped off the tree limb, dropping to the ground. Landing on his feet and crouching to soften the impact, he never loosened his hold on her.

A moment later, she found herself on her back, cushioned on a soft mattress of moss and cotton. Startled, she looked down to see a blanket spread across the forest floor. "You did plan this location!"

He chuckled. "Did you think I'd let another male catch you this time?"

"Well, you did threaten to let Gregory have me."

"An idle threat and you knew it. You are mine, Irina. Don't forget it."

She grinned and pulled his head back to her, kissing him again. His hands glided along her sides to her hips and his grip tightened. His cock, once again erect, pressed hard against her thigh. She was wet and ready, eager to feel him slide inside her again.

But he had other ideas. His mouth followed the path his hands had forged, gliding across her neck, over her shoulder to her breasts. He lingered there only a moment, long enough to suck one nipple into a hard peak, before kissing the skin on the side of her breast and following her ribcage to her waist. When his mouth teased the sensitive skin along the side of her abdomen, she arched up. He applied just enough pressure to drive her a little insane and her core clenched tight. Licking a wet line to her hip, he slid lower, positioning himself between her legs. The brush of his breath over her hipbone sent tingles of anticipation across her stomach.

He glanced up long enough to catch her gaze. The sparkle in the dark depths of his eyes made her smile. Then his mouth was on her, and she closed her eyes in satisfaction. The tease of his tongue against her, then moving deeper, made her moan. He avoided her clit at first, licking and fucking her with his tongue enough to excite but not enough to complete. She panted and groaned and dug her fingers into the blanket, moving her hips to guide him closer to her clit. He continued to resist until she thought she might roar in frustration. The feel of his soft, deep chuckle against her wet heat did make her growl.

"Tease," she accused through clenched teeth.

"Do you want me to make you come like this, love?"

"Yes."

"Now."

"Yes!"

"A pleasure to oblige."

And to her infinite relief, he did. He lips closed around her clit and he sucked eagerly, flicking her sensitive flesh with his tongue to increase her pleasure. Night air washed across her skin, adding to the growing build of tension. And when his fingers closed over one nipple, squeezing hard, she cried out, coming in a loud explosion of shuddering sensation. His final lick made her shiver as her muscles continued to twitch and tingle in the aftermath of her orgasm.

The feel of his hot body sliding up hers, settling over her, made her smile and she opened eyes she hadn't realized she'd closed. "I love when you do that," she murmured.

"I'd be happy to do that every night if you'd just move in with me."

"Tempting. Very tempting." She groaned as he slid into her, clenching at his tight ass to pull him even closer. They fit so well, they had from the very beginning. And she loved nothing better than having Max's thick cock deep inside her. The friction of his slow, languid rhythm made her sigh and close her eyes again so she could savor every moment.

He was right, three days wasn't enough. She wanted him all the time, day and night, weeks, months, years. She wanted to grow old with him. And she didn't want to run anymore. The run held a thrill of excitement, which added to her estrous lust. But her lust and desire were settled on Max and she didn't need the run to want him.

When his steady thrusts increased, she opened her eyes and locked her gaze with his. Wrapping her legs around his hips, she rocked with him, matching his pace, urging him on. She watched his control slip and the need in him take over as his hips slapped harder against hers. Her channel tightened around him, increasing the friction and making them both groan. And when he slammed hard and fast into her, she finally closed her eyes to lose herself to another orgasm just as she felt him pulse and heard his shout of completion.

"I love you," he murmured against her ear, so quietly his voice was almost inaudible. "Marry me."

She smiled into the night. "Yes," she whispered back. "I'll marry you. But we have more to talk about. The run . . ."

His fingers pressed against her lips, silencing her. "Nap. You're tired, I can hear it. We'll talk more later."

He rolled to his side and pulled her tight against his chest, wrapping her in his incredible heat and strength. She was tall, just over six feet, but he was taller and larger and he made her feel safe and feminine and infinitely loved. "Later, then," she agreed. "Wake me when you're hard again."

He chuckled and kissed her forehead. "Count on it."

She grinned, pulled in the heady mix of their combined scents and drifted off to sleep. Early morning darkness still shadowed the forest when she woke with his mouth on hers. She smiled into the kiss, snuggled closer and opened her mouth to tangle her tongue with his. She was so caught up in his kiss, the feel of his strong body, the scent of their mingling pheromones, she missed the change in the currents of the air until it was too late.

"Get up," a quiet voice ordered.

Irina knew the instant that voice disturbed their peace exactly who it was; his scent was very familiar. "Gregory."

She and Max rolled to a standing position to face the intruder.

"What are you doing here, cub?" Max said, his voice quiet and calm.

He placed his big body between her and the other tiger, a protective move that made her smile.

"The run is finished," she said. "Max won again. Why are you still in this territory?"

"Because you never give the rest of us a chance," he growled. "And don't you dare call me a cub, old man. I'm your equal in the run. I'm your equal."

"No. You're not." Max's voice didn't change from the even tone.

"It's not fair," Gregory said, taking a step closer. "It's not fair that we run every season and no other male gets a chance."

"The run isn't about fair," Max said. "It's about being the strongest male."

"Let's test that theory."

Gregory's pale eyes glistened in the darkness, and Irina sucked in a breath. Something about that look and his threat had her pulse pounding. This wasn't right. Males didn't challenge each other over females anymore. That was the reason for the run. She sniffed the air again, taking in Gregory's familiar scent and analyzing it with her heightened senses.

"You don't really want to fight me, do you, cub?" Max asked even as he pushed Irina further behind him.

"Oh yes, old man. I do. And when I win, I expect you—" he nodded at Irina "—to fuck me as you should."

"No." She didn't bother to embellish her answer. Her choice in mates had been obvious from the beginning.

"Then I'll have you by force."

"No." She'd no intention of allowing him to rape her. She would fight with Max and make sure Gregory lost.

"You're walking dangerous ground, threatening my mate that way." Max stepped closer.

"She's not your mate yet."

"Yes. As of this night, she is."

"Liar. Now fight!" Gregory roared, a sound that echoed in the trees, and started to shift to his tiger form.

Irina prepared to shift too, but Max stopped her with a grip on her forearm. "No. You get into the tree and stay safe. I'll take care of him."

"Max, you can't. He's not right. I can smell it."

"And you can't shift anymore. You're pregnant. I can smell that."

She widened her eyes and straightened her shoulders. She sucked in a breath and the change in her and Max's mingled scents registered. He was right. "But . . ."

"Irina, your job now is to protect this." He settled his hand on her lower abdomen. "My job is to protect you. That's the way it is. Now get into the tree."

She nibbled her lip, hesitant, but she knew he was right. And his willingness to protect her made her chest tighten with love. "Don't get hurt," she ordered, then hurried up to the tree branch she'd settled on earlier that night, leaving Max to shift.

Gregory, in his full tiger form, waited for Max to finish shifting, a nod to the fight ritual she wouldn't have necessarily expected. Males, when they did fight, followed a certain set of rules. But Gregory wasn't right, there was something wrong with his chemistry, so what rules he adhered to and which he disregarded was anyone's guess.

Irina remained near the trunk and watched as the two huge male tigers circled each other, sizing up their animals. Max was taller, but Gregory looked a little heavier in this shape. Other than that, the two looked evenly matched.

She knew Max was right, she shouldn't shift now that she was pregnant. If she wanted a future with him, a legitimate future that didn't go against every custom and law of their people, she needed to protect the new life they'd created. But she wouldn't have a future with Max if he got killed. And not helping him went against her every instinct.

With her heart pounding, she clenched the rough bark and waited for one of the males to make a move. Gregory broke the stand-off, lunging forward with an earsplitting roar.

Max met the attack head on, both males coming up on their back legs and slashing at each other with their front claws. They broke apart and this time, Max launched himself at the younger tiger first, catching him off balance and sending him rolling over the forest floor. But Gregory regained his footing effortlessly and charged again. The two met in a fury of aggression and angry sound, swiping at each other's heads with powerful paws as each struggled to reach the other's neck with wickedly sharp teeth.

They moved at speeds far faster than a real tiger could move, their striped coats blurring in the predawn shadows. Irina followed the flashes of white fur covering their stomachs. In an ordinary fight, one male would eventually give up and roll onto his back, showing submission to the winning tiger. But Gregory's imbalance left him unpredictable. And she knew Max would never give up and submit to the younger male. Not after Gregory threatened to rape her. Unless Gregory gave up, this was a fight to the death.

Her fingers dug deeper into the bark under her palms,

the thick wood crumbling in her grip. Sweat dripped down her temples, despite the cool early morning air. When Gregory pinned Max to the ground, she rose from her crouch and barely contained the shout of distress clogging her throat. Max didn't need the distraction. Her knees bent as she readied herself to leap from the tree, but Max slashed a paw across Gregory's nose, drawing blood and forcing the younger tiger back. Swallowing the bile in her throat, Irina held her place. For now.

She couldn't allow Max to die. They'd conceived once, they could do it again, as early as her next cycle if this pregnancy didn't take. So long as they survived.

The roars and growls of the fighting males filled the forest, echoing through the trees. They choose this particular part of the central Appalachians because humans didn't frequent the area. But any ambitious camper that did make it this deep into the forest would no doubt be confused and terrified by the snarling sounds of a couple of large cats battling.

Gregory got the advantage of Max once again, and Irina hugged the tree, hissing in a sharp breath. She was mere heartbeats away from beginning to shift, when Max flipped the young tiger, a move so sudden and fast, the motion blurred. The next thing she knew, Max pinned Gregory on his back and had the underside of his neck clamped between his powerful jaws. Gregory growled and hissed, even risked a brief struggle. But then he fell quiet, lying passively under Max, submitting to the superior male.

For a split second, as Max continued to hold Gregory longer than was necessary, Irina wondered if Max would actually kill the young tiger. Gregory wasn't right. Something would have to be done about him eventually. But would Max take that task into his own hands, or would he pass the responsibility off to the elders? Did he risk releasing Gregory? Could he kill the younger man in cold blood after he'd submitted in the fight?

Irina held her breath. She wasn't sure which outcome she wanted. After a long, silent, still wait, Max finally released Gregory and slowly backed away. Blood coated Gregory's coat on his side and near his neck, wounds Irina hadn't realized he'd received. She turned quickly to study Max, but he seemed unharmed. A sound pulled her attention back to Gregory in time to see him begin the shift.

With the males in human form, she jumped down out of the tree and hurried to Max's side. "You're not hurt?"

"No."

"But he pinned you. Twice."

He glanced at her quickly before focusing on Gregory again. "Strategic allowances on my part," he said with a slight smile. "Only way to get close enough to cause his injuries without him noticing."

She followed his nod back to Gregory. The young man was fingering the wound in his side. A vicious set of claw marks scraped along his ribs, but the gashes had already stopped bleeding. He'd be fully healed by mid-day.

"You've lost," Max said, his voice calm and even once again. "Go. Find another female to chase."

Gregory snarled up at them. "The elders have a lot to answer for."

"I'll be sure to pass that message on to them."

Gregory's eyes widened and for the first time, he looked nervous rather than defiant. He climbed slowly to his feet and backed into the woods, not taking his eyes off Max until the shadows swallowed him. They stood listening to his retreat, waiting for the sound of his running feet to fade with distance.

Only then did Max turn and take her into his arms. "I want us married within the week," he said without preamble.

She let out a breath of disbelief. Then started to laugh. "So impatient! We have plenty of time." She pressed his hand to her lower abdomen and smiled. "No one can argue with our mating now."

"I'm not taking any chances. This was your last run, Irina Gorban. You and I are meant to be together. I'm going to make sure no one else can dispute that."

She rose and pressed her lips to his, melting against the heat of his body. He was coated in sweat from the fight, making his hot skin slick against hers. Despite the conception, her need for her mate started to rise and she snuggled closer to make her intentions clear. He chuckled against her mouth before angling his head and taking the kiss deeper. Irina sighed and wrapped her arms around his neck as he lifted her off her feet and carried her back to the blanket.

No more running. Her true mate was finally hers.

Girls' Night Out
By J. G. Faherty

The wind turned my black leather coat into a cape as I walked down the empty street. The spring air carried a hint of moisture, just enough to deliver a tingling chill to exposed flesh.

It was looking to be a bad night for this vampire. Not because I was in danger; no Van Helsings or Buffys on my tail. No, I was simply horny, bored, and hungry—in that order—and I hadn't found a man to satisfy any of my cravings.

I was on my way to the Dungeon, the newest, hippest place for the "in crowd," if you happened to enjoy dressing in black, avoiding the sun, and listening to dark alternative rock. I'm talking retrogoth and the associated wannabees, not some kind of supernatural hangout. We're not really into that. But with my tight leather pants, sheer top with no bra, and knee-high black leather boots, I blended in well with the disciples of the church of Morrissey and the Cure. Normally I avoid fringe culture hang outs, preferring to find my fun in more traditional settings like sports bars, dance clubs, and even poetry readings. It's hard to attract someone's attention when you don't look any different from the rest of the crowd.

However, tonight was different. Not that I couldn't have taken home any one of a dozen testosterone-loaded, self-proclaimed studs I'd met at various bars, but even I have standards. Unless I'm starving, which I wasn't. No, it seemed to be a night for loud mouths, bad breath, and crude come-ons, none of which were high on my attraction list.

My wanderings had led me to The Dungeon. Considering how the night was going, I didn't have high hopes, but it was the last bar on the strip. If this didn't pan out, I intended to just go home and take matters into my own hands, so to speak.

When you're young forever, there's always another night.

I descended the cracked cement stairs and 'suggested' to the bouncer that I'd already paid my ten bucks cover. As soon as the thick metal door opened, deafening music assaulted my ears. It took almost a full minute to grow accustomed to the din and recognize the song as Shreikback's one big hit, "Coelacanth." A golden oldie for the dark and depressed.

The bass line vibrated through my three-inch heels and across my pelvis, doing things to me more appropriate for hands than music. I was glad I'd worn leather.

It doesn't stain.

My eyes had no trouble adjusting to the darkness, which was broken by randomly placed black light tubes on the ceiling and the fake stone pillars that contributed to the ancient-castle feel of the place. The room was about half-full, with more people crowded around the bars and cocktail tables than on the dance floor. I pushed my way through a sea of black makeup, pierced bodies and faces, and hair that looked like Edward Scissorhands sculpted it, thinking I'd get a drink before beginning my hunt.

My sensitive nose picked up the odors of hair dye, unwashed armpits, semen, K-Y jelly, puke, piss, alcohol, and dope. All overlaid, as always, with the sweet tang of blood. For a vampire on the hunt, a crowded club is the equivalent of entering a kitchen at dinnertime, and I felt my mouth—and other parts—grow wet.

At the bar, I ordered a double Remy. On the house, of course. Why pay if you don't have to? I took a small sip, savoring the burn, and then turned around to survey the crowd.

As I'd expected, the girl-guy ratio definitely skewed to the female end of the spectrum. It only took one glance to see the pickings were slim to none. Manhood seemed represented by short, skinny college-age boys, most of them probably going through a rebellious phase. Even if I wasn't a vamp, I'd be afraid to bed one of these wisps, for fear of breaking him in two. A drunken frat boy sidled up to me and mumbled a come-on that I barely understood. His words rode a wave of puke-breath that made my stomach roll, so I took my drink and headed towards an empty cocktail table, hoping he'd take the hint and move on to less-particular prey.

The latest single by Interpol erupted from the speakers

and a few more partiers headed down the steps to the dance floor. I positioned myself so I had a good view of the bar and the lower level. I could people watch and scope out any potential meals-on-heels at the same time.

A burst of feminine laughter distracted me from the dancers. A giggling, slurring group of hardcore avoid-the-sun girls occupied the table next to me. Early to mid-twenties, barely a trace of color except black on any of them, unless you counted the wide assortment of tats and piercings. Typical, except for two of them who seemed way more into each other than the guys around them, judging by the heavy make out session they had going on.

I sipped my brandy and turned my attention back to the dance floor, where some dude was trying to impress the ladies with his dance skills. I was surprised no one had mistaken his gyrations for an epileptic fit and called an ambulance.

That's when a hand grabbed my ass.

I turned around, ready to smack some schmo to the floor, then stopped, fist halfway up, as one of the lezzies from the next table held up her hands in apology.

"Oh, like, sorry. I saw you checking us out and I thought you wanted to join the party, you know?" She gave me a muddled smile, unaware she'd almost ended her night with a face full of broken bones.

I lowered my fist and stared. They'd thought I was flirting with them? Were they that drunk, or was I so horny I was sending out the wrong signals?

"Hey, no harm," I said. I backed this up with a smile of my own. "Nothing personal, I don't swing that way."

The girl laughed. "You don't, or you haven't tried it yet?"

"Same thing, in my book."

"Sweet tits, you have no idea what you're missing. None of us here are strictly lez, but look around. You can count on one hand the decent guys in this place. Half of them are queer, and the other half wouldn't know how to use their dick if they had an instruction book. Sometimes you just want someone who knows exactly what you need."

She gave me a brazenly appreciative once-over. "And the way you look tonight, I think you're ready for some real fun. All night fun."

The Elvira wannabe ran a long, violet fingernail across the mesh of my shirt, trailing along one of my nipples, which instantly grew hard and started to tingle.

Damn, I must hornier than I thought. My brain tried to take back control of my body from my baser emotions. I placed my hand over hers, intending to push it away, but all I did was press it harder against my breast. At the same time, I was unable to control the growl that rolled from my throat. It was a combination of annoyance and repressed lust, and as I opened my mouth I felt my eye teeth growing, extending downward. I knew my black eyes were probably shifting to red at the same time.

I'd lost control, and there was no reason for it. I shut my mouth, knowing it was already too late. Now I'd have to get her away from her friends and erase her memory of me. I expected her to step back in horror, maybe scream, but she surprised me again.

"Oh, shit, you're a vampire!" the girl exclaimed,

clapping her hands. "That is so wild. You're my first, you know. Keisha over there," she pointed to a tall, Asian-looking girl in a leather skirt and jacket with nothing on underneath, "she's been with a couple of vamps. Both of them were guys, and she told us that when they bit her, she had, like, the most ultimate orgasm of her life. Is it always like that with vamps?"

A thousand replies raced through my head, creating a traffic jam that prevented any of them from reaching my mouth. Finally, one broke free. It wasn't the one I would've picked, if I'd been thinking more clearly, but the girl's rapid-fire, non-stop patter, together with my own lust, had me in a tizzy.

"Wait a minute, you know about vampires?" I asked, simultaneously validating her knowledge and forgetting to protest her fingers.

"Sure. Keisha's old girlfriend knew a chick who knew about a bar where someone said vampires sometimes hung out. This was in Boston, before Keisha's parents tossed her out and she moved here. Anyway, they started hanging in this bar, you know, hoping to get lucky, and one night she met these guys and went back to their place for a threesome. She said she came like ten times that night."

I was willing to bet it was true. I've been with other vampires, and I can vouch for the unbelievable intensity of the orgasms our bites can bring. Plus, I've done it to plenty of guys myself. Doing the biting is almost as good, and when two vampires get together, watch out. Tantric sex doesn't hold a candle to a good bite, suck, and fuck session.

My new friend was still talking. I tried to follow her

twisted, alcohol-influenced chain of events, but combined with her Long Island accent and mile-a-minute speech pattern, I soon gave up. When she finished her story by saying that ever since her friends' encounter, they'd been searching for vamps of their own, I held out my hand and stopped her.

"Enough. My name's Sofia."

The goth chick grabbed my hand in both of hers, and as she introduced herself she scratched a fingernail across my palm. The feeling sent an unexpected, massive shiver through my body, and I only half-heard her introductions. "I'm Cassie, and this is Rain." She indicated the girl she'd been making out with earlier.

They could have been twins, although Cassie definitely had the bigger breasts, which were practically spilling out of her artistically-torn black t-shirt, while Rain's crop-top t was so tight you could see her nipple rings through the thin material.

Cassie stroked my palm again, as if she knew how it had affected me the first time. "You know, this place is pretty lame. What say we go to my apartment and have a real party? You can tell us all about being a vampire, and we can show you how much you don't need a man."

She still hadn't let go of my hand, and from the look in her eyes I had a feeling she didn't want to do much talking. I glanced at Rain. She was staring at me the way a hungry man stares at a steak. I knew that stare. I'd given it to plenty of guys over the decades. She licked her lips and smiled when she saw me looking back at her, no shame at all on her face.

"Sure, what the hell. I'm ready to party." The words left my mouth before I even realized what I was saying.

Cassie pulled me away from the table and towards the door, Rain following close behind. They didn't even bother to tell their friends they were leaving.

In the back of my mind I heard a voice telling me, *It's cool, don't worry*. You don't have to do anything when you get there. Hell, it's not like two human girls can force a vampire to do something against her will. You can take a quick nip and then hypnotize them both to forget the whole encounter.

Unfortunately, a sinking feeling in my stomach told me that my best-laid plans might just come to naught.

Tonight, my will didn't seem very strong at all.

It was a short walk to Cassie's place, a basement apartment in an older-style brownstone. The decor matched my expectations completely: dark, sensual, and comfortable. A black second-hand sofa and two matching love seats filled the center of the living room, surrounding a long coffee table littered with candles, a bong, and some ashtrays.

Art store posters decorated three walls, while the fourth held two large, framed movie posters: one from the vampire thriller Underworld, and one of Johnny Depp in Pirates of the Caribbean. Heavy black fishing net separated the living room from the bedroom. The apartment was clean and tidy, and I tasted hints of pot, incense, and sex in the air.

I liked it.

Cassie grabbed a half-finished bottle of cheap red

wine from a cabinet and guided me to the couch. Rain immediately crammed in on my other side, making a particular effort to rub her supple breasts against me. I was the center of a girl–girl sandwich, but somehow it didn't seem as uncomfortable as I would have thought a few hours earlier. I'd already taken off my leather trench, and the feel of soft, feminine skin pressing against my arms made my undead flesh break out in exquisite shivers. I felt myself growing moist and hot, the way I'd only previously felt when I had a particularly well-endowed man under my spell.

Cassie pulled the cork out of the bottle with her teeth, took a hearty swig, and passed it to me. I gulped down a mouthful, the taste of her lipstick mixing with the sweet yet acidic wine. I turned and handed the bottle to Rain, and as soon as I looked back, I found Cassie's face right in front of mine.

"So much for the party," she whispered. "Now for the fun."

Before I could say a word, she leaned forward and kissed me, grinding her lips into mine and forcing her tongue into my mouth. I responded instinctively, entwining my tongue with hers and letting my passion take over. I closed my eyes and devoted myself to frenching Cassie, forgetting all about Rain until a pair of hands circled me from behind to roughly fondle my breasts. Cassie had one hand in my hair and the other stroking my leg. I made a half-hearted effort to push her away, and my hands found two rock-hard nipples under the thin material of her t-shirt. At that point, I lost the last vestiges of my control. I squeezed and pinched them, and Cassie moaned in response.

The sound of her excitement drove me crazy. I wanted more. I grabbed her shirt in both hands and tore it away from her body. Her flesh was hot against my palms, and she groaned again as I stroked and tweaked her. Through it all, she never broke our kiss. As a vampire, I don't need to breathe, so the passionate kiss was no problem for me. But I couldn't believe how long Cassie could suck on my tongue without coming up for air.

Behind me, Rain hooked her fingers into the mesh of my shirt and ripped it in half, pulling it down and away in one fast motion. An instant later, her bare breasts rubbed against my back, their twin points firming as she pushed herself against me. She licked my neck, while one hand continued to caress me. I wondered where her other hand had gone, and then the mystery was solved as fingernails stroked me through the tight leather of my pants.

I leaned back into Rain's embrace, breaking my lip lock with Cassie, who stood up and slid out of her pants. She stood in front of me, totally nude, and I found myself unable to look away from her little landing strip of hair that pointed down to a pair of damp, swollen lips.

Cassie moved forward until she was only inches from my face. The sweet smell of her filled my brain, and when she placed her hands on the back of my head, I needed no further urging to lean forward and part her with my tongue.

I'd never done anything remotely sexual with a woman before, but I attacked her as if I'd been born to it. Cassie cried out softly as my tongue made contact, and she spread her legs apart, placing one foot on the couch to give me full access.

I moved forward, grabbing her ass with both hands and grinding my face into her as hard as I could. The sweet, musky taste drove me crazy, and I tried to reach every square inch. I put everything I had into it, wanting to see what made Cassie scream and cry the most.

While I explored Cassie's fragrant depths, Rain undid my pants and guided me from one knee to the other so she could pull them off. I'd never even noticed her removing my boots. Suddenly her hand was between my legs, her thumb massaging while two fingers plunged inside. I had no time to brace myself for the jolt of pleasure that rushed through me, and I let out a moan as I arched backwards. However, Cassie wasn't done with me yet and grabbed the back of my head and drew me forward again, and I forced myself to concentrate on pleasing her while Rain's fingers sent wave after wave of ecstasy crashing through me.

Lights and colors flared behind my closed eyes. I'd been with many a man in my ninety-plus years and I thought I knew every trick in the book, but Rain was amazing. Every movement sent shivers through me, and before I knew it, she had a third finger in me as warm wetness ran down both my thighs.

I felt my body twitch and spasm, and then I was screaming into Cassie, never taking my mouth away from her even as I felt the world spinning around me. The vibration of my cries sent Cassie over the edge as well, because her voice joined mine, shouting out my name as she dug her fingernails into my shoulders.

When her orgasm subsided, Cassie fell away from me, pushing the coffee table out of the way and collapsing onto the floor. I lost my balance and fell off the couch, but I wasn't ready to end things so soon. Someone else had taken over my mind and body, someone definitely not the me I'd known all my life.

"Poor Rain, we've had our fun, but now it's your turn." Was that my voice speaking those words?

I spread Rain's legs and I rotated my body over hers, assuming a classic sixty-nine position. I went to town on her, using my tongue and both hands to touch every sensitive place I could reach. Underneath me she was busy doing the same to me. I felt her nails claw flesh of my ass cheeks, and I knew I was bleeding from the scratches, I could smell it in the air, but it just added to the excitement, making me lick and suck even harder.

When Cassie's tongue entered the one place I'd never let anyone enter before, I didn't even flinch. I just wanted more and more. I was drowning in pleasure, and when I came for the second time, I lost control completely. My fangs sprang out and I bit into Rain's thigh. I retained just enough control to nip rather than bite deep for food. She gave a shout of pain that quickly turned into a scream of pleasure, as the vampiric aphrodisiacs in my saliva worked their magic. The taste of her blood, mixed with her salty-sweet tang already coating my tongue, filled my mouth, and my second orgasm rolled into a third.

I think I must have blacked out for a moment, because when my sight and senses returned, I found myself on my back, Cassie straddling my face.

"My turn, do me!" Cassie yelled as she lowered herself onto my mouth.

I didn't hesitate in granting her wish. When I sensed she was about to peak from my tongue's attentions, I pulled her down tight, biting at the same time. Even with her legs squeezed tight around my ears, I heard her screams, and I wondered what her neighbors were thinking. Then my fourth orgasm of the night hit me as the taste of her blood sent me over the edge once more and left my whole body shaking and quivering uncontrollably.

Cassie collapsed on the floor next to Rain, panting and crying. One of them groped around the table for the bottle of wine, and we passed it back and forth. Our faces were smeared and sticky, and I savored the mingled flavors of both girls on my tongue. To be honest, it tasted a helluva lot better than having some man's bitter spunk in my mouth.

"Holy shit, I've never felt anything like that in my life," Rain whispered, still sounding as if she'd run a marathon. "Are you sure you never made it with a girl before?"

I shook my head. My voice wasn't much stronger. "Nope, but I think tonight was a good beginning. Is it always like this?"

Cassie laughed. "Depends on the girls. But a lot of it was you, babe. God, I never came like that before. It was like, different. More intense. I could feel things happening all over my body, not just between my legs."

I nodded. "Yeah, that's the old vampire mojo."

I felt a different type of tingle course through my body, and I looked at my watch. It was almost four in the morning.

"Say, you guys don't mind if I crash here, do ya? I can't

go out in the light." I didn't like staying away from home. I never feel really safe anywhere else during the daylight hours, but I didn't have the strength to make it up the stairs, let alone go back to my apartment.

"Crash? Sofia, what makes you think we were gonna let you leave yet? We're just getting started. This was the warm up; now it's time to go to the bedroom for some real fun!"

As I looked at them in awe, Rain leaned forward to whisper in my ear. "Have you ever tried anal beads?"

I smiled.

"You've got an hour to teach me."

The Best Man

By Elizabeth Thorne

"I wish werewolves were real."

Marla choked on her coffee, spilling some of it on the table and making quite a production of cleaning the mess.

"Well that was the non-sequitur to end all non-sequiturs," she responded as she regained her composure.

"Not really," I sighed. "We were talking about men and playing in the woods, and that made me think about sex, and that made me think about werewolves."

"Maggie, honey," Marla looked at me like I was the one trying to pull off a mocha-stained white blouse as a fashion statement, "you are a very strange girl."

"No," I answered, "I'm just a hopeless romantic," and we went back to discussing the details of her upcoming wedding.

Truth be told, it was her fault that I'd had the thought in the first place. A barefoot wedding in the woods with an offering to her favorite goddess and a wolf watching party the night before—which would be the full moon—would make any fantasy-obsessed, romantically-starved woman start thinking about werewolves. They were, after all, the sexiest creatures in the supernatural canon.

I'd never understood some women's sexual obsession with vampires. It was a bit creepy, I thought, wanting to be seduced by an animated corpse. Personally, I'd always preferred the werewolf myths. I loved the idea that, instead of the vampire's terrifying gift of an inescapable eternal half-life, they had been blessed with an existence more abundant and more intense. I loved the idea of a man who the world would have to work harder to take away from me, a man who couldn't be felled by cancer or a bullet from a gun.

Of course, I was also attracted to the power and virility inherent in a creature who was half beast, half man. Looking at my past relationships it was clear that my sexuality had always tended sharply towards the dark side. I gravitated towards partners who liked to play with knives, who liked to bite—men who enjoyed holding me down and taking me roughly while I happily fought and struggled beneath them. The fight was what turned me on, that and the sheer animal passion of two muscular bodies struggling for dominance. It seemed to me that a werewolf would be the perfect lover, all tooth and claw, with the size and strength to use me in the ways I most desired. If only they were real.

Two weeks later, it was time for the rehearsal dinner. Marla's family lived in a luxury compound in the woods. It was a beautiful, peaceful place, and I'd never seen anything like it. Behind a rustic stockade, houses in various styles spread out along a climbing mountain road. At its top was a majestic log building that was the community hall. When we walked inside, I discovered that the whole back wall was made of glass so that the forest dropped away beyond it to create an unbelievable view. Looking out that window it seemed as though you were existing in a world untouched by human hands—a primeval forest that stretched out to eternity.

I was drawn to the window as though nothing else in the room existed, and I stood, mesmerized, and stared at the endless forest.

"Incredible, isn't it?"

I jumped at the sound of the man's rich voice coming from close beside me. I had been so absorbed in the view that I hadn't heard him approach.

Turning my face away from the window, I found myself standing next to a very compelling man. He seemed to be around my age, or possibly slightly younger, and although he wasn't conventionally attractive, there was something about the way he stood that drew the eye. He had that spark of charisma that powerful men use to command the attention of the room, but it was tempered with the light of sincerity and a sparkle of humor in his leaf green eyes as well as by the tousled mess of his shoulder-length brown hair.

"You must be Margaret," he said, reaching out his hand to grasp mine.

"Yes," I answered, confused but liking the feel of his warm, strong grip on mine, "but how do you know?"

"You're one of very few people coming to this wedding who isn't a local or part of the family, and you're the only one of those who was supposed to arrive this early." He smiled, "I'm Marla's brother, Matt. The best man."

I stared at him the way I'd been gaping at the forest moments before—astonished. This polite, handsome man was the pesky younger brother that Marla had complained about so often when we were rooming together in college? If I looked closely, I could see the mischievous boy from her childhood photographs, but he was nothing like what I'd expected.

Matt laughed at the expression on my face. "Marla's been telling you stories I see."

I started to sputter and deny it, but he interrupted me with a laugh.

"No, I was an enormous trial to her when we were growing up. I can't deny that I was quite a pest. Fortunately," he grinned, "I've mostly grown out of it."

"Only mostly?" I matched his smile with one of my own.

"Well I'd hate for anyone to think I'd become boring," he replied. "Besides, I have to keep in practice so that one day I'm ready to torment my wife."

I raised an eyebrow at him, "So what you're telling me is that, in your universe, women like to be tormented?"

He slowly bent over my hand, holding my eye in a way that made my heart beat strong and my knees go weak. "They do when I do it right," he responded, and then, keeping my gaze, he turned my hand over to place a soft kiss in the center of my palm. "That's why I need all the practice."

"Yes . . . Um . . . Well . . ." I stuttered. "You do seem to have quite the technique."

Matt gave me a delighted grin, stood up straight, changed his hold on my hand to a more traditional grip, and started to pull me towards the door.

"Hey!" I protested. "Where are we going?"

He kept leading me towards the door. "For a walk in the woods," he replied. "You know you want to."

It took me less than a second to throw off my doubts—go for a walk in those beautiful woods with this beautiful man or stay here and risk getting shanghaied into flower arranging or some other sort of wedding planning hell. "Can I leave my bag here?"

"Just drop it in the corner." Matt grinned at me. "No one will touch it. Everyone here is family."

I did as he suggested and we escaped out of the building and into the forest. It seemed like we'd made it just in time since as the door shut behind us I heard someone asking if there was anyone around who knew how to fold napkins into swans. I laughed as we ran down the steps and thought *Free!*

Still holding my hand, Matt led me into the forest. It was so beautiful and peaceful that for a while neither one of us felt the need to speak. We just walked, watched the birds, and listened to the way the sounds of the woods changed around us as we moved deeper into the trees.

Suddenly Matt stopped and, before I could ask him why, he put a finger to my lips to keep me quiet. Then he caught my eye and directed my gaze to a clearing a short way off the path on which we wandered.

I drew a quick breath and tried to stay as silent and still as possible to avoid disturbing the scene unfolding before us—a red fox and her kits were tumbling around in the grass. It was enthralling, like watching kittens play.

I don't know how long we'd been standing there when I felt the breeze change and lift my hair. All I know is that at that shift in the wind, the adult fox froze, scenting us, and, with a quick bark, gathered up her kin and ran off into the trees.

We stood in silence a moment longer, watching the place where she'd been, when suddenly I realized how tightly I'd been clutching Matt's hand. With an embarrassed smile I released my grip with a sigh, taking a step forward towards where the foxes had disappeared.

I shook my head. "How could Marla leave something like this, someplace this magical, to go live in a CITY?"

"Marla, as you may have noticed . . . ," Matt's voice sounded rueful as he stepped up behind me to place his hands on my shoulders and lean his body against mine, "is not exactly a 'magical' woodsy sort of a girl. I love my sister, but she's more of a fashion-forward, ruthless-practicality type."

I laughed. "True enough. There are times when I'm amazed that we stayed friends after graduation. Our priorities are so different that sometimes we might as well be living on different planets." I stepped out of Matt's arms, turned to him, and shrugged. "Make no mistake," I continued, "I love her. I just don't always *understand* her."

Matt barked out a laugh that sounded like nothing so much as the fox's call to her kits and said, "Story of my life, babe, story of my life." Then he took my hand once again to lead me deeper into the woods.

It was a wonderful afternoon.

We didn't speak much. Mostly we wandered through the forest enjoying the sights and sounds, occasionally touching each other to draw attention to a particularly fascinating animal or plant. It was oddly comfortable, and familiar, the way he would stroke my hand with his thumb as we walked along.

At one point, as we crested a hill and briefly moved into sunlight, I heard a wolf's howl in the distance and turned to look longingly towards the sound.

"You're not afraid?" Matt looked at me with a surprisingly serious expression on his face.

"I think they're beautiful," I responded. "Although I know enough to keep my distance, I wish I didn't have to."

I thought I heard him mutter to himself "I know the feeling," but when I asked him what he'd said he shook off the question, and we slowly walked back to civilization.

That night, the full moon, Marla and her mother led a small group of guests into the woods. It was mostly women and, although the groom was there, Matt and most of the other groomsmen were nowhere to be seen.

When I asked Marla where they were, she looked annoyed and said "boys will be boys," and I assumed they'd gone to a bar because they thought an evening in the woods was too tame for them. I was slightly disappointed in Matt, because this trip to look for wolves seemed to be just the sort of thing he'd enjoy, but what did I actually know about him? We may have had a wonderful afternoon together, but the truth was we'd only just met.

Eventually the group came to a clearing and stopped.

"The wolves often run up along that ridge," Marla's mother said, gesturing up into the distance as we stared at her expectantly. "We'll wait here and watch."

It was a beautiful spring night. The full moon lit the clearing and shone along the ridge that ran above us so that the forest seemed to sparkle with silvery light. Small groups began to drift into conversations and, not wanting to get caught up, I wandered back to the edge of the forest.

Time passed, and I had fallen into quiet contemplation of the sights around me when suddenly someone gasped. I looked up to see a group of wolves running across the ridge. They were so beautiful I could hardly breathe, and I felt my heart skip a beat as, silhouetted against the moonlight, one stopped, threw his head back, and howled.

The others joined him in song, and I stood mesmerized until I was jolted back to awareness by the feeling of something warm and wet brushing across my palm. I looked down and froze. Standing next to me was an enormous russet wolf whose leaf green eyes sparkled as they met and momentarily held mine. Then his tongue swiped across my palm once more, and I gasped as he took off to join his companions, his thick fur brushing against my arm as he ran past.

Several of the guests screamed as the enormous wolf dashed through the clearing, and I could have sworn I heard Marla's mother laugh as she calmed everyone down and led us slowly back to the house.

I was finishing breakfast the next morning when Matt came in with the other groomsmen, looking surprisingly well rested for a man who, according to his irritated sister, had been out playing with his friends until the wee small hours before dawn.

"Have fun last night, ladies?" Matt asked, swiping the last slice of bacon from Marla's plate and then dashing around to my other side to dodge the smack she aimed at him in repayment. "See any wolves?"

Marla glared at him more than I thought his thievery warranted, and the silence at the table was beginning to feel uncomfortable when I responded. "It was amazing. One brushed right past me as he came through the clearing. He was the most beautiful thing I've ever seen, and his fur was so soft . . ." I grinned. "I think I'm in love."

Marla choked on her coffee, and Matt jumped up to pound her on the back saying, "Breathe, sis. Breathe."

He then turned to me, and as he once again bent down and flipped my hand over to kiss my palm I momentarily flashed back to the moment in the woods where the wolf met my eyes.

I have an overactive imagination, I thought and then happily wrote it off as a lack of sleep instead of insanity when he said, "See you later, nature girl," and went to get some breakfast of his own.

The wedding that afternoon was beautiful. It was like stepping into a story. A circle was called, a god and goddess were invoked, and all of us took a moment outside of time to celebrate the love and union between Marla and her groom. It was a joyful and unexpected experience and when her mother, acting as priestess, bound their hands in silk cord and bade them jump over a broom into their new life together at the end of the ceremony, we all cheered.

When it was all over and people had started back towards the road, Matt stepped up behind me and said, conversationally, "You know, traditionally they can't untie that cord until the wedding has been consummated."

"Can't beat a religion that includes a little ritualized bondage," I quipped, and then turned bright red as I realized what I'd just said.

Matt gave another of his barking laughs, but then his face turned serious and he took my hands in his and turned me towards him. "We have a few hours before the reception," he said, "and I can't help feeling there's something here between us." He raised one hand to lift my still blushing face to his. "My sister might not approve of my asking, but . . . do you want to find out?"

I considered the question for a moment. He was charming, funny, attractive, and there was something about him that resonated deep inside me, something I didn't understand. It confused me, but I realized that even if I never figured out what it was, I liked the feeling of his strong hand on my face and wanted to feel it lower down.

"Yes," I said, and he led me down a path in the forest to a small cabin that I assumed was his own.

The second he opened the door, I was in his arms. It seemed as though I had been thinking about his lips on mine for years, although I had only known him for a little over 24 hours. He pushed my back against the door to close it and I fisted my hands in his hair and kissed him until I couldn't breathe.

He pulled back for a moment to give us both air and said, "Hi."

We were both flushed and breathing hard as we stared at each other wonderingly.

"Bedroom?" he asked.

"Floor," I said, and I tackled him onto the rug that was spread out behind him.

Without even thinking about what he was doing, Matt growled, rolled me off of him, and pinned me hard to the ground. I grunted with the force of his action and he quickly backed off, faster than I would have thought possible, to lean against the couch.

"God," he said, "I'm sorry. I'm so sorry. Reflex reaction. Please don't be scared of me." I crawled over to him and sat back on my knees to touch his face where he held it in his hands.

"Matt. Don't worry. It's okay."

"No, it's not. I shouldn't be violent with a woman. I'm sorry. It won't happen again."

"Not even if I want it to?"

Matt looked at me in confusion, "What?"

I blushed and admitted, "I'm a bit of a pervert. I like a little wrestling for dominance as part of my sex. I like playing with strong enough men that I know can fight them without being worried that I might win. I'm not a small girl, and I found the fact that you could throw me around that easily incredibly hot."

He started to look like he was feeling better, and as a predatory smile crossed his face, I began to be the one to scuttle back, "You did, did you?"

"Um, yes, I. . . ." I squeaked as he pounced me again.

Matt pinned me to the floor with one hand on my

wrists and let his other run up under my dress to feel the dampness that was already soaking through my underwear. "Why yes, it seems like you did."

I moaned as he played with me, enjoying the sensation of being able to use my full strength to struggle against his hands without worrying I might get free. "Please," I babbled, "you're talking to a girl whose biggest sexual fantasy involves supernatural predators."

"Vampires? Truly? You like VAMPIRES?" Matt's voice sounded vaguely disgusted although he didn't stop nuzzling his face in my neck and nipping at my throat.

"No," I purred happily as he switched to pinning my legs with his own so that I could feel the hard bulge of his groin grind against me as he moved the hand that wasn't holding me down to my breast, "werewolves."

Suddenly he froze against me, his body tense against mine. "What did you say?"

"Werewolves," I said. "You know? Men who turn into beasts at the full moon? Teeth and claws and animal hunger?" I sighed. "I wish they were real."

"Mmm." Matt seemed to relax again, and then I decided I must have been imagining the earlier tension as he pulled down the top of my dress and began to kiss his way down my neck.

"I can see how that would be a hotter fantasy than vampires. What do you imagine them doing to you?"

I sighed happily as his mouth closed tightly over my nipple. "Mostly just wonderfully rough, violent, animalistic sex," I whispered in his ear and moved my body against him, gasping in pleasure as he slowly bit down on my nipple, and sneaking my legs free to wrap them around his waist. I wanted to feel the heat of his groin snuggled up against my own.

Suddenly he got to his knees, flipped me over, and pulled me up to all fours. I pushed back against him as he reached around to grab a breast in one hand and slip his other into my panties. He growled in my ear "The kind where the wolf man buries his teeth in your shoulder as he penetrates you roughly from behind, the bristly hairs making you scream?"

"Exactly," I moaned at the thought and then screamed in a sudden orgasm as his fingers found the right pressure on my clit while he ground up his still pants-covered cock against me.

"You know," Matt said, pulling back from me and quickly removing his tuxedo, "we are both wearing far too many clothes."

I started to get up to take off my maid of honor dress, but he pushed me back down to my hands and knees.

"Stay there," he said. I heard the sound of a condom wrapper opening and, as he came back down to my level, gasped once more as he pushed the rest of dress up around my waist and ripped my underwear from my body.

Matt then spread my knees farther apart and pulled my hips back far enough so that I could feel the tip of his penis barely touching the entrance to my body.

"You want this?" he asked, his fingers toying with my clit and playing with the wetness our earlier wrestling had inspired.

"Yes," I said, pushing back against his hand and trying to direct his body into mine. "You want me to take you like an animal?" he kept touching me, tormenting me, but wouldn't come inside.

"Yes, oh god yes, please," I begged.

"I think I'd like that," Matt responded, and he slowly began to push himself into me.

He was a very well-endowed man, and it felt incredible as he worked his cock into me. I loved the sensation of being stretched, being opened, a feeling of pleasure so intense that it was very nearly pain.

Finally he made enough room for himself inside me and we both took a moment to luxuriate in the feeling of his hips snug against my own and his cock pressing deep against my cervix.

Then he grabbed my hips in his hands and slowly began to move. In and out, it felt like each time he entered me he moved deeper, filling more of the space inside me. He shifted my hips again and suddenly his cock was sliding up against my G-spot. I came explosively from the sensation, and he laughed.

"That felt good," he said and started to speed up his rhythm, aiming his thrusts to rub against that place that felt so good. "Do it again."

I think it surprised both of us when I came at his command and suddenly he began to fuck me fast and furious. He pushed my torso down towards the rug and used his hands to keep my hips up as he fucked me harder and deeper until I began to gasp from the intensity.

"Do you need me to stop?" he said, slowing down.

"No!" I cried out. "More! Please, hurt me with your cock if you want to. Just use me. Fuck me. Please."

"Gods," he growled, and sunk his teeth into my shoulder as he continued to drive his cock inside of me. The pain and intensity of his pounding made me come over and over again, including at the very moment he came inside me, thrusting deeper than I would have thought possible as though he could push through my cervix and come out the other side.

Matt collapsed on top of me, and I could feel his cock still throbbing deep inside me as his weight pushed me deep into the rug.

I made happy contented noises as we both tried to catch our breath, and then gasped as he pulled out of me and rolled over to snuggle me into his arms.

"So that would be yes to there being something here, then," he said, after we'd both had a moment to calm down.

"It certainly seems so." I replied. "Who would have guessed?"

"Not Marla," Matt said, and then smacked himself on the head. "Oh god. The reception. We should talk before we go any further but . . ."

I looked at the clock on the mantelpiece. The event had started thirty minutes before. "If we don't get there soon, she's going to kill us."

"You're not kidding," Matt quickly stripped me out of the rest of my dress, hoisted me up over his shoulder, and carried me laughing into the shower.

Fortunately we made it to the reception before the

end of the cocktail hour, and so we escaped the terror of Marla's wrath, although she did give us quite a glare when we came in together with our hair still damp and our clothes somewhat mussed.

Seeing his mother motioning to him from across the room Matt looked at me and said somewhat urgently, "We really do need to talk, but right now we both have responsibilities to my sister. Can you find me after it's all done? There's a clearing near a lightning-split oak tree about a ten-minute walk down the main path into the woods. I'll meet you there after the final song plays."

"Of course." I nodded.

I wondered, for a moment, what was so important for him to discuss with me—an ex-wife? an incurable illness?— but the question quickly slipped my mind as I dove into my duties at the reception. I gave my planned toast, laughed at Matt's, made sure Marla got enough to eat, danced with the small children, and generally had a fabulous time. By the time the bride and groom danced their last dance and headed out to leave for their honeymoon, I was happy and exhausted. I told Marla's mom I'd be back in the morning to help clean everything up and then headed out into the forest.

The moon was still full and the forest sang with the noises of its nighttime creatures. Perhaps I should have been frightened, but the woods felt so welcoming that it was easy to wander deep into their embrace. After about ten minutes of walking, I found the clearing. It was empty and I sat down in the moonlight to wait.

I must have been exhausted, because the next thing I

knew I was waking up to sunlight and the feel of warm fur
against my back.

Fur? I thought and slowly and carefully rolled over to
see an enormous russet wolf curled up behind me, asleep.
His nose was tucked underneath his tail, and as I sat up in
shock he yawned and stretched.

I knew I should be frightened at the sight of those huge
teeth, but he had clearly been there through the night,
and I could find no fear. Instead, I sat extremely still as he
sank back down to open his eyes. They were leaf green, so
familiar, and I gasped in sudden recognition as he pushed
his nose under my hand and flipped it up to lick my palm.

"Matt?" I said uncertainly

The wolf licked my palm again, and then wiggled under
my hand so that I could scratch behind his ear.

"You're beautiful."

He rolled over and showed me his soft underbelly, and
I stroked it gently as he wriggled and yipped in pleasure.

"I can't believe you're real."

The wolf lay on his side and put his head in my lap.

"This is why you were so shocked last night, at my
fantasy."

The wolf licked my toes and made me laugh.

"Oh my god. Does Marla know? Is this why she freaked
out when I said that I wished werewolves were real? Is
this why she choked on her coffee when I told her how
beautiful that wolf the other night was . . . that wolf who
was you?"

"This is what you wanted to tell me isn't it? This is
what you were so strange about. Oh god. I can't believe

I told you about my werewolf kink. I'm so embarrassed. How could I use your reality as my fantasy for sex?"

All of the sudden the wolf growled and pounced, knocking me onto my back. He was enormous, with the weight of a full-grown man, and I was terrified and excited as he put his enormous jaws to my throat. I felt his teeth close gently around my larynx and closed my eyes as I lay frozen in shock. Then I felt something change. When I opened my eyes a moment later, Matt was lying above me in human form, his teeth still around my throat. He bit down gently and then released me.

"Don't be embarrassed," he said, rolling onto his side and looking up at me. "Do you have any idea how hard it is for us to find women who can accept us? Only the men of our kind change, but our wolves mate for life. What we have is special. I feel lucky to have found you.

"Not many of us find women who can accept both sides of us—in the bedroom and out. Marla has never been comfortable with what our father is, what I am. That's why she escaped to the city. Her husband is a normal. She hopes her kids will be too."

I was speechless.

"I don't want to pressure you," Matt continued, "but I felt like there was the possibility of something amazing between us. I'm not asking you for a commitment. I just didn't want to risk us falling for each other without your being fully informed.

"Are you okay?" he asked.

I thought about it and slowly nodded. "I just can't believe you're real."

Looking at him lying naked beside me, I continued, "God, you're so beautiful. In this form, and as the wolf. How can you be so beautiful and strange? It's like a dream to want you this much."

Matt smiled hesitantly. "You still want me?"

I ducked my head shyly. "I want to touch you. Playfully as the wolf." I ran my finger down his muscled abdomen. "Dangerously as the man."

"Dangerously, huh?" Matt rolled back on to me, pinning my hands sharply above my head.

I moaned happily and nodded.

"I have a third form, you know," he lay his weight upon me and whispered in my ear. I could feel him growing hard against me as he said, "Do you want to see it?" He darted his tongue into my ear and I writhed underneath him and nodded. "Close your eyes."

I did, and when I opened them, there was a beast above me. Long-clawed hands pinned mine to the ground, and a creature stuck halfway between wolf and man was poised above me on powerful limbs.

My first instinct was revulsion. Although his other two forms were pure and beautiful, my mind could not, at first, parse the beast man as anything but obscene. Slowly, however, as I looked at how he perched above me, I began to find his shape exciting.

The beast man was the same height as Matt, but with more powerful limbs. Muscles corded thickly beneath his skin and the claws that replaced his finger and toenails were long and appeared sharp. His face was fascinating, with a mouth full of sharp pointy fangs inside soft human lips, and his whole body was covered with a short, dense coat of russet fur.

I stroked my hand down the soft fur of his chest, loving the play of texture over muscle, and soon found my hand hovering near the beast man's penis. It was long and firm . . . and covered with fur. I licked my lips, and my breathing got heavy as I imagined it pushing inside of me. I felt myself start to grow wet.

The beast man breathed in deeply as he caught the scent of my growing arousal. Then he growled deep in his throat, moved one clawed hand to my chest, and used it to rip my dress to shreds.

I was still naked under it from our adventures of the night before, and the beast man smiled. It was a terrifying grin to see, exposing those terrible teeth, and yet somehow it excited me. I shivered in fear and delight and tried to keep from moving as his claws wrapped around my breasts and squeezed lightly, their points pushing into my skin. I moaned quietly in appreciation as he slowly tormented my breasts, teasing my nipples with the sharp tips of his claws so that they became more sensitive and erect.

When I could no longer keep myself from writhing beneath his touch, he used one hand to pin me to the ground, claws at my throat, and scratched the other slowly down my abdomen. Then, suddenly, he used his furred thighs to push my legs apart, and moved those clawed fingers between my legs.

It felt like someone was drawing a knife along my sensitive skin as he slowly ran the edges of his claws along my labia, and my hips moved under his hand. Then he pushed his thumb up under the hood of my clit, the claw pressing against me so hard that I was afraid if I twitched again he'd draw blood.

The sensation was both frightening and intensely arousing. Even more intoxicating was the fact that I could see it was affecting him the same way. As I watched, a soft pink head slipped from the tip of his furred penis and began leaking fluid. It seemed to be getting even bigger, and I bit my bottom lip as I imagined how it would feel to have it inside me.

The beast man saw where I was looking and moved his hands to my hips. I could feel his claws digging into my ass as he raised me up to a convenient angle to begin his penetration. He hesitated, for a moment, so I took my ankles in my hands and held myself open to invite him to continue.

At first, he slid in easily. I was so wet, and the beast man was actually narrower in this form than Matt was as a human. Then he began to pull out, and I felt the burn of his fur inside me being rubbed the wrong way. It hurt and felt incredible, like I'd been fucked for hours and was deliciously raw from being used. As he slid back in, the friction from the fur stopped, but it still seemed though I were being stretched wider. The sensation was so confusing and intense that I reached one hand down to the juncture of our bodies and realized it was true. He was growing inside me.

In this form, it seemed, his penis was like a wolf's. He had penetrated me, at first, using just the bone inside his penis, and only now was he starting to come erect. I whimpered as he pulled out of me again, the combination of size and friction almost too much to bear. Then he pushed deeply back inside of me and stopped.

For a moment, all I was aware of was the sensation of the tip of his cock pressed deep and achingly against my cervix, but then I realized something else was happening too. As though he were truly canine, a bulb at the base of his penis was swelling up inside me, locking us together, and pressing against my g-spot. I came hard from the feeling and the sheer glorious delight of living out a sex scene I had only imagined in my dreams, and that elicited another canine grin.

The beast man changed the position of his right hand on my hip, and reached out his thumb so that his claws were once again playing with my clit. The combination of pleasure and pain with the intensity of him still being swollen inside me made me come again. Then he rolled onto his back so that I was astride him, forcing me to bend my knees or pull agonizingly against where he was locked inside my cunt.

He started playing with my breasts again, using his claws and scratching at my nipples, and I whimpered and moaned as I realized I couldn't get away. I was trapped with him inside me as he teased and tormented me and made me come over and over again until I was crying and begging him to stop.

It was so overwhelming that I closed my eyes to try and find some way to process the sensations, and when I opened them everything had changed. The beast man was once again the best man, and Matt pulled out of my sore and swollen cunt, grabbed my scratched and bruised breasts, and fucked the space between them until he came in a glorious rush of heat all over my chest. Then he rolled off me and collapsed, breathing hard.

"So it was good for you too?" he asked me, watching as I rubbed his warm, slick fluids into my aching skin.

"I think you could say that," I smiled, and as I closed my eyes to curl up against him, I felt the wolf's tongue gently cleaning my skin.

I fell back asleep with the warmth of his fur underneath my hands.

And Ye Shall Eat the Fat of the Land

By Jan Kozlowski

"My God, look at that HOG!"

"Thar-she blows!"

"Holy shit, is that even human?"

Maddik did his best to block out the puerile gibbering and focus on the zaftig Goth barrista he was toying with, but eventually, curiosity overcame hunger and he glanced upward at the wide-screen television to see what had set the cretins off. It was tuned to an all news channel and there, in all her high-definition glory, was the largest, most breath-taking human female he had ever seen.

The audio was muted, but the crawl at the bottom of the screen labeled the woman as Lolly Randall, forty-five, of South Paxton, Connecticut. The graphics further identified her as something called a Food Porn Star and as being responsible for an Internet video that had gone viral and pissed off some powerful people.

Maddik was mesmerized. The station looped the report, playing it every fifteen minutes for the rest of evening. Eventually he pieced the story together out of sheer repetition but dismissed it as unimportant. Only she was important. He couldn't take his eyes of her. By the time the coffee bar closed, he had memorized every curve of her face, catalogued every mannerism and lost himself in her minutia, like the way her abdomen popped and shivered when she laughed and the rhythmic undulations her upper arms made when she coyly waved to the camera. Maddik had had thousands of humans, male and female, in his long existence but this fluttering inside of him, this quickening was a new experience.

It wasn't merely hunger, although he couldn't deny that was part of it. It had been days since he had last fed and to see that much lovely adipose in one place, buttery and luscious, it was like asking a chocoholic not to drool at the sight of Fudge Mountain. But there was so much more about Lolly Randall that fascinated him. Things he couldn't remember noticing before in any other human. Her luminous, gold-flecked eyes. Her throaty, effervescent laugh. And something indefinable that was turning his normally logical and careful brain to mush.

He hurried through the steaming Arizona evening to the anonymous gray haven of his air-conditioned Buick and fished his cell from his pocket.

"Franklin, I need you to get me to South Paxton, Connecticut, ASAP."

"Yes, sir." Electronic squicks and beeps signaled that Franklin was doing his thing.

"Phoenix to Hartford is the most direct, but JFK or Logan will naturally be safer."

"How much time will it add?"

"Not an appreciable amount compared to the risk of you being spotted at a small airport like Bradley. I can get you into JFK and have a car waiting for you. It's only a two hour, thirty-three minute drive from there."

"All right, book it but I need the first flight out. I don't care if it's a party plane for the International Society of Talk Show Hosts, got it?"

"Yes, sir."

"And I also need you find every pixel of data available on Lolly Randall. Two L's in both names. Age 45, from . . ."

"South Paxton, Connecticut?"

"You're good, Franklin."

"Yes. I am. You'll have the file to read on the flight, which is leaving in exactly eighty-seven minutes. I've already loaded the optimum route to the airport on your GPS."

"Thank you, Franklin." But he was already gone.

Lolly Randall settled all 473 pounds of herself at her kitchen table and flipped open her laptop. The video stuff was fun, but it wasn't going to pay the rent, at least not yet, so it was time to get back to work. She made sure that both the camera and the Internet connection were working and then turned her attention to the triple-tiered Argentinean caramel cheesecake dripping in chocolate ganache and dotted with white raspberries that had arrived by special delivery earlier today. She didn't need to read the shipping order to know who had sent it, or what he wanted to watch her do with it. Bob was one of her oldest and most enthusiastic clients, as well as one of the easiest to satisfy.

When the small ding announced that Bob had successfully signed in to their private connection, Lolly reached forward and ran her hand lightly across the cake's shiny dark surface, stopping to teasingly finger the little white nubs of fruit before grabbing a large handful of cake and shoving it between her bright red lips. Bob liked a slow build, so Lolly played with the cake a little, squishing one finger after another deep inside of it, pulling them out slowly, licking and sucking and allowing pieces to slide down her white cotton V neck and land with a small plops deep in her cleavage.

Bob always paid top dollar for a full hour, but Lolly knew he was a thirty-eight-minute guy, so she paced herself accordingly, allowing her moans and gasps to hit a crescendo at the 37:15 mark and sure enough, another ding at 38:02 announced that Bob had disconnected. Two minutes later an email confirmed that her MoneyBuddy account had been credited what amounted to a month's care for her mother at the Paxton Alzheimer's Center, plus a generous tip that would more than cover that camera-mounting bracket she needed to if she wanted to film those drive-bys from her cycle.

Lolly let her thoughts drift to her plans for the next video as she scoured up the remains of Bob's session. Maybe now would be the time to do a sequel to This Is Your Brain on Mac and Cheese Dust, the video poke at addictive food additives that Senator Pork Panties and her cronies had gotten so tweaked about.

As she brainstormed, she cleaned. Sweeping, wiping, scrubbing, crumbing, bending, and moving, Lolly worked up quite a sweat by the time she was done. She was meticulous and missed nothing . . . except for the open video feed left over from her session with Bob.

The eyes that appraised Lolly as she tidied up were neither lustful nor appreciative. They were flat and calculating, measuring what they knew about Maddik and the odds that this woman would be enough to flush him out of hiding and into their hands.

"Dhampir, Chicago is on line one. She wants a status report immediately."

"Put her on speaker."

"Dhampir, where are we on Maddik? Are we close?" She may have been one of the richest and well known women in this time and place, but the need and pain in her voice sounded like every other woman Dhampir had worked for over the years.

"Madame, thanks to the video access you were able to obtain for us through Homeland Security, I was able to identify him as one of the passengers that disembarked at JFK two and a half hours ago. We did our best to follow his path through the HLS SecCam network, but lost him just north of the Connecticut border. We believe though that he may be heading toward a small town in the south western region of Hartford County called South Paxton."

"Why on earth would he go there?"

"We believe he may be trying to make contact with a woman named Lolly Randall. Ms. Randall appeared on National News Network's Daily Recount show last night as part of the DIYVid flap Senator Hamilton has gotten herself into."

"Why would he be so interested in this Randall woman that he would risk traveling in the open to reach her?"

"We're not sure exactly, but part of the puzzle is obvious from the news footage. It is estimated that Ms. Randall weighs approximately 500 pounds."

"Is that enough to draw him out? Surely, he's run across people that large before? God knows I've had at least a dozen on my show over the years. She couldn't be THAT much of a novelty?"

"Actually, people of great weight are a relatively recent phenomenon and a rare public find for a creature like Maddik. As you yourself know, most people of this size are by nature and necessity shut off from the rest of the world. Naturally, Maddik's interest would be piqued."

"If he does find her, how long would he be able to feed off of her?"

"It depends on his heart."

"His heart? What does his heart have to do with it?"

"Madame, while Maddik is more than capable of taking what he wants and needs from any human body, his tastes are refined and his emotions are even more so."

"You've lost me. My producers said he was just a vampire that developed a taste for fat instead of blood. Are you saying their research is inaccurate?"

"Not inaccurate, Madame, just incomplete. There is more to Maddik and his kind. They are complex creatures . . ."

"Dhampir, I don't care about Maddik's complexity, or his heart or his delicate sensibilities. I have the reports.

I have photos of his work. He has the ability to suck ten pounds of fat a day from two tiny holes anywhere on the human body without leaving any marks, bruises or skin flaps. I need this creature. I want this creature. And since only creatures of YOUR kind can see him in his true form, and I am paying you a great deal of money, you will bring him to me. There are no limits to the money I will spend, favors I will call in, or laws I will break in order to obtain him. Do you understand?"

"Yes, Madame, I understand, but . . ."

The phone was already dead in his hand. "Tessa," he called over his shoulder.

"Yes, sir?"

"I need you find the Dunpeal for me."

"But sir, you know she is never available for consultations."

"If my gut is right about what is going on with Maddik, trust me, she will make herself available."

"Sir?"

"Tell her we may have an Eros Effect on our hands."

Lolly had set the alarm for seven, but Benje, her sound guy and web master, obviously missed the memo.

"Lols, have you checked the overnight site stats on LollyBounce.com yet?"

"Benje, it still IS overnight you psycho. Me need sleep you bye now."

"Lolly, no. Wake up. Listen to me. Your little sound bite on NNN has registered huge. We've got over 50,000 hits in the eight hours since it ran. And other stations are picking it up."

"6am is too early for bullshit, Benje."

"No bullshit, Lolly. It looks like you might be riding a perfect media storm here kiddo. According to the overnights, it seems that the good Senator is involved with even more disgusting and unethical stuff regarding the American food stream than we ever imagined and all the channels are beginning to launch investigations. Until they get their own packages though, guess who's little video masterpiece they're running."

"Holy shit."

"And that's not counting the emails and phone messages. The service called me at oh-four-fucking-thirty because their people were overwhelmed with overseas messages asking for comments, interviews, and quotes. I've only had time to scan the emails, but it looks like the press on this side of the pond wants you too."

"Wow. My head is spinning. I need food and coffee before I can process any more of this."

"Understood. But we need to get the whole crew together and figure out how to handle all of this."

"Yeah, absolutely. How about everyone meet for lunch over at Del's?"

"Lunch . . . Lols, I was thinking of rolling by to pick you up in like a half hour. We can get as many people together as possible, maybe Skype in the rest and get our collective asses to the masses."

"Benje, look it's Tuesday. Mam expects me and you know it throws her off if I don't show up on time."

"Lols, sorry I completely spaced on the day of the week. Sure, we can wait until after you see Mam.

Give her a big hug and kiss for me. And call me when you're done. I'll come pick you up and we can go from there."

"Got it. Later bye."

Lolly's head spun but she made herself stick to her Tuesday morning routine. An hour later she was reasonably awake, clean, fed, and ready to face Mam at the Paxton Alzheimer's Center for their Tuesday Morning Chair Fitness Jam.

Since the Center was only two miles down the road, she made the executive decision to take her mutant cycle. It was a scooter/motorcycle hybrid that her friend Elinor had modified for both her comfort and so they could use it for drive-by filming. It had a wide seat, three oversized wheels, a back step for a passenger or equipment, a 24 volt rechargeable battery and a range of about 20 miles. The other cool thing about taking the mutant was that the Center classified it as a therapeutic vehicle and let her drive it right into the facility.

Mam was in her usual spot in the hallway, sitting between her neighbors Mrs. Collins and Ms. Traytek but none of the three even noticed her as she puttered to a stop a full five minutes early. They were all staring hypnotically at a man who Peg Dandrow, the all-business Center administrator, had by the arm and was introducing around the nurse's station.

"Who's the hottie?" Lolly whispered to her mother as she pulled up next to her chair and leaned over to peck her on the cheek.

"Hottie?"

"The guy that Peg's got in an arm lock and that you three ladies can't seem to stop staring at."

"Oh, him. No dear, we're not staring at him because he's attractive, we're all just wondering how he eats breakfast without a face."

"Mam, have they been experimenting with your meds again? Or maybe there's a new dispensing system that they haven't gotten quite right?"

"I don't think so, dear."

"Maybe he's an alien and he eats with his ass," Mrs. Traytek offered.

"I bet he uses his fingers like straws and has eyes in his hands. I saw that on a book cover once. I think it was by that horror chickie with the cake, Gina McQueen."

Got to be the medication, Lolly thought as the three continued their discussion. The man was standing not fifteen feet in front of her and he most definitely had a face. And a pretty damn fine face it was . . . not to mention the smoking bod it was attached to. Tall, lean, a little weathered, middle-aged Eastwood, with a touch of Swayze thrown in, all her favorites in one long buffet. Yum. It flitted through her mind that this was unusual behavior for her, but by then Peg, her guest and their expanding entourage had changed direction and were moving toward her. Two nurses aides on the outside edge jostled by her as they scrambled for a better view.

"You're crazy Keesha, he looks like Jared Leto in Fight Club."

"You hookin meds from the patients again, girl? That guy is Denzel all day."

"I don't know what drugs YOU'RE on but I'm telling you nobody's a bigger Jared fan than me, and that guy could be his clone."

"So you're telling me that not only are you color blind, but you need a seeing eye dog too now?"

Lolly's brain tried to wrap itself around what the aides were arguing about but when she looked up, the man in question was standing in front of her.

"Oooooo, Lolly, I have someone you just have to meet. Lolly Randall, this is Mr. Maddik. Mr. Maddik, this is Lolly Randall."

"Mr. Maddik."

"Ms. Randall."

Lolly reached for the hand he offered and thought she would melt from the surge of energy that slammed through her body. Nerve endings that she didn't realize she possessed exploded into a swarm of horny bees that engulfed her from hair roots to heel spurs and left her gasping for oxygen and physical relief. She wanted this man and if they didn't get off somewhere private she would hump him dry right here in the hallway with her mother and the nurses as their cheering section.

The two stood, hands, eyes, and what felt to Lolly like their souls, locked together. She had had men before. Lust was an old friend, not to mention a well paying one. She had even thought she was in love once but none of that prepared her for this complete body jacking of her head, heart, and genitalia.

Maddik knew he should drop Lolly's hand. Even the more distracted patients were beginning to stare, but he couldn't bear to break contact with her. All of his existence he had been the one who manipulated his quarry's emotions. His powers tapped into their fantasies and hyper stimulated their brain chemicals until they were swept away on waves of passion that not only allowed him to feed easily, but actually sweetened the taste of their lipids.

Bolts of need shot through him. He wanted her. He wanted to taste her, to savor all the parts of her body, to feast on nothing or no one else until the end of his days. His hunger was problematic though. It had been so long that it was almost at an uncontrollable level. He recognized that he was dangerously low on nourishment, but he needed time to explain, to make Lolly understand who and what he was and how he needed her.

"LIMO! LIMO! LIMO! LIMO! LIMO!" Mrs. Collins's screeching burst through their cocoon like a nuclear bomb blast.

Maddik and Lolly both turned to stare out across the facility's manicured lawn as a black limousine and a long line of black SUV's exited the highway ramp across the street and snaked their way up the driveway.

"Maddik, what's going on?"

"Lolly, we have to go, now."

Her first instinct was to question, but one look at his face pushed her to action. "Maddik, get on the back of the cycle. I have an idea."

The extra weight and the obstacle course of a hallway made the trip slower and more difficult than Lolly expected, but by taking a short cut through the library and another more inappropriate one through the physical therapy room, they made it to the kitchen unchallenged.

"CHEF! CHEF! Need your help here!"

"Lolly Bounce! What do you need, sexy girl?"

"We need a place to hide. Bad people will be coming through in a few minutes looking for my friend here. Can you help us?"

"No worries, got your back. Roll this way. We got a nice big storage room down deep in the back. Slide on in and we'll pile some buckets and brooms in front of the door and no one will ever know it ain't a janitor's corner."

"Thanks Chef, I'll owe you one."

"I like the sound of that, Lolly Bounce. Tuck in good, I'll come and get you when it's safe."

The room was large, dimly lit and filled with a collection of dry ingredients, canned goods and other necessities of a busy industrial kitchen. Lolly motored over next to a three-foot high pallet of 100 lb flour sacks and dismounted. Maddik stepped off the back, but as he turned to reach for her hand, he slumped forward and sat down heavily, puffing a small cloud of white dust up around him. Lolly rushed to his side.

"Maddik! Are you hurt? What happened?"

"Not hurt, just weak. Days since I've fed."

"Fed?" The word, along with bits and pieces of other conversations and observations clicked against each other inside her brain.

"Lolly, it's easier and quicker if I show you. May I please?" He held out his hand to her.

"Show me what . . . how . . . ?"

"Who and what I am. I promise I won't hurt you and you'll be able to understand so much better if you'll let me explain it this way."

Lolly nodded and slipped her hand into his. He took it tenderly and brought it to his mouth, brushing the palm with his lips and then clasped it to his chest, over his heart. At first all Lolly felt was a rushing, like he had placed her hand in fast moving water, but then, closing her eyes, images began to flow, ones she realized he was sharing with her. They told his story, his vampiric beginnings, his evolution, his wants, his needs and his mistakes, as well as the code he now abided by and finally his feelings for her. The picture show ran until she had absorbed what she needed to in order to understand him. When it wound to a stop, she lifted her hand from his chest and caressed his face.

"I want you to take what you need from me, right here, right now."

"Lolly, are you sure? If you have any reservations or fears, I'll find another way."

"No, please." She stared into his arctic silver eyes. "I want this. I want to do this . . . for you and for us."

"Us. I like the sound of that word, it's one I've never had a use for before."

Maddik drew Lolly to him and she felt his kiss to her bones. She waited for pain or discomfort somewhere in her body to signal that Maddik was feeding, but all she felt were his lips and hands traveling the length and breadth of her body, igniting it into a carnal flambé. The heat rose with every touch, every caress, and every flick of his tongue. Through the haze she became vaguely aware of Maddik rolling back her right sleeve and she squirmed a little. Her upper arms were the body parts she was most embarrassed about, but he didn't seem to notice or care. He kissed every inch of skin between her elbow and shoulder, finishing up at the thick crease that cut across her bicep. She felt a tickle as his silken hair brushed against skin and then a sudden pinch as he pierced her, followed by complete sensory obliteration as an orgasmic tsunami swept her off the edge of self and sanity and left her floating in soft, warm darkness.

Lolly had no idea how long it took her to remember to function inside her body again. She cracked her eyes open to find Maddik smiling down at her. His eyes were diamonds in the half-light of the storage room, shining with energy and pleasure and just a hint of amusement.

"Wow," she sighed.

"Wow, indeed."

"Is it . . . are you . . . is this always . . . like . . . THIS?"

"No. I'm told it's usually pleasurable for my partner, but no one has ever said Wow before."

"How about for you?"

"Are you asking if it was good for me too?" Maddik said, smiling.

"Yeah, smartie, I am."

"Lolly, feeding for me has always been just a biological function."

Lolly's head dropped and as much as she wanted to be as cavalier about it all as he was, she felt tears begin to gather.

Maddik reached forward and lifted her chin back up. "Until today, Lolly. I felt everything you felt and I never want to feel anything else.

"Oh, Maddik . . ."

CRASH. The storage room door flew inward so hard it bounced off the wall behind it and flew off its hinges. High kilowatt spotlights cut through the gloom and pinned Lolly and Maddik in place like butterflies in a display case.

"Chef, are these the two that asked you to hide them?"

"Yes, sir."

"Chef, how could you?" Lolly called out.

"Sorry Lolly Bounce. They promised me something a little more substantial than jack off material. Maybe a spot in her kitchen. Maybe my own book or TV show deal. Man's got to look after his own interests, sexy girl. And besides, it's not like they want to kill you or your man. They just want to talk, they said. A few minutes of jawing is surely worth a nice career for your old pal Chef, now isn't it?"

"Thank you, Chef," a disembodied authoritative voice said. "Now please go back to your office and wait for us to finalize the arrangements." Lolly and Maddik could hear him muttering as he moved off.

"Now, please escort these two back out to the kitchen. Dhampir is on his way in to make his official ID and then we'll set up a transportation plan."

"Who is Dhampir? What is this all about?" Lolly whispered as they stood, hands entwined, in front of the massive stove, lunch's enormous cauldron of soup stock simmering away, forgotten on a back burner.

Before Maddik could answer there was a fluttering in the smartly dressed black and purple ranks. They parted to allow a short, soft man with enormous dark eyes through. He moved slowly and silently, his loose-fitting clothes and long hair flowing around him like a caul. He glided to a stop less than a foot in front of the couple and paused for a moment, his eyes trying to focus on something that seemed just beyond his sight. Then he reached into his pocket for his cell and punched in a single number.

"Madame, it is not him. Yes, I am standing in front of Ms. Randall and her companion. I cannot positively identify him as the one you are looking for. Yes Madame, I am sorry as well. I understand. Yes, I will be back in Chicago before nightfall." Dhampir lowered the phone from his ear and hit a series of numbers. After a squint at the screen he turned to Lolly.

"Ms. Randall, my apologies for interrupting your morning. My employer wishes to compensate you for your inconvenience and any embarrassment we may have inadvertently caused you, your mother or your friend. A check has already been cut and as of . . . right now . . . has been deposited to your personal checking account." He turned the screen so that Lolly could see the display. "Here is your new balance. Do you find this fair and acceptable?"

Lolly choked out an affirmative reply, or at least she thought she did. She had never seen that many zeros in anything but a math problem.

"Good."

Dhampir raised his hand over his head and with a single circular movement all the black and purple drained from the room. Lolly expected Dhampir to float out after them, but he remained until the three of them were alone.

"Mr. Maddik, I want you to know I did not lie to my employer. As you may be aware, the biological changes you have under gone recently have compromised our identification capabilities. That doesn't mean that I don't know who you are, or that I can't recognize what you are, but the rules of our game are very specific and I will not violate them no matter what these humans pay or command. So you may go, for now. But be assured The Dunpeal and I will find another qualifier and when we do, you and I will see each other again. "

Lolly and Maddik watched as Dhampir floated back through the swinging kitchen doors.

"Do you often get amorphous threats from weird little dudes who can make a million dollars appear in a stranger's checking account?" Lolly asked when she could breathe again.

"Yes, I'm afraid I do. Is that a relationship deal breaker?"

"Nah, you'll find that us ex-Food Porn Stars are pretty cool with stuff like that. Especially if you'll let your full time video producer girl friend roll film on his ass next time he and the Gucci storm troopers drop by for visit."

Maddik laughed and pulled Lolly into a deep embrace. "I think Dhampir may regret the day he ever messed with my girl."

"As long as you never do, Maddik . . . as long as you never do."

Cupid, Cuspid: What's the Difference?

By Lois Gresh

Even Felicia was surprised when they named a new type
of sex addiction after her. I mean, she knew that she was
addicted to sex with Tremorna, and she knew that it was
Tremorna's fangs and claws that turned her on; but *still*, it
was such an *honor*. As her human lover, I went with Felicia
to the award ceremony, and let me tell you, honey, we've
both been gushing about it for months.

Of course, Tremorna had to stay home. She's been
pouting for months, and nothing Felicia and I do seems to
placate her. This is what happens when you have a three-
way love affair with two humans and one *Unguscrotemnacae
pecorthosuperiosum*.

That's longhand for the Tripods—you remember,
those creatures that clawed their way out of the Incan
ruins a few years ago.

Felicia and I fell in love with Tremorna at first sight,
and now the National Sexual Association, aka NSA, has
defined *Feliciadnaughtium* as "characterized by longterm

romantic and physical intimacy with a member of the Tripod species."

The NSA agents guard the house twenty-four hours a day. Tremorna whines that it's claustrophobic to be surrounded constantly by guards. Felicia maintains it's an honor and gives us all respect in the eyes of neighbors. As for me, I'm totally psyched about *Feliciadnaughtium* but want the household bickering to end.

I brush my blond hair and fluff it around my head the way Felicia likes it. I check my makeup and primp a little. It never hurts to add a touch of blue shadow when you have big baby blues like mine. I accentuate my high cheekbones with dabs of peach blush. Guys have to look good these days. We have a lot of competition.

Felicia's at work, so I decide to tackle Tremorna first. If I can get Tremorna to see Felicia's viewpoint, then Felicia will be happy, and our household will rock back to normal.

I leave my dressing room and gaze down the long hall toward the door labelled, POOL. The sconces cast an amber glow across the blue silk carpet. They also cast relaxation vibes into the air, and by the time my toes leave the softness of the dry carpet, I'm tranquilized.

I step onto the wet rug by the pool door. My toes curl. I drink in the musk of chlorine, seaweed, and moss. I'm getting hard. Just knowing I'm about to see Tremorna does that to me.

My god, why doesn't Tremorna know much I love her?

I swing open the door, and there she is in all her splendor:

The Magnificent One.

I tremble from the excitement.

To be near her, to touch her, to be enveloped by her—

Tremorna hears the door and shifts her weight to two of her three legs. She grumbles at me. "Have you come to gloat, Harold?"

"No," I say. "I've come because I love you. I want things to be the way they were before the whole . . . *Feliciadnaughtium* . . . thing, I mean, award. Come on, Tremorna, let it go. You're hurting all three of us."

Tremorna's neck curls like a snake on top of her body. Now, she unwinds the snake and dips her head so we're eye level with each other. I give in to Tremorna's four coconut-sized eyes. My head starts whirling. Any human who has ever gazed into the eyes of a Tripod knows how intoxicating it can be: like looking into a child's kaleidoscope while high on narcs.

I feel the warmth of Tremorna's breath on my knees and thighs. "They should have named the award after me, Harold. You know how I feel about it. *I'm* the Tripod, not you or Felicia. It's longterm romantic and physical intimacy with *me* that matters."

I stroke the calico fur coating Tremorna's cheeks. I feel the nubs of Tremorna's fourteen cheek fangs. I quiver. My hands move to Tremorna's forehead tail and caress a cluster of claws. The tail curls down, and the claws rake strands of hair from my face. I quiver again. "Tremorna, please. This is still a society run by humans, so they called our love a human name. What does it matter?"

Tremorna stomps one of her three hooves on the pool tiles. The whole room vibrates. Her neck zooms back up the ceiling. Her coconut eyes disappear from view. The room stops whirling. I blink a few times, clearing my vision. Tremorna says, "What am I, an animal? Do I have no respect, no rights? They didn't even hold the awards ceremony in a hall large enough to accommodate me. And *I'm* the Tripod!"

"Jealousy does not become you," I say.

"Well, la-de-*da*, Harold." About half a mile over my head, Tremorna's lips purse. Calico fur everywhere, even on her tree trunk legs, softer than a cat's belly. At least two hundred fangs embedded all over her body, legs, and three arms included. At least five hundred claws—at last count during the romp the three of us had at the beach last season—on the forehead tail, neck, paws, and rump.

Tremorna is a *Beauty*.

"How about we all go to the beach again?" I say. "We had so much fun there, remember?"

"Sure, I remember, Harold. But that was before the award. Now we're surrounded by NSA agents. We can't go anywhere."

"I'm sure we can work something out. It's not as if they're forcing us to stay in the house. I mean, Felicia leaves the house all the time. She's at work as we speak!"

"She's human. She has rights. So do you."

"You're being ridiculous. You're allowed to go outside, Tremorna."

"Won't matter. If we go to the beach, we'll have no privacy. The agents will be there. They'll watch us have sex, Harold."

Tremorna sinks her tons of flab, tails, hooves, and fangs

into the pool. The water is deep like a lake. Seaweed splashes all over me. The coconut eyes stare at me again. "Care for a swim, Harold? A small dose of *Feliciadnaughtium*?"

My heart beats faster. "Oh yes, Tremorna!"

A snicker. A sly grin. Then Tremorna dips her snake of a neck beneath the water, and lights flicker through the pool windows a mile away. I know the NSA agents are recording everything we do through those windows. I imagine them—lank and skinny, faces like ugly curses, all wearing black suits and ties, wishing they had even one mild sexual addiction. Hell, I doubt anyone in the NSA even *has* sex. They probably all still live with their mothers.

I slip out of my clothes and toss them on the bench by the door. My chest and torso are hairless and bronze. I'm branded, a thousand times over from a thousand sexapades with Tremorna, with her imprint: whirligigs of cupids and cuspids are etched into my flesh from my shoulders to my feet, tattoos from the bas relief designs on her hooves. I didn't even feel the branding when Tremorna did them. I was too intoxicated by her love.

I glance down and wonder if Tremorna finds my appearance sexy. Can a Tripod feel that way about a human? My body is toned from daily six-hour workouts on the FlubGrinder and ButtWhacker in Felicia's Goddess Room. Thanks to the publicity surrounding the *Feliciadnaughtium* award, I'm slated to be the official spokesperson for both FlubGrinders and ButtWhackers, and other than being with Felicia and Tremorna, the promo gig is just about the best thing that's ever happened to me. I haven't told Tremorna about the gig yet, and I don't plan to tell her any time soon.

I sit on the edge of the pool, then slide into the water. The seaweed and moss stroke me with velvet caresses. I'm dizzy from the high of the chlorine, the prospect of having Tremorna to myself for a few hours before Felicia comes home.

Tremorna's four coconut eyes rise from the water, and her forehead tail twines around my body, then releases me so I spin through the water like a top. I'm giggling as I pluck the seaweed from my shoulders, and then Tremorna unfolds that heavenly tongue and brushes dozens of cuspids across my face. "Your blush is running, and there's a trace of blue eye shadow on your chin—let me get that for you." *Lick lick*, and the cuspids rake down my cheeks and across my forehead and chin. I gaze into the whirling multicolor eyes, feel the tang of narcotics in my blood as the cuspids prick me in a hundred places.

I grab the calico fur on Tremorna's belly and sink my head against my favorite set of claws. The NSA video lights stream through the windows at all angles. They'll probably post our sex video on the internet tomorrow, but what do I care? Tremorna's the shy one of our little threesome.

The claws, the fangs, the eyes, *my god*, and then Tremorna presses me to the moss on the bottom of the pool and flattens me under one of her hooves. I'm branded again with the imprint of The Magnificent One. I'm numb from narcotics, and the pressure and pain are making my head float, and I'm no longer in Felicia's pool of seaweed and moss and chlorine, but rather, I'm adrift in the Mediterranean Sea, surrounded by aquamarines and clear green, a froth of bubbles, a curl of wave, warmth warmth *warmth* . . .

The sun kisses me, and all is still: I hear a bird chirp, see it flit through the pink haze of the sky. Tremorna's hoof releases me, and hundreds of claws lift me back to the surface of Felicia's pool. I gasp for air, and my head starts clearing, but my body is still thrumming in heat. I need Tremorna. I can wait no longer.

"Please," I whisper, "give me the eyes."

"And in return, Harold," Tremorna whispers, "what will I get?"

The murmurs of humans replace the stillness of the Mediterranean and the chirp of the bird. Black coats and ties surround the pool. At least fifty of them: all lank and skinny with faces like ugly curses; the NSA agents are watching us up close, the videos are no longer enough for them.

With a jolt, I realize that the NSA agents have the addiction. Bad, bad cases of *Feliciadnaughtium*.

Some are already stripping and heading for the pool's edge. Hairy bodies in need of the toning equipment in Felicia's Goddess Room. This flesh is imprinted by nothing, not even by human hands. I can almost smell their naiveté. Old with pocked acne cheeks, some of the agents are balding already, but still, they have the look of teenagers on their first sex high.

"Sickening, isn't it?" growls Tremorna. "That they come and watch me, that they name their desire for me after a human, that they study me as if I'm in a cage. Yet I should be the one in control, Harold, shouldn't I?"

"You should," I agree, "yes, you have all the power, all of it." I grasp her fur, trying to tug the long snake neck down so I can stare into her eyes. I want the NSA to leave us alone, but I want sex with Tremorna more than I care about these pathetic weenie agents. Let them get their rocks off watching us, what do I care?

"I can give, and I can take. Harold, if I give you the eyes, what will I get in return? You still haven't answered."

I shove an NSA agent away from us. He falls into a pocket of seaweed, and water splashes. They're coming at us like zombies, drugged just by Tremorna's *appearance*. I kick off another one, he has a clipped beard and no hair, pimples on his chest, no muscles.

The National Sexual Association definitely needs to up its standards when hiring agents. My god, what does an award mean when it comes from a bunch of sexless zombies?

"I want to be loved for me, Harold, not just for my fangs, claws, and big eyeballs."

"But I *do* love you, Tremorna, with everything in me."

"You only like the way I look, the hormonal surges you get. It's all lust, Harold, nothing more."

"No. I *love* you, Tremorna. Oh, *please*, just give me the eyeballs!"

She growls and stomps her hooves on the bottom of the pool. A giant wave splashes onto the tiles and slams several NSA agents against the walls. They're so deep under the spell of *Feliciadnaughtium* that they don't notice that their foreheads are gashed and their skulls are oozing blood. Seaweed flies up and slaps me across the face. I scrape green slime off my cheeks.

I'm about to tell Tremorna again that I love her when the pool door whips open. It's Felicia, home from her long day at Flint, Buster, and Weesle, the hotsie law firm downtown where she's general counsel, whatever that means. "Honey doll," she says to me, "whatever's going on in here? Your hair's a mess, your shadow's all smeared." Felicia's nostrils flare. She's drinking in the chlorine, the seaweed, the moss, the sex perfume of Tremorna. "*Darling*," she gushes at Tremorna, "I've missed you so! Tell me all about your day!"

I'm not jealous. I'm used to this sort of thing. Being humans, Felicia and I are close as companions, but both of us are addicted to Tremorna. I cling to a paw and suck on the protrusions: voluptuous bulges tipped by points, Tremorna's claws are everything a man could possibly desire. As my mouth sucks, the claws swell with heat and effervesce with love perfume that further clouds my mind. The paw is throbbing in my hands with dozens of claws opening in my mouth like rosebuds. She's so sweet, so pure, like nectar, and my mouth is drenched in her fluids, my nose filled with her scent.

And now Felicia is beside me, holding onto another paw, sucking the claws and spreading her legs across Tremorna's stomach. Felicia is gyrating, and I know she's getting off on the rub of the calico fur.

"If you really want to know, my day was fine," says Tremorna.

I release her paw. Poor Tremorna. She gives and gives, and like she was trying to tell me only moments before, what does she ever get in return?

Felicia lifts her head from a claw. Her lips are red and plump. Her brown eyes glow, her wet hair clings to her breasts and back. "I'm sorry, sweet thing. Tell mama what you did all day."

Tremorna rolls four eyes. "I sat in the pool while NSA agents masturbated to my every move. What did *you* do?"

"I dreamed about being with you and Harold."

Tremorna snorts. "Yeah, right."

"But why don't you believe us, Tremorna?" says Felicia. She gazes around the pool room at all the NSA agents slumped against the walls and floating in the water as if knocked out with sleeping pills. "What are we going to do with them?"

"I want to be with another Tripod, someone like me. A member of the *Unguscrotemnacae pecorthosuperiosum* species. Male or female, I don't care which."

"But you're infertile, Tremorna," I point out.

"I don't want children. I want love." She pouts.

"This is impossible. There are only a few Tripods on the whole planet. You're being difficult. You have a good life here with us, and we *do* love you. Why can't you be satisfied with what you have?" Then Felicia gestures at me, and we both pull ourselves out of the pool and sit on the edge. Felicia whispers in my ear, "What can we do to persuade her already? She's driving me crazy, Harold."

I nod. It is a bit much the way Tremorna has been carrying on since the *Feliciadnaughtium* award. On the other hand, Tremorna has a point. I love her mainly for the sex, but I *am* very fond of her and I'm much happier when she seems to like me.

"I want to go to the beach," whimpers Tremorna. "You can disguise me so nobody knows it's me."

Felicia laughs, gets up, grabs a towel from the Goddess Rack. She tosses me an extra fluffy towel the color of clouds. It matches my eye color, and Felicia casts me a lascivious look that lets me know she notices. I feel my cheeks go crimson. I love it when Felicia notices me.

"Listen, doll baby," she says to Tremorna, "you're half a mile tall. What do you want us to disguise you as? The Empire State Building?"

Tremorna sighs, and I fear that she might start crying. Maybe her misery is more serious than I thought. Could it be that she's depressed? In need of a psychiatrist? But who can we get who specializes in the sexual frustration of Tripods?

Felicia's the smart one of our little threesome. She's a general counsel. I'm just a pool boy, basically, and Tremorna's like a big sex kitten. Felicia suddenly grabs my arm and jumps. "First I'll call the NSA and get them to remove the agents. And this reminds me of something, Harold. I was talking to the NSA president, who said they're trying to figure out just what it is about Tripods that makes humans addicted to them."

"Honey, I don't understand—" I start to say.

She cuts me off. "Imagine if they can reverse-engineer the sex chemicals in Tremorna!"

"Meaning?"

"Meaning," said Felicia, "they might be able to come up with the exact reverse, something for Tremorna that lets *her* get off on *us*!"

"Absurd," says Tremorna. "If they reverse-engineer my love fluids, all they'll get is an antidote to *Feliciadnaughtium*. Is *that* what you want?"

Felicia and I stare at each other. Tremorna has out-smarted Felicia. Of course, Felicia is intoxicated right now on the very love fluids we're discussing, but still, neither of us thought Tremorna was even capable of understanding the notion of reverse engineering. We've always thought of her as . . . well, as a bimbo.

"If you love me," says Tremorna, "then you'll pleasure me as I pleasure you."

It does seem like a fair exchange, but we don't have a clue how to arouse a Tripod. After the NSA grunts come and carry off their agents on stretchers, Felicia and I try our hardest to arouse poor Tremorna. We want her to be happy. We want her to feel pleasure.

We rub the two hundred fangs that coat her body. We suck on the five hundred claws. We massage the forehead tail, cover the calico fur with scented oils and massage her flab. We show her lewd photos of other Tripods, but the pictures only make her eyes tear. Being infertile like a donkey, she has no sexual organs, and trust me, honey, we know her body well and there are simply no cavities other than her mouth and nostrils and nothing remotely resembling my penis.

We play soft music. We light sconces and cinnamon candles. We give her special treats to nibble, everything she loves: roasted seal chunks, saltwater taffy, and ninety-five pounds of peanut butter and jelly sandwiches. Strawberry goo is stuck to her fur. We lather her in citrus shampoo, wash her fur, condition it, and run our fingers through it to make it smooth. Nothing seems to help. Tremorna remains as depressed as ever, and she isn't getting off on anything we do.

By now, it's midnight, and Felicia and I are both exhausted. We need to curl up in bed beside each other and fall asleep. Felicia has a big day tomorrow at the office. She's suing the governor of some state for cheating on his wife with a goat and three chickens. And I need my beauty sleep. "We have to go now, Tremorna," I say. "I'm so sorry."

"But I want to go with you. I don't want to sleep all alone," Tremorna whimpers.

"Well, we could try to sleep on the pool floaties again," says Felicia. "It's not very comfortable for us, but for you, Tremorna, we'll do anything."

"Please," says Tremorna, "let me cradle you in my forehead tail all night."

We climb onboard her beautiful furry body, and she lifts us to her forehead tail, which curls around both of us and hugs us tightly. Tremorna is warm, and I can feel her heart beating beneath the soft calico fur. Felicia and I snuggle together. With Tremorna.

And then The Magnificent One, the Beauty of all Beauties, she gurgles with contentment, and I feel her breath stroke my face as she rakes her cuspids across me. Oh, that feels good.

As Felicia and I doze off, I hear the voice of an angel. Tremorna. "Some people give," she whispers, "and some people take. Always, I give. And my two lovers give to me. They can call it whatever they want. *Feliciadnaughtium* or *Tremornacosis* or something else. In the end, my beauties, the three of us are addicted to the same thing."

Will Power

By Cecilia Tan

We vampires are creatures of will, for wasn't it willfulness that caused Lucifer to turn from grace and fall? If that is, indeed, where we come from; I do not claim to know. I do know that nothing happens in a vampire's life that is not an act of will. Humans beget other humans by accident. They die by accident. Not so with us.

There is only one way to make a vampire, and only one way for us to die. Don't believe the myths. A stake to the heart? A painful way to punctuate a chapter in eternal life, but not the end. Get staked, though, and it is certainly time to move on to another place, another hunting ground. Sunlight? Painful to immolate, painful enough to drive some mad, but we coalesce again once night falls.

I have never been staked. Perhaps this is because my human servants always served me with true loyalty, not the mere compulsion of my will. Served me and my needs in every possible way, as serfs, as dragoons, as butlers, and nowadays as collared sexual submissives.

Like Geordy, who would let me do almost anything to

him. It would not be unusual to see him hanging slack in
his wrist cuffs, his blond hair darkened by sweat, his entire
back red and speckled from flogging. No individual welts
would stand out if I had given him a thorough tenderizing.
I would step forward with a piercing needle in my hand.
He would shiver as my fingernails played lightly over his
skin and he'd whisper "Mistress," not to get my attention,
but purely for the pleasure of naming me, of reveling in
his submission.

The first time I pierced him was in a public dungeon
in the city, and an overzealous dungeon monitor put a
stop to it, not because of the blood, but because he feared
Geordy's circulation would be damaged by how he hung
in the cuffs.

We could not very well explain to a mere human that,
as a vampire servant, Geordy was far more difficult to
damage than that. Geordy had been a callow youth of
eighteen when we first met. Twenty years later, thanks to
regular tastes of my blood, he appeared to have aged only
to his mid-twenties.

In private our usual game was to lay him down and
tie his wrists and ankles to the bed, then bind his cock
and balls so that his quite sizable prick would be swollen
and straining. Do you know what happens if you pierce
an erect penis? Especially one that is bound? Blood
everywhere. But a vampire needs blood to stand in for all
bodily fluids, and if I wanted to fuck him—and I always
did—I needed to feed.

There was such ecstasy to take him in my mouth and
pierce him with my teeth, and feel the hot jet of high

pressure fluid into my throat. Then I would mount him, his blood coating my insides as I pushed myself down onto that eager, pulsing cock.

Each time we made love in such a way, in his eyes I saw his love deepen and his devotion take hold more tightly. You can see why I entertained the thought of making him mine eternally.

But just as with a human baby, no single vampire can make a new child. It takes two. I could not Turn him alone.

My petition was rejected. We are few in number by design, as it is important the hunting population must not outpace the herd, so I knew there was always a chance they would deny me. But after five hundred years I have never Made another and I thought they would consider this in my favor. As I stalked from the underground council room, I held in a sob. Geordy's death would be forty or fifty years off, and yet in that moment it was as if I could see him dying before my eyes.

I made my way through the tunnels toward the surface half-blind with unshed tears. I had just reached the ladder to the subway platform when I heard the scrape of a sole against the concrete behind me.

I turned, wary, and my wariness only increased when I recognized the figure coming slow step by slow step toward me. There was no mistaking his panther-like demeanor. "Favian. What are you doing here?"

"Mara," he said, coming close enough that now I could see his face. His hair was as raven-black as always, and it hung straight and lank over his shoulders. He had been dark-skinned when he had been turned, and so retained a bit more color than some. "Just passing through, tending to some council business."

He said no more, as if daring me to demand a fuller answer, or perhaps hinting I deserved none. I turned from him and began to climb the ladder.

"Mara!" It was the sudden undertone of urgency in his voice that stopped me, moreso than his hand on my arm. "I heard of your petition."

I jerked my arm free, looking down on him from the second rung. "Then you heard it came to nothing."

Looking up into my eyes, his held surprising sympathy. "Perhaps it doesn't have to," he said.

There once was a time when I had trusted him. A long time ago. A small argument sprang up in my head, reminding me on the one hand that trust was long since gone, and on the other that it was so long that surely he might have changed . . .? "You have a proposal?"

He glanced behind him as if to ensure we were alone. "Not here."

Was I going to trust him? Not enough to bring him to my haven, where Geordy was waiting. Not enough to go with him to any domain of his, either. "Come have coffee with me, then," I said, and climbed the rest of the way up the ladder without looking back.

The city has no shortage of places to have coffee and an intimate conversation in the middle of the night. He followed me to a diner on the east side, where I could have my coffee espresso-dark but adulterated with chocolate and hazelnut both. Vampires do not eat, but we can pass liquids easily enough, and flavored coffees were among my recent vices. He settled for tea himself, facing me in the booth with one hand on the Formica table as if he wanted to take my hand, like we could be any pair of ex-lovers talking.

"Your proposal?" I pressed, once we were settled with our drinks.

"You have been so wrapped up in your human life, you may not realize how much influence I have with the council," he said, his voice oddly devoid of bravado. "I can make a deal that would allow your wish to be granted."

When two people, humans or vampires, know each other as well as Favian and I once did, it isn't necessary to spend a long time working up to a point of negotiation. "What is your price?"

He chuckled. "Aren't you curious about what machinations might go into—"

"Favian. What. Is. Your. Price."

He sobered then, looking at me. "Be mine again for a night," he said, his voice low. I could almost taste the longing on his tongue as he spoke the words. "Just one night, wear my collar again."

"I never wore a collar," I pointed out.

"Metaphorical or actual, I don't care," he said, lifting his teacup. "One night on my terms, with your complete obedience."

"And if I am disobedient? Will you punish me by breaking the deal?"

Now his laugh sent a wave of gooseflesh down my back, and set other parts of me tingling in anticipation.

"No, dearest, I will have many other ways of punishing you before the sun rises. Some of which you might even like. I suppose if you disobey I will have to assume you do."

"Bastard," I hissed. He knew he had me. He knew I wouldn't say no.

"And of course for this to work, I'll need to be your other Maker." He sipped now, only looking up at me from under hooded eyes.

"I figured as much," I said, hoping he was disappointed that he hadn't managed to shock me with that part. "But Geordy will never be anything of yours. Once he is Turned, he will be mine and mine alone."

Favian shrugged. "I have no interest in your boytoy, I assure you." He set down the teacup, and I heard another sound, a tiny metallic clink. When he lifted his hand I saw he had put down a small key. "At sunset, then," he said, in a voice that already presumed I would obey.

And damn him if he wasn't right about that.

Geordy awaited me at sundown as he always did, naked, on his knees beside my four-poster bed, waiting for me to draw the curtains aside. His face, though, was drawn and troubled rather than beatific as he looked up at me.

I had told him when I'd woken him before sunrise what was going to happen. He didn't like the thought of me spending the night with Favian, which was wholly appropriate—if he hadn't been jealous and territorial I would have considered him nothing more than a slave to my whims and not a mate at all. He also questioned whether Favian could actually deliver on his promise to have my petition reconsidered, and granted, and was disappointed that I had not pressed for details of his plan. The plain truth was that I believed Favian, and I believed in Favian, and Geordy was right when he said I trusted him too much.

I don't know why I trusted him. Perhaps because I thought I understood his motivations. One more night with me, perhaps for retribution? I did not tell Geordy our whole history, or he would have likely fought even more vehemently. I had once loved Favian the way Geordy loved me. I had been a human servant to—for lack of better words—a vampire king and queen, and they had made Favian into their vampire prince. It amused them to see their prince dominate their female servant, playing out scenarios of lust and pain before their eyes night after night. I loved him and he loved me, I have no doubt of that.

But love is no guarantee of happiness. In fact, I might say Favian feared both happiness and how intensely he loved me, and he was short-sighted in his pursuits of pleasure and power. He broke the promises he had made to them, sleeping with the queen. The king would not stand for this, of course, and cast Favian out, and then forced his queen to help him Turn me before casting her out as well, and making me queen in her place.

Do I even need to tell you when or where this was? I do not think so. The country where it all took place does not even exist any longer, and as you can imagine, this underground kingdom did not long stand. I did not love the king and he did not love me, and after a short span of years in misery, he finally took his own life in the only way we can. I shall never forget the way his eyes seemed to turn to glass, his skin becoming translucent as he suffered toward his final days.

It was long ago. I have been submissive to no man since, though I never lost my taste for what today people name "bondage" and "sadomasochism."

In the end Geordy bowed his head before me, though. For all I let him argue and express himself, ultimately I am still his Mistress. My word is law, and this is what calms his heart and makes him truly mine. I kissed him and left him kneeling by the door, promising him I would return before sunrise. But as I went out the door I wondered if I would be much changed the next time he saw me.

I had debated what I should wear. In the end I had decided on a simple black dress, which would be good enough for seduction and simple enough for submission. No underwear. The seduction came first, as I fed on a stranger before taking the key in the palm of my hand and letting it lead me where it would. Favian had given me no instructions, so I assumed he would want me at my peak. With fresh blood in my veins, my nipples would harden when pinched and I could become slick between my legs.

The doorway I came to was in a basement, and I leaned my palm against it as I tried to catch my breath. The key tingled in my palm, even as other parts of me did, too, with phantom sensations of pleasures and cruelties of the past recalled.

All those years ago, I had been the one to betray him to our sovereigns. I had been hurt and jealous that he had taken up with the queen. But had I truly been Favian's, and been loyal to him, would I have told?

I reminded myself that I was the one who was wronged. His transgression is what destroyed the order of things. But that didn't change the fact that if he believed himself the wronged party, I might be handing myself to him for a night of revenge.

Fine, I thought. We will both get what we want. He shall finally get retribution for my betrayal, and I will finally get the eternal companion I deserve. If only I have the nerve to walk through this door.

I slipped the key into the lock.

"Lie down and spread your legs."

His tone was cold, yet his voice seemed to come from right beside my ear and I jumped, startled. I knelt where I was, not even bothering to remove the black cocktail dress. I had kicked my shoes off inside the door and made my way in pitch blackness to what I had guessed was the center of the room, wondering if it was some power of his that was keeping me in blind darkness.

I lay on my back on what felt like a padded rug, my knees bent and my feet about three feet apart on the carpet.

"Wider," he said, and I knew exactly what he meant. "Hands behind your head. And now hold still."

I expected to feel the touch of a blade at any moment, some kind of cold steel, for this was exactly how we had performed for our sovereigns in the past. Only then I was blindfolded and made to follow the sound of his voice around the room, sometimes taking the sting of a lash as I stumbled about, until eventually it would always come to this, with me lying passive and awaiting him.

"Favian—"

"Silence." I flinched at a touch on my cheek, but it was his hand, not a dagger. "You're warm. You've fed."

"Yes."

"You presume much about what your master wants."

I felt myself flush with embarrassment. I had tried to use his name instead of his title, as if I didn't know better! Still, I could not shrink before him. "Given your lack of instructions, *Master*," I said, emphasizing the honorific, "my presumptions were all I had."

His hand slid down to my breast, toying with one nipple, and I heard him break into a chuckle. "Which just goes to prove how well you know me, Mara. Even after all these years." He coaxed that nipple until it was stiff and nearly aching for more than just his teasing touch, then moved his hand to the other. I whimpered a little, my breath growing ragged. "And I see your body lost none of its responsiveness when you became immortal."

I gasped. He still knew just how to touch me to set me afire, alternating between touches so light my skin yearned for more and sudden pinches that sent arousal blossoming all through me.

His fingers ran over my lips. "Isn't it funny, how our bodies remember what it was to be alive? How when we are afraid, our breath speeds up and grows uneven, like yours is now, Mara?"

His voice was as soft as his touch and I did not answer, assuming his question to be rhetorical. The next one he asked, though, required an answer. "Are you afraid of me, Mara?"

"Y-yes, Master."

He bent to kiss me then, as if he wanted to taste that word on my lips, and I could have cried it was so sweet.

I had forgotten what it was like, to sink into the well of submissiveness. I had expected pain, I had expected him to tear me to pieces. But he never did more than I was ready to take, leading me ever deeper through some flogging, some pain, some predicaments, some pleasure. Indeed, he put me through the same paces I would have put a submissive through and had he not I feel we would have both been disappointed. After the kiss, the darkness lifted, and I saw we were in a room outfitted as a modern bondage dungeon, and very few of the implements I saw hanging on the wall went unused.

I enjoyed all he did, far too much for anything to feel like revenge.

But time moves forward, the Earth turning its face ever toward Heaven, and sunrise was coming inevitably. With his fist in my hair and his breath in my ear he said, "You have pleased me well, Mara. For a reward, you may choose the position I fuck you in."

"Yes, master," I answered, though my mind was racing. What position? He had never allowed me to choose before, and I felt there must be some significance in my answer. He let go of me then, and took a step back, waiting for me to assume whatever position it would be.

I could bend myself over a padded horse, lock myself into a pillory, get on all fours on the floor, lean against the wall and lift one leg . . .

No. I knew how he wanted me. And how I wanted to be taken.

I moved to the open center of the room again, and lay down on my back, spreading my legs and putting my hands behind my head, just as he had bade me do when I had first entered. As I closed my eyes I heard him whisper, "Very good, Mara."

Approval washed through me like a cleansing rain.

"You know what comes next?" he said, from very close. He must have been kneeling or sitting beside me now.

"The knife," I answered. "Please, Master."

I nearly opened my eyes to look at his face as I heard his breath catch. "Y-yes, the knife, dear one."

He touched it to my cheek then, the needle-sharp point of it, not to cut me, but to heighten my awareness of the threat the blade represented. The next place I felt it was on my shoulder, and this time he drew a light line with the tip down my arm, making me shiver.

If you have never been loved with a knife, I do not know that I can convey how sublime the sensation is. A more arousing caress is hard to imagine, for it stimulates and pleases the skin when done lightly, and then burns not with pain but with passion when applied with slightly more force. That certainly had not been what I expected, all those years ago, when he had laid me down upon an altar as if I were a ritual sacrifice, and proceeded to make me cry out in pleasure and lust using just a dagger.

And it was not entirely what I expected now. I was not the inexperienced virgin any longer, and not the fragile mortal he had enthralled with his power and his beauty, then, either. Yet still the blade in his hand could thrill me.

"Don't move," he admonished, as he drew the point between my legs, pressing it lovingly against my clit. My heart no longer beat as it did when I was mortal, but full of mortal blood my flesh responded as it once had, the nub throbbing as he subjected it to gentle torture with the blade.

I felt the very tip pierce the skin, just enough to let a ruby red droplet of blood well up, and then his tongue replaced the dagger, lapping at the tiny wound and making me cry out again with the intensity of pleasure.

And then he lifted his head and said, "Don't move" once again, and I sighed with pleasure as I felt him slide the blade between my labia, easing it into me as if my body were a well-oiled sheath. He fucked me as gently with it as if I had been mortal again, making my legs quiver.

"Master," I gasped. "Please."

He slowed the motion of the blade even more. "Please what, dear one?"

My voice failed me, then. I was not sure I could beg. There was still a vestige of pride in me, after all.

"I can guess," he purred, "but I should not have to. I've seen the size of the cock on your boytoy, you know. Is that one of the reasons you chose him? Surely it must be."

I did not know if that was mere talk, just something he

said to get a rise out of me, or if he truly had observed me with Geordy at a public dungeon.

"Oh, and now you are thinking of another man's cock," he said, "Aren't you? Don't lie."

"Yes, Master. Yes, I am." It was one of those games, and I knew it, for how could I not think about what he was describing? But it was a game I had once enjoyed playing endlessly, and I remembered how to now. "Please let me make it up to you."

"And how will you do that?"

"Let me please you, Master. Let me worship your cock."

I felt the knife withdraw and heard his satisfied grunt. We swapped positions then, and I worshipped him with my mouth, licking and sucking him. Somewhere deep in the back of my mind I wondered whom he had fed from to have the blood for such a prodigious erection. Did he have a human servant, too? Or had he fed on a stranger like I had?

"Enough, dear one," he rasped, and I realized I had been sucking him for a long time. "If you make me come I will leave you unsatisfied."

I pulled off him quickly at that, and lay back again. He positioned himself atop me, sliding the slick head through the ooze of fluids from my slit but not entering me yet. He teased me with the tip of his cock the way he had the point of the knife, until I was close to coming.

And then he plunged into me and took me so hard and fierce I cried out, my own wail drowning out what he murmured, but it might have been, "How I've missed you."

Or maybe that was only what I wished he'd said. For after five hundred years apart, my body molded to his like we had been fashioned to fit together.

I barely made it home in time, the birdsong coming from the park as I rushed into the building as menacing a sound as the growl of any predator. But inside the apartment it was cool and dark, and I was leaden and sleepy as I put my hand onto the bowed head of Geordy, waiting there for me as if he had not moved all night. Although I appreciated the gesture of loyalty, his role so long as he was human was to do the daytime tasks we needed.

But soon enough we would have to find a new servant.

"Favian will help me Turn you," I said.

"I can smell him on your skin." Geordy wrinkled his nose.

"And I will smell him on yours," I answered. "For all eternity."

That cowed him. "Yes, Mistress."

"One week, then we begin." I said, and then I went to my bed, to sleep the sleep of the dead.

It was a long week. I was restless and irritable, as I always was before making any major change. Living for centuries had only made me more apt to cling to routine and the familiar when I had it. A few times I took blood from Geordy so we could make love, but I did not shackle him or flog him. I told him I was saving that for the night of his Turning.

I took the time to be sure he understood the full implications of immortality, as well. I had not told him until then what it took for a vampire to die.

"I thought we couldn't be killed," he said, frowning at me as he ate a plate of tortellini in cream sauce, one of his favorite foods that he would soon no longer find so appealing.

"We cannot be killed, but we can die, if we choose to," I said, sipping a cup of rose-petal tea. "It's a slow process, and supposedly quite painful. You stop drinking blood and start drinking holy water instead. After you reach a certain point of saturation, which takes a few weeks at least, then you immolate on the steps of a church. If you've drunk enough holy water, you don't re-coalesce."

"Do you know anyone who died that way?"

"Only one," I said.

Geordy put his hand atop mine. "You look sad."

I shook my head. "It was a long time ago, when I was newly Turned," I said. "And he was ancient."

"What made him decide to finally give it up?" he asked, as brimming with naiveté in that moment as he was with fresh blood. I had been Geordy's first and only love. How could I explain it to him?

Perhaps I couldn't. I could merely tell. "Someone broke his heart," I said with a shrug.

It would take three nights to Turn Geordy. On the first night he would drink from both of us. On the second night we would drink from him. And on the third night he would drink from us again. In the end I decided our apartment was the safest place for it and invited Favian there.

Favian arrived at the door looking somewhat worn out, but laughed it off, saying anyone would be worn out after wrangling with the council, and then producing the decree with a flourish. "The official grant for your pet's Turning," he said.

I plucked the paper from his fingers and ushered him inside, wondering why I felt so annoyed when he called Geordy a pet. Perhaps because he did it to annoy me, always diminishing Geordy like that.

"Where is your boytoy, anyway?" he said, as he took a seat in the living room. "Can't start the party without the guest of honor."

"He is learning a lesson about time," I said, taking the seat across from Favian. "And patience. If we're to spend hundreds of years together, surely he can learn that impatience does not become him."

"Oh?" Favian's eyes lit with curiosity. "What sort of lesson?"

Now I had to laugh, because of course it occurred to me that the lesson I was teaching Geordy was nearly the same as one Favian had taught to me. "Do you remember," I asked, "the time you plugged my ears with soft wax, and bound my eyes, and suspended me with ropes and cloth so that I was weightless . . .?"

His smile was warm, and perhaps a little wistful. "And the only way you knew time was passing was my touch. My very . . . occasional touch."

I could not blush, not having fed yet tonight, but I could lower my eyes as I recalled that the only place he had touched me was between my legs, and that a mere feather-light caress of my most sensitive spot. I do not know how long I hung suspended—minutes, hours, days—only that each time his touch returned, my sensitivity increased tenfold.

When he finally took me, keeping me suspended and bound but pushing his cock into me, I had been dripping and aching for him for what seemed like eternity. And then I had been completely overwhelmed with the feeling that I had been nothing but an ethereal cloud, made flesh for one purpose, and that was to give his cock a home, a place to fit.

I stood abruptly. "Well, he's been down long enough."

"Surely? The sun set not two hours ago . . ."

"It will feel like ages to him," I said with surety. "Come on."

I led him to our playroom. Along one wall sat the sensory deprivation tank I had Geordy in. On the opposite wall was a low king-sized futon, and opposite the door was a standing frame with an open pair of wrist restraints hanging. The walls were hung with various toys and implements of ours, and the shelf above the bed held a collection of dildos and buttplugs.

Favian picked up one of the glass plugs and examined it casually. "I think the hardest I ever came was once while fucking you when you had something like this in," he said, voice cool as he set the hard object back down.

I couldn't be as cool suddenly. "That was . . . five hundred years ago," I said, frozen in my tracks in the middle of the room. "Surely you've—"

"Had better?" His hand slipped into my hair as he was suddenly close. "No, Mara. Not better than you. Not in half a millennium."

Well, I've had better than you, I thought, but I found I could not say it, not even just to sting him. Possibly because it wasn't true. "Have you . . ." It was an effort to speak at all. ". . . tried many?"

"Hundreds," he said, staring into my eyes. "Girls, boys, men, women, slaves, masochists, whores, submissives . . . None compared."

I desperately wanted him to kiss me then. He had fed. I could feel the hardness of him throbbing against me. But instead he said, "Go on, tell me. Tell me you've had a hundred masters better than me."

I shook my head. "You don't understand."

"What . . .?" he breathed softly.

"I never looked," I answered. "I never tried another. There was only you. I've had a hundred lovers since then, but no one I would bow to."

"No one . . .?" he seemed to whisper it almost to himself as he forced himself to step back from me. He shook his head, whether in disbelief or to snap himself out of it, I don't know. "Time's wasting. Wake up your boy and let's get this over with."

I closed my eyes where I stood, trying to control the surge of emptiness I felt, both in my heart and between my legs. "Fine," I said. "You don't have to stay. Cut your wrist and let a little of it flow into his mouth, I'll do the same, and you can go." *And then I'll ride Geordy's cock all night long until I've forgotten what yours even felt like*, I thought, but I had to look away as I thought it.

I opened the door of the tank instead. Geordy's eyes and ears were blocked, but he felt the air move. "Mistress?"

I tapped on his lips and he opened his mouth obediently. The touch of a small straight razor from our collection was sufficient to start the flow from my wrist down my fingers, dripping into his mouth. He convulsed with pleasure—a vampire's blood is ambrosia to mortals.

Favian stepped close and held out his hand. "Go on," he said, urging me to cut him.

I took his hand in mine to steady it, holding the razor in the other. I could slash him and hurt him out of spite if I wanted.

But I didn't want to. I just pressed the razor gently against the veins of his wrist and it sank in ever so slightly, as if he were butter. A few drops went into Geordy's mouth.

And then I was closing the door of the tank, and lifting Favian's wrist to my mouth, lapping away the excess and then healing the wound. And then he was crushing his mouth to mine, all reserve gone, both of us consumed by a need for each other that we had both thought long since dead. We should know better, in a world where the dead rise again.

He took me there on the floor of the playroom, surrounded by every plaything of power you can name, but all he needed to dominate me and make me his again was his hands, his voice, and his cock.

We slept entwined upon the futon, too exhausted by the time we finished to do anything but collapse, and it was too close to dawn to risk leaving the windowless room. When next we woke, the sun had set, and Geordy was no longer in the tank. I stood beside it, staring into the empty chamber in disbelief that he had freed himself.

Favian donned his already worn clothes in a hurry. "There's somewhere I must be."

I pulled on a robe myself. "How long will you be?"

Geordy appeared in the doorway, then, fully dressed. "Or will you just have a quick bite before you go?" he quipped.

Favian laughed, but it sounded forced. "My apologies for not treating your Turning with more ceremony," he said. "But it's not the ritual that does it. It's the blood."

Geordy sighed in a very put-upon way and held out his arm. Favian unbuttoned Geordy's shirt cuff, baring half his forearm, and then running his nose and cheek up and down the tender underside as if appreciating the aroma of a fine cigar. Just as Geordy seemed to relax, he bit him, and a moment later Geordy slumped onto the futon.

Favian licked his lips. "Whoops, sorry, I lose control of that one sometimes."

I moved Geordy into a more comfortable position, then sat beside him. "I didn't know you had the ability to put your victim to sleep with your bite."

He shrugged. "I developed the power about a hundred years ago. That and a few other mind-control tricks. Just goes to show, there's always more one can become."

"Favian," I stood, intending to thank him for his help and see him to the door.

I found myself pulled into a kiss, flavored with the sweetness of my own human servant's blood. "I'll be back for the final bite tomorrow," he said. "And that is the last time you will see me."

I jerked a little as what he said stung me. I had just become used to the sight of him again, to the sound of his voice, to the idea that maybe the betrayals of five centuries ago were long enough ago that now we could look back with some fondness or mutual respect. "You don't have to disappear," I said, "on my account."

He shook his head. "In two days, you will have a newly fledged vampire to occupy your time and your bed. Neither he, nor you, will thank me for being in the way of your happiness."

But as the elevator doors at the end of the hall closed behind him, I wondered why happiness was not what I was feeling at all. I went back to the playroom to wait for my fledgling to wake, so that I could feed from him. I drank deeply of him that night, and all the wicked plans I'd had for his emergence from the tank, I enacted. But nothing we did felt to me like it matched the passion of just one of Favian's kisses. Favian was right, I thought. The sooner he was out of our lives, the better.

The third night arrived and I dressed in high fetish fashion, with a leather "tennis" skirt and matching corset, a favorite outfit of Geordy's. I wasted no time putting him into standing bondage. He had taken blood from us, we had taken it back, and now we would give it back once more, at its most potent. I wondered if he would inherit Favian's ability to cause somnolence with his bite.

I teased him, flogging him lightly and binding his balls, and telling him all the while what a good boy he had been. He would get a drop of blood from Favian, and a drop from me, and fall into a swoon and die as the sun rose. At sunset he would rise as one of us.

I left him in bondage, a leather hood over his head and his cock and balls in a Cat's Cradle of silken cords, while I went to let Favian in.

He looked worse, with circles under his eyes as if he hadn't slept, which was ridiculous since vampires do not so much sleep as lie undead all day. I could not help myself. I slid my hand along his cheek and pulled him close. He tried to pull away, and that was probably what made me examine him even more closely.

"Favian, you don't look well. Have you fed?"

He waved me off with a smile. "I've fed. Where is your boytoy? Are you going to let me have a piece of him tonight, Mara? Or should I keep things polite?"

"Ha. If anything he should have a piece of you."

His chuckle was the same as always. "Yes, how about this piece right here?" he joked, hefting his cock and balls.

"I'd like to see that," I said, daring him.

"Mm, think I won't put my cock in your boy's mouth?" Favian began stripping out of his clothes, there in the entryway, until he was standing there in nothing, his skin pale and marble-like. I ran my hands down his chest, examining the pattern of blue veins. He was paler than I remembered. Was that just the effect of a few hundred more years without sun?

Or was it something else?

I slid to my knees, my hands settling at his hips, and I took his cock into my mouth. He was flaccid at first, but soon he was quickening, filling my mouth. I felt his hand in my hair, encouraging me to take him deeper.

If I had not known him so well, if I had not so recently

reacquainted myself with the flavor of him and with the scent of his skin, I might not have noticed anything different. Geordy would not have, for he had no basis of comparison. But there was something floral, something that reminded me of incense . . .

I didn't believe for a moment that he had suddenly developed a liking for soaking in bath salts. And the flavor wasn't just on his skin. It was intensifying as fluid began to leak from the slit as I licked all around the head of his cock.

"You're . . . so good to me," he whispered.

I looked up at him, stroking him with my hand. "Why?" I asked. He played dumb.

"Why what, dear one?"

Dear one. He used to call me that, when we were alone together, all those years ago. Never when our sovereigns were watching. "You said this is the last time I'll ever see you."

He nodded, closing his eyes.

"I can taste the holy water, F— *Master*," I said.

I saw a pang cross his face, though whether it was of pain or regret, I could not tell. "Why?" I pressed.

He opened his eyes and stroked my hair then. "Because I have spent the five hundred years since my exile searching for someone worth spending my life with, and have found no one," he said. "And I owed you a debt. Tonight, I'll pay it, and die in peace. You and yours can have the happiness I denied you years ago."

"Idiot," I hissed in anger. "What makes you think I'll be happy that you're dead?" He shook his head. "The deal I made the council is that we'll have zero population growth. You can turn Geordy because I'll be gone."

I don't know what came over me. I knocked him down and pinned him to the floor under me; he didn't fight. "You're insane! Do you know how painful it's going to be? I watched Kemal kill himself this way—"

"You won't be watching me, though."

I slapped him across the face, and saw a flare of his anger in his eyes. "Stupid! How could you think I'd let you go through with it?"

He caught my hand as I was about to hit him again. "Forgive me, but usually when someone hits someone else it's because they hate them. I've been under the impression you've hated me for centuries, Mara." *Hypocrite*, I thought. *You only spanked me because you loved me, not hated me. I know that.*

"You betrayed me, destroyed my life, and took yourself away from me," I said, gritting my teeth so hard my fangs dug into my gums. "I hated how stupid you were. I hated that I mattered so little to you that you'd throw me away like that. But now you're telling me I do matter. I matter enough that you'll sacrifice yourself to make me happy."

He merely nodded.

"Idiot," I repeated. "I hated what you did to me, but I have never stopped loving you." The truth of it hit me hard as I heard my own words, and if I hadn't already been on all fours I probably would have sunk to the floor. "I have never . . . stopped trying to be loyal to you."

He pulled me down for a kiss then, hard and tender at the same time, his lips and tongue soft while his grip was like iron. I straddled him where I was, then cried out into his mouth as he pushed in suddenly, filling me.

Oh, yes. There was a rightness in him taking me like that I hadn't felt since before the Ottoman fleet had defeated Venice. He let go of my face and I reared back, pushing him deeper, riding him. Part of me knew it might be the last time, and yet having finally said the words to him that I had wanted to for so very long, I felt ecstatic and free, even as he made me his all over again, for a little while, at least.

I cried out as I came, my hips jerking violently against him before I fell limp against his chest, his erection still deep in me. He cradled me with one arm as aftershocks ran through my body.

"Dear one," he whispered, and kissed my hair. "I was so wrong."

I raised my head at the sudden sound of something hitting the floor behind us. I turned to see Geordy standing there, his cock still trussed as I'd left it, and the leather restraints still on his wrists. He had pulled the leather hood from his head and thrown it to the floor. "Mara!" he exclaimed. "What the hell were you doing leaving me in there while you . . . you . . ." He stalked toward the door, so I could see him now without craning my neck. "I could have suffocated!"

I could feel disapproval radiating from Favian, but he said nothing.

"You have the blood of two immortals running through your veins," I pointed out. "You cannot die so easily."

His face was livid with anger. "I cannot believe you expected me to—"

"To do as your Mistress bade you?" I said.

"While you're slutting around out here with this ex of yours!" The skirt I was wearing was too short to hide the fact that Favian was still inside me. Geordy started trying to untie the cords around his cock and balls, but he couldn't get the knot started. "Five hundred years! How many more like him are going to show up and expect you to spread your legs? Is this what you promise me? An eternity of—"

"*Silence!*" I had never had to use the Voice on my human servants before. His mouth moved like a fish's, no sounds coming from his throat. I never used the Voice because I had always, I thought, convinced them to serve me of their own free will. They served me and obeyed me because they loved me. Didn't they? Or did they do it because I became everything that they wanted? The perfect Mistress. It was no hardship to serve me if I never challenged their loyalty.

I looked down into Favian's eyes and saw sympathy and sadness there. "Do you want to die?" I asked him in a language I had not heard spoken in five hundred years.

He reached up and touched my lips, tears of holy water leaking from the corners of his eyes. His answer came in a whisper. "Not if I can have you."

I leaned down and kissed him in answer, then climbed slowly off him, aching from the emptiness but knowing what needed to happen now. "Take him, then," I said to Favian. "Fuck him until you eject as much of the water from your system as you can. Bite him at the same time, replace it with blood. How long have you been taking holy water?"

"Just a few days." He remained where he was on the floor, though, looking up at us. "Good." I switched back to English. "Geordy, what did you think I meant when I said you were mine? You may speak now. Do you want to be mine?"

He was a little meeker now, but he still held his ground. "But I am yours," he said, hands folded in front of him.

"And what does that mean?"

"It means I'll do whatever you say?" he said tentatively, like a schoolboy who is unsure of his answer in front of the class.

"I have the power to make you do whatever I like," I said. "While you are human. But when immortal?"

It was too much for him. It was all too much. "I won't stand for being cuckolded," he said.

"I sympathize with you," I said, running my hand over his cheek. "I truly do. And perhaps if you had expressed your unhappiness with me in some more respectful way, I might have seen it as reinforcing my bond of ownership over you, instead of tearing it down and throwing it away."

He looked frightened now. "Th-throwing it away?"

I merely nodded. I wondered if I should use the Voice, or if perhaps now that he was cowed, Geordy would freely give me one last act of submission. "Bend over the back of the couch, Geordy," I whispered.

"Okay," he said. Not "yes, Mistress." But he did as I asked, bending over and spreading himself for Favian.

We showed Geordy mercy . . . after we had our fill of him. The poor thing, it was not his fault I'd been deluding myself all that time that I could be happy with a pretty lapdog. I had fooled myself into thinking so, and even fooled my own master, who knew me better than any soul alive, dead, or undead. Favian altered his memory so that I had been nothing more than a fling, a rich, eccentric Mistress who had left him with a fabulous apartment and a chunk of money in a bank account. He would live a healthier, longer life than most mortals, but not long enough to be more than a passing oddity. We left him asleep in the four-poster bed, the curtains all drawn back to let in the sun.

Favian dressed me in a simple black dress and then lifted me in his arms, carrying me out of the apartment to the elevator.

He carried me across the threshold at his hideaway, as well, a brownstone that faced the river, and up to the top floor, where the blackout curtains covered the windows. We were both beginning to tire as we felt the sunrise coming.

He set me down on the bed and then climbed up alongside me, resting his head on his hand.

"No human servant?" I asked.

He shook his head. "I haven't been able to bear anyone close to me at all for quite some time." He traced the edge of my face with one finger. "I . . . am still not sure I deserve you."

I leaned up and kissed him on the lips, then fell back. "I will give you the chance to prove every single day how much you deserve me, Master."

His smile was as warm as the sunrise neither of us had seen in a half-thousand years. "Every day, forever, dear one."

Good Boyfriend
By Gina McQueen

The fields are beautiful, rolling green, and the sun is high in the baby-blue, cotton ball sky. Not too hot, not too cold, not too shabby, this weather. I say so.

Jim smiles.

"God, I love it here," he says.

"Imagine that." Smiling myself, in my little sundress. "How much of this is yours, again?"

"As far as the eye can see."

"I have pretty good eyesight."

"Good for you. How's your hearing?"

"What?"

"Excuse me. I can't hear you!"

"WHAT?" And then we both laugh, because we're both ridiculous creatures.

Today is a very nice day.

I like Jim. I really do. He's goofy, kicked-back, and super-sweet. Making friends with him was easy as chewing garlic mashed potatoes. A very relaxing older gent, and not unsightly, in his jeans and sneakers and button-down short-sleeved shirt, two buttons open. His gray hair is copious, down past his whiskered chin. He is wiry and trim. He has Siberian Husky eyes.

I gotta admit, I've been thinkin' about it.

And clearly, so has he.

Twenty years of age difference is a lot, in human years. I clock in at thirty. He weighs in at fifty.

But he's not desperate. He's not clingy. There seems to be some sort of emotional sanity at play. He's not basing his life on my next facial expression, demanding an answer for what it might mean.

I feel safe around him. This is not a bad thing.

And after three months of occasional friendly bump-intos, he's invited me over.

"I gotta tell ya," I say. "I had no idea."

"About what?" His eyes are smiling, though his lips are quizzical.

"That you're doing so well. You don't talk about that. Most guys with this much acreage would claim bragging rights."

"Bragging rights are for assholes."

"You think?"

"Yes, I do."

Can't argue with that—I live in Hollywood—so I don't. "You never talk about what you do."

"That's right."

"How come? Are you, like, a pot grower? I don't see any weed here."

"I buy mine medicinally, like everybody else."

"Oh, really. And your symptoms?"

"It helps me get through the changes." And with this, he intensifies just a little. Not coming closer, but subtly closing the psychic space.

I look in his eyes.

He looks into mine.

"Sarah Lee, do you mind if I tell you something?"

"What?" I say, feeling my short hairs start to stand. Not with apprehension, precisely, but very alert. And liking how he just said the first two-thirds of my name.

"What if I were to tell you . . ." he says, clearly wrestling with the words, "that I . . ."

I wait as long as I can stand it.

"SPIT IT OUT, for fuck's sake!"

Jim laughs, robust, at his own sudden pussy-assness. "Alright! Alright! Jesus!"

"Do I have to punch you?"

"No, you don't!"

"Okay then, Mr. Grownup." And I waggle my hand, in a get-on-with-it manner.

And just like that, he begins to change.

At first, it just looks like he's flexing his chest, and his face goes red, and I wonder what the fuck? This was not what I expected.

Then the buttons start to pop.

And his hair grows down his face, down his neck, down his chest, across the broadening shoulders suddenly exposed by the shredding fabric of his suddenly entirely superfluous shirt.

I suck in breath as he grows taller, stronger, and less human with every second. And then I smell him.

He smells incredibly good: a pheromone charge that puts Axe Body Spray to shame.

My own animal awakes, as he changes. My nipples suddenly hard as ice, the rest of my flesh growing hotter and hotter.

"I love you," he says, through a mouth elongating, less wolf than coyote, with a long lolling tongue. Snout wide enough to spread me without breaking me open.

I am pulling off my sundress. "Good boyfriend," I say.

Fixation

By Dana Fredsti

"Quick, agile, and powerful enough to take down the largest prey in the jungle, the jaguar is the largest of the big cats in the Americas and one of the most efficient and aggressive predators."

My fellow docent, Beth, held forth to the group of first graders crowded in front of Dandy's enclosure. Tall and gangly in a droopy, Olive Oyl way, Beth wore her frizzy red curls clipped in a poof that bubbled out of the back of her baseball cap. While she droned on in front, I covered the rear to insure none of the kids wandered off where they shouldn't.

Dandy, a melanistic jaguar sometimes referred to (incorrectly) as a black panther, sprawled at the edge of his cage and watched the kids. They were all small enough to count as prospective prey to a jaguar, although toddlers would be even better. At the Feline Preservation Center (henceforth referred to as FPC), the docents and keepers referred to babies in strollers as 'meals on wheels.' Dandy, although raised by hand instead of mother-raised, had all the instincts of his wild brethren and was no doubt sizing up which rug rat to cull from the pack, should the opportunity arise.

"Endowed with a spotted coat and well adapted for the jungle, hunting either in the trees or water, making it one of the few felines tolerant of water, the jaguar was, and remains, revered among the indigenous Americans who reside closely with the jaguar."

The kids weren't quite slack-jawed with boredom, but Beth's auto-spiel, delivered in her nasal drone, was so far over their heads, she might as well be flying above in a jet plane. Beth is very knowledgeable when it comes to all things exotically feline, but not exactly a people person, especially when said people are under eighteen.

Mind you, I'm not a huge fan of school tours. If I wanted kids, I'd find a guy and spawn a few. I love animals, especially cats large and small, and would rather spend my time doing cat rescue and volunteering at FPC than dealing with either children or men. Unfortunately working with the exotic felines wasn't all picking up leopard shit, chopping up frozen horsemeat, and scouring sinks free of congealed chicken fat. It also meant patrolling the 'zoo' portion of the compound during the hours we were open to the public, making sure none of the visitors ran, screamed, tossed things into the cage, tried to pet the animals or otherwise harassed our feline residents. *And* it also included docent duties, i.e. answering questions and giving tours to groups ranging from geriatric motorcycle clubs to Scout troops to classroom tours of all ages. Usually one docent was enough to handle any one tour, but when there were twenty-plus hyperactive first graders on the loose we worked in pairs.

Speaking of tours, the little natives were getting restless. Beth was focused on Dandy and spouting off dry statistics about the jaguar populations in South and Central America, while the teacher was too busy talking on her iPhone to notice one curly-haired blond, blue-eyed tot in the rear trying to climb the iron safety fence so she could "pet the kitty." I scooped her up just as she reached the top of the fence and plunked her back down on the sidewalk. Her face began that inevitable 'just bit into a lemon' collapse that all kids get when they're about to let loose the mother of all tantrums. And me without my earplugs.

I squatted down in front of Miss Curly Locks just as her mouth opened to begin squalling. "Can I show you something really neat?" Without waiting for an answer (which would probably be an ear-piercing screech anyway), I reached out and pulled a battered, chipped, and scarred blue sphere from what was originally a cement ashtray. "Do you know what this is?" I held the ball up in front of her.

Shirley Temple circa 2010 shook her head so I rolled the ball over in my hand to expose three holes in the other side.

"Well, it *was* a bowling ball. Then it became a toy for baby jaguars. Feel how hard this is." The other kids in the back crowded around, anxious to not be left out of the fun. I held the ball out so they could touch it, feel the cracks and gouges in the hard resin with their little pudgy fingers. "Baby jaguars did this with their claws and teeth. So if a baby jaguar can do this to something as hard as a *bowling* ball . . . imagine what a grown up jaguar could do to your skin." I looked Miss Curly Locks straight in the eye. "This is why you don't pet the kitties here, okay?" She nodded, eyes round.

"Well, I could . . . I could beat up the jaguar before it bit me!" This came from a pugnacious little ginger-haired boy who'd been reprimanded more than once for running, yelling at the cats, and wandering off. I also happen to know he had a rock in his back jeans pocket and had been waiting for the chance to throw it at one of the cats without getting caught.

"Really?" I turned my attention his way and locked gazes with him. I have a great hypno-stare.

"Jaguars fixate," I said. "Do you know what fixate means?"

I looked at the kids gathered around me and got mostly silence punctuated by a few shy giggles. One little boy picked his nose with a single-mindedness that rivaled a jaguar's.

"When a jaguar fixates, it means if it decides it wants something—anything—, it will go through whatever is in its way to get what it wants. If it wants your shoe, you'd better take it off 'cause a jaguar will take your foot off so it can play with the shoelaces. The jaguar is the only cat in the world known to fight to its own death before admitting defeat. Its jaws are strong enough to crush your head in one bite." I gripped the little brat across his skull with my free hand to emphasize my point. "Trying to beat up a jaguar would be a very bad thing."

He gave me a sullen stare. "You're stupid."

I dropped my voice so no one else but the kid could hear me. "I'm sure your parents would miss you when the jaguar ate you up, starting with your head. *Crunch!* Just like a piece of popcorn. Except with blood sauce instead of butter."

Just for added oomph—and because I could—I sent an image into his head of just that.

His eyes went wide and he took two staggering steps backwards before falling on his butt on the grass next to the walkway. He was quiet the rest of the tour.

I thought about this a few hours later in the staff trailer as I gathered my things for the drive home and couldn't help but smile at the memory of the little snot monster's expression when I'd zapped him. Okay, yes, I realize that when one possesses certain abilities they should use them for good and not for evil, but this kid had needed a lesson and I don't even pretend to be a nice person when I'm cranky. Besides, FPC is all about the cats and if scaring the kid stopped him from doing something potentially harmful, I was technically using my psychic ability for good, *not* evil.

Shut up. I know I'm rationalizing.

Walking across the hard-packed dirt towards the employee parking lot, I was almost to the gate when someone shouted my name across the open space between assorted office, staff, and supply trailers. "Hey, Maya!"

I turned to see Jeri Callahan, one of the founders of FPC, waving at me from her office door. Jeri possesses a slightly weathered beauty, with the sun-streaked blond hair and tanned skin of someone who'd spent most of her life outdoors. I like Jeri. She's tough but fair when it came to training the largely volunteer staff. There's no room for ego when you're working with potentially lethal animals and Jeri won't put up with any shit or stupidity from her crew.

For example, one idiot gal, Kiki, was caught texting when she was supposed to be holding the pulley bar to a leopard's den box while another docent pulled dirty dishes from the enclosure. The leopard had managed to paw the den box door open three inches before someone noticed. Jeri threw Kiki's iPhone in a dumpster filled with bags of cat shit and told Kiki she could dig for it if she wanted. I'm not sure if Kiki retrieved her phone, but she never came back to FPC.

I retraced my steps and met Jeri at the foot of the office trailer steps. "What's up?"

"Any chance you can stick around tonight? We just got word this afternoon the jaguar's coming in a week early. Patrick's gone to pick up him up from LAX."

Patrick, an ex-movie exec turned conservationist (I know, it's crazy but true), is Jeri's right hand man. If a movie were made about his life, he'd be played by Fred Ward. He still has the personality and drive that earned him the nickname 'The Tiger' back in his Industry days, but I understand he's mellowed a bit. I get along fine with Patrick 'cause I can always tell a mile off if he's in a temper and I know how to stay out of his way. Those without hereditary empathetic psychic ability, however, are shit out of luck on Patrick's bad days.

"Is this the one from Belize?"

Jeri nodded. "Yup, the mate for Sandy." Sandy is Dandy's littermate. Yes, they have a brother named Randy. Thank goodness there hadn't been another girl 'cause she would have been stuck with Candy.

I took a quick mental inventory of my plans for the evening. Go home. Shower. Have a glass of wine or a G&T. Watch a stupid movie on SyFy Channel or one of my Netflix DVDs. Have another glass of wine or G&T and get maudlin over the recent loss of my beloved cat Luna, taken from me at age twenty-one by kidney failure. Have another drink and get maudlin over breakup with boyfriend of six months. Fall asleep on the couch as goofy CGI sharks or whatever terrorized bad actors on my flat-screen TV. "Sure," I said. "I'd love to help."

Jeri heaved a sigh of relief. "Good! We'll be putting him in the empty cage in quarantine for the night. Kyle's coming out tomorrow to check him out before we put him next to Sandy." Kyle is our vet, a rugged-looking Aussie with an accent to die for. I'd had a total crush on him until I realized he wasn't interested in my type. As in female.

"If you want to spend the night," Jeri continued, "the extra bed in the staff trailer is free."

"I have my sleeping bag," I said. "Mind if I sleep outside near the new kid?"

"Even better," said Jeri. "You can keep an eye on him."

Sleeping under the stars on a temperate evening is one of my favorite things to do at FPC. And even though she'd never admit it, Jeri knows I have a calming influence on the cats. She doesn't know why and I don't try to tell her. She wouldn't believe the truth. And honestly, who would?

"What's his name?"

"Nagual."

"Cool name."

Jeri nodded. "Yup. I have no idea what the fuck it means."

I took a shower in the staff trailer and changed into clean jeans, T-shirt, and a hunter green hoodie. I always carry a change of clothes in the car, along with bottled water, energy bars, and a heavy-duty maglite that subs as a blunt weapon. When you live in earthquake territory and drive through hinky neighborhoods, it pays to be prepared. My short honey blonde hair required approximately thirty seconds of attention; most of it involving a brisk towel dry before I left it to its own devices. I have regular features, neither homely nor beautiful, but my eyes are a rich, dark brown and rimmed with long, thick lashes visible without mascara. I used to use a lot of makeup to emphasize them, but makeup makes me look like a TV evangelist's wife and I wised up. Now I just used a little bit of eyeliner on the inner lash line. That and a bit of blush-colored lip gloss pretty much completed my makeup regime. At five seven I was not exactly a delicate flower but I told myself it was mostly muscle. Which it was. Mostly. Whatever. The natural look works better for me anyway.

Patrick and Nagual showed up in Patrick's truck around seven. Jeri and I met them in the back quarter of the compound by quarantine along with the two full-time keepers, Meg and Farrell. Meg and Farrell are both short, dark, and wiry, with mellow temperaments. They look and act so similar they're often asked if they're twins, which they're not. They're just one of those couples that start to morph into one another as the years go by.

I'll spare you the gory details of all the swearing, sweating, and straining that occurred getting Nagual situated. PG Reader's Digest version, I only got a brief glance at Nagual through the grate of a wood and metal crate before we muscled the thing from the truck bed to the quarantine 'airlock' (picture a cage with inner and outer doors, the inner door with a guillotine gate, which can be opened and closed from the outside of the structure via a pole and pulley system), but I could feel his stress and fury at being caged up all too sharply.

Patrick unlatched and opened the crate door as Farrell slid the guillotine gate open. A low grunting noise reverberated from the crate. A brief pause and then a truly magnificent jaguar exploded from the crate into the quarantine area. The guillotine gate slammed back down the minute Nagual's tail cleared the opening.

He gave a low rumbling growl and bared his teeth at us, his eyes glowing lambent gold in the lights. Jaguars are built like bulldogs on steroids, with sturdy chests, strong stocky legs and shoulders. Nagual was no exception. I stared at him as he sprang from one side of the cage to the other, up onto the den box and then back down again, muscles coiled steel beneath his glossy coat, classic brownish-yellow with black rosettes, smaller markings inside each rosette. He was simply one of the most beautiful things I've ever seen.

"Oh, you beauty," I said under my breath, trying to project waves of soothing calm towards him.

Nagual stopped dead in his tracks, landing from mid-leap to the cement floor where he hunkered down and stared straight at me.

Whoa. This was a first. I mean, yes, I am capable of projecting feelings and images to both animals and some people, but I'd never had either react this way before.

I moved to the side.

Nagual's eyes tracked my every movement.

Patrick waved a hand in front of the cage.

Nagual ignored him.

"Guess we know what *he* wants for dinner," joked Farrell.

You okay, fellah? I reached out cautiously, trying to put the words into images. Jaguars don't speak English, after all.

Nagual continued to stare at me as if I were the only person or thing in the area, totally fixating on me. Kind of flattering and kind of spooky.

What's up with you? I wondered.

Suddenly my head filled with images and feelings not mine, as if someone had shoved out my mind and replaced it with theirs. The images flickered like a Power Point slide show on hyperdrive.

Damp heat. Moving through the jungle at night, low to the ground, afraid of nothing. A dark clearing lit only by torches. A woman, fierce and beautiful as a jungle cat.

The smell of piñon or some other fragrant wood-based incense. Flesh against flesh. Fur and flesh mingling. Darkness. Trapped in a small space. And rage, unforgiving and implacable.

The images and feelings vanished as suddenly as they'd come, leaving me dizzy and confused.

"Maya, you okay?" Meg put hand on my shoulder.

I shook my head to clear it. "Yeah . . .just a little dizzy. Should've had a bigger lunch."

"Let's finish up here and go to El Puerco." Meg grinned at me. "I could use a plate of those carnitas. How 'bout you?"

"Sounds good."

I stared at Nagual, who continued to stare back at me as if I was the only other thing in existence. What the hell were some of those thoughts doing in a jaguar brain?

"Maya, get your butt in gear and help Farrell pull the crate." Patrick barked orders like a drill sergeant, breaking the mood. "Meg, get him some food and water." He paused, staring at the jaguar, now pacing back and forth in the front of the cage, making the coughing noise that constitutes a jaguar's roar. "Damn, he's one fine cat."

No one argued.

Farrell and I pulled the crate out and loaded it back in the truck. As I got in the cab and shut the passenger door, Nagual started up a series of urgent bellowing coughs, long and throaty. These were followed by a succession of shorter, more rapid grunts. Some of the bottle-fed jaguars do this when Jeri is around and they want her attention.

Farrell gave me a sideways glance as he started the

truck. "I know you're good with the cats and all, but that bad boy definitely has a thing for you."

I shrugged and grinned. "Don't they all?"

We drove to the supply shack where Farrell helped me take the crate off the truck, then left me to clean it out in the dim light of the three-walled structure. This means checking to see if the former occupant left any little surprises, and taking out water dishes or any toys, etc. Nagual had indeed left some tokens of his esteem (not surprising after a plane ride from Belize). I grabbed a small rake and retrieved the stinky prize, then gave the box a quick hosedown before poking my head and shoulders in, rake in hand, to get the metal water dish and anything else possibly hidden in the shadows in the back.

I wasn't expecting to find anything beyond a stray piece of poop, so when the rake hit something with a dull "thunk," it surprised me. Leaning in a little further, I hooked the tines around whatever the object was and rolled it out.

Roughly oval in shape, kind of like a bumpy egg with one side partially flattened, it looked to be made of reddish clay. I picked it up, holding it closer to the single light bulb on the ceiling. About three or four inches tall and about three quarters that in width, it was roughly in the shape of a seated figure, arms clasped around bent knees, head resting on the forearms. The face was odd, with blunt features that could be human or feline . . . or both. It looked old, the clay pockmarked and weathered.

How the hell it got into Nagual's crate was beyond me. Anyone with any knowledge of jaguar physiology and behavior would know better than to put anything so fragile in with the cat. Teeth that can take chunks out of bowling balls could make short work of hardened clay, especially during a long and no doubt boring plane journey. The fact Nagual *hadn't* trashed it was a bit of a miracle. It had to have been a mistake, an oversight on someone's part.

Now the question was what to do with it. I mean, should I play finders keepers? No one else knew it'd been in the crate. And it *was* awfully cool. Or would that be unethical?

Too physically wiped to think this one through, I decided to table my decision until tomorrow. Tucking the little idol in my hoodie pocket, I forgot about it for the time being and went to meet everyone for carnitas and a pitcher of margaritas at El Puerco, the little Mexican restaurant down the road.

A couple hours and two margaritas later, I made my way just a little unsteadily by the light of sparsely placed solar-powered lights to the patch of grass in front of the quarantine enclosures. An iron barred fence separated the grass from the cement walkway outside the cages, so there was no danger of rolling too near Nagual even if I tossed and turned in my sleep.

I peered into the cage . . . and found Nagual sitting smack up against the front. Staring at me. Again.

"You're a strange one," I said.

He grunted, almost as if in response.

A cold wind had kicked up while we were at dinner, cutting right through the layers of T-shirt and hoodie. Throwing my sleeping bag and pillow on the ground, I wriggled into the warmth of the down-filled nylon, turning so I lay on one side facing the cage. Something jabbed into my ribs, a rock or something. I sat back up again and felt under the sleeping bag, finding only grass. I patted down my jeans and hoodie and found the culprit hiding in the pocket of the latter: the little idol I'd found in Nagual's crate. "Got you, you little devil!" I pulled it out and lay back down on my side so I could see Nagual through the gaps in the protective fence.

I set the figurine down in front of me. "See what I found?" I said to Nagual, pointing at it. His gaze actually followed the direction of my finger. And stopped when they came to the statuette.

As if that wasn't strange enough, what happened next was just too weird to believe. Nagual's eyes actually narrowed; then his mouth opened in what I can only describe as a grin. You know, that happy, almost dopey look dogs get when the world is their oyster?

I looked from him to the statuette and then back again to Nagual, who appeared to be doing the same back and forth between it and me. "Is this yours, big fellah?"

He let out a short coughing grunt . . . and I could swear he nodded.

I shook my head. Something very out of the ordinary was going on with this jag, but I was too tired from the long day and the two margaritas to try and figure it out. I snuggled down into the warmth of my sleeping bag and shut my eyes . . . then opened them again as I felt the weight of Nagual's stare. "Would you please knock that off? It's really creepy trying to sleep with someone staring at you."

And I'll be damned if he didn't hunker down onto his belly, rest his massive head on his front paws and close his eyes.

"That's better," I said as a yawn nearly unhinged my jaws. I was asleep within minutes.

"What is your name?" The deep, male voice slid into my mind and wrapped around me like warm caramel.

"Maya," I whispered.

"Ah . . ." The word wafted out on an exhalation. *"Open your eyes, Maya."*

My eyes flew open as I woke up, startled from a deep sleep by a dream I couldn't remember. For a few seconds I didn't know where I was; then the deep quiet of the country punctuated by the occasional grunt or growl from one of the cats penetrated my consciousness. I relaxed back into my sleeping bag with a relieved sigh.

"Maya."

I sat bolt upright, hands clutching the top of the bag to me like the heroine from a turn of the century melodrama shielding her bosom from the mustachioed villain. Was I hearing things? It sounded like—

"Maya, look at me."

The voice, exotically accented, unmistakably male, and as decadent as a box of See's Candy, came from Nagual's cage. Slowly extracting myself from the sleeping bag, I turned my head towards the quarantine . . . and realized I was still dreaming.

Inside the cage stood a tall, dark, and, yes, handsome man with glossy black hair past his shoulders. Lean, well muscled and . . . well . . . naked. I caught a glimpse of his penis and even by dream standards it was impressive. He looked like he should be modeling for those paintings of Aztec warriors holding the swooning maidens you always see in Mexican restaurants. El Puerco has several. His nose was gently aquiline, a slight bump at the bridge and slightly flared nostrils. Lips full without being feminine, almost impossibly sensual. I've never seen eyes like his before, green with flecks of gold, intense and glowing in the light of the cage. Which didn't have any lights, so where was the weird amber shimmer coming from? For that matter, where was Nagual?

Oh. Right. Dreaming. I'd almost forgot.

He stared into my eyes and smiled. I knew that smile . . . didn't I?

"Where is Nagual?" Seems like I didn't need to speak out loud either.

"He is here." He touched his chest.

"Do I know you?"

"I have known you forever . . ."

His voice and the words he spoke caressed my nerve endings like the rough tongue of a jaguar. I felt a sudden heat unfurl inside me and realized I felt the same way about him.

"You have something of mine, Maya." The way he said— no, *thought* my name; his lips didn't move—in that exotic, unplaceable accent was like a caress along my skin. I shivered with pleasure.

I held up the little figurine. *"This?"*

He nodded. *"Would you bring it to me?"*

I got to my feet, shivering as the cold air penetrated my clothes. No climate control in a dream, I guess.

The iron of the fence chilled my hands as I hoisted myself over it onto the cement walkway, tucking the figurine back in my pocket as I did so. Once over, I approached the front of the cage. *"Who are you?"*

"My name is Balam."

He pressed his hands up against the iron of the cage, the openings not quite big enough for him to slip them through. Without thinking, I put my hands up against his. I felt something like a low-level electric current run from his hands up into my arms, coursing through the rest of my body. Thin, cold strips of metal pressed into my fingers and palms, but the heat of his flesh against mine burned the cold away.

"Are you human?"

He smiled, showing remarkably long and sharp canines. *"Sometimes."* His fingertips caressed the palms of my hands. My knees went weak and my nipples stiffened beneath T-shirt and hoodie.

"Why are you here?"

"Trapped by an enemy who I thought was a . . . friend."

Sudden images of the beautiful fierce woman played through my head. I saw her face underlit in the glow of lit torches, triumphant and cruel as I . . . he lay on the ground before her. She held something in her hand, thrust it forward so he could see it better. The little crouching figurine. She chanted in a language I didn't recognize, but Balam did, and I felt his horror as he realized what she was doing.

The dream within a dream ended and I once more stood before the cage, hands still touching Balam's.

"*I must have it back.*"

"*What does it do?*"

"*Without it I am trapped in only one form in the waking world. I cannot go home again. Evaki would do much damage in my absence.*"

"*She's the woman who trapped you?*"

He nodded. "*Will you help me?*"

"*Of course.*" Reluctantly I pulled one hand away from his and retrieved the figurine. "*Here.*" I poked it through one of the openings, taking care not to let go of it until Balam had it in a firm grip.

His face lit up in triumph not unlike the expression on Evaki's face when in my vision, and his features seemed to shift back and forth between human and feline, the characteristics of both melting into one another and then morphing again even as I watched. This was too freaky, even for a dream. My breath caught in my throat and I took a step back, then another, getting ready to run.

"*Wait.*"

Somehow both a command and a request, the single word stopped me from bolting.

"*I need you, Maya. I am weak and must replenish my magics if I am to break Evaki's spell. Will you help me?*"

That question again. But this time I hesitated. "*What do you need?*"

His face totally human again, he gazed at me with a mixture of tenderness and lust I'd never seen before. "*I need you.*" He held out his hand as if expecting me to take it and I would have if not for the cage bars that . . . that were no longer there. *"Come to me."*

It was a dream so I went with it. I took Balam's hand and he drew me towards him into another place.

We stood on the edge of a perfect clearing nestled against the edge of immense trees draped with vines. Soft grass replaced the cold concrete that had been under our feet. Warm sunlight, improbable tropical flowers with multi-colored blossoms so bright and fragrant they seemed almost alien. A waterfall splashed down into a small crystalline aqua lake with a tiny strip of white sandy beach sparkling up against the water.

Why didn't I have dreams like this *every* night?

"Do you like it?"

"It's perfect."

"No, Maya. You are perfect." With that Balam leaned down and kissed me, lips firm and oh so real against mine. When his tongue slipped inside my mouth, I met it gladly with my own, my body melding against his as he pressed a strong hand against my lower back to hold me closer to him. I felt the heat of his groin through the denim of my jeans, suddenly hyper aware of his nakedness . . . and magnificent body.

Why did I still have clothes on? Shouldn't I be naked in this kind of dream? Or at least wearing a whisper-thin slip of silk clinging to my curves and flowing to the ground?

Balam's hands slipped under my T-shirt to the clasp of my bra, unhooking it with experienced fingers. I guess this jaguar got around. He gently pulled both shirt and hoodie over my head, trapping my arms in the fabric with a firm twist of his hand. I gave a small gasp, heat coiling in my stomach, anticipation mixed with just a hint of fear as he lowered me to the ground, drawing my arms and hands above my head, his green-gold eyes staring into mine.

"What are you doing?"

His lips curved in a seductive smile. *"Whatever you want . . ."* His mouth descended on mine in a soul-shattering kiss, lips, tongue and teeth doing things that drove me wild. I arched up against him, arms straining to be free so I could wrap them around his torso and pull him even closer.

He nibbled on my lower lip, planted little butterfly kisses on my jawline and neck. Then he moved lower, tongue like rough velvet tracing a path from my neck to my collarbone, then down to my breasts. Licking first one nipple and then the other, my dreamworld lover used that deliciously rough tongue of his to tease them both into stiff buds, so sensitive to the touch I almost came on the spot. Balam laughed softly, his warm breath on my skin like an aphrodisiac. One hand slipped down to the waistband of my jeans, unhooking the top button with clever fingers, pulling the zipper down with deliberate slowness, prolonging our anticipation.

His fingers slipped inside my lace thong, teasing the edges of my most sensitive area but never coming into real contact. I growled softly and thrust my hips against his hand, wanting more.

"What do you want?" He smiled down at me, canines lengthening as I watched.

"You."

I pulled my hands free—or maybe he let them go—and wrapped both arms around his back, feeling the muscles that rippled underneath like steel cables. I nipped at his neck, tasting spices and the salty-sweet flavor of his sweat.

"*More*," I growled, not sure if I was thinking or talking out loud at this point.

"*You will have more.*" He made a guttural sound that could have been a laugh or a growl or both. With one casual sweep of his hand, he ripped my jeans and thong off my body, literally shredded the fabric with a hand that now had claws. The tips grazed my flesh with a slight stinging sensation just short of pain. My nipples stiffened even more, so hard and sensitive that the slightest brush of his skin against them made me squirm with desire.

My hands, caressing the sleek smoothness of his skin, felt coarse fur sprouting under my fingers, growing impossibly fast like a time-lapse film of a flower unfurling. I looked up into Balam's face as his nose flattened, his teeth elongated, and his green-gold eyes took on a feral expression that should have terrified me . . . but instead aroused me to the point of no return.

I could smell the scent of our arousal in the air; an earthy, musky smell as heady and intoxicating as the fragrance of expensive perfume or melting chocolate. I felt myself growing warm and so wet I thought I'd die if he didn't fuck me then and there. But Balam had other ideas.

"*Wait.*"

He ran that gloriously rough tongue across my breasts

again, then moved lower, tracing a path down my stomach to my hips, flicking the sensitive area around each hip bone, taking tiny tastes of my flesh with gentle bites. He ran his fingers/claws down to my legs, teasing the soft skin of my inner thighs while his mouth and tongue traced a warm path between.

I moaned and arched into his mouth as he explored my most sensitive parts, tongue plunging inside me and then lapping at my clitoris with a smooth, steady rhythm guaranteed to drive me crazy.

"*Now.*" I reached down lower and took his shaft in one hand. No fur, just a hot, thick, throbbing cock. *Mine*, I thought as I carefully guided him to my center, feeling the tip pushing against me.

"*Yes. Yours.*" With one sudden movement, Balam thrust inside me, filling me completely. I screamed as I came, the sound deepening even as it came out of my mouth, lengthening, coarsening to the bellowing roar of a jaguar.

Balam suddenly bit down on my neck, teeth closed around my jugular in a grip that meant business. I gasped, then growled again and dug my nails into his back, nails now curved in deadly talons that could take chunks out of a bowling ball.

Balam withdrew from me and I laughed with a primal joy as I felt my body changing, shifting, and morphing into something wild and ferocious, strength coursing through my body. I lifted a hand to see rough yellow-brown fur, patterned with rosettes, replacing my skin. Half hand, half paw, finishing the morph into paw even as I watched.

"*Do you like it?*" Balam, now totally in his jaguar form, hunkered down next to me. I grinned at him, an open-mouthed jaguar grin giving him the answer he sought, tail (tail?) lashing back and forth with excitement.

"*Shall we swim?*"

"*Oh, yes!*" I took off like a shot, reveling in the feeling of strong muscles propelling me towards the enticing crystalline water. I felt rather than saw Balam (Nagual?) catching up with me, racing along at my side. We both reached the lake at the same time, plowing into the water like two feline cannonballs.

It felt like cool liquid silk, like heaven.

We played in the water like frolicking cubs, leaping on each other to see who could duck whom under the water; racing from one side of the lake to the other, then back again just because we could.

After we swam Balam took me for a run in the jungle, letting me stretch my muscles and stamina. I reveled in the power and grace of my feline form . . . and the beauty of my companion. At one point he outpaced me, vanishing amongst the dense foliage. I ran after him, then stopped, disoriented and suddenly frightened he'd left me alone in this strange place. I let out a mournful call that echoed through the trees. And was suddenly sideswiped by several hundred pounds of frisky jaguar.

His mouth lolled open in an annoyingly satisfied grin. Both angry and relieved, I growled and swiped at him to let him know I was not amused. He boxed my ears in retaliation, then wrestled me down to the ground until I was on my stomach, his teeth sunk into my nape as he fucked me from behind. Quick, but satisfying, although it hurt when he withdrew. Stupid feline barbed penis.

Eventually we ended up back in the clearing where I collapsed in an exhausted heap, ready to sleep. *"Rest now, Maya . . ."* Balam gently washed my face with his tongue, like a mother cat with her kitten, soothing me to sleep in a cocoon of total security. *"Remember . . . I'll be back for you."*

Reality and wakefulness did not come easily. I felt sunlight on my eyelids trying to urge me to join the world, but I felt such a wonderful languor from my dreams . . . I didn't want to wake up. Then something started buzzing around my face, landing on my nose. I lazily swatted at it, then stretched out the full length of my body from head to . . . to tail.

My eyes flew open.

Iron bars in front of me. Cement floor beneath me. Paws instead of hands.

I opened my mouth to scream, but the only thing that came out was the guttural cough of a jaguar.

I was a jaguar, it was broad daylight and I was locked in the quarantine cage at FPC.

I looked outside at the patch of grass. There was no sign of my sleeping bag.

This had to be a dream!

But what if it wasn't? What if the little figurine I'd found held a secret magic? Something strong enough to imprison a man in jaguar form? What if this man used it . . .used me . . . to free himself, trapping me in his place?

Bastard.

I started pacing back and forth along the length of the

cage, tail lashing in outrage, bellowing roars of rage and abandonment with each circuit I made. No jaguar at FPC had ever made the fuss I was making now. I would wake up the entire compound until someone came to . . .

To what?

Who would know who and what I really was?

This realization only set up an entire new round of barking roars, accompanied by frantic leaps up on the den box and back down, running around the perimeter of the cage, only to repeat the pattern again and again.

Footsteps approached, but I paid them no heed, too caught up in my cycle of misery and betrayal.

"Maya!"

I stopped mid-leap as I recognized Balam's voice. Running to the front of the cage, I leapt up, front paws against the bars as he strode towards me, my Aztec warrior now dressed in jeans and a crisp white cotton shirt. He was followed closely by Jeri and Patrick.

Balam leapt over the protective fence before Jeri or Patrick could stop him.

"Señor Cadejo, I wouldn't—" Patrick stopped and shook his head as Balam pressed his hands against my paws, putting his face up to the bars next to mine. I licked him frantically through the bars, ecstatic he hadn't abandoned me.

"Maya," he whispered. "It is going to be fine. I've come to take you home." With a quick sleight of hand, he pulled the figurine seemingly out of the air and held it in front of me. "I'll take care of you, I promise." Another gesture and the figurine vanished.

"How the hell did your people send us the wrong damn cat?" Jeri came up beside him, understandably pissed off and confused.

Balam shrugged. "I was out of the country and one of my keepers is new and didn't bother to check the gender of the jaguar sent to you. He is no longer in my employ."

"So you're saying this one isn't even male?" This was Patrick, as pissed off as Jeri.

"Most definitely not. This is Maya, a female who I myself raised from birth."

More or less true, I thought, giving his face another lick through the bars.

Balam chuckled. "You can see she knows me."

Jeri gave a grudging nod. "Obviously. You said her name is Maya?"

Nodding, Balam reached in and scritched my forehead. "Just like your docent."

Jeri gave him a sharp look. "How the hell did you know that?"

"Ah, that is quite simple. Once I discovered the mistake, I flew up here from Belize immediately and arrived at your compound early this morning. I didn't want to intrude, so I waited in my car in the parking lot. Your Maya came out there quite early and I told her who I am and why I was here."

Patrick nodded slowly. Something about Balam's soothing voice made anything seem plausible.

"But why did she leave so early?" asked Jeri, frowning.

"She was ill," said Balam. "She said something about a . . . a migraine? . . . and needing to go home to get medicine. She asked me to let you know."

Jeri nodded, satisfied.

"So now I must take my Maya home with me." Balam smiled at me. I rubbed up against the bars, running back and forth before dropping to the ground and rolling on my back.

"What about Nagual?" asked Patrick.

"Ah, Nagual . . ." Balam looked at me as he spoke. "You know that Nagual is a name for a spirit companion in the form of a jaguar, yes? The shamans believe these companions protect them from evil spirits while they traverse the worlds between the spirit realm and the Earth."

"That's all very interesting, Señor Cadejo." I could tell Jeri was trying very hard to keep her temper. "But it doesn't answer the question."

Balam turned to face her. "Quite right, Miss Callahan. My apologies. I will arrange to have the correct jaguar sent to you tomorrow on one of my private jets, at absolutely no expense to you. And for the inconvenience, I'll also arrange for a donation of fifty thousand dollars to your compound."

Jeri and Patrick looked at each other, then back at Balam. Jeri was the first to speak. "That's very generous of you, Señor Cadejo, but not necessary. The jaguar will be more than enough to—"

Balam waved his hand in friendly dismissal. "I must insist. You already paid for the transport of my little Maya here. The mistake was made by my people. Let me make up for it."

"Well . . ."

"I insist."

He turned to me. "Maya, are you ready to go home with me?" His green-gold eyes shimmered with an unearthly glow. "It's been an eternity. I will never let us be separated again."

I gave a soft grunt in reply. I wanted to go home. And home was with Balam, in this world . . . and any other.

The Red Devil Lounge

By Melanie Thompson

My name is Claire Davenport and tomorrow my life ends. I've been forced into marriage by my parents. I'm being sold to the highest bidder. My parents' choice is Drake Johnson, a shipping tycoon and a man I've never met.

"Snap out of it, Claire" Victoria, my outspoken scandalous friend, glared at me from her corner of the carriage. "We all must accept our parents' choice. Marriage is merely a contract between two people for the purpose of procreation. It doesn't mean your life has to end. This night is for us. Stop moping around and let Lucy and I show you a good time."

When the carriage pulled up in front of our friend Lucy's uptown mansion, I saw the San Francisco Bay and smelled crisp salt air. Before the driver could open the carriage door, Lucy was there.

"Let me help you in, Miss," the driver said, with a polite bow.

"I've got it," Lucy replied, a sweet smile on her lips.

With her blonde curls bouncing, Lucy climbed in and blew a kiss at the driver. "Thank you anyway."

Lucy settled her voluminous skirts on the tufted cushions, twitched a taffeta fold into place over halfboots of the finest leather and immediately started chattering. "Claire dear, it's so wonderful you're getting married tomorrow. I'm just pink with envy."

I settled against the soft cushions and groaned. "Please do not remind me of my upcoming demise."

"But, Claire, if I was getting married, I would be the happiest woman ever." Lucy's deep sigh was filled with longing.

"Maybe you should trade places with me." Briefly, I entertained the thought. How lovely it would be. She'd be tied to a man she'd never met, and I'd be blissfully free, living with my aged aunt in a lovely mansion at the very hub of San Franciscan society. "He's never met me".

Lucy stared at the cream and gold satin ceiling of the luxurious carriage and sighed again. "I'd love to help you, Claire, but I will only marry for love. You know Aunt Hendred will never force me to marry against my will. Besides, your parents chose Mr. Johnson to be your husband. I don't think they'd like me to steal him away."

"Then stop your prattling. For a moment, I had hope. This type of conversation does nothing to improve my mood."

Lucy pouted. "Fine. Are you ready for your adventure?"

"Whatever do you mean? I thought we were going to a play. Pray tell me what could be adventurous about such an endeavor?"

Lucy and Victoria exchanged a knowing look. "Yes, darling, we're off to see a play."

Claire grabbed Victoria's small hand. "What are you up to?"

Victoria squeezed her fingers. "Don't worry your pretty head. Lucy and I have arranged everything."

The carriage bounced and lurched back and forth as we traveled down the cobblestone street. I rubbed my temples and put a scented handkerchief to my nose to block the offensive odor of manure and piss emanating from the road while I contemplated what mischief my two friends could be up to.

The carriage turned down a dark alley. I leaned over Lucy to gaze out the window. Aside from the dreadful odors, the alley was also dark and in a part of San Francisco I'd never visited. The driver stopped the carriage and all I could smell was the sewer. We must be deep in the heart of the city.

The carriage belonged to the Conners family, Victoria's parents. The driver was an old family retainer. When he opened the door, the whites of his eyes were huge in his dark face, his forehead wrinkled and he seemed agitated. "Miss," he said to Victoria. "Are you sure this be where you wants to go?"

Victoria glared at him. "Henry, do not doubt my instructions. Of course it is. Are you questioning me?"

The driver looked around. "I was just a thinkin' yer pa wouldn't want me to let you out here. I was just . . ."

"Just what?" snapped Victoria.

Henry shuffled his feet and carefully examined a hole

in the toe of his boot. "Never mind, Miss. I'll have me a chew while I wait."

Vicki waved. "Don't wait, Henry. Return for us at two."

Henry tipped his hat. "Yes, Miss."

Henry's concern for his youthful charge gave me pause. What was he worried about?

The old black man helped the three of us out of the carriage and then climbed back onto his seat and picked up the reins. He slapped the horses on the rear with the lines and left us there. The sound of the horses' shod hooves ringing on the cobbles gave me goosebumps. I shivered. My friends were up to something. I knew in my heart I should call Henry and get back into the carriage and go home.

But when I thought about what the morrow would bring, I said nothing. Anything my friends had planned could not compare with the horror of marrying a man I'd never met. He was rich, which no doubt meant he was fat and old and ugly.

The three of us stood there for a few moments staring at the building.

There were two large picture windows in the front. Both had been painted black, a flat color so dense I could see no light shining through from within. Bright moonlight broke through the cloud cover and illuminated a sign hanging from an ornate metal rod above the door. In red writing on black wood, swinging back and forth in the sea breeze, it said Red Devil Lounge.

I grabbed Victoria's arm. "Where are we, Vicki? What the hell is this place?"

Her hazel eyes lit with a look of pure longing and excitement. "We have arrived at your surprise. Trust us."

Victoria grabbed the huge brass knocker and banged on the black door three times.

I got the feeling she'd done this before.

The door swung open immediately. A tall bulky man stood there. A black cloak covered him from hooded head to his booted ankles. As he stepped into the moonlight, I noticed how pale the skin of his face was, like he hadn't seen the sun in a decade.

"Do you have tickets?" he asked.

Victoria promptly pulled three tickets out of her clutch. "Of course we do, Merlin. It's so nice to see you again."

A smile lit his face. "Miss Victoria, as always a pleasure."

I couldn't stop staring at his face. His eyes were the color of ice reflecting off water and his teeth were longer than any I'd seen before. Against the alabaster skin of his face, lips the color of bright summer cherries seemed odd.

As we walked through the door, I felt his eyes trailing me. A shiver went up my spine as the hair on the back of my neck slowly rose.

I heard Lucy giggle and jumped at the sharp sound in the deathly quiet of the entryway. When I looked behind, I saw Lucy staring into Merlin's eyes with hunger.

"Victoria, where are we? It doesn't look like a theatre to me and I'm sure I've never heard of one in this part of town."

"Claire, you must trust me. I assure you, you will have the time of your life."

We walked down a narrow hallway. Alternating red and

white candles flickered above our heads from black sconces. The red light gave an erotic feel to the place. I reached out and touched the red-and-black wallpaper. It was satin.

As we approached the end of the corridor, a long red velvet curtain blocked our way. It automatically opened to reveal a small theatre. There were ten rows of cushioned seats; eight in each. The rows were filled with costumed men and women all wearing bizarre masks. There were three empty chairs in the first row next to the stage.

When I stepped through the door into the small theater I noticed the walls were draped in red and gold velvet tapestries depicting scantily clad or naked people in various displays of lovemaking. My face flamed. I'd never seen such acts before.

But even though I was shocked, I couldn't stop staring. The males were depicted with huge jutting organs while the females had thrusting breasts with large red nipples. The pictures excited me in a way I could not explain. My breathing sped up and my heart raced. I smelled wine, perfume, and something musky I did not recognize.

Blushing, I turned to Victoria. "What kind of theatre is this?"

"Relax, my dear friend. You have this one last day of freedom. Enjoy it."

Leading us to the front row, Victoria turned to Lucy. "You sit on the end. We'll put Claire in the middle."

Lucy smiled at me as she slid into her seat. "Of course, Vicki, that way Claire will feel safe." She winked at me. "No worries sweet, this is going to be so much fun."

Lucy's eyes smoldered with what I could only describe

as anticipation. Her expression reminded me of my little sister's on Christmas Eve.

Music started playing, a mixture of drums, piano, and flute. It began softly, and was as soothing as a lullaby.

The curtains on the small stage parted to reveal a burgundy chaise lounge, four blazing candelabras and a white bear skin rug.

Two women entered the stage from the left, both clad in undergarments I had only read about in my mother's secret stash of erotica. One, a beautiful tall blonde with legs for miles wore a black bustier, fishnet hose, garters, and short high-heeled boots. Her partner was a petite woman with red curls piled on top of her head. She wore her emerald-green satin corset open at the top to expose round pale breasts glistening in the soft candlelight. The privacy panel of her white pantalets was gone allowing the audience full view of a fleshy white mound of Venus with no hair. I grabbed my hot cheeks and gasped.

"Shhhh!" Victoria hissed.

The two women swayed to the soft music. They moved closer to each other, their eyes half closed, their lips parted. The tall blonde pulled the redhead into a tight embrace. As they kissed like lovers, she rubbed the redhead's bottom and moved one hand to cup her naked sex. Then she gently pushed Red back onto the chaise lounge, where she caressed her breasts. Red moaned and threw back her head in pleasure, while the blonde sucked each pert nipple into her mouth. The tips of Red's breasts swelled, lengthened and grew rosy with each sucking stroke of the blonde's mouth.

Heat filled my most private place. The feeling was new for me. I had never known the pleasures of flesh before. I discovered I couldn't take my eyes off the two women as they kissed and fondled each other. I knew it was wrong, but I didn't care. When I looked at Victoria, she was rubbing her breasts with both hands. I turned to see how the show was affecting Lucy, and saw her transfixed, eyes glinting with desire.

Victoria nudged me. "Claire, drink this."

She handed me a glass of dark red wine. It smelled like sweet musky grapes.

I realized I was very thirsty. My mouth felt filled with cotton. I guzzled the wine as the music rose to a crescendo. The drums pounded with the beat of my heart. I stared frozen in place as the blonde pulled off Red's bloomers, spread her legs and lowered her mouth to the junction of her thighs. Red grabbed the blonde's head and shoved it to her crotch, moaning.

My nostrils flared as I smelled the women's excitement. We were so close I could see the pink interior of her sex. I leaned forward to get a better look.

A tall man with slicked back dark hair appeared on stage so fast it seemed as though he materialized out of thin air.

When he turned around, I gasped. It was Merlin, the doorman.

My heart raced. "Vicki, what are they going to do?"

When she looked at me, I saw Vicki's hazel-gold eyes blazed with lust. She flicked her pointed tongue across her lips. "The show is just starting, sweet one. The fun is about to begin."

I wiped beads of cold sweat off my upper lip and brow. "What fun?"

Lucy nudged me gently. "Shhh. Be quiet and enjoy."

The pitch of the music grew even stronger and the drums beat faster. Merlin pulled the two women into sitting positions on the chaise, knelt between them and spread both of their legs. He bent his head between the blonde's legs, while he ran his right hand up Red's thigh.

Both women stared at him as though mesmerized. His back was to us so we could clearly see him open the blonde's sex. He glanced over his shoulder once to stare at us, grinned, and then shoved his face against her center. While he busied himself with the blonde he stroked the red-haired women's moist opening, using his thumb to stimulate her clitoris. I held my breath as she screamed out in pleasure. The wet sounds of his sucking could be heard over the music.

Merlin suddenly pulled his head away from the blonde's sex and showed off his long fangs. Blood dripped from their tips onto the white bear-skin rug.

"Vicki, that's pretty realistic. I've never seen a makeup job that good."

When Vicki turned to me she smiled and I gasped. For the first time, I felt real fear. Small fangs gleamed from between her full lips.

She smiled and I shivered. "What makes you think he's not real?"

When I realized I couldn't move, I screamed.

"Vicki, you've drugged me. Please don't hurt me! We've been friends for years."

"Be quiet, my baby," she crooned, stroking my arm with ice-cold hands. "No one is ever going to hurt you. Vampires and humans have coexisted for years. We do need your blood, but we don't like to kill."

Merlin stood up and for the first time I saw the bulge in his tight pants. He turned to the audience, spread his arms and grinned. "Who wishes to join us on stage?"

I looked around the theatre and for the first time really examined the audience. I wondered how many were human, or were they all vampires? It was impossible to tell with all of them hiding behind their elaborate masks.

"Vicki, I'm scared. What does he mean?"

"Don't worry, my darling Claire." She held the goblet to my lips. "Drink more of this wine."

I allowed the soothing red liquid to slide over my tongue. It warmed my stomach and filled me with a strange energy. But all I could manage to do was squirm in my seat.

A wave of pure pleasure coursed through me as the potion in the wine took control.

"Lucy, Vicki has given me some kind of drug."

My bouncy, ebullient friend hissed at me. "Shhhh. It's only something to loosen you up. Relax. Feel the music and enjoy the show. Tomorrow you will belong to someone."

The tempo of the drum increased. I turned my head so I could see the stage. Men and women poured from behind the curtain and entered the audience. Their faces were also masked and they wore shocking, elaborate costumes. Some were open to reveal a naked rump. Some of the men's organs jutted from their tights. Bare breasts jiggled, nipples were rouged improbable reds and pinks.

I felt the anticipation of the crowd. Was I the only one unaware of what was about to happen?

I swallowed the last of my wine and glanced to my right at Lucy. She swayed back and forth to the music, eyes closed, lips slightly parted. Even she knew what was coming.

A tall black-haired man in a peacock-blue mask stepped off the stage and strode toward me. He had skin-tight black pants on and no shirt. His well-muscled chest tapered to a small waist.

"My darling, your sparkling green eyes have drawn me to you from across the room. I could stay away no longer."

His voice was as smooth as the caress of silk across my skin. He reached around my head and pulled the ivory comb out of my auburn hair. Loose, it cascaded down my back.

Feeling had returned to my body. I discovered I could move. I tried to reach up to stop him from touching my hair, but he grabbed my wrist.

"Why so shy, beautiful one? Don't you want me to touch you?"

As I stared into his dark-blue eyes all thoughts of stopping him flew away. They were as bottomless as the deepest ocean.

I heard moaning all around me. I felt lost in the pulsating rhythm of the music. The scents of musk, lovemaking and blood filled the air.

I turned to check on my friends. Lucy had her yellow skirts thrown up around her shoulders. She writhed in her seat as a man with wild blonde hair knelt between her legs and rammed his enormous cock into her. She wrapped her legs around his waist, clutched his thighs and moaned.

I looked to my left at Victoria. The chairs were gone and so were her clothes. Naked, she rode a man dressed in a confederate soldier's costume. Bending low while riding his cock like a jockey, she ripped the buttons off his shirt with her teeth. Exposing her fangs, she buried them in his neck. The man bucked and screamed beneath her. "Give me more, harder, harder."

My stranger gently grabbed my face and turned it so I looked at him. "Does it excite you to watch your friends in the act of love?"

His sultry voice made my sex ache and swell. I squirmed.

"Yes," I whispered, dropping my gaze beneath his heated look. "I've never seen lovemaking before. I know nothing of the art. I am a virgin."

"Then, you must allow me to teach you."

I slowly nodded my head. What was I doing? Confused emotions warred within me. I wanted him. I wanted to know what love was like. I wanted one night of passion before I entered a loveless marriage. But everything raging around me went against the dictates of my upbringing and all that I knew was right.

When he pressed his cool lips to mine, I opened my mouth and allowed his tongue to delicately touch mine. He picked me up and carried me through the churning mass of humans and vampires on the carpet and in the chairs having sex. I saw men on men, women on women, threesomes and couples in corners alone. The music pounded and my sex throbbed as I buried my face in the clove-scented body of my captor.

He carried me to an alcove. The curtains magically moved out of our way. Behind the red velvet, a golden room glowed. Candles on the wall cast shadows in the corners of a room strewn with plush pillows.

He gently laid me on the cushions and fell beside me. "You have the softest skin," he said as he caressed my shoulders. "I must taste you. Will you allow this?"

Even though I wanted this with every fiber of my being I shook my head. "I can't," I whispered. "I'm promised to someone else."

My need for him was so powerful I felt like screaming with frustration. Why had my parents forced me into marriage?

He pulled me into his arms and I realized if he wanted me, there was little I could do to stop him. He slowly removed his mask, his face so close I could feel his breath on my cheeks. He was the most perfect man I'd ever seen. He possessed piercing, deep-blue eyes, a straight nose, square jaw, and full sensual lips. I groaned.

"Beautiful one," he crooned in my ear. "You owe this man no loyalty."

When he kissed my neck, I couldn't stop him.

He kissed his way from my neck to my mouth and then thrust his tongue through my parted lips. I moaned as all of my protests slipped away.

He stared into my eyes. "I'm going to pleasure you now."

My body shuddered in anticipation.

He grabbed my evening dress and ripped it off my body. Staring at me with those eyes, he removed my corset, gently loosening each string.

I let my instincts take over. I wanted to see what was under his pants. I pulled them down his legs. His organ sprang forth. It was the first time I'd seen one this close. I grasped it, bent my head and took his large cock into my mouth. I was surprised at the way it felt, silky skin over steel.

He pushed me away. "Stop, I want to look at your perfection."

He gently cupped my small breasts. "They are delightful," he murmured as he thumbed the aching buds.

When he looked at my most personal spot, it felt like a flame ignited inside me.

His hands wandered over my body slowly, touching, stroking, squeezing. He kissed my breasts, then down my ribs and past my navel. He parted my scorching sex; inserted one finger and stroked my core while he used another finger to stimulate my clitoris.

"I want to be inside you," he whispered in my ear. "Your smell is making me crazy with need."

"Please," I moaned, weak with hunger for something I'd never experienced. "I don't know what to do."

He needed no more motivation. As he hovered over me, he spread my legs and pushed deep into my sex.

I screamed in joy and agony.

He stopped. "I know there was some pain, my darling. For this I beg your forgiveness. But it will pass. I'll go slowly until you become accustomed to the size of me inside you."

I nodded, unable to speak. The feel of his organ, spreading me open and filling me was indescribable. I wanted to cry and scream. I writhed beneath him. I wanted him to move to ease the aching need, but did not know how to ask.

I gazed into his smoldering eyes, then down to his parted lips. His fangs were partially exposed. "The smell of your virgin's blood has aroused me. I hunger for it."

He began to move inside of me, slowly at first, then faster. I hung on to him as the pain turned into pleasure. I rode the waves of his thrusting organ. Wrapping my legs around his hard ass, I dug my heels into the flesh.

I felt his lips on my neck and then a small prick as he gently bit me. Pure pleasure flowed from my neck into my sex. My body exploded with excitement. His huge cock coupled with his lips and teeth on my neck sent wave after wave rippling through me.

I felt him shudder as he pulled his mouth from my neck, threw his head back and yelled. His organ bucked with spasms as it spewed into my yielding flesh. Finished, he rolled off of me onto his side.

He pulled my face close to his and forced me to look into his face. "You will always belong to me."

The look in his eyes left no doubt. He meant it.

He held me, stroking my face, our bodies pressed together. The smell of sex still hovered in the air.

"Sleep, little one," he crooned in my ear. Languor filled me from the sex and loss of blood. My eyelids drooped and I fell into a blissful sleep.

*

Sunlight touched my face and I smelled the salty tang of the sea. Stretching, I yawned. Then it hit me; the memories. What had I done? I bolted upright in bed. "Where am I?"

When I looked around I saw my dresser, my mirror, my window. How did I get in my room? Did I dream the whole experience?

I threw back the covers. I was wearing my oldest nightgown, the flannel one embroidered with pink roses. When I reached down and gently touched my sex, I winced. It was sensitive to the touch. I felt my neck we're he'd bitten me. It was tender.

I leaped out of bed and ran to the mirror. Two small puncture wounds stood out on the white skin of my neck. How did I get home? I had lost part of the night.

I suddenly smiled as I realized it had happened. I was no longer a virgin. Drake Johnson had bought himself a wife, but not a pure one. Then the dread set in as it dawned on me. This was my wedding day.

The double doors of my room swung open and my mother burst in. "Claire, get up! You don't want to be late to your own wedding."

The next three hours were a blur as I was plucked, pulled, coiffed and squeezed by my mother, her snooty dresser, and my maid. I had no time to think or wonder about the night I'd spent with my mysterious lover.

As my mother settled the stiff white dress over my head, I begged. "Please, Mother, I don't want to get married. I don't know this man. How can you be so cruel?"

"Claire dear, we've been over this a hundred times. The family needs his money. He's promised to save your father's business and pay all his gambling debts. You know your dear father, he's always at his club and he's run up some steep obligations we just can't pay. You must do this for him, my dear. And I'm sure you will like Mr. Johnson."

"Mother, we've never seen him. All you know about him is what he wrote in his letters. He'll take me away to his home in England and I'll never see you again."

"Yes, dear, but this is how things are done. He's seen a picture of you, and offered us anything for your hand. He said he fell in love with you the moment he saw your face. He can't be all bad."

There was no arguing with her. I was just a piece of property to be sold.

I brooded over my fate and the fact I would never see my mystery man again. A black hole opened where my heart used to be.

When I was dressed, my mother led me outside and helped me into the carriage. I was a walking corpse, numb with disbelief. I prayed for death.

I sat in a small room inside the church waiting. Everything was ready. The church was filled, my family in their pews. The door opened and Victoria swept in. She winked at me and took my hand. "Come with me, sweet. It's time."

Lucy placed my veil on my hair and pulled it over my face. I was glad. No one could see me crying. Victoria handed me my bouquet and we walked into the church.

The music started, but all I could hear was the pounding of my heart.

My father took my hand and began to lead me down the aisle. Victoria walked in front of me. She was so tall,

I couldn't see over her head. My mouth was dry and my throat swollen with fear. I wanted to see my new husband and dreaded my first look all at the same time.

As Victoria moved to the left to take her place at the altar, I saw the back of my new husband's head. He was tall with dark hair, but I still couldn't see his face. I looked at the toes of my white satin shoes when my father took my hand and placed it in the stranger's.

"Look up, beautiful one," my new husband whispered.

My heart leaped inside my chest as I looked into blue eyes, eyes I easily recognized.

"Did I not tell you? You will always belong to me."

Jan's Punishment
By Sascha Illyvich

Prince Faolan hated this. He sighed as he sat in his chair with the paper and a lit cigar, the end of which he'd nearly chewed off. An empty glass of cognac sat on the table beside him. The wolf inside him growled in irritation at that stupid faery living in his house. Slumping against the chair, he folded and set the paper down on the table beside him and put his cigar in the ash tray.

The aroma wafted in a plume of smoke that smelled like earth and cocoa.

He groaned.

Anya's words rang in his head. "You have to punish him. You agreed to be his dominant and teach him to behave while Millie is away."

He lowered his head to his hands and sighed heavily. The poor bastard fae liked it rough in bed and was his only source of sexual satisfaction when Miss Millie wasn't around.

The Fae Lust had taken an interesting turn when Faolan realized that Jan's mouth or tight asshole could sate the disease that caused him extreme pain throughout his body. That disease, a faery invention, was designed to propagate the species but no one knew what far-reaching consequences it had since the doctors in Faery never researched it.

Those who contracted the disease were usually banished from the Unseelie City-State.

Previously, the only known cure was for the infected to fuck the being who had infected him, who was ultimately that being's mate. Luckily, Diana's Curse, the Moon Goddess's equivalent of the Fae Lust, hadn't made Faolan uncannily fond of Jan.

As Prince of the Protectors, Faolan couldn't have a mate. Fate had gifted him with more than one partner who could help, it seemed.

That was fine with the prince, he supposed. But couldn't Fate have given him another woman? Did the Fates have to go give him a gay faery?

And must Jan whine so much? Or talk shit about his mate?

The trash talking was a serious respect issue.

Faolan could deal with Jan's fashion sense, he supposed. And his taste in food wasn't so bad either. But the five-hundred-year-old faery needed to learn some damn respect.

Faolan shifted his weight in his chair and crossed his legs. He growled.

The door to his study opened and Anya lead Jan in on his hands and knees, dressed in black leather shorts that rode up too high for Faolan's taste. Dark leather straps that crossed his chest clashed against his pale skin. His tri-color eyes gave away his Seelie heritage.

Jan had been thrown in prison when Faolan was in the Unseelie City-State and had been separated from Millie. They had expected the wolf to kill the young-looking faery, probably intending to set another example of why wolves and faeries were a bad pairing.

Jan didn't buy it. Instead he took all of the rough sex Faolan could dish out and begged for more.

Faolan sighed again. He hated the needs of his body sometimes.

Something had to change to make Jan respect Faolan as dominant. The young fae truly needed to get it.

Brutality didn't work. Jan had taken his fair share of savage kinky faery sex. The Unseelie fae were known for their brutality in their sexual expression. That worked fine for Faolan. He could be ferocious and, in fact, loved that side of himself. Millie recently helped him explore a softer side.

Maybe Jan needed that.

He looked up. "Anya, what do you want?"

The scent of cayenne and black pepper mixed with something Faolan recognized as fear hung thick in the air. Anya stepped forward and threw the leash at Faolan's feet. "You fucking you deal with him. I'm tired and need to make dinner. He's in the way and irritating as usual. I can't believe—"

Faolan cut the air with his hand, a signal that he'd heard enough. "Fine. The little bitch needs punishing anyway. I'll not stand for his blatant disrespect."

Jan looked up, fear in his eyes.

Faolan sighed. He hated having to deal with Jan, but a

deal was a deal. He couldn't teach Jan how to be a faery—
wolves weren't faeries. But he could teach the boy to be
humble and learn to serve.

That had been the goal once he accepted that Jan
would rather die than be left out in the cold. Truth was, he
wasn't a bad guy.

He was just young and stupid.

Discipline could correct that problem. Hell, it might
even make him stop whining too.

Faolan growled. "Stand up."

Jan nodded and stood tall. His posture straightened but
his gaze remained fixed on the floor.

Faolan waved Anya away.

She snorted. "Take that bullshit, wolf."

He glared.

Jan shivered visibly.

"I bet you're just like Millie, aren't you?"

Jan shook his head in defiance. "No. Nothing like her.
She's a girl."

"Obviously, fool. And you're a boy."

"Your boy."

Faolan withheld a groan. He couldn't show weakness
in front of Jan, not right now. The boy needed a keeper as
much as Faolan needed a mate. He offered a faint smile.
"Why do you persist in annoying my charge, and my
mate?"

Jan looked up, met Faolan's gaze.

The wolf wouldn't fall for the sensual curve of Jan's lip
or the multitude of colors flashing in those normally tri-
colored eyes. The Fae Lust would propel Faolan into pain

if he didn't resolve this issue soon.

Flecks of gold sprinkled deep red and purple irises. The scent of cinnamon and clove drifted towards Faolan.

Jan was aroused.

Jan was acting out to get his attention, even if that came in the form of displeasure. Now he needed to admit that.

"Tell me why you continue to pester me. I've given you a safe home, clothes, use of necessities. You shouldn't want for anything. Yet you argue and annoy me frequently while insulting my mate"

Jan's lower lip trembled. He spoke weakly. "I don't know."

Faolan let out a long slow breath. A slow build-up of energy flowed around Faolan's cock, signaling arousal. "Damnit." He let out a low whisper.

"I can take care of that problem if you'll let me." Jan seemed overly eager to assist.

"No." It was a command.

Jan frowned.

Seeing the faery's reaction, Faolan thought for a moment. Separation from the Seelie world meant Jan wouldn't have the prudish notions of his people. Since he'd been living in the Unseelie world, a world where sex wasn't frowned upon, his inhibitions were low to begin with.

That meant he was ruled by his sexuality.

A slow smile crept over Faolan's lips. "We can do this the hard way, or the easy way. Judging by the fact that you like the roughness and beatings I've given you, and are fond of all the bloodletting, we're going to try a different tactic. One that will make you behave properly. Tell me you understand."

Jan quickly nodded. "Yes, my prince."

Faolan cleared his throat. "You are to go to the dungeon with Anya. She is to secure you naked on my favorite table. Then she is to leave to fetch scotch."

Jan swallowed. "Of course, my prince."

A few moments later, Faolan managed to dress himself in black leather jeans that fit snugly and no top. Jan was a sucker for a sexy chest and a healthy-looking cock. Faolan certainly had both of those.

As he made his way down the stairs into the dungeon level of the house, he considered the type of punishment Jan deserved that would teach him to respect Faolan's mate.

Faolan scoffed at the idea. The thought of having to let that sissy Fae touch him . . .

He shuddered even as his cock grew hard.

Faolan looked down and saw the bulge in his pants. What could he really do to the Fae that wouldn't make him crave more?

Jan liked brutal punishment, a result of his having lived most of his life in the harsh reality of the Unseelie kingdom. Life was cold there, rough and mechanized due to the influx of technology introduced by the CyberMage and his ilk. Hell, Faolan recalled, not that fondly, of meeting Jan in the dank prison cell where he'd been left to rot for crimes against nature. The guards had shoved Jan in, hoping that Faolan would fuck and kill the faery and give them something solid to charge him with.

Thankfully, the little faery could take a great deal of pain. Faolan skull fucked him so hard that if he were normal, his head would have been in pieces. Though the need existed to satisfy the Fae Lust, Faolan hadn't wanted any part of it. But here he was, with not only a queer faery who disrespected his mate, but a house full of shifters, and a sensual yet smart-assed submissive who happened to be both his mate, and a faery.

She often offered to share with Jan but the boy merely cringed and swore he was queer.

It didn't matter. Faolan had to become the master of both the smart-assed Millie and of this boy who craved attention.

As he reached for the heavy metal door's knob, Faolan inhaled sharply. He needed something.

Then it hit him.

Basic needs hadn't been met or even acknowledged.

His lips turned upwards in a smile. He could do this.

Hell, his cock wanted this too.

Just a simple exercise. That would make Jan obey.

Pushing the heavy door open, Faolan waited for his eyes to adjust to the darkness of the room. Anya was a sucker for atmosphere and had been ever since he'd picked her up off the streets of San Francisco and brought her back to be his personal assistant and more.

Now she had Virus to deal with.

Faolan snickered at the thought.

His supernatural eyes adjusted to the sight of the room. Red lamps hung in corners providing the only light for the entire dungeon.

Whips hung from one rack along the far wall with a mix of very heavy-duty floggers. A first aid kit rested on a wooden table near one of the corners. The room was empty except for the one table that had been padded for comfort and a couch along the back wall.

Jan lay sprawled on his back on a table, restrained and motionless. His legs were spread apart. His ass rested just at the edge of the table, slightly tilted up for insertion purposes. His arms rested straight out.

Lights gave his alabaster skin a softer hue, mixing with the blue and purple vines that appeared all across his flesh. Hair fanned out behind him like a long colored cloak.

In daylight that hair was a deep crimson when Jan used glamour.

Faolan's eyes traveled down the length of Jan's body, noting muscular development. He chuckled. "You look good that way, quiet and still."

Jan didn't move or respond. He knew the way this was supposed to work.

As harsh a master as he was, Faolan only had a few rules in the dungeon. Keep quiet, obey, and answer all questions.

Even Jan could handle those rules.

"Do you think you look good with the extra muscle, Jan?"

Jan lifted his head up and replied in a soft whisper, "Yes sir."

"Good." Faolan's eyes continued down Jan's body, stopping at his impressive cock. Faolan had never let the boy put that anywhere near him.

The damn kid was fairly well endowed but Faolan

suspected he had no idea what to do with such a tool.

Besides, for Faolan, Jan was always a bottom.

Faolan closed the door, making sure that it shut with enough noise to wake the dead.

Jan flinched, but only the supernatural could detect that slight, yet quick movement.

The air filtration system kicked in long enough to clear the room of the previous dank smell of sex and old blood that hung in the air.

Faolan took a deep breath, then let it out slowly and walked towards Jan. He had to get over his fear of touching other men. Several times during their escape from the Unseelie kingdom Jan had offered up his life so Faolan could live.

The bastard had sacrificed himself and it pissed Faolan off. The Protectors were a proud race of wolves that needed no one to save them, but Jan stepped into the line of fire repeatedly to protect Faolan.

The air system shut off. Faolan walked closer to Jan, keeping a level hand. He touched the faery, setting a hand on the boy's stomach and felt Jan's muscles contract.

In a stern voice, Faolan spoke, "You will relax. There is only one type of pain here you will endure and it will be at my hands. Do you understand?"

Again Jan lifted his head and replied, unable to keep the shakiness from his voice, "Yes, Master."

Another tiny tremble shot through Jan.

Faolan's touch eased.

Jan settled, the muscles in his body relaxing ever so slowly.

Still maintaining an even, low tone, Faolan continued, "Good. This will be a different type of pain than you have ever experienced."

Jan didn't respond.

Point for him.

Lightly, Faolan trailed his fingers across the faery's skin, skittering them across so that his nails grazed the flesh but did not cut.

Again the muscles in Jan's stomach worked, this time visibly.

Faolan repeated the movement in the opposite direction, applying slightly more pressure. He kept his eyes on Jan's reaction, hoping the boy would just be still enough to enjoy the touch. It still freaked Faolan out, but he had to do what was necessary in order to maintain control.

Jan's body quivered, but he remained silent. His lips parted and his nostrils flared.

That cock of his grew hard and lay straight against his taut stomach.

Faolan continued to work light caresses over Jan's body but kept his hands away from Jan's cock. He bent down and blew hot air over Jan's swollen cockhead.

The faery's eyes opened, revealing beautiful tri-color irises that sparkled like diamonds in bright sunlight.

Faolan remembered the first time Jan had been exposed to the warmth of the Earth sun. His body radiated with colors just like now, those purple and blue vines down his skin glowing in response to the sun's heat.

He traipsed a few more fingers across Jan's skin.

The quick movement of flesh amused Faolan. "You cannot hide even the smallest twitch from me. From this point on, I want to hear your responses and see them. Understood?"

Jan nodded.

Eyes narrowed, Faolan snuffled. "I didn't quite hear that."

"Yes, Master. I will respond in kind."

Just to test him, Faolan grabbed Jan's cock and gave it a gentle squeeze.

His hips arched upwards and he responded with a groan.

Faolan let go of the faery's cock and watched it fall back only slightly. The damn thing stood angled and proud. He choked out the words. "You've got a beautiful cock."

Jan replied, "Thank you, Master."

"The lesson here is simple, Jan. You must learn to communicate your needs better, rather than acting them out. So," Faolan unzipped his leather pants and let his own cock fall forward. "You're going to ask for what you want. If you're a good boy, perhaps you'll get it. If not . . ." He let the words trail off while remaining focused on Jan's response.

His mouth hung open. A pink tongue flicked over plump lips.

Faolan hated to admit that he enjoyed those plump lips wrapped tightly around his cock but the Fae Lust had changed something inside of him. He'd grown slightly more open to playing with the same sex, thanks to a disease that forced frequent sex between mates.

Walking towards the head of the table, Faolan remained aware of Jan's heated, hungry gaze locked onto his cock. He was hard, the head now slick with precum. Taking himself in hand, he gave a pump before stepping closer to Jan. "Do you want this?"

Jan nodded. "Yes."

Irritated, Faolan slapped him across the forehead with his cock. "You forget yourself."

Jan's eyes widened. It appeared that the faery indeed remembered some of what he had been told. "I'm sorry. I want your cock, Master."

Faolan grinned. "Perhaps. But I don't believe the tone in your voice is adequate to prove your desire." He pumped his cock a few more times while looking down at Jan. His eyes widened and appeared to glaze over. He recognized this as Jan trying to escape into himself when he thought he was about to be abused.

Slapping Jan's forehead again with his cock, Faolan growled. "You will remain here with me, present as always. Do you understand?"

The frightened look in Jan's eyes left and worry lines faded away.

Power surrounded Jan's body.

Annoyed, Faolan cut a hand through the air just above Jan's body. The power forming dissipated. "You're powerless to do anything other than respond. You should always respond. Even Miss Millie understands this now."

"Yes," Jan's voice trembled with a hint of arousal though definite fear remained present. "Master, I am to respond."

"Yes." Faolan nodded. "What do you want, Jan?" His

eyes traveled down the line of Jan's body before stopping at the hardened prick still angled up. The head now glistened with precum.

Jan's legs remained spread, hips tilted up and arms stretched out to the sides of his body.

"You answered me a moment ago, Jan. Get out of your head." Faolan moved to the side of Jan's body and grabbed his cock. "Now tell me again what you want."

With a groan, Jan lifted his head up and met Faolan's gaze. "I want . . ."

He didn't finish.

The key to the Fae was their sexuality. Control Jan's release and Faolan could probably get more obedience out of him. He pumped Jan's cock once, very slowly.

Jan groaned.

Faolan repeated the motion, slower this time. His thumb caressed the smooth roundness and slicked more precum around.

Eyes rolled back in Jan's head.

Squeezing him tighter, Faolan pumped him even slower now. Each upstroke, Faolan squeezed the bottom of his hand along the shaft, then on the down stroke he let up the pressure while his thumb worked over the wet head of Jan's cock.

Jan's groans became louder.

Faolan barked the order. "Tell me what you want or I'll stop."

Jan's head slammed back against the cushion and lolled off to one side. His eyes slammed shut. "Hurt me," he whispered.

Faolan growled. "No!" The days of pain-filled sex that left one or both parties bleeding were over for Jan. He'd seen enough violence, even at Faolan's hands, to last him several lifetimes. "You'll not get that lie. Now tell me," he stroked Jan's cock again, "what you want."

Jan's hips arched up to meet Faolan's hand but the faery remained trapped by whatever horrific images remained in his head.

Faolan was going to lose this battle if he didn't do something quickly. The stupid faery wasn't capable of focusing on anything but pain. Too much time spent in captivity by the Cyber-Fae had to be undone before he could get proper submission from Jan.

But he didn't have that time to fix things slowly. There was a war of attrition going on in the Unseelie Kingdom now. And Jan's submission would ultimately mean he could live under Faolan's protection.

Releasing his cock, Faolan decided to try another tactic. He dug his nails into Jan's thighs.

The faery hissed through gritted teeth. His hands clenched into fists and his toes did the same.

"Good. Now I've got your attention." Letting go of muscular thighs, Faolan used the palm of his hand and his fingertips to trace circles around Jan's thighs. Each circle inched higher and higher towards Jan's groin.

Swallowing hard, Faolan looked at that large cock before him. He wasn't about to do what he saw a glimpse of in Jan's head. Millie was better suited for sucking off huge cocks. Still, he kept his touch light as his hands played over Jan's smooth skin.

Jan's body shook violently under Faolan's touch. Aroma of chamomile filled the air and mixed with beads of sweat that formed on Jan's skin.

"You're overworking this process, Jan. Ask for what you want."

Weakly, Jan responded. "You'll beat me."

Faolan kept his voice low and spoke through gritted teeth. "I might beat you if you don't obey."

An eyebrow arched. "Master, I . . ."

Taking Jan's cock in his hands, Faolan caressed the long shaft and cupped the faery's balls. Giving them a tug produced a low sound from Jan.

Faolan repeated the motion and earned another groan from Jan.

"Now I see." And he did. The faery needed just what Faolan guessed, softness with that hard prick. "I never did bother to watch what you do while servicing me."

"If I had my hands free I could—"

Faolan glared at him.

Jan shut up instantly.

"I didn't ask. This is your punishment. Feel the sadness surround you at not getting what you want, all because you refuse to ask. Feel desperation take hold while you cower in fear of a reality that's no more." Faolan kept tugging Jan's balls. He leaned forward and blew warm air over the tip of Jan's cock.

Jan grunted and bucked against the hand that pumped his cock.

He'd kept his tone neutral. Still stroking, faster and faster, Faolan watched sweat drip down Jan's face. "I am your prince and will give you what you want if you'll only ask, Jan."

Jan's chest heaved and he lifted his head up. Angry eyes stared at Faolan, eyes smoldering with desire and violence. Jan's voice dropped several notches and held an air of command. With each word that came from his mouth, power filled the room. "I want your mouth on my cock. I want you to suck me."

Something was wrong. The faery hadn't ever had a backbone before and now Faolan stared directly at him and saw heat.

Faolan let go of Jan's cock. "You dare to challenge me?"

Struggling against his bonds, Jan roared and stiffened. "No, Master!" He whimpered.

What was going on inside Jan's head? The baby faery desperately tried to hold himself down against the table. "You promised me anything," he replied in a hushed voice.

Those angry eyes now closed. When they reopened, the look of sadness in them pained Faolan's heart.

"You'll reject me eventually." Jan whispered.

Faolan started to agree but stopped. His mouth went dry as realization hit him. The faery was waiting for the other shoe to drop.

Just like Millie used to.

His heart ached at the sight of pain felt by someone he was responsible for. "I won't let you feel those emotions, Jan."

"But . . ." His lower lip trembled.

Faolan leaned forward and hated himself for giving into the weakness that was love. Wolves mated for life and often were monogamous but not many of the Protectors who had found mates.

And apparently not Faolan, either.

He'd kept his emotions locked up so tightly and here was Jan reflecting them like a mirror.

Faolan's heart unlocked that chamber in which he kept those feelings bottled up. A tear slid down his face. He smoothed his hair back and took the time to look at Jan, really look at the faery.

The hue of his body showed off perfectly muscled abs thanks to Faolan's muscle training. Tight nipples peaked and begged for touch.

Faolan ran a hand over Jan's chest, keeping his touch gentle. The faery had suffered too much hardcore kink. "Light touches are the most effective." His voice was calm now.

Jan's shudders slowed. His features softened and his lips trembled.

"Do you crave calmness, Jan?"

Jan shook his head but his eyes held their truth.

"Tell me honestly. Do you crave submission?"

"To you," Jan whispered.

Faolan narrowed his gaze. "And only to me, you crave this?"

"Yes."

He tried to hold the restraint from his voice. Millie the Fae was his heart mate, as Jan would become if he chose to open himself to what could be. "What will you do with Miss Millie?"

Jan started to respond but stopped.

Faolan saw the look in those perfectly tri-colored eyes, as though he could actually see the thought processes working in Jan's mind.

"I want . . ." He stopped.

Faolan straddled him. "She is a part of me forever. Will you open your heart to your true nature as I have done to you?" His cock hung heavy between his thighs, resting now on Jan's chest. He took himself in hand. "I will keep my word if you'll open yourself to me."

Jan nodded. "Yes, Master. I'll . . . accept Millie. I'll try harder. I promise. I'll—"

Faolan closed his eyes and fell forward, letting the sweep of his hair engulf Jan in darkness. His mouth fell on the faery's lips, capturing them, pressing his body into Jan's. The wolf inside Faolan rebelled only slightly at the prospect of more love and protection, but power swirled around inside Faolan with a renewed strength.

He licked at Jan's mouth, nipped the faery's lower lip and pulled back to see surprise in Jan's eyes.

The taste of faery whiskey, caramel with a hint of enhanced magick lingered on his lips. "Now, will you tell me what you want? Open to me, Jan. I'll only guide you as a dominant should."

"I want you to suck my cock, Master. And I want to taste yours. I need it." Jan's voice held more conviction.

Faolan's body stiffened. The statement held more power in it than before, a move that amused the arousal in him. "So be it."

Sliding off the table, Faolan slipped off his leather pants. Brushing his dark hair to one side, he climbed back on the table and straddled Jan's body. His cock hung heavy between his thighs just above Jan's face.

The faery could lift his head up and taste him, which he did.

Faolan hissed a breath at the contact of heat around his hard shaft.

Cautiously, he lowered his head and opened his mouth. He'd never sucked cock before, doubted it would be a regular thing. But a master had to be true to his word, had to remain as honest as he could be.

Circling his lips around Jan's velvety shaft, Faolan slid his tongue up and down the length, while Jan's tongue did the same to Faolan.

His hand tugged Jan's balls, pulling them from his body. The faery was shaved smooth, an order from Faolan. That taut skin around the base of his cock tasted of power and magick that was fairly old. Faolan would have to remember to ask about that later, but for now, he continued to work his lips up and down Jan's cock.

Jan mimicked Faolan. It took less time for Faolan to get near the point of no return than it did for Jan, but in a few moments both men had established a rhythm and worked each other into a sweaty frenzy.

Jan's tongue slipped up and down Faolan's shaft, swirled around the thick head of his alpha's cock.

Faolan moaned and slid his palms over Jan's powerful thighs. Popping the head of his dick out of his mouth, he bent and kissed the tip.

It bobbed back and forth, amusing Faolan, but arousing him more. This new side of him was unexpected but welcome at a time when he still felt lonely, even among his charge and mate.

Taking as much of Jan's cock in his mouth as possible, he drew the shaft up slowly.

Jan grunted and his hips bucked, forcing his dick deeper into Faolan's mouth.

The beast inside Faolan roared with eagerness and the desire to come. But Faolan kept it in check, aware that he had to give in order to get.

It was how respect of one's dominant was earned.

Pumping harder, Faolan kept his hands on Jan's thighs, fingers stroking balls, tongue caressing, and mouth opening to take him in deeper.

"Master," the pop of Faolan's cock pulled his attention from Jan's dick, "I want you to shoot in my mouth!"

Nodding, Faolan released his control. Power spilled around them in a blinding flash that warmed both men. Sweat broke out on Faolan's forehead, strands of hair stuck to his muscled back and Jan's skin. He could let the fae have what he wanted. "Certainly. We'll go together."

Pumping his hips into Jan's mouth, his balls slapped the faery across the face but Jan didn't seem to care.

His mouth worked along Faolan's hard prick with precision, driving his pleasure higher and higher.

Faolan mimicked Jan's movements, stroking with his hands and pumping into his mouth. Lips sealed over the swollen head before Jan's cock quivered.

At the same time, Faolan's prick shook, and his balls drew up against his body.

Both men grunted and violently unloaded cum inside the other's mouth.

Jan swallowed, slurping and sucking harder and harder.

His mouth filled with a thick, creamy load that tasted of sweetness and salt while orgasm wracked Faolan's body, making the wolf inside howl in pleasure. Tightness in his gut released pent up tension.

Before letting his hips sink onto Jan's face, he slid off and continued pumping Jan's cock, enjoying the sounds the faery made.

Jan whimpered and an orgasm was triggered inside. Those stomach muscles, thighs, ass, and hips tensed. Another load shot high in the air and splattered all over Jan's stomach. Panting, Jan's eyes slammed shut while his mouth remained open. He spoke, wordless sounds that made sense only to Faolan.

A few minutes later, Faolan had retrieved his pants and sat with a sobbing Jan in his arms. He'd taken a blanket from Anya and wrapped it around Jan.

The faery sobbed hard, letting out years of frustration, anger, desperation, and disappointment.

"There, there," Faolan stroked Jan's back, fingers tangled in the silky smoothness of that long faery hair, "it's okay now. You're here now."

"I can't feel the storm anymore," Jan hiccuped. His voice was mostly gone, harsh from having cried so much after his second orgasm. "I can't feel anything in me from where I used to."

Faolan understood. The anger had left, the fuel that fed a storm of rage and violence, that cried for punishment as a way to get attention, had been destroyed. In its place was left coldness, an empty feeling that Jan would have to work through.

Days later, when Jan woke up from the healing sleep Faolan was about to send him into, he'd remember the incident and the last words spoken to him.

"I'll love you differently than Miss Millie, but I'll love you, Jan."

Love Bites: A Survival Guide
By Kilt Kilpatrick

It's not a perfect situation.

Don't get me wrong; I know how lucky I am to be here. It's just that, well hell, there are just too many of them, and they never stop showing up, and it's down to just me left. I've been basically under siege ever since the Infection broke out—for just how long, I've lost count, exactly, but it's been just a bit over two years, eight months. And all on my own for most of that time. Well, just me and Charlie, and he's not always there.

Like the real estate guys say, the three things are location, location, and location. Little Kitsap Island isn't exactly a prime Puget Sound tourist destination; most folks have never even heard of it. But when everything was going screaming batshit crazy in downtown Seattle, we made a beeline straight for it. Not much here besides lots of trees and the Clackamas Station lighthouse—and no way to get there but by boat. Perfect. Or so we thought, anyway. Wrong on both counts.

Now I'm running low on supplies. No more ammo,

batteries, or vitamins, and not many canned goods, dried meat, candles, gasoline, kerosene—aw screw it, you name it, we're out of it or running short of it, and for most of them, once they're all gone, that's it, isn't going to be any more. Ever. I worry about that. I worry about tetanus, lockjaw, and scurvy. I worry about all the million weird-ass diseases out there I don't know jack about. I worry about what month after month of sleep deprivation is doing to my body and my brain. I worry about going crazy. I worry about dying alone.

I worry that I may be falling in love with a zombie.

Shit! I hear the sound of the trip lines and I'm wide awake again, just like that. Old fireman's reflexes; not that I can ever sleep more than a few minutes at a time these days anyway. It's the sound of a cowbell, not jingle bells, tin cans or forks and spoons; that's how I tell the trip lines apart. Cowbell means the main pathway, about twenty-five yards out. I get up from my perch at the top of the lighthouse, unlatch the little door on my old brass bullseye lantern and swing its beam of light towards the sound. Often it's nothing, just the wind or a raccoon, but over time I've developed a knack for telling when it's cause for alarm. Like now. Gleaming red eyes glitter back at me. Just three dead men walking this time, two of them on the small side. Nothing too serious.

I hang the lantern, adjusting it until the beam is fixed on the yard, then head downstairs. The old gun rack by the door now holds a small armory; mostly former firehouse equipment-turned-hand weapons. My first choice is the Halligan bar—it's a fireman's favorite; a high tensile strength titanium rod with a heavy forked claw on one end, a combo wedge blade and tapered pick on the other. Perfect for tearing through doors, walls, cars, or zombies. But after a quick deliberation, I pull down a long pike pole, they're the hook in "hook and ladder," and one of the fire axes. I set them against the wall just long enough to stretch my arms and loosen up, then I throw the heavy bolt and unlock the main door. Grabbing my tools, I kick the door open wide and stride out to greet the guests.

I worry about the big fellah first. I heft up the pike in a javelin-throwing stance, take a few running steps and then hurl it at him with all I've got. Practice pays off; it catches him right below the ribs and goes through him like he was made of wet cardboard. It won't put him down but it should slow him down long enough to deal with his two friends. Running now, I switch the axe to a two-handed grip and bring it down on the head of the second. He splits right down the middle with a squelchy sound and I pull the axe back up for a swing at his buddy who's already closing in on me with purpose. Batter up. I connect nicely, and his ugly head goes flying with a trail of black blood.

I take a second to scan the yard for sight or sound of any more coming, but the coast seems clear. I stay there longer than I should, hoping to catch a telltale glimpse of white, hoping like an idiot that she's out there again tonight. Nada. Nothing else out in the woods tonight but darkness and fog. I get it together, chew myself out for being stupid, and get back to deal with my shishkabobbed friend. He's encumbered and having trouble with the new addition to his torso, but there's still plenty fight left in him; I circle around behind him while he hisses and growls at me and swipes at me as best he can.

It's not enough. While he struggles to un-impale himself, I get a good chop at his leg and then he's down. I come forward and put my boot down on his shoulder, pinning his arm down so I can get some solid whacks in at his head. It only takes two to do in his skull. I take up the axe and take another look and listen for more. Zombie #3's decapitated head is somewhere in the yard, I can still hear him making gurgling noises and gnashing his rotten teeth. It's too dangerous to go fumbling around in the dark looking for him; I make a mental note to go out in the morning and pick him up.

I slip the axe in my belt, quickly reset the trip line and haul the two halves of Zombie #2 inside. When the door is securely shut and bolted, I take the mess up to my crow's nest at the top of the lighthouse and toss them over the railing. The ropey bits of ragged flesh and bones twist down to the dark water below. Sometimes I wonder how many skulls and bones must be piled up down there below the waves, growing barnacles and housing little crabs.

My antique lantern doubles as a hand warmer; I don't like to think about how I'll manage when the oil finally runs out. So I don't. Instead, I settle back into the blanket-covered deck chair and keep watch again, and catch a little sleep with one eye open. In my spare waking moments I play around with long strands of cedar bark fibers. The local Suquamish Indians wove cloth from the stuff; if I could figure out how they did, I might be able to come up with more rope, and wicks for the candles. Sitting there in the predawn gloom, cursing the uncooperative threads, a sneaky little movement near my boot catches the corner of my eye. At first I think it might be a rat, and my stomach gurgles in hungry anticipation at the thought of catching him.

But no such luck, damn it. It's only a little man, about five and a half inches tall. His baggy black pants and oversized shoes are a size too big, his natty little coat two sizes too small. He pokes his head out, then waddles up in that goofy way he does, twirling his skinny little wooden cane. He doffs his tiny derby hat to me politely and wiggles his little mustache. I'm trying to focus on my work, but I don't want to be impolite.

"Oh, hey, Charlie. How's it hangin'?"

He rubs his empty tummy and looks at me imploringly, hat in hand.

"Yeah, I know what you mean. I could use a bite myself. Hate to say it, but I was kinda hoping you were a rat just now. Good thing I didn't stab you by accident."

His eyebrows arch with alarm, he makes an "o" with his mouth and shivers theatrically at the thought.

"But since we're *sans* rat, that means breakfast will have to be some stewed nettles, the rest of that can of dog food and some strawberry preserves. Not much, really, but I guess not enough is better than none any day. You're welcome to join me if you want."

He gives me a jaunty wave of his hand in appreciation, and then climbs up to a perch on top of the lantern to supervise my ropemaking attempts, directing me with his cane when I do it wrong. I don't know what I'd do without him some days. He's been with me for quite some time now; first showed up a few weeks after the last of my fellow survivors defected to the other side. He keeps me sane. But I was going to tell you about her.

This happened just the other morning. I had gone farther from the house then I should have, but I was really hoping to find some more bird eggs, and needed firewood besides. I caught a whiff of rot, a branch snapped behind me, and boom—there he was, a big ugly bruiser of a corpse right on me. I tossed my armload of firewood in his face and jumped back, pulling out my hatchet. When he moved in, I gritted my teeth and made a quick chop to his eyes as hard as I could. It sunk deep and twisted out of my hands. Luckily, it was deep enough to do the job; he stiffened, then slowly crashed to the pine needles. I quickly snatched up one of the dropped branches, and wielded it like a baseball bat, my breath steaming while I try to catch it back again, listening hard and peering around for others.

Now I was turned around. Which way back to the house? Nothing in sight but fog and half-seen trees, but I could hear more approaching. Make that several of them: that god-awful death-rattle moan and clumsy blundering through the underbrush close by. I tossed the worthless stick, bent down and stepped down on his head to pry my hatchet free. I got up again, and that's when I saw her. She was walking right through a knot of them without a care in the world, perfectly serene, completely at ease, looking right at me, walking up casually right towards me. The zombies ignored her as if she wasn't there at all.

She was a vision: tall and long-limbed like a supermodel, like a queen. Long, pure white hair, dressed in a pale moonlight-colored dress that looked like it was spun from cotton candy. Her face was so beautiful, and yet at the same time so indescribably ancient and sad. Her almond eyes seemed a bit bigger than they should be; it gave her an exotic, alien beauty. We locked eyes . . . and it brought tears to mine. It's been so long since I had seen intelligence in someone's eyes. Hell, just to see a face that wasn't trying to eat me . . . I'd forgotten what that was like.

"W-who are you?" I stammered like a clod. She didn't answer; only stood there and shook her head. Though her mouth never moved, it felt like I knew exactly what she was trying to tell me. *Not yet. Soon.* She pointed behind me, off to the right. *That way. Hurry back now.* I couldn't bear the thought of leaving her, but the undead motherfuckers were already shambling past her to get at me, totally oblivious to her presence. Over a half dozen of them, and hungry ones, too. I turned in the direction she pointed and hauled ass back home, double time. I spent the rest of the day in the crow's nest, picking them off with the crossbow. But she never appeared again.

I've been thinking about nothing but her ever since. I look at Charlie for guidance. He pays close attention, resting his head in his hands. He's a good listener.

"You don't think she's—one of them somehow, do you, Charlie? Not some kind of, what is it, mutation or something? I mean, how could she be? She's so beautiful . . . besides, she talked to me. Well, not really talked, but she still had her mind intact, right? And she did save me from them. No, she's got to be one of us, another survivor. But how *the hell* could she just waltz through them like that?"

I gnaw on my knuckle, frowning, trying to make sense of her.

"And where is she now . . .?" I wonder. We look out into the dark, smelling the mix of pines and sea air. Across the Sound, I see where the lights of Seattle used to be, now just more darkness. The night is cold and damp and doesn't have any answers for us.

"You don't think she's . . . I dunno, like an angel or something, do you? I mean, don't get me wrong, I'm not really churchy or anything like that, but I mean, what if she's . . . something—you know . . . *supernatural.*"

The word sounds dorky and lame to me even as I say it. Charlie just sits there on top on the lantern clasping his hands, wiggles his little mustache thoughtfully and shrugs. Another uncomfortable thought occurs to me. "Or maybe I just imagined the whole thing." Charlie screws up his face like I'm talking crazy and waves a dismissive hand at me. He's right. I nod, exhale sharply, and get back to work. I keep working on the rope for a few more hours, dozing off a few times before first light.

Charlie's gone again when I get up for good, yawning, but I'm pleased with my progress on the ropemaking; I've spun not quite a foot and a half of good, solid triple-strand. Feels like I've turned the corner and finally getting the hang of it. Nice start to the day.

I come down from the tower, wash my hands and face

in the kitchen's water basin, and take breakfast in what's left of the dining room. The station is basically a two-story house attached to a lighthouse tower and a water tank. A little oil house and the remains of Mom's rose garden stands on the other side. The roof was engineered to collect rainwater for the cistern; as long as I keep on top of it and don't go crazy with water use, it works beautifully. Just one more little thing to observe. I know the rules well; I grew up in this house. After the lighthouse was mothballed and abandoned, first by the military and then in the 60s by the Parks Commission, my folks tried to make a go of turning the station into a B&B. It was a labor of love. They never quite broke even on it, but my mom stayed there her whole life, even after my old man died. Bridgit and I were going to get married here in the yard.

After breakfast, I peer through all the arrow slits and the pretty little art deco peephole on the front door to check the yard. It's clear, so I take the spiked groundskeeper's stick my folks used to pick up litter and cigarette butts with, and poke around for that stray head from last night. I finally find it deep in the grass; he's still staring and trying to bite me when I head up, no pun intended, to the rail of the crow's nest and slide him off the litter stick into the Sound along with the rest of his corpse. I retrieve my pike from the big guy and cut him into pieces for easier disposal, too. It makes me a little sad to look up at the lighthouse from the yard. Its enormous, never-to-be-lit-again lens looks like a giant dead eye now, like the whole thing is a monument to the zombies, our new overlords.

I take a catnap on the couch after that, and then spend another hour or two dipping candles. Then I scour the kitchen pantry for anything better to eat for lunch. A couple forgotten twists of squirrel jerky turn up, which makes me happy, and I bolster that with powdered milk and half a can of dog food. Then it's catnap time again, until I'm awakened by a scratching sound. A thin, dead, greenish-gray arm is actually reaching through one of the arrow slits in the wall, fishing around in the air with its remaining fingers. Yawning and rubbing the sleep from my eyes, I pull a machete off the rack by the door, take the arm by the wrist, hack it off at the wall and throw it in the trash. I wipe off the machete and return it to the rack, then take down the scythe and poke it through the same slit to do some fishing of my own. It's tricky, but at last I manage to hook the blade around his head and give it a good sharp tug, which takes care of that. I head up the stairs to see if there are more of them about. There are four doors in the hall upstairs, including the one I never, ever open anymore—the one that goes to Dan's room.

I go past it and open the next one, which leads to the master bedroom. I peer out the barred windows, but the yard is clear. Good. I know I have more important chores I should get to, including cleaning up the armless, headless mess on the porch, but for some reason, I have an irresistible urge to tidy up this room instead. It's the nicest room in the house, with all the old Victorian touches: an elegant vanity table, a matching armoire and nightstand, and a genuine one-hundred-and-sixty-year-old canopy bed with four heavy mahogany posts carved in thick, majestic spirals. I never sleep here. To be honest, I'm scared to; if I get too comfortable at night, I might sleep too deeply or too long, either of which might get me killed. The house is safe as I can make it, but it's no Fort Knox.

Still, it couldn't hurt to take a minute to straighten up. So I do, for a half-hour. For some reason it feels nice to have the best guest room shipshape. Then I go downstairs to toss out our new doormat and spend the rest of the afternoon keeping watch on the yard and sharpening all the arrowheads, axes, machetes, and knifes. But once it starts getting dark out, I get a hankering to go upstairs again with one of the freshly sharpened knives. The candle-lit Victorian bathroom is warm, more so now that I've fetched the big cast iron kettle from the fireplace downstairs. I don't have any vices left; no cigarettes, no booze, no drugs, no caffeine, no chocolate, no deep-fried foods. And I've had to re-think the meaning of luxury items: a fresh-caught crab or fat chipmunk, matches, toilet paper, and that one last bullet in the little pistol I always carry; the one I'm saving for myself, for when I'm having a really bad day.

And hot water—god, how luxurious that feels these days. I warm my hands over the steaming kettle, and strip off my thick fisherman's sweater and thermal undershirt, unbuckle my heavy belt and set it down with all its sheaths, pouches, holsters, loops, and clips—you talk about utility belts, Batman's got nothing on me. I sit down on the rim of the antique claw foot tub and pull off my boots and peel off the wool socks. Ahh . . . better. My heavy-duty logger pants feel like chain mail when I let them drop to the floor. Then I peel off my boxers and stretch my aching back. When I dip the washcloth in the hot water and start to scrub the dirt off, it feels so good I think I might pass out. I start with my hands and forearms, then my face, and work down to my chest, under my arms, my stomach. No fat on me at all these days; the Zombacalypse Diet really does tone you up. Maybe a little leaner in the ribs than I need to be. I wash down my thighs and haunches, and the rest of my legs all the way down to my toes.

Feels like old times when I splash extravagant handfuls and handfuls of water over my head, soaking my hair and beard, stubbornly refusing to think about how many days worth of drinking water I'm using up. I take the scissors from the medicine cabinet and wipe the steam off the mirror with my hands, then go to work on my hair and beard; I'm sick of looking like Paul Bunyan. I don't quite give myself a prison boy cut, but it's plenty short; I don't want to give the zombies anything to grab hold of. I snip off the beard in big, wet chunks, and then take the knife to my chin and cheeks and shave as close as I can. It takes forever, but it's worth it to see a reasonably good-looking guy in the mirror again. Even drying off with the big fleecy towel feels like a treat.

I stride naked into the master bedroom, scrubbing my hair dry with the towel, and decide, what the hell, let's lie down on it for a little while. What a decadent night this was turning into . . . But then, like the Japanese say, if you're going to eat a poisoned meal, you might as well lick the plate. I stretch myself on the cloud-soft quilts, flat on my back, arms and legs out, reveling in a perfect moment of pure bliss. Lying here, I could almost forget all the bad things outside and all the problems inside. I want to take just a few minutes to plan out what needs to be done tonight—but before I even realize it, I'm sound asleep.

In my dream, I open my eyes, awake again. She's back. She's floating above me in her long white dress, with her long white hair streaming like a veil. Impossible as it is, she's reclining on the billowing cloth of the canopy bed ceiling, looking back down at me looking up at her. Her big eyes are beautiful and unblinking, staring into mine. She smiles her sad, faraway smile and spreads her arms, imploring. I'm suddenly aware of my nakedness, but for some reason it doesn't feel weird to be naked below her, or for gravity to be working in reverse for her. I can feel myself becoming aroused, my dick stirring for the first time in months.

She's descending like an angel from heaven, her body drawing closer to mine. Her lacy nightgown first fades into gauzy cobwebs, then vanishes into trailing streams of mist. Her long nude figure seems brighter and more insubstantial as she comes to me. At the moment I expect the touch of her body on mine, she's no more substantial then fog and light, but I still sense her presence somehow, and my body reacts to her. My skin tingles, my chest draws in a sharp gasp of breath, the hairs on my arms and legs rise, and so does my cock.

I feel like I'm being fucked by a ghost, and maybe I am. I hear her voice in my head the way I did the first time I saw her. *So warm*, she purrs, *Need your warmth*. It's making me crazy not to be able to touch her, but I can still feel her in the marrow of my bones, feel my heat and strength pouring—somewhere. I sense, more than hear or feel, her pleasure as she takes in my essence. It's the most intense dream I've ever had, even more than the nightmares where I jerk awake in a sweat, crying out because the zombies have finally gotten me, or crying because in my dream I was back with Bridget in Seattle and none of this had ever happened. I feel drunk, I feel ecstatic, like I haven't felt in almost three years.

My whole body tenses; I clench the covers in one hand and my forehead in the other. I can almost feel her body there with me, in me; I can see her looking at me in pure lust, hear her sighs and feel her shuddering orgasm, even if she is just a ghost. Then I come, with a full-body intensity so sharp it's almost painful. With a sudden flood of awareness, I know what she's feeling. She loves me, she wants me, she's drinking me in like wine. She even knows my name—and I know hers. *Tanna*.

I love her.

Jesus, what a wild dream . . . I wake up on top of the covers, still naked, still erect. I have a moment of pure adolescent panic when I realize I had a wet dream on the good guest bed covers—but Mom won't kill me, and besides that, there's actually no mess at all; not on me, or anywhere on the covers. Guess it wasn't a wet dream after all. My second burst of panic hits when I realize it's the dim light of morning. Fuck! I've slept the whole night through— something I haven't done since the first night of the Infection. I run over to the barred window, hoping that the yard below isn't crawling with zombies.

It is.

A split second of shock, then reflexes kick in: Move! No time to think—Suit up: pants, belt, fuck the socks, one boot, other boot move it move it move it! Run downstairs; anything breaking through? The boarded-up shutters on the front windows are rattling, but holding. Keep moving—Tower: up, up, up the spiral stairwell; grab the box of Molotov cocktails (I flash on The Rule: Never Use More Than One at a Time; you'll burn the house down). I look out and see the yard filled with shambling, groaning, rattletrap bodies with horrible dead faces. There're enough of them to tear the house apart—Fuck it, it's Alamo time.

Outside on the rails of the crow's nest, the noise from all their low guttural moans is like bagpipes from Hell; music to drive you insane by. The corpse stink of so many of them together is foul; it makes my stomach queasy. I get out my prized Zippo and go through the numbers: light the rag fuse, wind up, and throw. I send the first one hurling far into the mob below. It impacts, engulfing walking human corpses with a fiery blossom and turning their moans to a shrill, keening shriek. Right now, there's no sight or sound so beautiful. I repeat the drill three more times, knowing with sickening certainty that if the wind picks up in the wrong direction the house won't survive an hour—and neither will I.

The undead swarm falters as whole clusters of them crash and burn. I thunder down the stairs two at a time; at the bottom I grab the crossbow and fire point-blank through a new gap in the boarded-up window into a rotting face. It'll take too long to reload; I drop it and switch to the bow; continue firing through the gaps and arrow slots as quickly as I can until I'm out of arrows. That done, I pull on my heavy Seattle FD coat and my old fire helmet, and grab the Halligan. Just like old times—time to put out this fire. I use the Halligan's pick to hook and throw the bolt, shoulder open the door and slam it closed behind me. It's now or never.

The battle is a blur; I sweep up the porch first; my bowshots have taken out several of the closest already, which makes bashing and chopping the remaining stragglers an easier chore. I move out into the burning, smoking chaos of the yard. The zombies aren't afraid of fire; they're as clueless about it as pretty much everything else, so it makes an handy obstacle I can use to my advantage. I know better than to walk through open flame; them, not so much. I chop and bash my way through whole knots of them with savage swings of the Halligan. After years in the service, it feels natural to be fighting alongside open blaze, almost like an old friend. Some I just shove into the flames as they try to get their claws on me, or bite through my coat; the fire seems to give life to their dead eyes even as it eats them.

Though, despite my worst fears, the flames are dying too. The damp and fog close in on the thatches of fire, blanketing them down into ragged patches of smoking, charred human remains. And I can feel my strength fading; I'm getting tired and clumsy. I feel a wave of despair and remember the pistol on my belt with its last lonely bullet. But I'm not ready for that yet—I want to take a few more of them with me first. I get angry instead. I holler at them and swing my gore-slickened Halligan in big roundhouse arcs, feeling like Conan, crunching two more skulls, then a third, and yet another—and then . . . it's over. I wheel around and around, panting hard, arms aching, eyes peeled for the next opponent . . . but incredibly, I'm alone again.

After the adrenaline buzz wears off, I'm completely exhausted and famished, but it's nowhere near time for a break yet. I restring the trip lines first, so that I can pile up the dead-agains for a big bonfire with less chance of being surprised by any late arrivals. Then I carefully walk the yard, double-checking for any signs of twitching from the dearly departed. One of the guys in the fire station once told me the word "bonfire" came from "bone fire," from back when the Church used to burn heretics at the stake. I don't know if that was just bullshit, but it's true enough this afternoon, anyway. After the last battered corpse is on the pile and the precious, irreplaceable gasoline reluctantly lit, I muse by the fire.

I beat my head over the usual burning questions. I don't get them, the zombies; I don't know where or how the Infection started, or how widespread it is now. The portable radio has been nothing but static every time I check it, makes me resentful for the waste of batteries. I don't get how they can move at all, even their pathetic excuse for locomotion. I don't get what keeps them going, either; for months I consoled myself with the thought they'd all be rotted away by now—but no; some get leathery like beef jerky, others all foul and rubbery and squishy, and some are barely more than walking skeletons. But they're all still here, god damn it.

The stench is as horrible as the worst kind of trash fire: garbage, filth, rot, old dead flesh. There's over fifty of them on the crackling bonfire; a new record. Over the course of the afternoon I have to kill three more who wander up on their own. I have no idea what's attracting them to this tiny island in the middle of nowhere. Could it really just be something as simple as the smoke from the chimney or the light of my lantern or candles? I can't really believe that. Or are they just like ants, simply wandering blindly in all directions looking for food?

I remember the first day they came out of the surf. There were five of us on the island then; originally supposed to be nine, but two didn't survive long enough to get to our little boat and two others were late getting to the pier. We had to leave them behind. So it was my mom, who had never left the island, Bridget and me, and our best friends Dan and Lindsay.

We'd been there about a week; we could see the fires still burning in Pike Place Market. Mom and the girls were looking for crabs. Brid told us Mom got dragged into the water first. At first the girls thought she had only fallen in, but when they went in after her, two zombies emerged from the water and seized Lindsay as well. Dan and I were trying to fix the emergency generator when she came screaming down the lane to the house. They're coming to the island, she kept sobbing, over and over again. We're not safe, they're coming, they're coming. And then there were three.

I stop reminiscing before it goes any further. The fire has done its job, and I keep careful watch on it as it finally burns out. It's been a long day. As I check on the ashes and embers, the evening sun is already turning crimson and dropping down to be swallowed up by the pines. I'm dead on my feet and haven't had a bite since yesterday's lunch. Still in a thoughtful mood, I do some quick zombie math. The population of Pugetopolis was over three million pre-Z. How many of them escaped? One in ten? One in a hundred? Thousand? How many survivors are still over there, holed up just across the Sound? Or are all three million-plus of them zombies now, spreading out in all directions, even wandering across low tide towards any sign of life, even on a podunk little island like ours—like mine?

Charlie pops out from some dying embers at the top of the bonfire's remains, punctuating his entrance with a pop of sparks. He does a little drum major routine, a victory march in my honor, triumphantly parading his cane up and down like a baton. I'm touched. I sit and watch him as he re-enacts the whole day's battle, putting up his dukes, swinging his little cane around like a broadsword at the pantomimed zombie horde. He mimes the vanquished zombies all falling down re-dead, and finishes by clasping his hands over both shoulders, doing the old "we are the champions" salute. I applaud and cheer, whistle as loud as I can. He takes a bow and blows kisses to the audience. Who needs a TV with talent like this?

Whoa there; I feel dizzy when I stand up again. There's not a square inch of my body that's not in pain—even my hair hurts. I've gone beyond hungry to some deep, hollow, ache that makes me feel like a nest of termites has moved in and is slowly consuming me from the inside. I stumble back to the house, and I have to really work to get the door open again. Seeing my rations of canned goods in the kitchen pantry triggers something like rage in me; makes me drunk with lust for food. I tear the lids off old cans of dog and cat food and scarf down the cold greasy contents in big greedy bites. But then my stomach cramps up without warning and I'm sick as a dog, retching all over the kitchen floor.

Pulling myself up from the mess on the tile floor, I get a couple handfuls from the bucket of drinking water and wash the stinging taste of bile from my mouth as best I can. I realize I'm crying, moaning just like a goddamn zombie myself. For the next few minutes, that feels like the only thing I can do; no, it feels like the *right* thing to do. But even that finally passes, and then, in another burst of clarity, I make up my mind to go out and find something real to eat. I strip off my firefighting-turned-battle gear, wash up and dress in lighter clothes—jeans, a camo T-shirt; things I can hunt in.

The door clicks shut behind me, and I realize I've never gone out after dark since—you know. I have my crossbow and a mental checklist of all the things I could eat tonight: chipmunk, seagull, rat, owl, snake, crab, raccoon, turtle, frog . . . I know folks who swear banana slugs are delicious if you know how to cook them right; the one time I tried to eat one raw, it tasted like the inside of a bicycle tire and the first lick made my tongue go numb. I wonder if there are still deer on the other islands. I creep from darkness to darkness through unsafe moonlit patches, never forgetting that there could be other hunters out tonight, and I'm also on the menu.

Eventually I find where the prickly bushes of blackberries are. Each bite is a little sugar rush of heaven. I gorge myself, ignoring the jabs and scratches from the scores of sharp little thorns. Encouraged by success, I plant myself down in the same bushes and wait for some more dinner to stroll by. It's cold, wet, and gloomy, but all the same I have a burning conviction that something good will come by in just a moment. I just have to be patient—and stay awake.

That second trick is harder than the first, and for the first hour or so I keep catching myself dropping off; my neck hurts from jerking back awake one too many times. As I'm shaking off the fatigue yet another time, a tiny pinpoint of green light appears in the dark, floating towards my small clearing. It bobs and weaves, erratically but leisurely, making its way towards me; it's the size of a zombie's eye, then the beam of a flashlight, but by the time it comes to a hovering stop in front of my hiding place, it's the size of a beach ball and bathing the whole clearing with its eerie green glow.

It's ridiculous to keep trying to hide, so I stand up, screening my eyes with my hand for a better look. The light totters off in another direction like a drunken balloon, but after a few yards it stops and waits for me. I hesitate; but finally I grasp my crossbow a little tighter and follow. It leads me on a merry little chase, but never gets too far away and continues to wait for me to catch up. I know there's a word for these urban legends, Will-o-wisps, foxfire, something like that. I forget if they're supposed to be good luck or bad. I seem to remember something about them and quicksand when it stops at another clearing and dissolves into dozens of fireflies flying off in all directions. And then she's there with me.

She's more *there* now, not as ghostly as in my dream before. I can see her perfectly fine, even in just the stray moonlight. She's dressed in a long-sleeved evening gown of rich, dark green velvet fit for a duchess; in fact, she looks like she just stepped out of a medieval painting. Her hair isn't a solid white anymore, but black shot with long streaks of silver; and it's no longer straight, but full-bodied, tied up in an elegant Mediterranean hairdo with strings of tiny pearls. Where she seemed ageless, sorrowful, and distant before, she now seems younger and more beautiful than ever.

Her sloe eyes are bright and just as striking as before; she never bats an eyelid. She flashes me perfect white teeth as if happy to see again, and then settles into a Mona Lisa smile. I remember the word from my dream and speak her name aloud for the first time.

"Tanna."

Like the rings rippling out from a pebble tossed in water, in my mind the sound of her name echoes strangely: *Tanna, Tanja, Tianna, Tannaz, Thana, At'tan-nat* . . . I get flashes of her portrait painted in oils, carved in marble, depicted in mosaic.

She puts a finger to her lips. *Don't speak.* Her luscious mouth never moves, but I can hear her voice all the same. Crossing her hands to her shoulders, she gently pulls at her dress. Like magic, it peels away with ease, slipping off like she's a snake shedding her skin. The material falls silently into a pile at her feet. Nude and statuesque, she steps out of the dress and comes to me, her arms reaching tenderly for me.

My crossbow is still in my hands with my finger on the trigger; absent-mindedly pointed at her sternum. I take a step back, then gently set it down on the ground beside me. She smiles again, and closes the distance between us. Her arms slip around my neck like serpents and her body presses against me. She stares up into my eyes. Her gaze never wavers; it's hypnotic, inescapable. Her lips remain unmoving, but her voice in my head tingles.

I'm stronger now, she says. Your love makes me strong.

She opens her mouth at last, bringing her lips to mine.

Soon we'll be together. Soon.

My whole body is taken in by the touch of her lips, the caress of her hands, the soft crush of her breasts and hips against me. There's a surreal disconnect though, almost as though I were only watching it all happening to some other guy, rather than really feeling it myself. Still, it's enough that I can feel her in me somehow, moving through me in a way that's indescribable. Her kiss is a drug; it makes me forget my hunger, my aches and pains, all my troubles.

It makes me forget everything.

Just before dawn, I find myself in the same tiny clearing, sitting with my back against a tree trunk. My crossbow lies on the ground, right where I left it, still armed. Of course, she's nowhere to be found. I sit there for a few minutes, not entirely sure I'm not still dreaming. I couldn't remember anything about last night after the kiss. But I did know that hadn't been a dream—or at least, it was a *real* dream, if you know what I mean. Something really happened here last night. And I have that feeling you get in dreams sometimes, where you just *know* things. For instance, don't ask me how, but I know now that even more zombies are coming on the next low tide than came yesterday.

But that doesn't bother me. Part of her is with me now; I can feel it. Even though I have no idea where I am now, I know I'll get through the woods and avoid the ones here already just fine. What I'll do about the house after that, I don't know yet. But I think she does. I notice a little brown bundle in the grass next to me. It's a rabbit, sitting perfectly still. I dart out my arm and I'd like to think it's my quickness that lets me catch my first real meal in days. But in my heart I know it wasn't going anywhere. It was sitting there waiting for me, a gift from her. I even know I'll have time to make a little fire and roast it before I head home.

And I'm right about that, but the same intuition also let's me know it's time to get moving when I'm about half way through my delicious roast rabbit breakfast. I can hear the familiar rumbling groan as I'm scooping up my crossbow in one hand, still munching on the rabbit in my other as I head off. I leave the fire burning; I'm hoping the smell will attract the bastards and keep them distracted. But I'm not really worried; now that I know angels are real. I have a guardian angel. And I can remember just one other thing she said:

Tomorrow.

It's a pleasure making my way back through the woods. I haven't been this relaxed outdoors in years. I stalk through the fogbound trees feeling like a wolf, feeling like a hunter, exhilarated, following my gut and enhanced intuition. A few times, I catch glimpses of them or hear their movement nearby, but I'm able to circle around them with ease each time. They'll never catch me. After a couple hours I reach the cliffs and follow them back home. I emerge from the woods just behind the old garden and the oil house, and peer around it to scope out the yard. There's a dozen or so Zs wandering around, but only a few on the porch. Right. I stride straight towards the house, shove two of them out of my way before they even know I'm there, march right up and put a crossbow bolt through the eye of the third. Then I open the door to my house and come home.

I probably should pick off the rest of them in the yard with the crossbow, but hell, it's only a dozen of them, and I'm just too excited about seeing her again, so I go upstairs straightaway. Everything else will have to take care of itself today; I want to make sure everything is nice upstairs. I spend the rest of the morning and afternoon on sweeping, dusting, and tidying up. While I'm straightening up the bathroom, I check myself in the mirror to make sure I'm presentable, too. I open the medicine cabinet—and there's Charlie, on the shelf right next to the dental floss. I've never seen him upset before, but he's on the verge of tears now.

"Charlie! What is it?" He stands up and points to the bedroom, then somberly shakes his head.

"What, Charlie?"

He makes a feminine outline with his hands, but there's nothing va-va-voom about it. He's dead serious.

"You mean Tanna? What about her, Charlie? You don't want her here tonight?"

He takes off his little black coat, makes a cape of it and does his best Bela Lugosi. I stare; then I laugh, harsher than I mean to. He's not trying to be funny, I realize.

"You think she's a *vampire*, Charlie? Is that it?" I shake my head and laugh hysterically; once I start, I can't stop. The very idea is so funny soon I have to bend over because my stomach aches from laughter. My eyes tear up; I hoot and sigh heavily, and wipe them off with my hands. But then something in me flips and it's not funny anymore—it pisses me off. I slam my hands against the wall and scream at the tiny little man.

"What the *fuck* are you trying to do, Charlie? She's an angel! *An ANGEL!* Are you jealous or something? Why are you trying to screw up the best thing that's ever happened to me? The one beautiful, perfect thing that's come out of all this fucking shit and you want to fuck it all up for me? What is your *fucking* problem, Charlie?"

Charlie stands there and takes my abuse without a word. Enraged, I slam the cabinet closed on him. The mirror cracks clear down the middle and the cabinet's door bounces open again. Charlie is gone.

I yell and punch the mirror; the crack implodes into a cobweb design. I stare at my new schizoid self-portrait. My knuckles are torn and bleeding but I don't feel a thing.

I'm shaking. I suddenly pull my fist back to punch

the mirror again; destroying it completely sounds so good right now. But I catch myself, and think about that a minute. Then another. I look at the crazy raging man reflected back in all the jagged shards. *My god. What's happening to me?*

For an awful lot of long, lonely, sobering minutes I stand there mourning a hope I hadn't really known I had, let alone lost. When I finally leave the little room, I'm so dazed and feeling gut-punched I can hardly walk. I can barely stand the thought, but now that it's been pointed out, I just can't deny it anymore. She's not an angel. There are no angels. She's a vampire.

I look out the master bedroom's barred window, not at the restless crowd of the dead, but at the rising moon. It's twilight already, and I need to get ready fast if I'm going to live to see the morning. So it's downstairs and rummaging for supplies. Number one on my list are wooden stakes; and that we can do. I take one of the old brooms from the basement and saw it into four foot-long pieces, then whittle sharp rough points for each. When I'm done I bring them upstairs along with a hammer.

What else: vampires hate garlic. I wish there was some, but we've been out of that for years now. They hate mirrors too, don't they, but do those actually hurt them? I start looking for some anyway, strategically placing them around the front room. What about silver—was that just for werewolves, silver bullets? Not like we have any lying around. I gather together what little cordage there is and slip a loop into my belt, and grab some of the heavy blankets and bring them into the front room too. Then I think of what I really need, and realize it's in the last place I want to go.

Dan's room.

Well, hell. For a few minutes I stall, debating the matter with myself, but there's really no way around it. So I light a candle and go upstairs, not happy about it, one heavy step at a time. In the darkening hall I stop at the door I had promised myself I would never open again. I look at the knob, make a face, and take hold of it. When I realize I'm holding my breath, I brace myself, count to three, then exhale briskly and open the door. Apart from two plain twin beds, a rustic wooden dresser, and heavy boards nailed over the shuttered windows, there's almost nothing in the modest old bedroom. It's completely unchanged from the last time I set foot in here; well, almost.

The only difference is that Bridget isn't lying dead on one bed, laid out neatly with a ring of roses around her head, her throat slit. And Dan isn't hanging from the ceiling rafters in a makeshift noose, staring at me with dead eyes. I guess it's possible they had something going on, I'll never know. But I'd rather think that Dan became fixated on her after Lindsay was eaten, and who could blame him for that? What I can't understand is why he had to take her with him.

The walls of the room offer the only clues, since damn if every square inch of them is covered in scrawled bible passages—he must have been in there scribbling them out for weeks before the end. In the flickering, uneasy candlelight I scan the mishmash spread all over the walls:

. . . Now this shall be the PLAGUE wherewith the LORD will smite all the people that have fought against Jerusalem; THEIR FLESH shall rot while they stand upon their feet, and their eyes shall rot in their sockets, and their tongue shall rot in their mouth. And it shall come to pass in that day, that a great TERROR from the LORD shall spread among them; and they shall lay hold every one on the hand of his neighbor, and every one will attack the other . . . I KNOW THY WORKS, THOU THAT LIVEST AND ART DEAD . . . And they of the people and kindred and tongues and nations shall see their dead bodies, and shall not suffer their dead bodies to be put in graves . . . WITHOUT THE SHEDDING OF BLOOD THERE IS NO REMISSION OF SIN . . . And the kings of the earth, and the great men, and the rich men, and the mighty men, and every servant, and every free man, hid themselves in the dens of the mountains; And said to the mountains and rocks, Fall on us, and hide us from the face of HIM that sitteth on the throne, and from the wrath of the LAMB: For the great day of his wrath is come . . . AND THEY OF THE PEOPLE AND KINDREDS AND TONGUES AND NATIONS SHALL SEE THEIR DEAD, AND SHALL NOT SUFFER THEIR DEAD BODIES TO BE PUT IN GRAVES . . .

I stop trying to read the long tangled bramble of crabbed words; it makes me dizzy and ill. I can barely remember that day now: screaming and sobbing. Carrying Bridget out and burning her body so that they couldn't dig her up and eat her. Drinking all the last of the booze and bringing the pistol to my head, repeatedly. Coming back to cut Dan down so I can throw his fucking corpse off the crow's nest for the crabs. His dead eyes coming to life as I came close, bobbing in the noose and making that horrible death rattle moan as he tried to tear my throat out.

I have to get out of there now; the insanity feels contagious. I grab what I came for: the big antique crucifix off Dan's pillow, and my mom's rosary beads from the Holy Land—Ireland, that is. I leave the bible and close the door behind me, renewing my vow never to open it again as long as I live.

Downstairs in the front room, I set my trap and plan my tactics. There are mirrors and shards of mirrors placed all around the room. I have the rosary beads around my neck, their little cross dangling front and center. I have the big hefty church cross in one hand and a wooden stake in the other. The other three are slipped into pouches on my tool belt, and I have a sturdy little carpenter's mallet tucked in a belt loop. There are only slivers of moonlight coming into the room, from the arrow slits, so I place a few hurricane lamps in the corners, dimming the flame so that it lets me see, hopefully without attracting too much attention from outside. I take up station at the front door's cute little window, a decorative peephole from the 20s with a thick fisheye lens about three inches wide.

There's a zombie casualty on the doormat; my old friend with the crossbow bolt sticking out of his eye socket. A couple of them are shuffling aimlessly on the porch. I keep still and hope they don't notice my little window; it would be such a hassle to come out and kill them. There're more in the yard; one is tangled up in one of my beautiful trip line systems and others seem distracted by the jangling tin cans he's dragging. I keep watch and wait. The moon is just beautiful tonight.

"Michael . . ."

"Michael . . ."

"Bridget?" My eyes snap open; I've fallen asleep on my feet again. Then there's a sound from the yard—a woman's voice. I'm not hearing it in my head, but with my own ears.

"Michael . . ." The hairs on the back of my neck rise at the sound of my name being spoken out loud. Through the little window I see her striding towards the house; the fisheye lens distorts the surreal view. I swallow, caught off guard. She is completely nude and unashamed. Her pale, perfect body is silver in the moonlight, her hair is full, rich, pure black, just like the v of curls below her belly. There's no trace of her sorrow or ancient age from before; tonight she's young and utterly irresistible; sultry and vibrant as a belly dancer, proud as a Brazilian samba queen, with a jungle cat's grace and strength and intent. She's calling my name. Even though I'm holding a stake in my hand to kill her, my body aches for her.

She glides through the dead effortlessly; I can't take my eyes off her as she steps up to the porch. Up close her big cat eyes are prettier than ever. She stands there, waiting for me, putting on a show for me. She knows full well I'm standing there looking at her, looking at those full breasts and long legs that make my mouth water; she's so fucking gorgeous. A zombie staggers up and gets too close to her in typical brain-dead fashion. In less than a heartbeat she gives a slight bend, plucks the crossbow bolt from the

corpse at her feet and with lethal grace slips it up under
the chin of the big clumsy undead oaf. The corpsemonkey
topples backwards off the porch with a loud thud. DRT, as
we used to say in the fire department. Dead Right There.

She gives me a playful Betty Page smile as though one-
shot zombie killing in the nude is just the kind of crazy fun
little gag she does for me. God, she's hot.

"Michael? Won't you let me in?" It's so strange to
actually hear her voice. She has an accent I can't place.

New contingency plans are forming and re-forming in
my head.

"Sure." I say, like it's no big deal, like there's no ongoing
debate on the matter going on in my head. My palms are
sweating. I put the stake in my teeth for a moment while
I undo the locks, then take it up again and use it to snag
the bolt of the door and pull it out of its bracket. I step
back and tighten my grip on the stake. I hold the cross up
prominently, change my mind and quickly slip it behind
my back, palm the stake.

"Come in . . ." I say invitingly. Inside my mind is racing.
Is this going to work? Am I really going to kill her? Is
she going to kill me? I brace myself, taking quick breaths.
Come on come on come on . . .

The door opens out. Nothing for a moment, and then
there she is, pulling the door with an intent look in her
eyes and a smile on her face. I smile too; I hope it looks
like a smile. It works. She steps through the doorway, her
eyes locked on mine, closing in. I almost forget what I'm
going to do, until the door swings closed behind her with
a sharp bang. The sound startles me into action. I whip

out the cross and lift up the stake. Her eyes go furious
with anger and fear. She hisses at the cross like an enraged
jaguar—flashing her unnaturally sharp canines—and
backs away towards the house stairs. Damn! Wrong way; I
was hoping I could pin her down in the lighthouse tower.

I improvise. Keeping the cross between us like a lion
tamer with his chair, I try to steer her into the corner of the
room by the fireplace. But she's fast; she crouches, feints,
then bolts for the stairs. I follow her up, swearing under
my breath, stalking her in the near dark. Upstairs the only
light is a faint glow coming from the master bedroom; just
enough for me to barely make her out. She's trapped at the
end of the corridor. When I take another step forward, she
dashes into the bedroom. I run down the hall after her, but
stop myself at the doorway. I wave the big chunky cross
around like it's a handgun, sweeping the room, coplike.

The place is a deathtrap; the only lights are the blue
squares of moonlight coming through the barred, half-
shuttered window and the dull red glow from the pair
of turned-down hurricane lamps. I take a few wary steps
into the room before I think to look up on the ceiling.
But she isn't there, either. She emerges from behind
the big Victorian bed, looking like a cornered animal.
When I move in closer, she snatches a hairbrush off the
nightstand; it's an antique metal one with a long tapering
handle that comes to a sharp, stylish point. She's wielding
it like a stiletto, and I have no doubts she could put it clean
through me if she tried.

I hold up the cross and stake like I mean business, but
we're at a standoff. We stare at each other. I improvise a

new plan. Slowly, slowly, I put the stake down on the bed. Then I look at her like it's her turn.

"Drop it, and I won't hurt you. I'm going to tie up your hands, but I promise I won't hurt you."

She frowns, and keeps her guard up. I'm surprised when she reaches over to the armoire behind and opens it. She keeps her weapon out and pointed at my eyes, but shields the rest of her body behind the cabinet's thick oak door.

"Back away," she growls.

I suspect she's fishing around in there with her free hand.

"Get away from there" I say, tougher than I feel. I wave the cross at her more. She hisses again and does back away—but now with one of Bridget's nightgowns in her hand. She stares at me with fire in her eyes, daring me to make a move while she slips into the nightie. It's a short silk number. It looks good on her. It looks real good.

I try to play it cool and take a slow deliberate step towards her.

"I said, drop it. And hold out your hands. You know I'm not going to hurt you." I'm surprised to realize even as I say it that it's not bullshit; I really mean it. She keeps looking at me; she never blinks, ever. Then she slowly raises the point of her metal brush up by her ear. I offer my palm for her to hand it over, but instead she snaps her hand down in a flash, throwing her stiletto past my ear. It sticks in the wall behind me with a solid thock sound. She cocks her head slightly with an innocent expression, then gently kneels and offers me her wrists. I place the cross on the bed and try not to look as shocked as I feel while she lets me bind her hands together as meek as a little lamb.

I pick up the cross again and take hold of her bound wrists with the other hand, pulling her up gently but firmly. I don't want to burn her with the cross by accident, or with the little one around my neck; so I take a moment and tuck the necklace of rosary beads inside my shirt. Then I lead her around to the foot of the bed and make her sit. For good measure, I take my last loop of rope and lash her wrists to one of the bed's big mahogany posts, feeling like the villain in an old-timey melodrama. She leans against it, resting her head, staring at me with an unreadable expression.

I place the cross prominently on the vanity in front of her, turn up the light from the hurricane lamps, then grab the chair and pull it around so I can conduct my interrogation. I'm surprised that I can see her perfectly in the mirror. Wasn't that a vampire thing, they don't cast a reflection? She reads the surprise in my face. I turn to her and jerk my thumb at the mirror.

"Hey, how come I can see you there? Is that because you regained your power to cast a reflection when I invited you in? You had to ask to be invited in, or you couldn't enter, right?

She sighs. "I had to ask permission because I couldn't get through the door if you didn't let me in. Because it was locked."

"Oh. But you are a vampire?"

"Don't call me that."

"We both know that's what you are. So why can I see you in the mirror?"

"In the old days, your elders thought the reflection in the mirror was your soul. Demon kind like me have no souls; ergo, we must cast no reflection. *Quod erat demonstrandum*." She smiles and adds, "Priests are fools. I know. I was once a priestess."

"How'd you get to the island? You have a boat?"

"No. I flew." I wait for her real answer, but she only adds, "Like a bird. In the shape of a bird—a great raven." She seems completely serious. Well okay, look who I'm talking to. I let it go for now.

"How'd you know I was here?"

"I sensed your dreams. I was alone and hungry before that. I was so happy to find you, Michael."

"Have you been in Seattle this whole time?

"What is that—Seattle?" Her pronunciation of the word is off.

Is she just fucking with me? I decide to take her at face value a little longer.

"This is Seattle—well, not here, the big city across the Sound. Isn't that where you came from?"

"No, this is my first time here."

"To Seattle?"

"To the . . . New World." She mistakes the look of disbelief on my face for confusion. "To this half of the globe, I mean," she adds helpfully.

"I knew what you meant. So you came here from where, exactly?"

"I was hiding in a mountain tomb in Styria, deep in

the forests." She sees that Styria means zilch to me. "Maybe you call it Steiermark? No? It is near Graz—you know Graz? No? Near Maribor? Carinthia? It lies in the Habsburg lands." I see this is getting us nowhere, so I drop it. She's getting frustrated too. She lifts her head again and gazes back at me intently.

"What are you going to do with me, Michael?" Her look is a plea, a challenge, another question altogether. I start to lose myself in those big beautiful eyes, but then shake myself out of it. Damn! If there's such a thing as Jedi mind tricks, she's a black belt. Okay then.

I go over to the armoire and pull out a black camisole, rolling it up as I return to stand in front of her. She knows better than to try a "who, me?" look. Instead, she gives me a knowing look and a little *can't-blame-a-girl-for-trying* shrug before I blindfold her. I take my seat again. She lowers her head and pulls her legs up underneath her on the bed. If she didn't look like a sacrificial lamb before, she sure does now.

You do know you're going to have to kill her, right? a part of me tells myself. Either you kill her or she's going to kill you—there's no two ways about it. My eye goes to the stake sitting next to her on the bed. I thumb the mallet on my belt. I really shouldn't delay this any longer. But it's awfully nice to have company for a change, even considering the circumstances. We both sit there, neither sure of what to say or what's about to happen. Outside the moan of zombies is as constant as the sound of the waves on the shore.

"Do you know the story of Shahrázád?" she asks.

"Sorry."

"She is the princess in *The Thousand Nights and a Night* who must tell half a wonderful story every night, or in the morning the Sultan, her husband, will surely have her beheaded at the dawn."

"Oh, the 1001 Arabian Nights, sure. Sinbad, Aladdin, yeah, I know about all that. So . . . are you proposing to tell me a story?

"I do know many stories. I know stories it would take a hundred years to tell."

"I don't know that we have quite that much time. Why don't you start by telling me what I should call you, if you don't like the word *vampire*."

She makes a face. "I hate that ignorant word. *Wampir, Nosferatu*, Witch, Succubus, Demon, *Lilitu, Lamia, Empusae*. All stupid peasant names. We are the Moon's Children. We are her chosen people, the born again, the resurrected. We are the *Alastores*, the wanderers, the nightgoers."

"The Children of the Night? Seriously?"

She draws herself up, like a captive queen. "Yes, that is what we are. And it is given us to prey upon you, the Children of the Day."

"That's real nice. So the zombies—they're just some retarded kind of nightgoer, or what?"

She's offended. "*Those* vile, diseased things? Are you joking? They're *nothing* like us! Zom-bie!" She says it like she hates the taste of the word in her mouth. "Another silly, stupid word. They've been around forever, like lepers. Unclean. They are *ghuls*—the Nabateans and the Egyptians knew them. They haunted the desert wastes and the ancient tombs. The Vikings called them the *Draug*. Even the Chinese in Hunan had them. They appear like a plague, kill everyone in their path, then burn out and disappear again, like locusts . . . Except this time." Her voice trails off; she's depressed at the thought. Tough.

"Yeah, you're so much better than them. Isn't that just what you wanted to do to me? Kill me? Drink my blood? Make me your supper?"

For a moment, she doesn't say anything. Then she says matter-of-factly, "Before this night is out, I promise you will give me your blood, happily."

If she's trying to piss me off, it's working. I pull another stake from my belt. "Not if I put this through your heart. That is what kills you, isn't that right?"

She laughs. "A wooden stake through my heart? No, haven't you read your occultic texts? It has to be a red-hot iron through the heart. No, a scythe blessed by a wise woman. No, silver daggers dipped in holy water—or burn me at the stake, or hold me down under running water, or tear my heart out, cut my head off, and bury me at the crossroads!" Her rant breaks down into more laughter, then she recovers. "Yes, pretty much anything through my heart would kill me—wouldn't it you?"

My turn to laugh. "Yeah, I guess so. But we're talking about you. What about garlic?

She snorts. "Peasants think garlic cures everything from mosquito bites to dying cattle."

"How 'bout sunlight?" That gets her attention; she sobers up at once and her voice gets quiet.

"It's . . . different for all of us. Some merely lose their

power during the day. And some of us it just paralyses, like *rigor mortis*, like stone. But others become sick and die quickly. And some of us it burns until we burst into flames. I . . . I'm one of that kind, I think. But yes, in one way or another, the Sun kills us all."

"So—there's more than one kind of you?" I ask, genuinely curious.

"Yes, many. Some are big, strong, and ugly. They live in caves or under bridges. Others can change their shape at night; some can make themselves look like other people, some become animals or half-animal, or fly like birds. Others can see things far away, or in the future, or walk in people's dreams, like I do. We all have our own special gifts and curses."

"And you all eat people."

"Yes, we eat people. Some of us can eat other things, but mostly we eat people. I can only drink blood . . . and drain the . . . the *energiapsychikos*, I don't know the word in English, in your sleep."

"In my dreams? You steal my soul in my dreams?"

"Yes, in your dreams you fed me. Thank you."

"You shouldn't talk to your food, you know." That does it; nowadays I'm half narcoleptic already; it's time to put an end to her before she completely sucks my soul out in my sleep. I get up, stake in hand, and fish the mallet from the belt loop.

I was trying to be quiet about it, but I can tell she hears me get up; her head tilts towards the sound. When she speaks next her voice has just a hint of desperation in it.

"I only took a little from you—you're young and

strong; you have so much. You've given me life again. Now I'm young and beautiful for you too."

"Until dinner time."

I realize it's going to be an awkward angle; maybe I should go through the back; or come from above and place the point just above her clavicle and hammer it down from there.

Her voice quavers just a little. "Wait. I've lived a long life, Michael. There's much I can tell you."

"No more stories." I need to do it quickly. I grit my teeth, raise the jagged point of the stake just a fraction of an inch above her collarbone.

"Michael . . ."

I don't answer. I focus all my attention on the point of the stake, bringing it gently down until it pricks her pale skin. She flinches and freezes. I freeze too. We both stay like that for a full second.

A second feels like a long, long time when you're about to kill someone. Or about to die. I lift the mallet over my head. My hand is trembling; I steady myself, then bring it down.

I bring it down slowly to my side, while I unpin the stake from the fresh dimple in her soft skin. I drop the stake and mallet to the floor. She raises her face to me, and I gently undo her blindfold. God, her eyes are large. And so gorgeous. I crouch down on the carpet so that I'm not looming over her.

"Look . . . I'm not too good with words, so I'll keep this short. I've been working my ass off just to stay alive so I could find somebody else. But if I kill you, I don't think there's going to be anyone else. So . . . this is it. I'm done. You win. I don't even care if this is all some hypno-trick of yours. If you need to kill me, eat me, you go ahead and do it. At least that way some good will come of all this. And for what it's worth, no matter how this turns out, I'm glad I met you. You're the most amazing woman I'll ever know. That's all."

Finally, something wipes that superior look off her face.

I can hardly believe it, but she seems genuinely touched. Her eyes are even bigger than when I flashed the cross at her. Then that exotic, beautiful face of hers lights up with a warmer smile than I ever imagined an undead bloodsucker was capable of. I can't even see those deadly fangs of hers. But she surprises me even more when she gives her wrists a little twist and slips her arms out the rope as quick and effortless as Houdini. With a wicked gleam in her eye, she takes hold of my rosary necklace and kisses its little cross. Her fingers do not burn; her lips do not blister. I have been totally misled.

"You sneaky little minx . . ." I start to say, before she closes her fist on the little crucifix and reels me in for a kiss, too. For the first time, I can really feel her soft lips, taste them. It shuts me up. Her lips are oddly cool against mine, but it's the most wonderful sensation I've felt in years; no, not in years—my whole damn life. She draws back, and the look on her face is pure lust.

"I want you, Michael," she says in that sexy, impossible-to-place euro commie accent of hers. "I know you're going to be so delicious . . ." I'm taken aback; and yet somehow

I'm still getting a hard-on, even though she's going to kill and eat me. I flash on half-remembered PBS specials about praying mantises and black widows. But I meant what I told her, and although I can think of a thousand worse ways to go, right now I can't think of any better. So I stand, take her face in my hands and kiss her right back, not even caring if it is the last kiss of my life.

She rises up on her knees and runs her hands up my sides and up around my shoulders, lifting herself up to kiss me better, deeper, opening her mouth to mine. We're hungry for each other; me for her body, her for my blood. She slips her hands under my T-shirt and pushes it up to get at my chest and stomach. We break off our kiss while I pull the rolled-up shirt over my head and off, and she doesn't waste any time pulling my torso closer to give kisses and little love bites to my chest and throat.

Her fingertips roam over my chest until they catch my nipple. They work it over while the nails of her other hand make a slow drag down from my collarbone to my belly; the sensations give me goosebumps. Then she wrestles with the clasp of my belt, giving a little grunt of victory when she gets it unsnapped and dumps the unwieldy thing. Leaning back on one arm, she reaches out to caress the front of my jeans. I'm stiff and constrained in there; she smiles as she makes it worse.

"Your shoes," she murmurs, and I kick off my boots and steady myself against the bedpost to peel off my socks. She purrs her approval, but she's not done with me. She pops the buttons on my fly one by one, then settles back in her catbird seat and orders me to take them off. I bend to slide them down my legs and step out of them. She leans in for a closer look, examining my Y-fronts like she's never been to the men's underwear rack before.

But she's more interested in what's bursting to get out of them. She hooks her fingers in the elastic waistband and pulls them down. I guess she's never seen a circumcised penis either. She reaches out and traces a finger around the tan ring of my foreskin scar; she's fascinated. I can feel that long black hair of hers brushing against my stomach. And I can't help but notice the amazing curve of her butt and the double curves of her cleavage as she bends forward to investigate me.

She looks up to check in with me. When she sees she's not hurting me, she grasps my shaft and gives it a loving lick, right along the scar. Her eyes turn to me again as she opens her mouth to take in the whole head.

"Watch the teeth," I warn her. Draining all the blood out through my jugular is one thing, but I don't want this goodbye party to end right here. I'm worrying for nothing, though; she wants more than just my blood. She smiles with her eyes and gets back to work on me, milking my rod with her hand while she does. I run my hands through her hair, slide them down the silk of her stolen nightie towards her ass. It's been way too long since I've felt so good. Less than a minute later I have to lean my head against the bedpost and hold on to it for support.

"Here I come," I tell her when I can't hold it back any longer. She ignores my warning and a second later when I do, she doesn't flinch; just drinks it all down, greedy bitch. She takes me out of her mouth and smiles like the cat who ate the canary. I smile back at her. We're both still hungry for more.

She rises up from kneeling on the bed and fiddles with the little bows on the front of the nightie. It falls open, flashing me her perfect belly dancer's body, full breasts, rock-hard stomach, those strong beautiful thighs, and oh yeah . . . everything in between. She lets the gauzy silk fall around her shoulders and leans in for a hug that presses her body against my chest. She rests her cheek on my heart, listening to it beat for her. The sound makes her happy.

My hands have a mind of their own; I don't even realize they're reaching for her as they stroke her head and hold her tight. Feels like a dream when I take over and run my fingertips down the nape of her neck, down her backbone, down the small of her back. I feel her draw in her breath when I cup her sweet ass—vampires can breathe. I let my fingers sink down to the backs of her thighs, and then close in and pick her up. She squeals like a real live girl and grabs her arms around my neck for support as I lift her to my chest.

With her in my arms I feel like a fireman again, coming to a beautiful woman's rescue, not that I ever carried anyone to safety quite like this. She throws her head back as I lower her down to the bed again, laughing with a pure, wild, joy that I sure as hell never heard come from any vamp in the movies.

She writhes on the bed like a hippy chick in a 60s porno while I spread her legs apart and bring my face down between her soft pale thighs. I gently push past her soft curly hair and down to the folds of her slit to breathe her in; the animal scent of her is making me harder still. I let my hands roam over the rest of her body while I kiss and suck on first her thighs, then her outer lips. I'm hungry for her; I tug on her hair and mound with my mouth, then use my tongue to get past them to the pink folds below. She's wet, which surprises me a little, but pleases me a lot.

When I start frenching her pussy, nibbling and tonguing her, she stiffens and grabs my arms to pull my face even deeper in. I torture her, teasing her clit with a few quick flicks and then tonguing her deeply and sucking her juices. I'm relentless, and the mewing, groaning noises of hers egg me on further. She buckles and twists in my hands. I like my work.

Her sighs become more insistent, she grabs on to her own nipples for dear life and makes sexy little unintelligible noises.

"T'e . . . t'e . . . ummm, T'e . . . Aiie, va . . . Va!"

Without warning she grabs my head with both hands and grinds my face into her. When the shudders stop she reaches down for my arms again and pulls me up to my feet with impressive strength. I take her by the upper legs and lift her butt up just a bit. Then I bring my hips into hers, guiding my cock down to her, then into her; a long, slow thrust that makes her grunt sharply with pleasure, and her eyes go wild. Even though I have her firmly by the legs, her heels on my shoulders, she keeps bucking her hips to meet me as I slide back and forth into her. It feels fantastic. She stretches her arms out and braces herself against the bedposts. Her eyes lock on mine as we fuck. Her breath gets shallow and her voice gets husky as she comes. She starts speaking in tongues. I don't know what she's saying but I don't need a translator; it's as sexy as fuck:

"Oh, ez az . . . a kurva életbe . . . a kurva életbe . . . Va! Omrdej mě na tvrdo!"

Her cries and shouts are such a turn-on; I have to be even deeper into her. I take her by the ankles and carefully bring her legs down until her feet are flat against my stomach. She seems to instinctively know what I have in mind; she lets go of the posts and wraps her arms tight around her shins. Now I'm able to sit up on to the bed, get my arms around her and pull her body into my lap. She can feel the difference; so can I.

Her breasts are right in my face now, and I can't resist leaning over and sucking on one while she rocks up and down on my cock, groaning and huffing. Soon she's coming again, and then it's my turn. At first I feel a trembling in my core, that quickly spreads to my bones, then my organs, muscles, and veins, and then sizzles through my skin. For the first time I'm aware of the energy my orgasm is building up inside me, and sense the power of it flowing out of me as I release it into her. Exhausting, but so worth it. Worth dying for, even.

With a sigh, she lies back on the bed, and I stretch out on top of her. She cradles my head against her breasts, and gently plays with my hair.

"You were magnificent, Michael . . . *Bene futuis . . .*"

"Benny what? What's that mean?"

She paused to translate. "It's Roman. It means . . . You

have fucked well." I can think of worse epitaphs. After a few blissful minutes pass, she rolls me over on my side.

"Is it that time?" I ask her. She nods with a gentle smile. I can't see any fangs.

"Do you want to lie back for me?" she asks softly. I do as she asks. It's been a good life. She leans in to me and slips an arm underneath my head, caresses my chest with her other hand.

"It won't hurt," she promises me, and lays her hand on the groove of my jawbone. She gently turns my head down and towards her, exposing my neck and throat. She leans over to kiss me. It ends too soon. Her hand underneath me holds my head still; the other presses down on my collarbone, and then I feel her mouth on me. At first, it's only the sensation of the kiss, then her fangs silently slide in and penetrate me. She's told a white lie: There is a flash of pain, followed by a rush of endorphins. I can feel the wet red warmth coming out of me; feel her tongue and mouth at work drinking me.

I feel her, like my consciousness is pouring into her mind along with my blood into her body. I sense the fear and desperate hunger of a vampire in a zombie's world. I feel childhood memories of a tiny Mediterranean village nestled high on a mountaintop amidst olive trees and grapevines. I see her hunting men, women, and children through ages of time; Greeks and Persians, Egyptians and Romans; Byzantine nobles and medieval pilgrims; monks and nuns trembling in their cells. I see her stalking through plague cities during the Black Death and battlefields during the Hundred Years' War. Seizing Gypsies, robbers, and highwaymen, and stray soldiers of Napoleon's winter campaign. Thousands upon thousands of faces, for twenty-five hundred years.

I feel the fear she felt when the Children of the Day began lighting their great cities at night, first with gas lamps, then the hateful electricity, lighting up the night like so many jewels. *She liked it better when the world was lit only by fire*, I realized. *When we were afraid of the dark.* I see her go into hiding from the machines and wires and horseless carriages, hibernating in a forgotten tomb for over two hundred years, living only off troubled dreams instead of blood, seeing the world go by through the eyes of others. I see her own dreams troubled by the Great War, and the greater war after that that. Most of all she feared the atomic blasts that came afterwards, one after another for decades; she was so sure that the world would end any day in a thermonuclear holocaust.

And then, after one unthinkable nightmare, the dreams all ceased. There was no one left dreaming. The people had turned *Ghul*. She thought she would never escape her tomb again. Until she one day sensed a dreamer, clear on the other side of the world. Me. Because I'm the last one left.

Michael? I hear her voice in my/our mind. *Come, it's not good to look too deep in your lover's heart—you may not like what you find.*

I open my eyes. She's still cradling my head, her hand over my neck, staunching the wound.

"You didn't kill me," I say needlessly. She smiles.

"No. I never said I would, but I love you for offering.

Rest now, I probably took too much. I was right—you *are* delicious."

I feel around at the wound. "Does this mean . . . I'm going to become a vampire now?"

She shakes her head. "I can't make you one of us—it's only those chosen by the Moon, and she only picks one in a thousand thousand thousand. But . . ." it occurs to her, "our children might be." I think about *that* for a minute. She catches a stray drop off my neck and licks her finger. I see her fangs slide back up again.

"I need you, Michael. We need each other. You and I— we are the last of our kind, I think. It's their world now, the *ghuls*. You must learn to be like a Nightgoer now. To stay hidden in the shadows . . . to kill them when you can." Her thoughtful look brightens for a moment and she smiles at me again.

"And . . . it's nice to have someone to talk to, isn't it?"

"You said it."

She takes her nail and expertly opens up a bright red arc on the side of her breast.

"Now take my blood. It will help you recover, and when you drink it long enough, you will live longer, too."

"How much longer?"

"Not long—only six or seven centuries."

I only hesitate a moment, but once I start nursing on her, the copper tang is irresistible. We stay like that a while, it's only fair after all. When I'm done we kiss some more, then we'll start making plans for our future.

*

Funny thing; I never see Charlie around anymore. Three's a crowd, I guess. So now, it's just her and me against the world. We've got our issues like all couples: a stressful environment, making ends meet, she has to work nights, I have to work days, wondering how we'll raise the kids, problems with the neighbors, things like that. I'm not complaining; we're both in it for the long haul. But like I said, it's not a perfect situation . . .

Welcome to the Black and Blue Ball

By Max Vos

"How in the hell did you score an invitation to the Black and Blue Ball, *the* hottest party of the year," Josh asked.

"I wish I knew," Ja'din answered his friend. "Only thing that I can think of is maybe that underwear shoot I did, but it hasn't even been released yet, so I'm not really sure."

"Becoming one of the most sought after male fashion models is already starting to pay off!" Josh jabbed and teased his longtime friend.

"Hey, this is just an added benefit," Ja'din murmured as he handed the invitation to the big gorilla-looking security guy working the door. "So far I've been able to pay for an entire year of school without having to take out any student loans, unlike *you*."

"Not everyone can look like you. Some of us are just plain or butt-ugly." Josh said as he adjusted the front of the leather jock strap he had on underneath the chaps he had borrowed from his best friend. "Are you sure this is okay? My whole ass is hanging out."

"Your ass is your best *asset*," Ja'din chuckled. "Trust me, you look great."

"You do know that I'm not really into all this BDSM shit, right?" Josh reconfirmed, a slightly worried look on his brow.

"I know—you just like the look."

"Wow, look at this place," Josh said. "I mean, I've been down East Seventy-Fifth before, but I never imagined that any of these places were single-family homes. This place is *huge*," he said in amazement as they entered the formal foyer.

"Gentlemen, welcome to the Black and Blue Ball. There is a bar set up in the foyer."

The man in a tux directing them seemed to be a throwback to a bygone era.

The two twenty-somethings made their way to the bar, their reflections looking back up at them from the highly polished Italian marble floors. Ja'din quickly noticed all the liquor was top-shelf.

Moving away from the bar the two stood and looked around, surveying the room totally lit by candlelight. A large bouquet of black roses and blue orchids adorned the center table.

"Whoever is throwing this shindig has got some major bucks," Josh commented quietly over his rum and coke.

Ja'din nodded, sipping his Kettle One vodka on the rocks.

"Man, there's enough dead cow in this place to carpet Yankee Stadium," Josh chattered, referring to all the leather being worn.

"Be careful, Josh—there are some pretty heavy players here."

"I can see, I think," Josh whispered, watching a muscled leather-clad daddy-type approach them.

"Hello. *Boy*," the man addressed Ja'din.

"Good evening, sir," Ja'din answered, bowing ever so slightly while Josh slipped behind his friend.

"Why don't you go get me another beer, *boy*," the daddy commanded.

"I may be a *boy*," Ja'din replied, looking directly into the man's eyes, "but I'm not *your* boy. Get it yourself."

The look on the man's face was first of shock and then embarrassment, realizing his faux pas.

"Damn, Ja," Josh said behind his friend. "I can't believe you just said that to that guy."

"Oh Josh, grow a pair, would ya?" Ja'din scowled at his friend. "Come on, let's go see what's going on."

Ja'din took his friend by the hand and led him down the hallway into a large living room, where most of the party-goers had congregated. Ja'din stood just inside the doorway, confident.

Josh had always admired his friend. He had a quiet self-confidence, even in high school, which no one else seemed to have. And why shouldn't he? He was one of the most beautiful people Josh had ever seen. Looking at him now with skin-tight leather jeans on that he'd got to keep after a photo shoot, a simple white T-shirt, a leather jacket and boots, he didn't even look real he was so beautiful. It was because of Ja'din that Josh had been one of the "cool" people in school. To this day he never understood why Ja'din had befriended him in their freshmen year.

There was a slight smirk on Ja'din's face.

"What're you grinning at?" Josh asked, puzzled.

"They're waiting," Ja'din answered, waving his hand holding the drink towards the room. "This is just a holding area I think."

"What are they waiting for?"

"I'd say that they are either waiting for a demo or a play party. Maybe both," Ja'din said before taking a small sip of his vodka.

"I'm not so sure I'm ready for all this, Ja," Josh whispered.

"You'll be okay, Josh," Ja'din smiled at him. "Just stick with me and we'll have a good time."

"I know you like all this—*stuff*—but it makes me nervous."

Before Ja'din could reassure his best friend again, a man dressed in a kid leather tuxedo approached.

"Good evening, sirs," he said with a slight accent that Ja'din couldn't quite place. "Mr. Harding," he addressed Ja'din, "your host, Mr. Brooks, would like to meet you— and your friend of course."

Josh saw, then felt his friend stiffen. It only took a moment to understand why. Ja'din didn't use his last name anywhere except in school and when he went home. He only used his professional name, *Beleza*, which is Portuguese for beauty. It was a pet name his grandmother had called him, who was herself Portuguese.

Ja'din nodded,

"Certainly, it would be our pleasure. Lead on."

Following the man who Ja'din and Josh assumed was a butler of sorts, they entered a wood-paneled library where a group of men, all dressed in leather, were smoking cigars and drinking. Ja'din nodded to the few he recognized before he saw their host.

Instantly Ja'din remembered him from the Spike Reunion party earlier in the year. It was the same man who had sniffed him like a dog would a bone. He never touched Ja'din, but ran his empty soft leather glove from his pubes to his neck, before he softly, like the wings of a butterfly, kissed him and left. It was one of the most erotic moments of Ja'din's life, which was evident by the tightening of the crotch of his leather jeans.

"Good evening, Ja'din—Josh," their host said as he approached, holding out his hand. "I am pleased that you could make it tonight."

Ja'din couldn't help himself. He instantly zoned in on the soft lips that he remembered barely touched his with a kiss.

"Let me introduce myself—formally." He looked directly at Ja'din. "I'm Edward Brooks, welcome to my home."

"It's nice to meet you, Mr. Brooks," Josh said, smiling and shaking his hand, obviously not bothered that the man already knew his name.

Ja'din and Edward Brooks looked at each other. Ja'din felt as if this Mr. Brooks could read his every thought. If that were true, he would know how much Ja'din wanted him, had wanted him from the moment they had first met, if you could even call it meeting.

"May I get either of you gentlemen another cocktail?" the butler asked, interrupting the stare down between the two men.

"Yeah, sure," Josh handed him his near-empty glass. "Thanks."

"Ja'din?" Edward Brooks asked. "Would you care for another drink?"

"No." The answer whooshed out of his mouth as if he had been holding his breath. "No. I'm good, thanks."

Josh, sensing that he was a third wheel, followed the butler, leaving his friend and Mr. Edward Brooks alone together.

Edward Brooks, with the back of his skin-tight-, soft-leather-gloved hand stroked the side of Ja'din's face.

"Such beauty. I understand the professional name you use, it fits you perfectly."

Ja'din shuddered slightly. Edward's deep, soft baritone voice washed over him like a warm ocean breeze. He pulled himself together before managing to say,

"It's nice to *really* meet you, Mr. Brooks."

"Please, call me Edward," he said as he took Ja'din's hand in his, but not to shake it. No, he just held it in his leather-clad hand. "All my friends call me Edward, and I hope that we can be more than just friends."

"Mr., um Edward," Ja'din, finally finding his voice, started. "Edward, as flatterin' as that is, I really do not have time for any type of relationship, I'm . . ."

Edward cut him off.

"Yes, I know," he dismissed with a wave of his hand. "You are a full-time student who also models as often as possible to pay for school. Very admirable of you, and ambitious, I must say."

"Okay, you're really starting to creep me out." Ja'din took a step back, pulling his hand out of Edward's. "How did you know my name and how do you know that I'm a student? And how do you know my friend Josh?"

"I had to know who you were after our first . . . encounter?" Edward took a step forward, closing the distance between them again. "I admit that I had you investigated, but it was only because you have infatuated me so. Please, take it as a compliment, Ja'din."

Ja'din looked into his blue eyes and remembered an advertizement he'd seen once for the Caribbean that described *azure* waters. These eyes he was losing himself in were azure blue. The straight nose that was just above those soft alluring lips, all this was surrounded by a reddish-blond mane, reminiscent of a regal lion. But it was Edward's lips that drew him in the most.

Josh's laughter broke Ja'din's self-induced trance. When he looked across the room, he saw his best friend talking to two other men dressed in what had to be custom-made leathers. The one with the lace-up-the-sides pants used to be a model. Although older, he still had a presence and was very attractive with salt-and-pepper hair.

"I think that Josh has made some new friends," Edward said, drawing Ja'din's eyes back to him, and his soft easy smile.

"What do you want from me?"

Ja'din wasn't a fool. He knew that Edward Brooks was someone of importance with a lot of money, and that always raised a red flag, as far as Ja'din was concerned.

"I only wish to know you better, Ja'din." Edward spoke easily, but matter-of-factly. "No tricks. No games. I am exorbitantly wealthy and can buy most everything I want, but the one thing I can't buy is love."

Run. Get Josh and run as fast as you can . . . Ja'din's mind screamed, but it was as if his feet were nailed to the floor.

The door opened behind Ja'din, causing Edward to break eye contact with Ja'din. A burly man in leather pants with yellow strips down the sides nodded to Edward.

Looking back at Ja'din, Edward said,

"Come, the entertainment is about to begin."

Ja'din started to go to Josh, when Edward stopped him.

"Let him be. It appears that he is having a good time. No?"

Ja'din only nodded, but thinking that he should be able to keep an eye on Josh just the same.

The large double doors at the one end of the living room had been opened into a dining room where a small stage had been set up with a Saint Andrew's cross on it. Restrained on the cross was an Adonis-like blond. Ja'din knew him only by seeing him around town. He was a power bottom who was always on the prowl.

Edward chuckled at the expression on Ja'din's face as he looked over at his friend, who was laughing quietly in between the two handsome leather men he had been talking to in the library.

"Don't worry. Josh will be fine," Edward said, leaning in close to Ja'din's ear.

Edwards's breath sent a chill down Ja'din's spine. His mouth went dry and his mind continued to scream, *run!*

The lights dimmed and a body-builder type stepped onto the stage wearing only a leather jockstrap, harness, boots, and a hood. He bent over and from behind the Saint Andrew's Cross he picked up what Ja'din knew to be a violet wand. When the man turned it on, its violet color, from which it got its name, glowed in the dimmed light. Ja'din's cock instantly got hard. He knew all too well the pleasure/pain that device caused.

Throughout the demonstration, Ja'din's dick was rock hard, his mouth dry. He wanted the man standing beside him, the man who had enthralled him months and months ago. He knew that Edward wanted him also, but there was something in his gut that told him that Edward was dangerous and he shouldn't be here. Normally Ja'din listened to his inner self, but this time he wished it would just shut up.

The popping and snapping sound the wand made as it was used, interspersed with the occasional scream of pain—or was it pleasure?—didn't help Ja'din's situation. However, when Edward would lean over and sniff him every so often, it was practically his undoing. Edward never touched him; it was their closeness without touching that was getting to Ja'din.

By the time the show was over, the blond hunk, sweat-covered with come smeared across his chest and abdomen, was helped from the cross by two men. The dom had known what he was doing and took the guy on a wild journey and back. Ja'din was about ready to crawl over Edward Brooks's frame, he was so horny.

"Hey . . . Ja . . . I just want to let you know I am cutting out," Josh whispered in Ja'din's ear from behind.

Ja'din whipped around to look at his friend.

"Wait, you sure you wanna do that?" Ja'din asked as he looked at the *two* former male models. Ja'din now recognized the other man who spoke to him,

"Don't worry, Ja'din, we know he's a newbie, and we'll take good care of him."

The brilliant smile Ja'din was met with didn't suppress his anxiety over his friend going off with them.

"Here's my card," the younger model said as he slipped a card into Ja'din's pocket. "It has both our names and phone numbers. I wrote down the address on the back."

"I don't know."

Ja'din wasn't sure this was such a good idea. Josh had no idea what these guys were about, and he wasn't sure he wanted to be left alone with Edward either.

"Edward can vouch for us," the older man said.

"That I can, Michael," Edward said, shaking the man's hand. Turning to Ja'din he said, "I think Josh is in good hands."

Ja'din couldn't do or say anything to the contrary without looking like a total idiot, so he nodded; hoping that Josh knew what he was getting into.

"Come, let's get another drink," Edward breathed into his ear once again, giving Ja'din the same effect as before.

When they got to the foyer where the bar was set up, Ja'din noticed that the crowd was thinning out, quite a few men were leaving.

"It looks like your party is breaking up, perhaps I

should be going," Ja'din said. His gut telling him that was the best thing.

His dick had other ideas.

Edward turned to Ja'din, with almost panic in his eyes. "Please. Don't go, Ja'din."

Ja'din took the drink that Edward offered him.

"Did you enjoy the show?" Edward asked as he maneuvered Ja'din down the hall back to the library.

"Yes."

Ja'din knew there was no point in denying it. It was obvious from the flush of his cheeks to the prominent outline of his hard dick in his leather pants.

"I know I would enjoy giving you such pleasure."

Without warning, Edward leaned toward Ja'din and breathed in deeply. This time, however, he followed by slowly licking him from his collarbone up his neck to behind his ear.

Ja'din felt the slight stubble of Edward's beard create a contrast between his slick soft tongue and his sandpaper-like stubble. He couldn't help but moan, his desire rising ever higher.

"Oh yes," Edward whispered huskily, his mouth by Ja'din's ear. "You taste as good as you smell. I've wanted you since the first night we met."

Edward took Ja'din's barely touched vodka from him, and set it on a table. He wrapped his arms around Ja'din and buried his face in the crook Ja'din's neck, where he breathed in deeply, before licking and sucking on it.

Ja'din's head rolled back with enjoyment at the sensation, before jerking slightly as Edward bit his neck. A sharp white pain ensued, but only lasted a second, before Edward went back to sucking and licking his neck. Ja'din trembled as the man massaged his ass with one hand, and held his head with the other.

Edward stopped, pulling him into a tight hug. Ja'din felt weak. He knew that he would do whatever this man wanted if he were to ask him right then.

Ja'din placed his palms on Edward's chest, pushing him gently away.

"I don't think that this is such a good idea right now."

"You are right, this is not how I would like you to get to know me."

Nervously, Edward turned and picked up Ja'din's drink, handing it back to him.

"Would you have dinner with me tomorrow night? Here?"

Ja'din took a large sip from the glass. He didn't answer for a moment, just looked at Edward. There was no doubt this man, who could have easily wrapped him around his finger only moments ago, was now nervous. *Was he afraid that he would say no?*

"Yes, I will have dinner with you tomorrow."

Edward seemed to sigh, his shoulders visibly relaxing.

"Would seven-thirty be good?"

"That would be fine, thank you," Ja'din smiled.

With his forefinger, Edward lifted Ja'din's chin and kissed him, his lips barely brushing his like their first kiss, but this time it lasted longer.

"I will look forward to our dinner tomorrow then, Ja'din."

*

Ja'din didn't know why he was so nervous. He had taken well over an hour deciding on what to wear, not something that was normal for him at all. In the end he chose tan linen slacks that hugged his ass nicely and a white cotton shirt that showed his light mocha skin off to perfection.

Standing in front of Edward's front door he hesitated before ringing the bell; then the door opened.

"Good evening, sir, won't you come in?" The butler asked.

"Thank you . . . ?"

"Gibbons, sir," the butler said, filling in the blank for Ja'din.

"Yes, thank you, Mr. Gibbons."

"No, sir, just Gibbons," the butler corrected as he took Ja'din's coat.

"I thought I heard voices," Edward said as he walked into the foyer, his loafers clicking on the marble floor. "Welcome Ja'din." He pulled Ja'din into an unexpected hug that was over as quickly as it had started. "How about a drink before dinner?"

"Uh . . . sure," Ja'din answered, hoping his nervousness wasn't obvious.

Ja'din inhaled the perfumed air from the lilies of the new floral arrangement that replaced the one from the previous night as he walked by. In the library, Ja'din sat on one of the brown leather sofas, the smell of recently cleaned leather enveloped him as he sat.

"Vodka on the rocks?" Edward asked.

Ja'din nodded, not yet trusting his voice.

Edward handed Ja'din the drink before sitting down next to him with his own drink in hand. "Did you have a good day?"

Ja'din cleared his throat before answering.

"It was okay. Got a lot of studying done."

"Very good." Edward seemed as nervous as he was suddenly, the cool self-assurance he had minutes ago was gone.

An uncomfortable silence stifled the air, before they both spoke at the same time.

"Please, go ahead," Edward deferred to his guest to speak first.

"I was going to say that I really like your house," Ja'din started, "but what I'd really like to know is what is it you want from me?"

"Nothing like coming right to the point." Edward grimaced. "I guess what I want is for you to get to know me. Me as a person, not as what the rest of the world perceives me as."

"Okay," Ja'din shifted, facing Edward. "But why? You went to a lot of trouble finding out all about me, which still creeps me out by the way."

"It is, or it has been, a long time . . ." Edward took a long swallow of the amber liquid in the crystal glass, not finishing his sentence. "I do not know how to say this without sounding like a lovesick puppy, but I see no other way." Edward looked directly into Ja'din's buttery brown eyes and asked, "Do you believe in love at first sight?"

The alarms went off in Ja'din's head so hard it was almost painful.

"No, I don't," Ja'din said as he stood up. "I don't think this was a such a good idea. I appreciate the invite, but I think it would be best if I left."

Ja'din walked around the side of the sofa only to be met by Edward. Ja'din shook his head slightly not believing his eyes. "How? You were just sitting—"

That was all he could say before Edward took his wrists, pushed them behind his back, and pulled him tightly against his own body, immobilizing Ja'din.

"What the fuck?" Ja'din struggled to get away.

Edward's eyes were intense as he looked at Ja'din. He closed the space between them, taking Ja'din's mouth with his own.

Ja'din still struggled to get away, but was held in place by Edward, whose arms, like bands of steel around his body, held his wrists tightly against his ass cheeks. The more he struggled, the tighter Edward's arms became, which excited Ja'din. There was no doubt that Edward felt his excitement through the linen pants. When Edward ground his own swollen manhood into Ja'din's, they both moaned in pleasure.

"I know what you want Ja'din." Edward breathed into his ear before licking his neck. "I can take you places you never dreamed about." Ja'din gasped as Edward nipped and sucked at his neck. "I saw how you reacted to the scene last night, I could see that you wanted to be the one on that cross."

"You . . . assume a lot," Ja'din managed to get out between his and Edward's moans of pleasure.

"Tell me that I am wrong Ja'din," Edward's voice

vibrated against Ja'din's neck as he spoke. "Tell me and I will stop right now."

Ja'din knew he meant what he said. Edward was giving him a way out, but did he want out?

No.

Edward ran his teeth along Ja'din's extended neck before he released his arms. Both were breathing hard, the air between them thick with heat and lust.

"I would like to show you something, Ja'din," Edward said seriously.

Ja'din gulped down the rest of the vodka, and nodded his assent.

"Follow me," Edward said, putting down his near-finished drink.

Ja'din followed Edward to the basement, to a black leather padded door. Edward looked at Ja'din for a long moment, before unlocking the door and stepping through it. Once inside, Ja'din was neither shocked nor surprised. He had already figured out that Edward was deeply involved in the heavier side of kink. Not only by who and what he saw during the Black and Blue Ball the previous evening, but by the way the man carried himself.

Ja'din walked around the room, examining the different equipment, most of which he knew about. Some he'd experienced, some not. Ja'din knew what he liked, but he also knew that he would have to have a lot of trust in a person to try some of the other stuff.

"You don't seem surprised," Edward stated as he sat on the leather-cushioned bondage table in the center of the room.

"I'm not, really." Ja'din picked up a single tail, smiled then replaced it. "Though it is one of the nicest playrooms I've ever been in." Ja'din sat on the table next to Edward.

"I am glad that you approve." Edward grinned, teasing Ja'din. "Perhaps you would like my own personal demonstration of the violet wand?"

"You think that you can do better than Hans did last night?" Ja'din quipped.

Edwards eyebrows rose.

"So you figured out it was Hans did you?"

Ja'din grinned evilly,

"I've experienced Hans' *talents*."

"Ahhh, I see," Edward replied as his hand undid the first button of Ja'din's shirt. "And do you think that each person who wields the wand is the same?"

"I think it would be basically the same," Ja'din challenged.

"Do you now?" Edward unbuttoned two more buttons. He explored Ja'din's bare smooth chest. "I would like to think that my technique is unique to me."

Jadin laughed softly, pushing his chest into Edward's palm.

"Perhaps I need to experience your technique and judge for myself?"

Edward leaned in and kissed Ja'din lightly.

"I would love to show you."

"Do I have to make an appointment?" Ja'din licked Edward's lips seductively.

"I will make myself available to you whenever you would like to . . . sample my proclivities."

"There is no place I need to be at the present," Ja'din whispered in Edward's ear as he licked the lobe.

Edward unbuttoned the rest of Ja'din's shirt after pulling it free out of his pants.

"Should I take that as you would like to find out now?"

"No time like the present, I've always heard."

Edward kissed Ja'din, forcing him back onto the table. When the model was lying flat, Edward kissed, licked, and nipped his way down Ja'din's muscled abdomen, but not before lightly torturing his dark nipples. When he reached the top of the linen slacks, he used his teeth to undo the belt.

Edward noticed that Ja'din was not only breathing heavily, but his excitement was also apparent by the outline of his nice cock. Wanting to make this his best performance, Edward did not rush things. Part of the pleasure/pain that he liked to inflict was the anticipation of what was to happen. Before he could get Ja'din's linen pants off, the young man was panting, his hips thrusting up into the air, a damp spot at the tip of his dick in his Andrew Christian white underwear briefs.

"I think that we may be ready to begin," Edward teased further. "Hold your hands back, Ja'din, and do not move your legs. Imagine that you are bound to the table." Edward spoke softly while looking directly into Ja'din's eyes.

The lust in Ja'din's eyes was enough to spur Edward on. He got the violet wand, attached the power tripper, and turned his body into an instrument of electrical titillation. An electrical current would flow from his body into Ja'din's whenever he touched him. Starting lightly, his hand inches away from Ja'din's nipples, he let a blue arc of current fly from his fingertips to the previously worked nipples, eliciting a yelp more of surprise than pain. The closer his hand moved towards Ja'din's body, the more intense the feeling.

Ja'din's back arched, increasing the current. Edward moved around Ja'din's chest and abdomen, taking his time, showing just how good he was at this. Ja'din's hard dick head peeked out from the signature band of his briefs, begging for attention, which Edward was more than willing to give.

Agonizingly slow, Edward removed the white briefs, the electrical current flowing from his hands all the way down Ja'din's lightly furred legs. He gave Ja'din a moment to catch his breath, and to calm down a bit. Edward could tell by the way his dark balls were pulled up tight to his body that he could come at any moment. By the time he stood next to Ja'din's head, he was ready to begin again.

Edward bent down, letting his lips hover over Ja'din's. The current flowing between them caused Ja'din to groan from the sharp sting of electricity. Closing the gap, increasing the current, Edward kissed Ja'din as he had that first time—like butterfly wings. As their kiss deepened Edward caressed Ja'din's egg-shaped balls, which now almost disappeared into his body. Rubbing the sensitive orbs, he moved his hands in such a way they were almost pulsing, sending electricity into the very core of Ja'din.

It didn't take long before Ja'din screamed into Edward's mouth, as he released long white ropes of come that painted his abdomen in white, creamy stripes. Towards the end of Ja'din's electric orgasm, Edward quickly moved down and took the head of his still-pulsing dick into his mouth, making Ja'din flail about on the table. The current still stimulated his balls and his now ultrasensitive glans, but Edward wasn't quite done.

Edward lapped up the still-warm load of Ja'din's come, moving up his body, the electricity arcing as he glided up the coffee-with-cream-colored skin. He finished by kissing Ja'din deeply, letting him taste himself. As he pulled away, a thin thread of come connected the two for a moment, then broke.

"I assume that you enjoyed that?" Edward asked, stating the obvious as he turned off the violent wand.

Ja'din rolled his eyes at him.

"What do you think? I can barely move."

"Let me help you up," Edward said as he reached his arm under Ja'din's neck, helping him up into a sitting position.

Edward took Ja'din's hand in his, as he sat down beside the naked man.

"Ja'din, as you know, I have thought about you a lot since we met nine months ago." He looked down where he held Ja'din's hand before he continued. "I also admitted that I had you thoroughly checked out because of that."

"Um, yeah . . . which really did creep me out, Edward."

"I can understand why it would, Ja'din, but trust me, I do have my reasons."

Ja'din sighed heavily.

"You know, I can almost understand why. A rich guy

like you, as hot as you are, probably has guys throwing themselves at him all the time."

Edward tilted his head back with laughter.

"Yes, sometimes, I do, but there is a little more to it than that." Turning more serious, Edward, with the back of his other hand, stroked the side of Ja'din's unshaven face. "I think I like you unshaven, it is very sexy on you."

"Thanks," Ja'din said, leaning into his hand. "I guess you've figured out that I think you're . . . well, it's just . . ." Ja'din had trouble describing what he felt.

"I believe what you are trying to say is that we have a connection," Edward suggested.

"Yeah, that's what I mean," Ja'din agreed. "But it's even more than that. I guess what I mean is I am attracted to you physically, but I am also drawn to you. It's almost like I don't have control of myself when I'm around you."

"Now maybe you will understand why I did what I did, Ja'din. I have the same feeling, which is something very rare for me."

They each stared into the other's eyes, enjoying the closeness of the moment.

"Mind if I ask you something?" Edward asked softly. "What, if any, hard limits do you have, Ja'din?"

"No scat, no animals, no children, no needles or hooks, and no necrophilia," Ja'din stated matter-of-factly.

Abruptly Edward stood up and walked towards the door.

"Then there is a problem."

"What? Which of those is the issue?" Ja'din was more than slightly taken aback by how abruptly the mood changed from ready to rip his clothes off to stone cold.

Edward turned back towards Ja'din.

"Necrophilia."

"You want to have sex with a dead body?"

Ja'din was dumbfounded.

"I have, and most likely will again," Edward answered before turning back to the door, opening it.

Ja'din jumped off the table and grabbed Edward by the arm, making him turn to face him.

"I think that you need to explain what you just said, Edward."

"Not only have I had sex with a dead person, but I was hoping that you would also."

The expression on Edward's face was of pure pain.

Ja'din's mouth dropped open; he didn't know what to say.

"What are you talking about?"

"Ja'din, I am one of those . . . dead people."

Ja'din couldn't help himself, as he busted out laughing. "Yeah, right, and I'm a zombie!"

Edward turned and, looking at the man he wanted to spend eternity with, said, "I speak the truth, Ja'din, would you like me to prove it?"

"You can't be serious?"

"Yes, Ja'din, I am quite serious." Edward wasn't surprised at the question.

"How would you prove it?"

"Stand here by the door, Ja'din," Edward said. "I will go on the other side of the room. All I ask is that you count to ten after I have proven myself. After I count to ten, I will let you decide whether or not you wish to leave."

"Um . . . okay," Ja'din said, not understanding him.

Edward walked to the other side of the room, and began to remove his clothing, letting it drop to the floor. Ja'din's mouth watered as he watched him strip. He couldn't help but admire his broad chest, the quarter-sized nipples, surrounded by whirls of hair. The thick trail from navel to pubic area made Ja'din want to lick it to its treasure. He shuddered a little at the sight of Edward's large endowment and low-hanging testicles.

"Ready?" Edward looked nervous as he asked.

Ja'din nodded, not knowing what to expect.

Edward looked to the floor, took a deep breath, and slowly exhaled. When he looked up Ja'din fell back against the door.

"What the . . . ?" Ja'din croaked.

Looking at Edward or what had *been* Edward he saw long fangs extended from the same smooth lips that he longed for. The eyes now blazed like yellow fire, veins stood out under his eyes and forehead. His chest seemed fuller, even more muscular. Ja'din gasped when he looked at the semi-erect dick that was even larger than when he first had admired it.

"Ja'din, please? Please count to ten?" It was Edward's voice, Edward's lips.

"One, two, three." Ja'din looked deeper into Edward's eyes. He felt the power coming from them. "Four, five, six." His legs shook as he counted, making him grateful for the door behind him. "Seven, eight, nine." He saw

Edward's dick become fully erect. "Ten."

Ja'din took a deep breath, held it then let it whoosh out of him. "Okay, I'm still here."

Slowly Edward walked towards Ja'din.

"I won't hurt you, Ja'din. I'd never hurt you."

"I believe you." Ja'din watched him now more with fascination than fear. "So . . . you're a . . ." He couldn't even finish the question.

"I am a vampire," Edward finished for him. "I am technically dead, but living.

"And you drink blood?"

"Yes, I must to survive. But I do not kill, Ja'din."

Edward slowly walked towards him, Ja'din was amazed how he changed from vampire back to the man he had kissed only minutes before. The only thing that did not change was the huge erection that pointed upwards.

Edward stopped a few feet from Ja'din, an agonized look on his face.

"Are you afraid of me now, Ja'din?"

"I . . . I don't know what I am," Ja'din answered honestly. He studied Edward, running his eyes up and down his body. Admired the well-developed pectoral muscles, the lightly furred blond chest and flat stomach, that big dick, the tip now moist, the shapely legs, also dusted in blond hair. Looking into Edward's eyes he saw the fear in them.

The fear that he wouldn't accept him for what he was.

Ja'din took the few steps that separated them, stopping only a few inches from Edward.

"I have to admit I am a little afraid, but I'm more drawn to you than afraid of you. If we take things slowly, let me have time to . . . I don't know, get used to the idea, then I think I'll be okay."

The relief on Edward's face was clear.

"I think that you will love me once you get to know me, Ja'din, as I know that I already love you." Edward pulled Ja'din into his arms, kissing him.

"Um, I think you have some unfinished business, Edward." Ja'din laughed easily.

Ja'din pushed Edward away from him, grabbed his hard dick and led him to the corner of the room where the sling was hanging. Ja'din lay back, placing his feet in the straps.

"You need to show me how a vampire fucks."

Marked
By Nikki Haze

Kat had been hanging naked from the shackles in the basement of her master's sprawling estate since the sun went down. A chain wrapped around her belly and trailed along the cement floor, disappearing into his casket. It was secured to his wrist by a shackle. She knew he enjoyed her being bound to him, even as the sun rendered him dead.

"Sleep, darling pet," Niklaus whispered the command with a kiss on her forehead as he slid into his coffin moments before the sun rose.

Kat slept, but it never came easy in the basement. Hanging limp in the shackles, her arms stretched uncomfortably high above her head, she had to stand on her toes to keep the shackles from cutting into her. When she did sleep she woke up with blood running down both of her arms. Niklaus said he liked to smell her fresh blood even when he was dead.

The sun was setting, and Kat felt her pussy become slick at the mere idea of Niklaus waking, his blue eyes wild as they settled on hers, alive again.

Kat's body dripped with sweat from the Louisiana summer heat. The sweat mixed with her blood, and stung his bite marks as the mixture trickled down her body, pooling on the ground below her feet.

It was getting dark, and she heard him stirring inside the wooden box. Niklaus tugged on her chain roughly, before he flung the casket open and hopped out. He let the top slam down in a loud boom that echoed in the small space. He was always flashy about his re-entry from death.

Niklaus' milk-white skin was illuminated by the full moon that poured through the small window. He sped towards her, yanking hard on the chain, and forcing Kat's body to arch forward. Pressing one finger under her chin, he positioned her head to meet his intense, icy blue eyes, which were feral as they assessed her.

As he moved closer to her, his sizeable erection stroked her thigh. He bared his fangs to her. Niklaus usually fed after waking, so she braced herself for the sharp pain of his bite. Instead, he unshackled her, and she fell into his arms. He carried her up the rickety basement stairs, into the bright light of the living room. Her eyes remained closed as she sagged against him while he sped through his expansive home and up the grand staircase.

Niklaus placed her on the cool marble floor of the bathroom and lit candles to illuminate the dark space. He unshackled the chain from around her stomach, locking the bathroom door as he did it.

You're mine, he mouthed to her.

"I'm yours, Nik." She arched her body, waiting for her first order. He started a bath, ordering her to remain still as he fixed it for them. As the tub filled with water, he licked the blood and sweat from her body.

His fangs dragged precariously up to her thighs, as she automatically opened for him. He lapped at her pussy, trailing his fangs sharply against her clit. Her body shivered and her cunt pulsed with impending orgasm.

"That's it, Love. Come for me."

He continued to lap at her cunt, wiggling his fangs into her clit, driving her wild. She exploded in his mouth, her body wracked with shudders as she screamed his name over and over again. He pressed his hand on her taut tummy to still her as he spread her legs further, sinking his fangs inside her thigh as she reached the height of her orgasm. She cried out, the pain extending her pleasure. Her pussy was dripping wet and throbbing with the last of her release.

Niklaus sucked her blood, his lips working the soft flesh in the ultimate kiss. He took long, hard pulls from her, keeping Kat just a little weak. He licked the wound before lapping once again at her still-quivering cunt.

"I'm in a mood tonight, Kat."

He pulled Kat to her feet, standing nearly a foot over her as his eyes solidified his moodiness. Kat tried not to smile, but she liked the way his mouth twisted when he was in a bad mood. She also craved that edgy pain, kneeling before him, still and silent, until he decided what he would do to her. Kat loved belonging to Niklaus above all others because he cared about her pleasure and knew just the kind of discipline she needed. He knew she would never leave him, even if she were given a chance. The charade of enslavement turned her on, and he kept it up for her pleasure.

He placed her in the large tub, and then got into the tub behind her. The water was pink from her open wounds.

"Mmm." He moaned into her shoulder, nipping at her skin. "I want the smell of your cunt and blood on me, always."

He washed her, ordering her to be completely still as he combed her black hair. Kat was good at pleasing Niklaus after so long together, and was completely frozen as he treated her like a doll.

He drained the tub and picked her up in his arms, both of them dripping onto the tiles. She remained still as he dried her body, running the towel over her hair at the end. She watched him in the mirror as he took care of her, broad-shouldered with the thick muscles she knew the feel of well. Those iron-hard muscles were covered with silky white skin, softer than any skin she'd ever touched, human or vampire. His wet hair, thick and dark, was swept back away from his face; his eyes were intense as he focused on caring for her. Abruptly, he looked up in the mirror.

"What?" he bit out. Oh, he was in a *mood* tonight.

"I'm just watching you, Nik."

He dropped the towel, sounding disapproval.

"I told you to look down, Kat. Did you think I was kidding before?" He wrapped the chain around her waist and shackled her to his wrist again.

She let out a deep sigh of anxiety she hadn't realized she was holding in. He pulled her into the bedroom, ordering her to kneel with knees spread on the white carpet. She did what she was told, eyes looking down as she was told. She eyed the edge of the all-white featherbed to her left and realized how much she'd missed sleeping horizontally. It had been months since he'd allowed her to sleep shackled to the bed, instead of with him in the basement.

"I'm giving this to you, despite your need for punishment." He knelt before her, one finger tipping her chin up to meet his.

There was a large white velvet box in his hand and he pushed it forward to her.

"Open it."

There was something in his voice she'd never heard before, some sort of uncertainty.

No, Niklaus doesn't get nervous, she thought to herself.

Niklaus had only ever given her the gift of his whip, which was more than she could ever ask for. All he'd accepted in return was the gift of her submission, which she gave to him with pleasure. Careful not to meet his eyes, she slowly opened the box and gasped, forgetting she'd been ordered not to speak.

"You're only earning more punishment for your lack of obedience tonight, Love."

The even tone of Niklaus' voice was even scarier than when he let her know he was in a mood.

Her mouth dropped open as she stared down at the beautiful gift. She gazed at the thick ruby and diamond collar, but all she felt was shame at having displeased Niklaus. Tears streamed down her face, blurring the extravagant collar.

He leaned forward, taking the box from her and kissed away her tears.

"You will accept your punishment, you always do, pet. Don't cry. *Here*."

He motioned for her to turn around and she did so quickly, spinning her naked body on the carpet. Niklaus secured the beautiful, thick collar of gems around her neck, before pulling Kat to her feet and dragging her over to the full-length mirror.

"Look," he whispered, his breath tickling her ear.

She held one hand up to the exquisite collar that hung tightly around her neck. It was heavy; something she'd never forget was there, like the chain around her waist. She'd always hoped Niklaus would collar her, as it spoke to a higher level of ownership. Kat never could have imagined there was a collar in the world that exquisite.

"You may speak."

"Thank you, Nik. It's . . . so beautiful."

"That's why it suits *you* so well, Love."

She couldn't help but moan at his words. *Love*. He'd only taken to calling her anything other than slave or pet last week, after he'd kissed her for the first time without biting through her tongue.

She'd grown to like the blood filling their mouths when they kissed, feeding him as their tongues tangled together. This kiss had been different, it wasn't a decadent exchange of fluids, it was reverent, and after he had gotten into his coffin without a word.

Kat tried her hardest not to think about it too much. She needed Niklaus desperately, craved his approval, dominance, and punishment. She liked having the privilege of nourishing him, yielding to him completely. There was no doubt in Kat's mind that she was in love with her master. This generous gift was making it harder for her to keep that feeling to herself.

"Look, Love." He cupped her high, tight breasts, flicking lightly at each nipple until they grew into dark peaks. He ran his hands over her tan belly, down to the small triangle of hair he'd allowed her to keep above the smooth lips of her cunt. She leaned back into him, moaning his name as he teased her clit. She watched in the mirror as he spread her pussy lips, stroking her slick folds with one long, knowing finger.

He was the most beautiful creature she'd ever beheld in a world with few remaining humans. Out of all the masters that had taken her, he was both the kindest and most ruthless. Niklaus was the only one she'd ever cared for as more than a master. He stopped abruptly, tugging at her by the chain so she followed him back into the kitchen.

He prepared a small meal of yogurt and berries for her, sitting next to her while she ate, sipping on a glass of red wine. She was starving and had forgotten all about it until the food hit her stomach and she realized how ravenous she was.

"I'll have Martin feed you while I sleep," he promised, tugging her off the stool by the chain.

Martin was Niklaus' servant, who Kat suspected was a different sort of slave. He often snuck down to the basement when Niklaus was dead and kept her company. He'd grown up in Wisconsin on a farm and missed his home, though everyone in the state had been turned into a vampire.

"I'm safe here," he'd whispered once.

Kat knew that no one was safe. She didn't care if she was turned into a vampire, but knew that Niklaus enjoyed feeding from her too much to do it. Plus, if she were turned, he'd take another human submissive to feed from.

Niklaus brought her down to the basement again, his favorite torture implements were laid out on the carpeted area by the window, illuminated by the moonlight. Kat loved when the moon was bright so she could see too, Niklaus saw as clearly in the dark as Kat did in daylight.

He sat on the leather chair, ordering her to kneel before him.

"Tonight is a special night, Love. I think you should choose your punishment."

She was silent for a long while as she thought it over. She liked how the whip made her bleed, so he would lick it away before fucking her face. The paddle was one of his favorites, and she loved the noise it made when it beat against her skin.

"Your hand, Niklaus." She wasn't sure why she had to think; it was always his hand she preferred. Kat couldn't figure out what he meant by a *special night*, but eventually settled on the significance of the collar.

He tugged on her chains, bending her over his knee, running his hand over the tight globes of her ass. Kat's muscles tensed as she waited for the first sharp bite of pain. Rubbing his finger over the opening of her asshole, he spoke instead.

"Why did you choose my hand?"

She answered him immediately.

"I like your handprint on my ass. Your mark. I love when you show me that you own me, Nik."

The strength of his hand hurt the worst, but she craved nothing more than to submit to that pain. His hand came down hard on her skin with a loud whack. She wanted to please him, and would take her punishment of choice without a single scream. Kat bit down on her lip, hard enough to draw blood. He spanked her slowly at first and then picked up his pace, the whacks mixed with his grunts, filling the air around them. His punishment was relentless, each spank one right after the other, his hand moving with preternatural speed.

Kat began to relax, melting over his lap as the heat of the pain spread through her whole body in a syrupy transition from pain to pleasure. She was barely aware of him spreading her legs and bending her over further until her hands were on the ground. He continued to hit her, again and again, moving his hand lower on her ass.

His hand came down hard on her sopping wet pussy, until he was smacking her clit. She spread her legs wide, hitching her ass up in the air to afford him better contact. She involuntarily shuddered, so lost in the painful euphoria of his dominance.

"Come for me, Kat." He was wild, screaming the words as she moaned, answering his command. His hand continued to spank her pussy as she melted away. Kat heard someone screaming and realized it was herself, but she was far away, lost somewhere on the moon.

"Get on all fours."

He brought her back down to earth with his command. His pleasure was hers, and he took his pleasure from her submission. She moved and the chain snaked around her waist as he tugged on it, pulling her back toward him. Her knees scraped on the carpet from the action, as she knelt on all fours and he slid his cock into her trembling slick pussy.

He held himself there, balls-deep inside her, moaning as he spanked her ass once. He began to fuck her ruthlessly, forbidding her from coming again when he felt her muscles tighten around his large cock.

"This is for my pleasure." He shouted the words and spanked her when he felt her cunt fluttering. Kat closed her eyes and focused on pleasing him. She wouldn't disappoint him again tonight. His speed was punishing, thighs slapping against her ass, on and on, until he finally slowed down. His cock pulsed; long spurts of come shot deep inside of her, the force of it nearly sending her over the edge.

"Lick my cock clean before I fuck your ass." She turned around to lick up and down the length of his still-rigid cock. She loved that he could stay hard for her all night if he wanted to, and he usually did.

He rubbed her chin and she opened her mouth wider, as he sunk deeper into her throat and released the last of his come in her mouth. She lapped up and down his length as he uttered his approval. Suddenly aware of the reason for it being a special night, she smiled against his skin. The weight of the collar, the chain, the come dripping from her pussy and the heady burn of his mark on her ass meant Niklaus owned her, and he was making sure Kat knew it.

Niklaus ordered Martin prepare Kat on the *special* cushion for him. She was ordered face-down on the fabric, but she turned her head to look up at Niklaus. He stood above her to watch, his beautiful cock in his hand. Her arms and legs were stretched wide and shackled in four-point restraints. She knew he loved to take her ass like this, her bound and helpless. Martin bobbed his blond head with an awkward goodbye before Kat heard him retreat up the stairs.

Niklaus knelt down by Kat, lifting her chin to him before kissing her in that same slow, claiming way that had shaken her so deeply last week. She opened her mouth to speak; she needed to ask him why he was kissing her like that, pouring his entire soul into hers. The question was well worth the likely punishment that would follow. But he shoved a ball-gag in her open mouth, securing it around her head before she could speak.

He stroked over her back and ass with his hands, the burn of his spanking ignited all over again with each stroke over her raw flesh. She heard the click of the chain as he used it to tug her pelvis up in the air, causing the restraints on all four limbs to cut into her recently healed wounds. She was beyond feeling pain, knowing her blood would nourish and please Niklaus. Pleasing him was all that mattered in her world.

He opened the globes of her ass further, and she could feel his eyes on her quivering flesh.

"You have such a nice tight pussy. The nicest one in my thousand years, and your ass . . ." He slid in one finger and then another, moving them in and out, driving her wild.

"I love your ass." He slapped her lightly, almost playfully. "So red from my hand. You pleased me tonight with your choice of punishment, you always do." He added a third finger, pressing deep into her ass, past his knuckles. His other hand massaged the heat of her burning cheeks as she bit down on her lip again to avoid from moaning.

He quickly replaced his fingers with his rigid cock, rimming her tight hole. He slammed past her resistance in one long stroke, sending himself in to the hilt. She knew that Niklaus liked her to remain still when he fucked her ass and she had to pull on her restraints to do so. To her surprise he didn't use his super speed. Rocking his hips slowly into her, his hands wandered over her skin as he moaned, indicating his enjoyment of her tightness.

She was frightened by the change in his behavior. *Why did he make tonight different?* She had always dreamed of being collared, but imagined it would be made of leather with a leash attached. This was decadent, speaking of care beyond their dominant/submissive relationship.

His slow strokes were relentless, his hips moving all the way out before he slowly buried his swelling cock deep inside her again and again. He covered her body with his as he fucked her tight hole. He brushed her damp hair aside, and without warning sank his teeth into her shoulder, taking a small sip of her blood.

He continued to bite all over her back, taking a small amount of blood each time. The pain from the sharp intrusion only heightened her impending orgasm. She counted fifteen bites as she held back her moans, edging closer. Blood trickled down her sides as he picked up his pace.

His body was still covering hers with brutal force, his lips pressed against the back of her neck in an endless kiss, leaving his fangs out this time as he ordered her to come. The gag muffled her screams, but his pleasure rang out loud, booming her name, over and over again.

"Kat, Kat, oh *Kat*."

He pulled out of her and began to release all over her back as she continued to pulse and quiver with the intensity of her orgasm. She loved the feel of his hot come on her bleeding back. He'd marked her in every way possible. Niklaus was still for a long moment before he collapsed on top of her, kissing her neck. She breathed deeply beneath him, the motion sending them rising and falling together.

He removed her gag but made no motion to unshackle her; he turned her face sharply to his and kissed her that same way, so she nearly cried at his tenderness.

"What were you going to say before I shoved that ball in your pretty little mouth, Love?"

She was quiet until she finally swallowed deep and asked the question she'd been begging to ask. What she really wanted to say was *I love you, Niklaus. My master, my world, I love you.*

He unshackled her and pulled her into his arms, kissing her again, come and blood trickling down both of their bodies. His grin was broad and toothy as his eyes met hers, and she just *knew*. He opened his mouth to speak; she held her breath as the words she'd been dying to hear poured from his soft lips.

He fucked her mouth for asking the question anyway, and she smiled with joy as she slurped down his come. That morning, moments before sunrise, Niklaus folded Kat inside the coffin with him and let her hold him as he died until nightfall.

Vamp-Hire
By Landon Dixon

I felt the chill first, then the hair stood up on the back of my neck in primeval warning. The door of my office opened, and a vampire stood there with two of his minions. They glided inside, the door closing behind them. "Count Fursting," the vampire said, taking a seat in one of the chairs in front of my desk. His two companions remained standing on either side of him. "The 'Count' is honorary."

"Brent Turner," I responded, playing it as cool as the temperature in the room. "P.I. The 'P.I.' is licensed."

"This is Timothy." Fursting gestured to the blond on his right. "And this is Cory." He gestured at the redhead on his left. "I'm a vampire." He stated the obvious. "And they are . . . recent converts."

They were both young, good-looking guys, slender builds, pale, and expressionless. Timothy was the taller of the two, with blue eyes; while Cory was shorter with green eyes. Both were dressed casually in t-shirts and jeans. Volunteer blood givers to the Darktown immortals.

I tapped my blotter with a pencil, my nerves doing most of the work.

"What can I do for you, Fursting?"

"There are a group of humans—'soul-savers'—they call themselves, who cross the lines from Brighton into Darktown and kidnap non-humans, forcibly removing them back over the border, for what they futilely call 'rehabilitation.' I want you to put a stop to it, Mr. Turner."

My pencil froze in my hand; I stared into Fursting's unblinking black eyes.

"Why don't you go to the police?"

The vampire's pale, emotionless face darkened slightly.

"The police will not help us. They are supposed to, of course, required to under the treaties we've signed. But they find the job . . . distasteful. Many on your side, Mr. Turner, still haven't reconciled themselves to the agreement that allows humans, of their own free will, to cross the line that separates us and become volunteer blood givers to vampires."

"To kill themselves, you mean. Become slaves to you people."

"You see, even you, with a reputation for very few ethics, are repelled at the idea of humans willingly becoming non-humans, labeling vampires as 'you people.' So, you can understand that the police will not help us. But *you* will *work* for vampires, will you not, Mr. Turner?"

I stabbed the blotter with the sharp, narrow wooden stake in my hand. Then I smiled, and sat back in my chair.

"I'm a realist, Fursting; in business to make money. What other people do with their souls is no great concern of mine. As long as vampires still trade in greenbacks, I'm willing to work on the dark side."

Fursting nodded as he pulled a black leather wallet out of his dark suit jacket, and five one hundred dollar bills out of the wallet. He placed the money on my desk, then snapped his long, pale fingers at Timothy and Cory. The "men" began to disrobe.

"As an added incentive, Mr. Turner," the vampire explained, "and to seal what some on your side of the border might term a dirty deal."

I watched Timothy and Cory pull off their t-shirts, revealing smooth and hairless chests with succulent, red nipples. Still expressionless, they popped open their jeans, skinning them down their slim legs. Their cocks hung enticingly from blond and ginger fuzz bushes respectively, smooth and clean-cut, surprisingly long even while soft. They kicked off their shoes and stepped out of their jeans, standing naked before me.

"Do we have an understanding, Mr. Turner?" Fursting asked. "Will you help me put a stop to these illegal soul-savers?"

I looked between deliciously nude Timothy and Cory, my eyes devouring their young bodies and adult cocks, picturing what their pert assess looked like from behind. I licked my lips and swallowed hard.

"We've got a deal," I croaked.

The vampire stood up and signaled to the two non-humans. I scrambled to my feet as they came around my desk. Each gripped one of my shoulders and pecs apiece, kissing me softly on the lips, first Timothy, and then Cory.

Then, while Timothy unbuttoned my shirt, Cory got down on his knees, unbuckling my belt and unzipping my pants.

Timothy unfastened the last of my shirt buttons, and pushed it back off my shoulders. He ran his slender hands over my bare, hairy chest, caressing my shimmering skin, his soft fingers buzzing my nipples. Cory breathed against the outstretched, straining length of my cock ballooning my white briefs, before digging his delicate fingers in and pulling my briefs down. My cock burst out into the open and bounced off his broad forehead. My veins swelled, pounding with hot blood, exciting both Fursting and myself.

Timothy licked my left nipple with his wet, red tongue. Cory gripped my cock at the base and spun his tongue all around the mushroomed tip of my dong.

I slumped with pleasure, they held me upright. Timothy sucked my rigid bud, tugging on it. I quivered with passion, though their breath wasn't warm by any means. But their tongues were damp and agile, and their mouths moist and velvety. I grabbed onto Timothy's blond head with one hand and Cory's red head with the other, thrusting my chest into Timothy's hands and mouth, my cock deep in Cory's mouth.

Fursting just stood there, watching, his hands folded over the front of his pants.

Cory bobbed his head back and forth in my hand, sucking on my shaft and hood, as I pumped into his mouth. Timothy bit into my nipples, then he got down on his knees, joining his fellow non-human at my cock.

Timothy popped my gleaming dong out of Cory's mouth, and into his. He bobbed his head even quicker, vacuuming my pole fast and tight. I rode his head with my hand, pumping my hips in rhythm to his sucking. My body blazed with feeling, my cock a naming staff of molten steel in his mouth.

They passed me back and forth between their young, sucking mouths. The one not vacuuming my organ would dip his head lower, jostling my balls with his tongue before sucking up the whole of my sack. They were good at blowing my cock, tea-bagging my balls, rapidly sucking to the point of my utter abandon and imminent release.

That's just when the vampire snapped his fingers again, both men instantly disgorged my cock and sack, leaving me hanging and dripping. Then they jumped up onto my desk, stretched out on their backs with their slender legs upraised, opening their cheeks to the bright, red entrances to their anuses. My gleaming cock speared up straight into the air.

There was lube in my desk drawer. I used it on my towering erection, on their petulant puckers, and then I plowed into Timothy. I gripped his legs at his bent knees, driving my glistening cap and shaft deep into his chute. He didn't utter a word, though I groaned with the enveloping good feeling with my balls jammed tight to his cheeks. Fursting bent over Timothy's neck, the vampire's sharp, shining, white fangs bared.

I felt the shudder go through Timothy's body, as Fursting bit into his neck. His anus convulsed around my submerged cock, as the vampire sucked on his jugular.

Fursting's throat worked powerfully, trickles of blood running down Timothy's slim neck below the vampire's grotesquely sucking mouth.

I wasn't horrified—I was electrified. I could almost feel the vampire's savage suck on my cock in Timothy's gripping ass. I sawed back and forth in Timothy's clenching chute, reaming his tight, satin anus. Fursting lifted his head and moved over to Cory's neck, sinking his crimson-smeared fangs into that man's jugular and sucked. I pulled out of Timothy and jumped over to Cory's ass, ramming my hood through his ring, slamming my shaft into his chute.

It was a fucking and feeding frenzy: human, vampire, and non-humans. My thighs smacked against rippling ass cheeks, my hands clutching Cory's quivering legs, as my cock thrust deep between both of their asses. My eyes locked on the bloodsucker getting his fill, until I bucked and cried out. I came harder and heavier than I can ever remember, draining my balls into the two young men, as Fursting drained the life out of their veins, licking his scarlet lips with a satisfaction that matched mine.

I headed down to Skid Row, the border between Brighton and Darktown. Orland Gitt was a "slaver," as some puritans put it—a guy who helped humans take the plunge over into the dark side, an undead existence in Darktown. He was versed in what vampires were looking for, and was as persuasive as a snake oil salesman at convincing conflicted humans to voluntarily give up their souls. He collected fees from both sides, so was equally despised on either side of the line. After gaining his attention with one of the one hundred dollar bills Fursting had given me, I garnered his cooperation with a second c-note. He told me a church on the corner of Main and First was running an "outreach program", ostensibly for troubled kids and young adults. But he suspected their activities extended right into Darktown.

"They're into rescuing souls from eternal damnation," he sneered. "Live ones and dead ones both. Pathetic, huh?"

My stomach churned just from being inside this greasy guy's grimy little back office, and I wasn't paying for his dirty opinions.

"Maybe they could help you, Gitt," I snarled.

He looked up from fondling the money I'd given him.

"Huh? Maybe you too," he shot back.

After reporting my findings to Fursting, I staked out the Calvary Cathedral that night. Some men and women went in and out of the two-story whitewashed building clutching prayer books, more staggered by on the sidewalk clutching bottles. It got quiet around midnight, just the occasional raucous yell of a drunkard on the Brighton side of the line. Or the occasional bloodcurdling howl from the Darktown side.

Just after two in the morning, four shadows slid out the side entrance of the clapboard church.

I got out of my car and tailed them on foot. Sure enough, the holy quartet slipped over the line, crossing Main Street into Darktown. They were hunting for souls to save.

I kept Fursting clued in via my mobile phone. So when the group of four met up with their first shuffling, dead-eyed non-humans a couple of desolate blocks into Darktown, there was a gang of six vampires waiting for *them*. I caught the glassy glint of their animal eyes in the blackened mouth of an alley from across the street before the soul-savers saw them. Too late, they were too busy coaxing a pair of non-humans to follow the path back out of the dark, and into the righteous light.

There was a furious rushing sound, as the vampires pounced. Human screams rent the night, as the soul-savers were surrounded. Their hands reached for crosses and vials of holy water. But the vampires were faster, moving at inhuman speed.

Tearing, rending, and spurting sounds cascaded across the broken street, washing up against the crumbling walls of the devastated buildings. I turned to go, slightly sickened, but was confronted by Fursting and three other vampires blocking me.

"I'm afraid you have witnessed us illegally turning humans into non-humans," Fursting intoned. "We can't let you report that to the authorities."

They advanced on me.

I pulled a silver-plated .38 out of my jacket pocket and pointed it at them. They stopped in their tracks, seeing the silver tips of the six bullets visible in the revolving cylinder of the gun.

"It doesn't pay to get too concerned with legalities in my line of work," I assured Fursting. "But I *will* require additional payment—to preserve client confidentiality in this case."

Fursting studied my face, and my gun. Both were

unmoving. He nodded, signaling to his three companions. They approached me, slowly, all of them tall and slim, with dark hair and dark eyes, ghostly pallors, sensuous red lips and long slender hands with long supple fingers.

I let the gun drop to my side, as two of the vampires opened up my shirt. The third got down on his knees and opened up my pants. Vampire sex, the ultimate in risky gay fornication.

I thrilled and chilled at the cool, caressing touches of the vampires. Their fingers strummed my bare nipples to buzzing hardness, wrapped around my engorged cock and pumped it harder and thicker still. I sensed their excitement at the heated pulse of my pounding blood, as I surged with a wicked eroticism borne of the utter depravity.

I was courting living death, a mere prick of their fangs enough to condemn me for eternity. All for a short, scintillating trip to a new, sky-high plane of sexual ecstasy.

The two vampires wove their fingers through the tingling hair on my shimmering chest. Their fingers were replaced with serpentine tongues that licked my jutting nipples. The vampire on his knees stroked my cock to raging erection, then placed his damp, red mouth over my bloated hood and down the entire length of my swollen shaft, swallowing me whole. He was not bothered by the gag reflex that applied only to the living.

I jerked in their arms, in his mouth, exulting in an otherworldly lust. The two vampires sucked on my nipples, lightly nibbling with their white, pointed fangs, smoothing their hands over my heaving chest and stomach. The third vampire kept me locked, quivering and pulsating, in the moist, suffocating confines of his mouth and throat. He pulled his slick head back, then pushed it forward, sucking tight and hard on my cock again.

I was so consumed by awesome bliss I didn't even notice Fursting get in behind me, until I felt his smooth, hard cock between my trembling buttocks, and his claws sink into my shoulders. He lubed my crack with whatever oil he'd applied to his cock, before he pulled his hips back and pressed his dick head up against my pucker. He pushed forward, bursting through and inside me. I tilted my head back, moaning like a wounded animal. The vampire's tremendous stake sunk into my anus, expanding my surreal joy with every driving inch, stretching my sensual delight to the breaking point.

My gun dropped out of my hand, and clattered to the sidewalk. Vampires worked my chest and nipples with their hands and fingers and lips and tongues, another bobbed his head in between my legs, sucking rapidly and expertly on my rock-hard cock. A vampire churned my chute with his relentless dong, pumping inside of me, his thin thighs smacking against my bloated buttocks, his cool breath bathing my neck, razor-sharp teeth grazing the vulnerable skin.

They sucked and fondled me harder, and fucked faster; I burned in their evil clutches with total abandon, surrendering myself to the overwhelming sensations. I knew *they* could go on forever. But *I* was a mere mortal.

The silver moon suddenly broke free of the black clouds, and beamed down on our frenzy. I erupted with absolute ecstasy, jolted by an earth-shaking orgasm. I spurted down the vampire's gulping throat, dancing in the vampires' claws, and convulsing on Fursting's pistoning cock with a wild intensity I'd never experienced before.

I lived barely through it.

Now, I take all the vampire-related cases I can, staking my reputation on it, an unabashed slave to outrageous and dangerous vampire sex.

Ladies of the Darker Nights

By Nicky B.

The highest tower in the castle was unusually warm for this time of year. Fredrick awoke from a long sleep with a start. Again. It was not a nightmare, he really was tied to a cross in the privileged dungeon.

"Welcome!" a husky voice greeted him from within the shadows.

He looked up, shaking the matted blond hair from his eyes, and longing for the ropes to be removed from his aching arms.

"Well, your highness, when you were invited to lunch you probably had no idea it would be you!" The husky-voiced maiden appeared from the shadows with a large, heavily melted candle. Her features would have made her very beautiful but for her evil sunken eyes and long, sharp canine teeth. She was dressed in a red dress that almost glowed in its ferocity.

Miranda was the chief concubine of the lord that everyone had referred to as "The Master," the head vampire.

Fredrick looked straight in her eyes; she returned his

gaze. Two shorter, less attractive females stood behind her, smiling and licking their lips.

"You are very honored: the master rarely dines alone on the blood of just one." She smiled while attempting to out-stare him. "Sorry, Duke, but tonight you must die."

He broke his gaze, glancing around the tall, dark room.

"There is no escape, sweet Duke, you are bound well."

Indeed he was bound very tightly to the cross that was mounted on the damp wall, with a window directly above. A single wooden support spanned the room, a final resting place for the living to be hung from as their blood was drained, along with their lives.

He couldn't help but find her attractive: her features were pure evil but her body was more stunning than the most expensive whore he had ever encountered.

"So you are your master's head concubine, Miranda?"

Miranda replied with a smile and gave a little curtsey.

"I am indeed, and I serve him well. He chose me specially for this."

"I have heard tell that you are not his best lover. You have the looks but not the mouth."

Her smile vanished quickly, the low growl of a large dog came from behind her closed lips. She quickly gathered her composure and smiled again.

Her two assistants approached him from behind, their heads level with his midsection. They closed in on his helpless state, it was time.

"Wait! Am I not entitled to a last request?"

The urgency in his voice was that of a frightened child. Miranda smiled widely, and her minions cackled.

He saw them in the dull candlelight, dressed only in short and tight petticoats that concealed stunning bodies. They were pretty but for their eyes, the blood-curdling laughs and their long fangs.

"So?" His urgency had changed to a plea.

"Very well! Speak your wish and I will consider," Miranda said.

They all stared hard at him, waiting.

"I wish to spill my seed over your breasts."

Silence.

"But how? You are tied up tight!" In eighty years, Miranda had never heard *this* request before. At the same time there was a stir in her sex that was above any the master had created in her, which unnerved her.

"Prove that you are an expert with your mouth; take my cock into it and make me spill all over you."

Her breath increased in speed and depth. After all, she was still mostly human.

"Very well." She approached the duke, placing the candle on a stool, as she raised her left hand in the air before him.

It flew down sharply and he gasped with shock. He looked down to see that she had slashed the groin of his trousers with invisible talons. The expensive material fell free and left a large section exposed. His cock shriveled from the cold, was in full view.

"Warm him up, my little sluts." Those two pulled their undergarments over their heads to reveal exquisite naked bodies. Miranda walked further away and lifted up one leg onto another stool and leaned on her thigh—watching intently.

The two maidens stood near the duke, then one of them stroked his shriveled cock while the other ran her fingertips over his testicles. One by one the wrinkles vanished as his cock started to fill, him watching as they gently massaged him. They both smiled as his member grew, his breathing growing deeper as well.

In no time he stood tall and proud with the candlelight enhancing the veins and his bulbous head in the shadows.

One girl slid her long, icy-cold tongue from his balls to the very tip of his cock, massaging the underside. The second girl took a testicle in her mouth, and between them, it was like ice being stroked over him.

The first girl moved her head back, and opened her mouth wider. Her fangs were exposed, and ready to strike.

The duke was oblivious as he watched Miranda undress.

"No!" Miranda shouted over with less than a second to spare. "Come over here and remove my corset." Disgruntled, the girl obeyed, shuffling her bare feet over the cold stone floor.

Luckily the duke had no idea of what had nearly happened, so he remained fully erect.

The second girl went to help Miranda as well. In no time, they were all naked with clothes strewn over the floor.

Miranda tapped the second girl on the shoulder, and pointed in his direction.

"You first!" The girl went back over to the duke and began to rub her cold hairless sex up and down his hardness.

He closed his eyes, though they darted open again to watch his cock vanish deep within her.

Inside her was like ice as he glided in and out. She took his full length each time, and pressed against his belly with each stroke. Their mouths panted in unison, as he stole a quick glance over at the other two.

Miranda had her elegant foot back up on the stool, the first girl was licking her sex. His hardness slammed in and out faster than ever, so that the girl threw her head back, and cried out through clenched teeth. She shook violently, then calmed as she lifted herself off his cock and jumped onto the stone floor with a big grin on her face.

Miranda pulled the head of the girl between her legs closer to gorge on her steaming sex, as she watched them. She moaned loudly, her hands gripping the girl's head even more. Then she threw her clear roughly, her tongue was still protruding and hung way below her chin.

"You! Take him now!" Miranda commanded the girl as she stroked herself.

The girl looked at Fredrick's hard cock and raised her hands in the air. She flew up unaided, gripping the wooden joist, like a trapeze artist she swung over and over just missing the leaking roof tiles. For a second she hung by her arms, and her lower torso grew. It stretched longer and longer, and angled towards him. Her middle got so long that her feet padded against the wall either side of Fredrick.

Before he had a chance to begin shrinking from fear, her pert bottom flew back and she was impaled on him. Her arms still hung on to the joist, as her lengthened middle fucked him with her icy chamber. She moved back and forth over his length, and he moaned aloud with pleasure.

The two other women stroked their own sexes with delight as they looked on.

Unperturbed by her freakish frame, he thrust his hips upward to fuck her in return.

They got faster and faster and all of the occupants of the room panted in ecstasy.

"Oh my lord! My seed is rising, it is nearly time to expel!"

Everything seemed to stop as the girl let go of his cock in time to release her grip on the joist. She returned to normal shape, and all three scrambled to him.

Miranda took his cock in her mouth. It was warm, almost burning in comparison to the other women. Her lips slowly slid up and down the length of his stiffness, while she gripped the base between her finger and thumb. The other women were close by her side watching and learning.

Fredrick threw his head back in pleasure.

"I heard wrong! You are unequalled with your mouth and I apologize."

She let his shaft slide out of her mouth, and it steamed in the cold.

"Foolish duke, why do you think I am head of these sluts?" Miranda returned to gorging on him.

"I am arriving! I am arriving!"

She felt his cock swell up in her mouth, she replaced her mouth with her finger and thumb which she slid up and down when he gasped out loud. The first spurt of his hot seed flew across the air and hit Miranda's face, dribbling into her wide grinning mouth. The remainder splashed over her breasts, covering them, steam rising from it.

Her two assistants licked it off, a breast each until she was clean.

Suddenly she and one of her sluts began to choke. Both coughing hard and wheezing, before falling to the cold floor. Their bodies convulsed, as they rolled around uncontrollably before the duke.

The coughing subsided and as quickly as they had started, the two women sat up and looked around. There was a loud slam from a closing door.

It was the master coming up the stairs.

The remaining girl jumped back up onto the thick wood support, clawing at it.

Fredrick smiled as he looked down at Miranda and the other girl. They both looked up at him in confusion.

"It is my family prophecy written many centuries ago, that our seed would cure the vampires of this castle of their illness." He beamed at Miranda and the other girl, who had gained normal features and were more beautiful than ever. "I wasn't sure if it was true, but I had to try once before I died. You are both free now—human again with thirst for nothing but fine wines."

Their elation was disrupted by the door opening violently.

The master stood in his fine suit, his long teeth bared, ready to conduct a massacre. He had heard the groans of ecstasy; only he should make them howl like that in his castle and he was irate. So intent on the cause of his rage, he did not hear the swish of air as the again-elongated body of the girl swung down at high speed from the joist. Clutched strongly between her feet was a stake made of wood, torn from the support, that thrust deep into his lifeless heart and out the other side.

Still gripping the wood, she lifted him and swung him hard across the room. He flew through the window and far into the distance of the dark valley. A loud explosion was heard: it was the disintegration his once-powerful form.

He was destroyed.

The girl gained her original shape, landing on the floor. She was normal again too, the women looked at each other and hugged. Now everyone in the kingdom would be cured, their smiles revealing ordinary teeth again.

"Can I be let down now?" said Fredrick. "I have released you after all, and feel that you owe it to me."

Miranda walked forward and lifted her hand high. Her frightening talons had been replaced with well-trimmed nails. Her quizzical look changed to delight.

Fredrick hung with his shrunken member dripping the last of his seed.

"So all those concubines in the castle are now normal humans? How many are there?"

"Hundreds! And I'm in charge of them now!" Miranda declared.

"Very good! Do you think one of them may possess a knife, some food, and a large bed for the night?"

"Maybe you should bathe first, Duke?"

How to Train Your Master Vampire

By Monica Corwin

"What can I do for you tonight, baby?"

"Well, baby, you can come home. Now."

"Caden, did you just waste $5.99 a minute to boss me around? You could have just texted me!" I dropped my head onto my desk, and took a deep breath.

"It doesn't have the same impact."

Checking behind me to make sure no one slipped through the cubicles, I said to him,

"I'll be there in fifteen minutes."

"It takes you five minutes to get to my house from your work—are you looking to be punished tonight, Aurelia?"

"Can't you get one of your other slaves tonight? I'm tired."

"I honestly can't believe you just asked me that."

Hell. I couldn't believe I just asked him that.

"Come home. *Now*."

Click.

I took off my headset and stretched my arms, it was going to be a long day.

1-800-UWF-ANGS is the only all-vampire sex hotline in the country. Caden Marcos was the CEO, coven master, and my future betrothed. Being one of the only females in the coven of pure-born blood, I was soon to become his bride if I survived that long. Caden enjoyed playing on the dark side, and he liked his women pure-blood, sexy, and submissive.

I got to the house in record time, hoping he wouldn't be angry at my outburst earlier. He stood waiting in the foyer, the shades already drawn for the impending dawn.

"Kneel."

His voice rang out, angry and loud, bouncing off the walls around us. The house was deserted, which made me worried. I met his eyes as I dropped my bag and keys on the side table. Slowly, slow enough to see his jaw clench as his teeth ground together, I got to my knees and bowed my head.

The chill of the marble beneath my knees seeped into my skin. While vampires usually run chilled, they don't run that cold. I didn't dare move, because he was in a foul mood and it would be so much worse if I challenged him again.

His aura curled around me as he approached, and instantly my body reacted to his presence. I didn't love him, and I didn't want a husband, but I wanted him.

"Do you want to be with me, Aurelia?"

"It depends on how you ask, Master."

"Ahh, honesty, it's refreshing."

Only inches away from me, his body was so close, and tendrils of his aura caressed my skin in heated licks. He leaned down so his mouth almost touched my earlobe.

"Tell me, why don't you want to be with me?"

"I don't like the idea of an arranged marriage. I don't like your attitude and your woman-hopping."

He snickered so close to my ear, I almost fell over at the assault on my senses.

"Are those the reasons you object to our union? What if we made a deal?"

My head snapped up.

"A deal?"

"You forget yourself," he growled.

I dropped my head back down.

"I will make you a deal. If you commit to me, I'll commit to you, for today only. If we both don't agree by nightfall, I'll let you go to another coven."

I really wasn't sure what to say. For Caden to make an offer like this meant he really wanted me, more than just for the prestige of having a pure-blood woman. There was only one answer to his offer.

"I accept, Master."

"Good."

He reached down and grasped my hands, pulling me up.

"Go up and bathe, eat, and I'll be up in an hour. Be ready for me."

He kissed the top of my forehead and left me. I exhaled a breath I didn't even realize I was holding. The stairs were right in front of me, yet my legs felt like they would give out if I made my way to them. Nerves and arousal battled for ground throughout my body.

It took a moment, but I got control of myself and made

it to my room. Each movement through my grooming process brought him closer. We had danced around this for some time now, him ordering, me always finding an excuse to weasel out of it.

This deal changed everything. I would submit to him.

Incense swirled in the morning air. I left the shade drawn but the window open. Birds chirped outside, but inside there was nothing but darkness.

I felt him before he opened my bedroom door. I knelt in the middle of the floor, my knees on plush carpet this time, trying to keep from shivering. Fear, arousal, or just plain anger. I didn't know which I one I felt.

"You are mesmerizing," he whispered as he closed the door behind him.

"Thank you, Master."

"Aurelia, I won't force you. Tell me what you've decided."

I looked up at him.

"I accept. I will submit."

"You don't think you'll like it? Or do you have a problem with me?"

I gazed at the floor again.

"I don't like the fact that women are always the weak ones, that we are the ones who always have to please our masters." I somehow kept my lip from curling at the thought.

He swirled around me, his aura already marking me, mixing with mine. My hair was long and loose down my back and his fingers in it made me jump, but I settled again when he just ran his fingers along the length.

"I hate to kill your notions of subservience, Aurelia, but it takes strength to be submissive. To give yourself over completely to another's control does not indicate weakness at all."

I didn't move, but merely waited for him to do whatever it was he would do.

"Aurelia."

The sharp bite to his word made me look at him. He didn't look happy.

"You will not think of yourself as anything less than the perfect, pure-blood female you are. I'll show you what it means to serve, and I'll teach you to enjoy it."

I inclined my head and stared back at the carpet.

He knelt down in front of me, knees only inches from mine. He was about a foot taller than me so if I kept staring at the ground, I looked right at his crotch. I glanced up but that didn't help, he wore a white shirt like no other man in existence.

"I can smell your arousal, I know you want me."

The smart-ass remark that came to my lips remained on my tongue. He gave me a choice, I agreed, so I could no longer act like it wasn't my decision.

"Master, what is your will?"

He leaned down and cupped my face, turning it until my head tilted enough to meet his lips. He swept in with gentle force, not pressing my lips into my teeth but making sure I could think of nothing but his lips on mine and his tongue in my mouth. He tasted of chocolate-covered strawberries and blood, a perfect combination. I reached up to cup his head and pull him closer, but he captured my hands in his before they made it.

When he broke away from the kiss my head swam. He held one of my wrists in each hand, as he stood up and pulled me with him so fast my legs didn't get under me. His speed was incredible, he wrapped my legs around his waist before I could even start to fall.

I anchored my hands around his neck and crossed my feet behind his back as he carried me to my bed. So far, so good. Sitting me down amidst the plush linens, he stepped back.

"Undress," he commanded.

I reached up and slid down the strap of the slinky dress I wore. It stretched around my curves as I scooted around on the bed and pulled it off my feet. Blood red heels and a matching thong were the only pieces of clothing left on my body.

I started to shake, my nerves finally catching up. I'd never been with this man, never truly touched him, and I didnt know how to play this game. Or how to please him. He must have sensed it because in the heartbeat of my hesitation, he was between my thighs, pulling my panties off for me.

"You are my slave."

"Yes, Master."

"Say it." He dropped my panties on top of my dress.

"I am your slave."

"Mmmm . . . I like those words on your lips."

He began to unbutton his shirt. I watched with rapt attention as his pale skin was exposed to the candlelit room. He was truly beautiful, long hair down to his butt that he kept it in a braid down his back, so black it looked blue like raven feathers. His body was wide and solid, muscular; his build was athletic from his life before he became a vampire. He had light blue eyes, full lush lips, and a penis I had been missing all my life.

"Aurelia, I want your pretty lips on my cock."

I climbed off the bed, wobbly on my heels, and knelt in front of him. I looked up his body as I gripped him, and he gave me a small nod before I put my lips against the tip of him. He tasted sweet and salty all at once. I sucked him into my mouth until my lips met my hand halfway around his shaft. I moved my hand down to his ball sack, carrying the moisture of my saliva along the soft flesh. He grunted, a noise of pure masculine appreciation.

I had wanted him before, but now my body was liquid and tight. Each inward suck of his dick rocketed my arousal even higher. I used my lips, tongue, and teeth on him until he stilled my head with his hand. With a final lick, I released him and sat back on my heels.

"Very good."

He tilted my chin up so he could see my fac and wiped a drop of pre-come from my lip with his thumb. I stuck my tongue out, and lapped it up before he even told me to. Maybe I *could* do this slave thing.

Doubt jumped back into my mind. Why did I have to do this? Why did I have to be the slave? There were so few female pure-bloods, everyone wanted us, why didn't they submit to me?

Anger infused my blood as I looked at him.

He noticed the change immediately.

"What is it?"

"Why am I on my knees?"

His voice went deadly soft.

"Excuse me?"

I stood up, drawing all the height I could. It didn't compare to his height, but it made me feel better.

"Why do I have to be the slave? Strength or not, I want to renegotiate our bargain."

He had the nerve to chuckle. I reached down for my dress, but he grabbed my wrist before I did. I looked at him and stated my case.

"My terms are simple. *You* submit to *me* for one night, then I will consent to be your bride."

His anger was harrowing, I almost cowered back from it, but held my ground. This was a pivotal moment in our relationship. If he had the "strength" to be my slave for a night, then he just might be a man worthy of me. Agreeing to this meant he owned body, soul, and me for the rest of eternity. It really was the least he could do.

He turned away. I heard his teeth grinding together.

"I submit only to my people. A pure-blood marriage would ensure the safety of our coven, it would ensure a wolf not be named to our house."

He turned back to me, dropping to his knees.

"Mistress."

I inhaled sharply.

This man, this powerful man was on his knees while I stood over him, it was all wrong and at the same time, so very right.

"What is your pleasure?"

I smiled, thinking of the one thing I had wanted since we met.

"I want to taste you, Caden."

He growled quietly at the idea but I wasn't deterred. I moved in and dipped my head, licking the spot where his artery ran. Blood play was usually only shared between committed couples. But however this went down, we both knew I couldn't walk away.

He tilted his head to the side and I nicked him with my tooth, watched as a drop of blood welled up, stark against his white skin. It slid down the curve of his neck. I caught it on my tongue.

The taste of his blood was heady, like drinking a shot of vodka straight from the bottle. I slipped my stilettos off my feet and studied him. He didn't bow his head but regardless, he was here at my pleasure now. Oh, the things I had fantasized about doing to this man, and this would probably be my one and only chance.

"Stand."

To my delight, he did. He didn't mock me, he simply stood before, his face unreadable.

I circled him, grasping the length of his hair as I moved behind him. It was silky soft. He growled again as I twisted it in my fingers.

"Do you like that?"

"Yes, Mistress."

I wanted to make him make that noise again. I moved around to his front, and scooted up and away on the bed. The coverlet soft under my thighs, I couldn't remember the last time I'd been completely naked in bed. I didn't dwell on that though, for a vampire it could be much longer than for humans. I patted the cover next to my thigh, and he joined me on the bed, sitting so his thigh ran parallel to mine.

Our bodies were so different. We were both pale, but his body had such controlled strength underneath the skin, like a tiger in a cage waiting to be released. I sat on the center of the bed.

"Put your face between my legs and don't come up for air until I tell you."

The command came easily to my lips, surprisingly enough. The sheer eroticism of saying those words to my future master was enough to make my knees shake. With his head between my legs, he nipped my thigh lightly, not breaking the skin. I squirmed and smiled at his attempt to put me at ease, until his tongue touched my clit. I nearly jumped out of my skin at the feeling of his mouth on my bare flesh.

He was more than aroused as well, his teeth were descended and he had to work between them, but the fact that they were there, so close, almost made me come before he made any real effort to do so.

His skin vibrated, as he gripped my hips hard between his hands. *He's enjoying this*, I thought.

He sat back, licking my moisture from his lips.

"What were you going to do to me?"

He smiled, a cross between a grin and a lecherous sneer.

"I was going to tie you up and have my way with the entire length of your body.

"Lie down."

"I don't know how well I will take to being tied up."

"Why is that?"

"I was tied up once, and it wasn't a pleasant experience."

"By a woman?"

"No, not by a woman."

"Would you have reservations if I expressed the same concerns?"

He went silent for a moment.

"No, I would have tied you up anyway and made you forget whatever happened previously."

He looked down at his hands, and then gripped the posts on either side of the bedposts. I tied his hands with the ties, and he became flaccid, his eyes wild.

I climbed on top of him, straddled his legs, and gripped his face in my hands.

"Look at me," I commanded.

His eyes locked with mine for a long moment before I kissed him, drawing small growls from him with each sweep of my tongue inside his mouth. I dropped my hand from his face, and ran it down his wide, firm chest. I could get used to this, if he didn't have a nasty habit of treating me like a possession.

I pulled back and looked down at him, he seemed calmer. I gripped his braid and started to undo it, the strands had a kink in them as I fanned out the length across his chest. His beauty stunned me, as I ran my fingers through his hair, brushing it with my hand.

"You are truly beautiful."

"Thank you . . . Mistress."

I smiled, shaking my head. This was just a game to him, but it was so real to me. I knew exactly what I wanted next.

I reached down, happy to find him hard again. I would him like a pony until he shouted my name to the house.

I lifted up and positioned him correctly, before slowly lowering my body onto his dick.

He hissed when I was fully impaled upon his lap.

"Caden, you are the CEO of Fangs, so I know you can talk dirty. That is exactly what I want you to do. Tell me exactly what you've always fantasized about doing to me as I ride your pretty cock. Then, when you shout my name and the whole house knows I'm in control, this one time, I'll allow you to come."

He swallowed.

"Yes, Mistress."

I moved up and down on him slowly, careful to postpone my own orgasm. I wanted to see the fight in his eyes as he retained his control, as he told me naughty things.

"The first time I saw you I wanted to lay you out like a feast across the hall table. I didn't, only because there were other masters present and I didn't want any of them coveting what would soon be mine."

I exhaled as I rose up and down. He stretched me in such a delicious way, I closed my eyes, surrendering to his words, to the sensations.

"The next time I saw you, you had that black dress on, and your skin looked like cream. It almost killed me not to be able to lick you as you passed by."

His words started to stumble out, each one a play at precision as he tried to maintain control. I clenched my inner muscles and a string of words in Latin poured from his lips. This control, it was a heady thing.

I raked my nails down his chest.

"Tell me more."

"Oh, Dea—." *Goddess?*

I liked the sound of that.

"At this moment, I don't care who is in control. Keep riding me."

I planted my hands on the hard muscles of his abs, using my arms to lift myself up and down on him. In utter bliss, I breathed heavier, as did he. I reached up and gripped his chin.

"You come before you shout my name, and I will punish you."

Something dark and dangerous flashed in his eyes before I let him go. I set a faster pace, my orgasm rising quickly. I would come all over him, and I couldn't wait to hear my name fall from his lips.

The orgasm crashed around me, like a maelstrom. Hard, terrible, and wondrous all at once. My body was caught up in it, and I forgot everything as I rode him mercilessly. I had just started to come down, never losing pace, when he shouted in Latin, his voice loud and all consuming.

"Aurelia!"

I had no doubt every person in the house knew exactly what was happening between us, and it was so much sweeter for it.

I rode him until he couldn't bear the sensation anymore. When I climbed off and untied his wrists, he looked down at his hands.

"I don't feel as if I gave up my masculinity. I feel . . ." He paused, thinking. "I feel exhilarated."

I smiled. There was nothing to say to that. I lay out next to him and he looked at me, truly seeing me for the first time.

"Slave, clean me up."

He growled, but got up and fetched a cloth, and cleaned me with soft gentle strokes until I was languid and sleepy.

"Now, you will spoon with me. We can figure the rest out at nightfall."

He curled up around me, his big body embracing mine.

"Aurelia, you are a wonder."

I smiled, almost asleep.

"Thank you, slave."

"Tomorrow, Aurelia, I'll show you what it truly means to be a master."

That promise swirled in my mind as I drifted off to sleep.

The Vampire's Embrace

By Lise Horton

They were ancient vampires of enormous power, and now she belonged to them. It had not been her choice, but then again, so little in her life had been. Nerissa stood silent, head bowed, as she'd been ordered, and shivered in fear.

The three Phralmulo came into the semi-dark room. Ancient Romany vampires, they were more powerful than the famous name all humans had known before the Coming of the Night. Before one and all knew the truth. The undead were among them. Dracula had been a mere underling in the world of vampires. Others, more terrifying, more ravenous, now ruled all humankind, and they demanded payment.

She was that payment.

Enslavement to the three vampires was to be her fate for all eternity. They were the most powerful, the most feared, and she had been given to them in sacrifice. In past days, those turned over to any vampires by terrified humans were never seen or heard from again. Virgins all, they vanished without a trace, their fates unknown, only whispered of in terror in the dark.

The tiny dark-haired woman who had prepared her had been ancient herself, yet still human. Perhaps she was their human servant, but she had not answered when Nerissa asked, only shushed her and told her the rule. There was only one.

"You will submit, no matter what. They are your masters. Your life is theirs."

Nerissa did not understand. Nightmarish images came to her but she could make no sense of what had so far been done to her, of what was to come.

Something changed in the air, as the Phralmulo approached and stood before her. Nerissa quivered in dread, desperately wished to see them, but obeyed the ancient woman's stern word. "Do not look, do not speak, until they have given permission. Submit. No matter what. They are now your masters."

"A beautiful slave, do you not agree, Fane, Vasile?"

"A veritable angel, Nikolæ. It will be a pleasure defiling her, no?"

Low, intimate laughter filled the room, the sound of it caressed her flesh. She flinched in surprise to find her body heating with desire.

Her masters.

"The humans must be especially fearful this year to have given over such a one as her to us."

"To our benefit, Fane."

"Yes, always good that they fear us. Courageous humans are dead humans."

The three voices were deeply rich, melodic, and mesmerizing. Nerissa swooned as she awaited her fate. Awaiting the death they would bring her, the death of fangs and blood. How would it feel as her heart slowed to a stop, as they drained her of her life force? Strangely her body yearned, even as her mind was filled with images of the horrible end she envisioned.

They closed in on her, and their hands reached for her naked flesh. She had been stripped of all clothing and adornments, had mortifying things done to her intimate places. Fear had overridden her sense of vanity, but now as their fingers touched and stroked, the heat of arousal bloomed and grew within her. She realized the first hands to touch her in lust were those of vampires.

"Ah, what sweet flesh for us to feast upon."

"Certainly a beautiful cunt. Look at how swollen the lips are, how pink."

"And her ass is that of a goddess. Supple, round, so pale and inviting."

The touch of cool fingers on her behind startled her. Yet as they probed, a cry escaped her.

"Always such a pleasure impaling a virgin in all her delectable holes."

One hand pushed between her legs, and into her. Another pulled at her nipple, twisting hard until she gasped. The pain like a sharp fang pierced her body, sending ripples of dark delight coursing through her.

"This will be a most enjoyable initiation." A tongue, strangely heated, ran up her neck, and around the curve of her ear. "I cannot wait to get started."

"Shall we begin our indulgence of her?"

"Certainly."

"At once."

They grasped her, and pulled her forward. Shocked, she raised her head. Where were they taking her? What was going to happen? Her gaze fell on them.

Her masters.

All three of the Phralmulo were like dark gods, Wicked beauty, pulsating power, and black eyes.

She was astounded at the sight of them, their hungry smiles, A they pulled her through the dimly lit room, and flung open a canopy of red velvet curtains to expose another chamber. A bed-chamber, but so much more. She took in the macabre vision that lay before her.

A massive bed covered in black sheets. Tall candelabras with flickering flames cast eerie shadows throughout the room, the chains that hung from the ceiling were tipped with manacles, and on the wall were hung a row of terrifying implements she recognized but could not believe. She was to be tortured by these creatures of incredible beauty.

Her masters.

Her legs betrayed her and she collapsed, only to be held up by three sets of inhumanly powerful arms. They dragged her relentlessly, into the room, to stand beneath the chains.

"Our beauty will learn the delights of pain, will she not, Nikolæ?"

"And then we will show her other delights, Fane."

"Let the Zapardin begin. We have so named our ritual, and now let us lead our slave in the dance of the vampire."

Nikolæ watched in satisfaction as Fane and Vasile chained their slave. Her delectable, nubile body begged for the touch of his whips, for the impalement of his cock, and his bite. Hair the color of a stormy sunset, dark and rich with auburn and gold, fell in a tangle to her waist, as if to direct the eye to her voluptuous ass. Her virgin ass. Fane paused to treat himself to a perusal of her breasts, his hands cupping, squeezing, tormenting the generous globes until their slave twisted in her chains. Vasile, as always, held back, preferring the self-imposed torture of delayed gratification. Yet when he chose to take his turn, he would be merciless in his torment of her flesh.

She was helpless in the chains, her arms trapped above her, her body theirs to punish. Theirs for the taking.

He strode to the wall and plucked his favored tool. The wicked cat-o'-nine flogger would wring ceaseless screams from her as he wielded it. Fane took his crop, and Vasile his long vicious switch.

First they would bleed her, bringing her to that special ecstasy only pain could create, then they would make her theirs. Their slave, their woman, their concubine.

The ritual began.

At the first lash of his flogger with its leather knots, their slave gasped. The second brought a short scream, and after ten she was writhing in the chains. His ferocious strokes had bloodied her skin and after the last lash fell, he began to lick the blood from her body. The taste was, as always, intoxicating. But this time somehow richer, more satisfying and intense. His cock, already hard in anticipation of their ritual, throbbed painfully. Laving her ass, pussy, and breasts, with long, lingering licks of his tongue, he cleansed her wounds and stood. Her eyes were wide, dazed, her mouth open in wonder. He pressed his bloodied lips to hers and thrust his tongue deep into her mouth, letting her taste her blood on his tongue.

After he took his lips from her mouth, Fane stepped forward and raised his crop.

The sharp, whistling lashes had their slave crying out again, yet this time Nikolæ detected the note of hungry yearning in her voice. Her body was being seduced by the pain, craving the next burning stroke that would leave her wet and dripping with her desire for them, and preparing her for their possession. Still, she twisted in her chains, but her head had dropped forward and at the end of Fane's lashes, her cries had turned to moans. As was his bent, he lapped at her like a wolf, his tongue sliding over her flesh, absorbing the blood and tasting the perfume of her skin. Capturing her head in his hands, he took her mouth, forced it open and thrusted his tongue deep inside, demanding her response and subjugation.

Vasile stepped forward, his punishment would be the most wicked. The switch was long, thick, and sturdy, and left bloody welts in a wondrous pattern of ownership. He set to work with a gleaming delight in his black eyes. He had always had been the most sadistic of their triumvirate. Certainly a master at wringing pain—and pleasure—from their slaves.

The hiss of the switch preceded the piercing shriek of their slave. He stroked her ass, leaving a criss-cross of slim, bleeding stripes. Up over her shoulders, over her breasts, he spared her no torture, whipping her until her curves wept. For his last strokes he turned his attention to her bared pussy. Their servant had done as ordered and stripped her bare of pubic hair, the better to bite her swelling lips before plunging into her virgin cunt.

The first stroke landed and her scream echoed through-out the room. Patient, he waited for her cry to end in a whimper. He lashed another stroke across her soft flesh, she cried out again. Her screams faded as he continued to punish her. Stroke after stroke across her delicate places, until her juices could be seen dampening her thighs, mingling with the blood, and running down her legs. Her screams turned to moans, then to sighs, and lastly to the groans of a woman desperate to be taken.

Vasile cleaned the wounds from her ass to her thighs, a carnal smile on his lips as he licked her and swallowed her blood. When he dropped to his knees and put his face to her pussy, savoring her fluids as he sucked and licked, Fane watched with rabid hunger.

He could wait no longer, the time to make her theirs had come.

He and Fane surrounded her, as Vasile released one cuff, then the next. Fane caught her in his arms as she dropped. Her hair trailing the floor and her eyelids half shut, Nerissa was limp, as if drugged.

"To the bed."

They all nodded, as Fane lay their slave down.

"We shall each possess her, once, again, and then thrice. We shall all take her until our essences mingle in her, then we will make her ours." Nikolæ said.

Fane and Vasile nodded, their faces dark with lust, their yearning so strong for the completion they had long sought. Nikolæ's own eagerness surprised him. They had shared slaves over the centuries, but had never succeeded in binding them with this ritual. Yet at first glance, the three of them had felt an identical, powerful urge to bind her forever. Bind her to them with all with rituals of pain and lust as powerful as silver chains. Unbreakable. The thought elicited a need so deep, so dark, in Nikolæ's tormented soul he wanted to howl with it. The others felt the same, he saw it in their eyes.

She was to be theirs.

Nerissa opened her eyes, feeling the heated stare of the three vampires on her body. They had abused her horribly, and she had screamed with agony until her body betrayed her. The pain was hot and horrible, yet grew into something beautiful. Something she wanted more of, something she craved with every fiber of her soul. Suffering pain at their hands became a trial, a test of her bondage. After they had bled her, tasted her, licked her, and kissed her, she suffered a torment of an entirely different sort.

She wanted more, wanted to feel the sharp, sweet sting of their instruments on her naked, willing flesh. Until the haze of pleasure and pain blended again into something that made her come alive.

Now she lay upon the bed as they stared down at her. Like wolves after prey, they came closer and closer. Her skin ached for their touch, other parts of her liquid with need.

As one body, they threw off their robes and their glorious bodies were bared to her eyes. Nerissa saw their height was matched by powerful, muscled bodies. Graceful limbs, swarthy skin, and large, erect members.

She was a virgin, but knew what was to come. They would take her; impale and possess her. They would own her, when they were done. Her heart pounded, her mouth dry with trembling lips.

She no longer feared it, but wanted it. Needed it. She needed to be consumed by their unearthly lust.

They prowled onto the bed like panthers, toward her body. Their skin shadowed in the candle's flickering light, dark hair sweeping across their shoulders. When they were upon the length of her body, with a soft sigh of surrender, she welcomed them.

The largest of the three loomed over her. He kissed her with firm ownership, just once. Then he stared into her eyes.

"I am Nikolæ, your master. You are mine."

He moved, and the second vampire took his place. His hair was longer, thicker, and his face a bit broader, but still hypnotic in its beauty. He kissed her fiercely.

"I am Fane, your master. You are mine."

The third came over her with a look of dark need, his kiss was deep, hard, and hungry.

"I am Vasile, your master. You are mine."

Nikolæ took her in his arms, twisting until he lay beneath her and she sat astride him. Fane knelt at Nikolæ's head, and Vasile moved to Nikolæ's feet. She had no idea of what was to come, yet she craved it with a decadent curiosity. They all looked at her as though she was the most glorious creature in the world. No one had ever treasured her as the three of them were doing now.

Nikolæ's gaze was riveting, as he moved his hands to her hips and lifted her as effortlessly as if she were a kitten. She leaned on his shoulders as he ploughed her and she felt the searing stab of him deep inside her.

Her other two masters sprang upon her as well, and one by one they took her, and took her, and took her.

Nikolæ thrust into her with ferocity, growling.

"Feel me, slave, feel my cock pierce your virgin's cunt as I take you and make you mine. I will fuck your tight hole, and fill you with come. Know I am your master."

Fane grabbed her head, and pulled her forward.

"Suck my cock, slave, and know that your mouth is ours to fill with our come when, and wherever we wish. Swallow my come and taste me. Know I am your master." He pushed his cock between her lips. There was no time to think, to plead, as his thick organ went deep into her throat and he thrust in tandem with Nikolæ.

She felt his thickness press behind her, impossibly pushing against the tight entrance to her backside, stretching, burning as he entered her.

"Take my cock deep into your ass, slave. Feel me rend your tight hole, as I make you mine."

One by one, they each took her. Fast and hard, all three plunged deep into her. Their lewd, ferocious words rang in her head, making her shiver with excitement. She wanted more, wanted to feel their cocks ripping into her, forcing her to take all they demanded, as their come filled her. Like a drug, their possession swept through her, the sharp pain, the rich pleasure, the scent of their musky heat, and the sound of their animal growls, as though she were being consumed by their lust. She was pulled under by the inexorable power of the three Phralmulo.

Nikolæ plunged his cock so deep into the cunt of their slave he felt the end of her womb. Above him he saw Fane's cock sliding into the moist recesses of her mouth, and the thrust of Vasile's cock deep in her ass could be felt against his own as they took her without mercy.

The whipping had been the first step of the ritual, they had said the words the ritual demanded, and now they were poised to complete the second step.

At the same moment, all three came with echoing roars of satisfaction. Their slave impaled by them and then filled with their come.

Each pulled free and exchanged places with one another. Nikolæ took up his position behind her, Fane beneath, and Vasile took her face. A moment later, they all plunged into her again.

Fane's face showed the dark glory he felt as he slid into the tight depths of her cunt. The virgin's body was tight and their forceful penetration drew cries from her that sent a thrill of sadistic hunger through him. This time his words would be first.

"Your cunt belongs to your master. To take, to use, to fuck, forever."

Vasile took her mouth, forcing himself deep into her throat, holding her firm despite her struggles until she accepted and swallowed him.

"Your mouth belongs to your master. To take, to use, to fuck, forever."

Nikolæ then spread the delicate globes of her ass and stared with hunger at the tight ring. He watched as his cock speared her, split her cheeks, spreading her wide to take him deeper and deeper. Like a fist her anus clenched around him, though she pushed her hips back, as if hungry for more of him. He shoved in hard, completely, and rode her with powerful thrusts.

"Your ass belongs to your master. To take, to use, to fuck, forever."

The three of them shared her body, filling all of her openings with cock and come again.

Withdrawing from her body, each stared as their semen seeped from her body. She hadn't been able to swallow all that Vasile deposited in her throat, so it dribbled down her chin. Fane's explosion on top of Nikolæ's inside her cunt left his come seeping from between her legs, which he watched with wicked excitement as their shared juices leaked out of her ass. They had anointed her, and now were nearly through.

Exchanging places once again, it was Nikolæ's turn at her mouth. He enjoyed the sight of Vasile burying his large organ in her swollen cunt, the lips of her pussy puffy and pinkened and glistening with their come. Her eyes closed, she gasped at the size of him as he penetrated her, his movements made her whimper with their force. Fane's face bore the look of rabid hunger as he directed his cock into her ass, roaring as he fucked her.

"Accept my cock down your throat. Accept my fucking. Accept me as your master."

Vasile screamed.

"Accept my cock in your cunt. Accept my fucking. Accept me as your master."

Fane's yell echoed his.

"Accept my cock in your ass. Accept my fucking. Accept me as your master."

Nikolæ pulled Nerissa's hair, yanking her forward. He squeezed her jaw until her mouth opened and he pushed inside. The heat of her tongue against his cock and the tightening of her throat made him shove deep, her struggling to take all of his thickness fully until her face was buried against him, her hands kneading his thighs.

Her body jerked with their punishment. She groaned around him as he sank deep into her throat. He watched as their three cocks plunged in and withdrew, filling each hole again and again, watched their ritual fucking until the moment arrived.

They swelled within her. At the pinnacle of the ritual, each cock grew larger in preparation. Holes that had been stretched now were spread further, to the point of pain as they took her. Each began to ram harder, more forcefully, into her depths. It was a subjugation, ensuring her enslavement as each of them battered her and demanded she accept him.

When the next stage of transformation arose before them, their eyes met. Each of them erupted with a roar, pouring their come in heated streams inside her. Around his cock she swallowed as his essence filled her mouth. Vasile's fingers dug into her thighs as he strained upward to impale her as completely as he could upon his now more massive cock. Fane's expression declared his satisfaction as he buried himself deeper in her ass, his cock twitching as it emptied itself into her depths.

Moments ticked away as they filled her, then it was time. Nikolæ motioned to them to pull out.

They pulled her up onto her feet and surrounded her, throwing back their heads and their fangs growing to their full length. Together they pierced her, their razor-sharp teeth penetrating her neck, as they sucked her sweet blood.

Nerissa felt the lightning-hot pain as their teeth sunk into her neck. Was this the end? Would she slowly watch the world grow black as they drained her?

Instead, a pulsing began to grow in the depths of her body. The places where they'd taken her, emptied themselves in her, grew tight, and her legs quivered. The sensation of their mouths drawing her blood stretched like a cord throughout her body as her muscles shook.

Suddenly, like a river overflowing its banks in a violent storm, she was swept up in a powerful sensation. Her skin tingled, and her cunt and ass spasmed. Without warning she wailed, high and long. She was responding to the feeling of their power, their possession, shuddering, they held her as she cried out. At the moment she thought she would go mad, when she could no longer stand it, they pulled free from her and shot their come across her burning, tingling flesh. Like the heated strands of a whip, it sluiced over her ass, her breasts, and her flayed skin.

She wept and writhed beneath the dark power of her masters. The words she screamed came to her without thought.

"I am yours. I am yours to punish. I am yours to bleed. I am yours to fuck. I am your slave. Yours!"

"Mine!" Nikolæ yelled.

"Mine!" Fane screamed.

"Mine!" roared Vasile.

For a long moment their cries hung in the heated air, spreading with a tangible power. The power swelled and burst over them in a fiery wave that did no harm.

All was silent and still.

Nikolæ, Fane, and Vasile stared at their slave. The ritual had been completed. Their simultaneous climaxes, their mutual commands, their simultaneous drinking, and their slave's surrender had worked the magic. She had come with them, never before had the ritual succeeded.

She was, now and truly forever, theirs. Nikolæ suddenly understood what had mystified him for ages.

"This was meant to be. She is our one and only slave. It was not that our ritual did not work, it was never the right one."

His wonderment was tinged with pleasure, knowing that after searching for centuries, they had found their slave. They would never be parted from her. Their magic was all-powerful, it would not be denied, and her willing cries sealed it. She had accepted tumnimos. The vampires' embrace. They had forged the final element of their triumvirate, and were now invincible. No enemy could stop them, and the ancient powers of the Romany vampires belonged to them, only them. They would reign supreme over the hordes of lesser vampires and their slaves would kneel at their feet.

She would scream in glorious pain beneath their lashes, and take them into her body in their bed.

They now gathered about Nerissa and soothed her with harsh caresses until, at last, she slept the first sleep of her new existence.

She was theirs.

In pain.

In pleasure.

For all eternity.

Blood Games

By J. G. Faherty

I got the call as I was leaving Emory's Dance Emporium. I'd just finished a quick meal upstairs, with a nicely built dancer named Pablo, who'd done a fantastic job of filling me up in more ways than one.

"Hey, sexy," I answered.

The number that had popped up on the ID was Cassie's cell. Cassie was one of my two main girls: one of two human friends, my regular party companions, and my favorite sex partners. I was kind of surprised she was calling, I'd told her and Rain I wouldn't be stopping by that night because they needed a night off from being blood donors. However, I figured maybe she was just drunk and wanted a little before-bed sex talk. It wouldn't be the first time one of them had done that.

"Sofia." The minute Cassie said my name I could tell something was wrong. She was whispering, her voice was filled with fear, and it seemed like she might be crying.

"Where are you?" I asked. Not that it mattered, I'd go to the ends of the earth to find her. If my girls were in trouble nothing would stand in the way of helping them.

"Bleecker and Third," she said. "Hurry. He's—"

There was a metallic clatter, which I recognized as her phone hitting the ground. *"You've been a bad girl!"* Someone shouted, followed by the distinct sound of flesh striking flesh. Then the connection went dead. I tried calling back, but it went right to voice mail.

Bleecker and Third. Way downtown from where I was. Half an hour by cab, fifteen minutes if I ran the whole way, but I'd be exhausted when I got there.

I pictured Cassie's terrified face.

I started to run.

There are lots of advantages to being a vampire: I'm stronger than any three people you could throw at me, I can hypnotize humans into doing what I want, I don't pay taxes, and I have the most fan-fucking-tastic orgasms you can imagine. I give as well as I receive, too. Most nights, it makes for a wonderful life.

But I'm not a superhero, even vampires have their limitations.

I arrived at the corner of Bleecker and Third just after midnight. I'd gotten across town in fifteen minutes but, as I'd expected, my strength was spent. I felt weak and tired, what I needed was a few minutes to regain my strength. But I didn't have them. Cassie—and probably Rain, they went everywhere together—were in trouble and I had to find them.

I glanced in both directions but saw nothing like a club. Knowing my girls, they'd found some kind of underground after-hours joint that had no signs outside. I looked around again. All the buildings looked the same: run-down fake brownstones with rusted fire escapes and bars over the windows. Further down towards Sixth Avenue cars still patrolled the streets, late-night partiers heading home and early risers on their way to work. The odors of exhaust fumes, garbage, booze, and vomit mingled with a hundred different kinds of food to create an olfactory stew.

The acrid tang of pot reached me from nearby Washington Square Park. The heady mixture gave me an idea.

I stepped out into the middle of the intersection and breathed in deep, turning in a slow circle. Nothing . . . nothing . . . there! The faint hint of jasmine and roses, Cassie's scent. Instead of perfume, she preferred an essential oil that she ordered over the Internet. Forgetting about how tired I was and how late it was, I followed her scent to a non-descript building half a block down Bleecker. The steps led up to a small stoop, and also down to a second entrance set below the sidewalk. I chose the downward stairs—something told me that if Cassie and Rain were in trouble, it was because they'd gone into a some weirdo's basement in search of a party.

It turned out I was right.

The door was locked but that didn't deter me. Even in my rundown state, it took very little effort to twist the knob off and open the door with my shoulder. Immediately, the twin aromas of sex and blood assaulted me. My body responded automatically, hunger pains in my stomach warring with a different kind of need down below my waist. For vampires, sex and blood are linked together. The taste of blood triggers a full-body sensation more powerful than any human orgasm. Combined with sex, the result is so intense it's been known to kill. That's where the nasty reputation vampires have started from some Transylvanian dude fucking poor peasant girls to death. We never take more than a couple of mouthfuls of blood when we drink. I know I couldn't even do more if I tried. If a vampire kills, it's either from sex or rage.

Right then, I was definitely in the latter category.

I made my way down a narrow hallway lit by two cheap red bulbs. At the end of the hall, I came to a door. A deep breath told me that Cassie and Rain were somewhere on the other side. I could smell Rain's more subtle perfume entwined with all the other scents: perfumes, sperm, lube, leather. Underneath it all was a delicious tinge of blood. Nothing too strong, there'd been no murders committed. At least none that involved a lot of bleeding, but there was definitely fresh blood.

I opened the door, prepared to vent my rage on whoever had hurt my girls, and for the first time in decades, found myself so surprised I couldn't move.

The scene before me was nothing like I'd expected. Hell, it was like nothing I'd ever seen before. Cassie was spread-eagle on a bed, thick leather straps holding her wrists and ankles to the metal bedposts. I knew it was her despite the black leather hood that was zipped up over her face. I'd sucked and squeezed her tits so many times there was no way I wouldn't recognize them. On top of her was a fat, hairy man who pounded himself into her. All I saw of him was his woolly back. From the waist down he was covered in tight black latex. The leather mask muffled her words, but from what I could hear she was very close to coming.

Even stranger was the sight of Rain, her arms and head locked in a medieval stock, a rubber ball stuffed in her mouth, and her naked ass up in the air while a second man spanked her with a riding crop. Red welts, some of them sporting droplets of blood, criss-crossed her ass cheeks. Yet after each blow, the man, dressed head to toe in shiny black leather decorated with dozens of chrome zippers and chains asked her if she wanted more and Rain enthusiastically nodded her head.

I stood at the entrance to the room not knowing what to do. I was no stranger to fetish sex: I'd played the dom with past lovers, used my fair share of toys, even had a few leather outfits myself. But S&M was something totally new to me. For a vampire, trying to act submissive just doesn't work, we're too programmed for self-preservation to give over control, too strong to be shackled, and definitely not interested in anything that involves blood without feeding.

I'd never really been interested in S&M, I didn't enjoy pain when I was a breather, and I don't enjoy it now. I know some vamps take on work as slave masters, building harems of submissives so they can have a ready supply of food and sex around at all times. But that wasn't my thing. I also never got into dressing up like a schoolgirl or a nurse, getting peed on, or any other of the thousands of sadomasochistic activities people enjoyed.

I just liked being a down and dirty slut. In fact, it was only in the past year that I started fooling around with women, thanks to Cassie and Rain. They'd opened my eyes to all sorts of things, but it was still just sex. We might dress as tramps when we went out, fuck each other silly in a bathroom or start a blowjob contest at a sports bar, but it was still just simple sex, and now here were both my girls, practically hog-tied and turned into fuck toys.

Yet as I watched Cassie and Rain get pounded, tweaked, spanked and whipped, my body ignored my brain's protests that this was wrong and started to responded to the smells, sounds, and sights before me. I found myself getting wet, and before I knew what was happening, one of my hands slipped under the waistband of my jeans.

Stop! I told myself. *Remember why you're here. Cassie called you. She was in trouble. Afraid . . .*

She doesn't look like she's in trouble.

That caused me to do a mental double take. It was obvious both girls were enjoying the hell out of themselves. If they hadn't been muffled and gagged, their screams of pleasure probably would have woken up the whole street.

So why did Cassie call me?

Time to find out.

I forced my hand out of my pants, and strode forward to the middle of the room.

"What the fuck?" I asked, raising my voice above the other sounds.

Both men stopped what they were doing and turned towards me.

"Is that her?" asked the one with the full-body suit.

Rain nodded.

The fat one climbed off the bed, and both men

approached me. I saw that both of their pants had holes cut in the front to allow easy access.

That's when I realized I was in big trouble.

The two men weren't human, which was obvious from the bright red color and gigantic size of their cocks, and the extra set of balls hanging underneath. It also explained my own reaction to their little sex show.

They were incubi.

I'd never seen one but I'd heard of them: sexual demons whose presence charmed women into willing slaves and also made them incredibly horny. The demons would fuck the women, draining a little life force each time until their victims were listless and weak. According to other vampires I knew, we were immune to the pheromones the incubi gave off because we were stronger than humans.

Except tonight my strength was near gone, thanks to running at full speed for several miles. Even fueled by rage, I wouldn't be able to fight a protracted battle with a pair of demons. Still, I couldn't let these two bastards suck the life from my friends, so I did what I do best.

I attacked.

The two incubi held up their hands as if in surrender but I paid no attention. I grabbed the first one and lifted him up in the air, although not as far as I normally could have. Instead of throwing him across the room, I had to settle for tossing him onto the floor next to the bed where Cassie was bound.

I turned to the other one, the fat, hairy fellow, and felt my legs grow weak. I knew I couldn't manhandle him, it took all my energy just to make a fist.

What the hell was going on?

"Stay back," the incubus said, still motioning for me to stop. I paused, as much to regain some strength as to gauge what he had planned. Then I noticed a tingling in my hands, and a similar, and much more familiar sensation between my legs.

I was getting horny as hell.

No! I couldn't let it happen, weak or not. I couldn't allow the incubi's supernatural aphrodisiac to overwhelm me. I took a step back, trying to get out of their zone of influence, and remembered the knife I kept hidden in my boot for emergencies. I reached down, drew it out, and flicked open the six-inch blade. The fat demon's eyes grew wide and fearful.

Good.

The masked incubus on the floor got to his knees.

"Please, wait." He reached up and unzipped Cassie's mask, pulled it off, revealing Cassie's beautiful face.

She was smiling, her cheeks were flushed and covered in sweat, but she was *smiling*.

A low growl climbed out of my throat. These fuckers had my girls so entranced that they didn't even know they'd been raped! At that moment, I knew I was going to kill both men. I think they saw it in my eyes, because they hurriedly retreated to the far side of the room.

"Sophia, no. It's not what you think." Cassie tried to wave her hand at me but the leather strap prevented it.

"You don't know what's going on," I told her. "They're not human, they're using supernatural chemistry to make you think this is okay."

Cassie shook her head and smiled again.

"We know *exactly* what they are. That's why we called you, we want you to join in."

"What?" I couldn't believe my ears. It had to be the influence of the incubi. No way my girls would trick me, lie to me, just to get me into an S&M dungeon.

Would they?

I remembered the time they'd brought me to a party where the host had a sybian, which turned out to be a giant vibrator that you rode like a horse. That had been something I'd have never tried if they hadn't tricked me into it, but after they had I was one happy vampire.

Across the room, Rain nodded her agreement, as the fat incubus untied her ball gag so she could talk.

"It's true," she said, her voice raw from shouting. "We met them at the club tonight, and knew they were different right away. I guess 'cause we've spent so much time with you. The whole lust thing, they explained it to us. It's not really different than when you bite us, it's like you're hooked up to some kind of orgasm machine."

"But they're incubi," I said, my thoughts swirling in confused circles, not knowing whether to be angry or relieved. "They'll suck the life out of you."

"No, vampire," the masked one said. "No more than you would. A little bit here and there, is all. Is that so much to ask for the hours of pleasure we give in return?"

I felt shocked to my core. The incubi weren't rapists? They weren't evil monsters? Were they really only doing what came natural to them, feeding the only way they knew how, just like . . .

Oh, shit.

Just like vampires.

The moment I thought it, my anger disappeared. How were the incubi any different from my kind? From me? They attracted their prey by giving off pheromones—I attracted mine by dressing like a whore and hypnotizing away any fears. They used sex as a way of getting the energy they needed to survive, and I used it to heighten the pleasure of my feeding.

In a way, they were vampires of a different sort. Sex and blood vs. sex and life force.

"And you called me because . . .?" I glared at Rain and Cassie, who turned red but didn't hesitate in answering.

"We figured if sex between vampires and humans is so awesome, and sex between incubi and humans is so awesome, just imagine how fucking totally wild it would be if all three were together."

I had no response, as Cassie lifted her rump off the bed and jiggled her pussy in my direction so I could see how wet she was.

"What about all this?" I gestured my hand around the room, indicating their outlandish paraphernalia. From what I knew, incubi got off on sex, not torture.

"That's just our personal kink," the masked one said. "Plain old fucking got boring a hundred years ago."

"We told the girls about our playroom and they insisted on trying it out," the fat incubus added. "It's up to you if you want to enjoy our toys. We understand if the idea of a little pain . . . *frightens* you." He said this last with a challenging grin, knowing he had me.

My human companions had already participated in all sorts of kinky shenanigans, and they were not only fine, they were ready for more. What kind of vampire would I be if I couldn't keep up with them? A fucking pussy, that's what kind, and I wasn't a fucking pussy.

I looked between Cassie and Rain, who stared at me expectantly. I narrowed my eyes to let them know I was still pissed, but I did what they wanted me to do.

"Take me." I held my arms wide.

The incubi got up on their feet, with each step they took, my lust grew stronger and my willpower grew weaker. The fat one got to me first, his still-erect member poked my thigh, as he pulled me forward. Just that touch was enough to make my knees buckle. He caught me, and his partner, who still wore his latex mask, motioned to the other side of the room, where empty shackles hung from steel bars bolted to the wall. A matching pair was welded to the floor.

The idea of being chained made me nervous, but moments later I was chained to the wall, my arms out to the sides and my legs spread as far as they could go.

Despite my anxiety, my body continued to betray me. My pussy dripped from anticipation, and all I thought about was getting fucked. The masked man moved close to me, close enough so that I could see the throbbing of the black veins in his crimson dick. Ready for action and jutting straight out a good ten inches, he wagged it at me. A few drops of pre-come slipped out, dangling before dropping to the floor.

"You want this, bitch?" he asked.

I almost told him to shut up. No one called me bitch like that, but I held my anger in check and played along.

"Yes."

"Too bad."

What?

"You're gonna have to wait," he continued. "Your friends begged for it. They said you wouldn't, said you were a tough bitch. You don't look so tough now, though. I bet we can make you beg."

He let go of his cock and grabbed my shirt. In one swift motion, he tore it off, exposing my breasts. I haven't worn a bra since the seventies, or panties, either, which my captors found out to their delight when they cut my jeans off me.

I was naked and helpless and, God help me, loving it.

A realization hit me: the pheromones of the incubi were more than just a simple aphrodisiac. They affected the entire body chemistry, triggering massive amounts of hormones. It wasn't a trick, a drug slipped into a drink, or sweet talk and chocolates after a dinner of wine and oysters. It was the real thing. Whatever it was the demons gave off, it produced the same effect on the opposite sex as honest to goodness lust. The kind of lust at first sight you feel when you meet a gorgeous stranger in a bar, and just know you're going to fuck his or her brains out before the night is over. The kind of lust that comes from crazy make-up sex, or the first time you try a threesome, only a thousand times stronger.

Fat Man held something in his hand, at first I didn't recognize it, and then he held it up. It was a giant vibrator;

thick, black, and shaped like a real penis. My legs quivered at the sight of it. I wanted it in me: in my cunt, my ass, I didn't care.

"Do it," I whispered. "Please, do it." I had no voice. For the second time in my life, I knew what it was like to be helpless. Unlike the first time, I found myself loving it.

He did as I asked, the vibrator growled to life as he thrust it forward, pressing it against my clit. I came almost immediately, a sudden spasm that caught me by surprise and made me jerk back and forth while he pushed it harder and harder against me. A second orgasm followed the first, as he ran the vibrator up and down my pussy lips, my juices coating the head of it. I moaned and moved my hips forward, wishing my cunt was a mouth so I could grab the vibrating shaft and pull it inside me.

Fat Man did me one better. He slammed it into me, rough and hard, I cried out from both pleasure and pain. He slid it out before ramming it into me again. And again. He moved faster, harder and harder, robotically impaling me on the gigantic phallus. I bucked my hips to meet it, frustrated at my lack of control but enjoying every delicious thrust. The incubus breathed in deeply, I knew he was inhaling my energy. His free hand grabbed my nipple and twisted, sending me over the edge once more. As I came, I saw his eyes turn dark red. When I was done, he withdrew the vibrator and walked away. I closed my eyes, still recovering. I'd never felt anything like that without blood being involved.

Cassie and Rain had been right: vampire and incubus sex was a *very* potent combination.

I heard the vibrator come alive again, heard Cassie's muffled cries. I closed my eyes, wondering why he'd gone back to her, left me alone. Then I felt a warm, wet tongue between my legs.

I opened my eyes, found the masked incubus lapping my thighs and slit like a thirsty dog. His tongue tickled over my clit and my body came back to life, eager for more. No sooner did my juices start to flow then he slipped a finger inside me. Then another, then a third. I screamed and twisted as he fucked me with four of his fingers. He tried to get his entire fist inside me, but my muscles clenched too hard so he settled for rubbing his thumb over my clit.

After that, I lost all sense of time.

At one point Rain whipped me across the breasts with a cat-o'-nine-tails while the incubi took turns impaling me with their gigantic members. Someone slipped a leather mask over my head so that I couldn't see before I was locked in the wooden stock and paddled until even my vampire flesh stung. Then Rain strapped on a double-ended dildo and fucked me from behind, while one of the incubi shoved his cock in my mouth and fucked my face. When he came, it was like a river, filling my mouth and spilling over my lips in thick, dripping waterfalls that made me gag and spit despite the fact that it tasted much better than human sperm.

I was on the bed, no longer blindfolded, Rain was on my face and Cassie was between my legs soothing my burning pussy with her tongue. Above me Rain sucked one demon and the other banged Cassie. The demon above me let loose another voluminous load which even Rain, who prided herself on her blowjobs, couldn't handle. The hot drops splashed between my tits, which Cassie lapped off of me.

After an hour? Three hours? They all stopped without warning. I started to ask why but all of a sudden I felt it, too.

Sunrise.

Like vampires, incubi are creatures of the night and with the dawn comes weakness. In my case, it also brings a desire to sleep. For the incubi, whatever power they have to incite unending lust fades away. Two ordinary fellows with oversized dicks and extra balls lie exhausted on the bed, surrounded by two equally exhausted women and one totally spent vampire.

I tried to stand, but the best I was able to manage was to push myself into a sitting position. The satin sheets stuck to my ass and thighs, glued there by our mixed fluids. I peered down at myself, saw I was so covered in demon jizz that I looked like the after pictures from a bukkake porn shoot. Cassie and Rain were no better, and not for the first time I thanked the gods that it was impossible for supernatural beings to get pregnant or impregnate humans. We also can't catch or transmit any diseases. In a way, we make the perfect lovers. If you're into unbelievably intense, no-strings-attached sex.

Believe it or not, some people aren't.

Cassie stroked a hand through my hair. We both started laughing as her fingers got snagged in knots and clumps of sperm. Rain giggled and snuggled against my leg.

"So, are you still mad we called you?"

I wasn't, but I couldn't give them the satisfaction of being right. Again.

"We'll see," I told them. "After round two tomorrow night."

Next to me, one of the incubi groaned,

"Maybe inviting a vampire to join us wasn't such a good idea after all."

We all fell asleep laughing, but I knew he was right.

I have plans for my two new friends, I just hope they can keep up.

Honey Blind

By Angie Sargenti

It takes a lot of trust to be a submissive and a vampire. People still look at us with fear and prejudice. Sometimes it's hard to tell what their intentions are, even though we can read their minds. Only their most predominant thoughts come through, and if they can think of something else they can throw us off the trail.

Bruce and I have been living together for a while; he's nurtured and encouraged me to become more adventurous. He's a natural dom, with a wicked dark side that makes me love him deeply.

Tonight, he stripped me and put me in the corner as soon as he got home, now he's come to take me out of it.

"I've got something special planned," he told me, sitting on the edge of the bed. "Stick out your hands."

I smiled and did as he asked, giddy with excitement. He took a couple of silk scarves out of his pocket and tied them around my wrists, binding them together with a long enough tail so I could be secured to the brass headboard of our bed.

Once he'd tied me to the headboard, he tied my ankles to opposite corners of the footboard. When I'm completely tied down, my legs spread wide, he whips out the *piece de resistance*—a black leather blindfold.

"Oh, no, Bruce. Not the blindfold, please."

"Hush."

After he places the blindfold on me, I hear him moving around the room, can hear him light a lighter. I catch a whiff of a scented candle, as I hear him walking around again. Blind, all I can do is trace the sound of his movement.

What the hell's he doing now? I turn my head in the direction of the sound of him, but can't figure out what he's doing. It takes a lot of courage to lie there helpless and at his mercy, but I trust this man implicitly.

Still, though.

"Bruce . . ."

"Patience!"

I lie there without another word as he continues to move about. I feel him near me, can smell the blood pumping in his veins. My own blood sings with erotic tension, my fangs are out and I know it, but I try to keep them concealed.

There's a certain amount of trust on his part too, since it's possible for me to tear through the silk scarves and rip his throat out any time I feel like it.

"I need you, Bruce."

He chuckles softly in the dark, and strokes my hair.

"Don't worry," he tells me. "I'll get to you yet."

It's hard to just lie there, wondering what he's cooking

up. I feel absolutely helpless, my undefended pussy spread open vulgarly as I lie there quivering in anticipation.

He can do anything he wants to me and we both know it. He can take pictures of me to post on the Internet, or e-mail them to all his friends, whip my tits with a riding crop, or even drive a stake through my heart if that's what he fancies. Anything, I'm his for the taking.

Of course, Bruce would never *really* hurt me. I have to stop thinking like that. He's a good man, and only doing this to please me.

I feel him near me again: this time he kisses me, his tongue gliding into my mouth as his free hand strokes my wet, swollen cunt. He lets one of his fingers into me, and finger fucks me to heighten my desire, pulling away before I can really enjoy it.

I groan in frustration and struggle in my bonds. Bruce chuckles, but he doesn't move away. I can feel his weight on the edge of the bed. He dabs something cold and gooey on my clit and my breasts, coating each nipple thoroughly. I can smell it, and know what it is.

Honey.

Bruce's lips meet mine and I kiss him hungrily, straining against the scarves as he moves away. He strokes the wet, sticky place between my legs and brings his fingers to my lips. I lick the honey-sweetened essence of myself from his fingertips. Once his fingers are licked clean, he kisses me again.

"You make me want to fuck you so hard," he says.

"Then fuck me."

"Not yet."

The bed creaks as he gets up. I hear the door open, and someone comes in. Someone whose scent I don't recognize.

"Who's that?"

"A friend. He's going to fuck you senseless, and then you're going to clean him up."

I imagine his name is Warren and he's never fucked a vampire before. He goes both ways and he'd like to fuck Bruce, too, but he knows Bruce would never allow it.

"Here's the catch," Bruce continues. "I have my clicker and the tawse. We're going to see how many strokes it takes you to get him off, and by God, you'd better not lose count or I'll double it."

We've played this game often enough, but this is a new twist. Usually he makes me take a dildo to myself. This is the first time with a real live person.

But the thing is, I grew up shy, and those inclinations don't disappear just because you're a vampire. They lessen, but they never go away. So I have a hard time getting off with someone else watching. I know it sounds stupid, but that's my predicament.

I hear the other man kick off his shoes and drop his pants, then I feel the bed sag under his weight as he crawls in. He sucks my tit hard, then he kisses me. His breath is sweet like honey as he fingers me, spreading me more. I hope and fear that he'll fuck me soon, sealing my fate. I'll be punished and rewarded at the same time, but I can't worry about that now. My need is too great and I'm hungry, if this man's not careful, I'll bite his goddamned head off and suck him dry.

"Stop it," Bruce tells me, and it seems he's the mind-reader now. "Don't even think about it."

"Please," I say.

"Just wait."

The man in bed with me pinches my nipples with a little twist, eliciting a cry from me.

"Sweet little vampire whore."

"I'm not a whore," I tell him, unable to recognize his voice. "I've never been a whore."

"We'll see about that."

He climbs on top of me and thrusts his cock in to the hilt. I gasp. He's huge, bigger than Bruce, probably hand-picked for this very reason.

I turn my face away.

"You're getting me in trouble," I tell him. "I'm going to be punished."

He laughs.

"I know."

He starts fucking me, his dick pistoning into me over and over.

"Don't lose count," Bruce reminds me.

"Six," I sob. "Seven. Eight. Come, you bastard."

The tawse is harsh. Thick, stiff, and rough on the backside, tough like rawhide. Tied as I am on my back with my legs spread far apart, I have a bad feeling about how he'll use it.

"Eleven, motherfucker. Twelve."

Where's he going to beat me, I wonder?

"Thirteen. Fourteen. Oh, God, why don't you come?"

"Calm down. You're making me nervous, I thought

vampire girls were supposed to be tough."

"I *am* tough."

"Then why are you freaking out?"

"She always does that," says Bruce. "Settle down, Antoinette. Behave."

So I become stoic, stop counting aloud or showing my fear. But I can't keep my fangs retracted anymore as I hunger for this man's blood, this man who is going to get me whipped unmercifully.

I'm calm enough to read his mind though, and I know he wants me to bite him.

"Come on, babe. Do your little vampire thing."

"May I, Bruce?"

"Go for it. He's your master for now. You do what *he* wants."

"Go ahead," says my temporary master. "Drink."

Bruce will punish me harder for enjoying it, I'm sure. Like he does when I get off too fast with the dildo or vibe, but I just don't care anymore. I reach blindly with my tongue, and the man on top of me kindly puts his throat within licking distance.

It's hard without the use of my hands, and he really has to press his throat against my lips before I can manage it, but I sink my teeth in at last.

He cries out. The blood forms a strong bond between us, I can read his thoughts better than ever. Being bitten hurts more than he thought it would, but it also feels a whole lot better than he ever could've imagined. He pumps into me half-heartedly, more wrapped up in the new sensation than he is with the sex, so I curse him and he renews his assault on my pussy. A few quick jabs and he's coming, shuddering to a halt with a pleasurable groan.

I take one last hard pull from his jugular while he's busy throbbing come into me, and when he's done, he tells me to let go.

I put away my fangs like a good little submissive, but my mental fangs are harder to retract.

"You're sweet," I tell him, conscious of Bruce's presence. "Sweet like honey. And you fuck good, too."

"I eat pussy better."

"Prove it."

I don't have to see Bruce's face to know this hurts him. He's growing jealous and doubting the wisdom of this encounter, but the guy is already down untying my legs.

"Stop," Bruce tells him. "That isn't part of the deal."

Bruce comes up beside me and pretends to check my hands, but what he really wants to do is lean down and whisper in my ear.

"Think you're smart, don't you? Now you'll pay for that," he promises.

He lifts me with his strong hands and flips me over, draping me over the side of the bed. He puts the tawse up under my nose, rough side up so I can feel it as well as smell it as he spreads my feet, tying them to the bed frame far, far apart from each other. He drops a single chaste kiss on my bare bottom and moves away. I hear a squirting noise, something cold and gooey oozes down my ass crack.

He's going to whip me, finally, but he must be going to take me in the ass first. He massages some of the goo in for lubrication, working my hole with his finger, opening me up for what's in store. When he's done, he slaps me on the ass hard.

"There you go, slick."

He laughs, but it's not a laugh that bodes well for me. I didn't expect my one cruel jab to hurt his feelings so much; now I feel apologetic.

"Bruce, I—"

"Shut up."

I hear squishy sounds behind me. He's lubing up his dick, I guess, and he stuffs it in me without much care.

"Watch me fuck my sub in the ass before I give her to you."

Warren doesn't say anything, but I can feel him licking his lips in anticipation. He's always wanted to do something crazy like this, but never had the balls to initiate it. Neither had I when I was mortal, but now that I'm outside of society, it doesn't matter what I do.

No one will ever dare reproach me.

The tawse is still under my nose and I turn my head, loving the texture and the warm smell of the leather. I wish we could skip ahead to the whipping, because I need it badly. We haven't had time to play in over three long weeks and I'm aching for it.

"I've missed you," I tell Bruce. I know it makes him smile, because he kisses the back of my head and snakes an arm around to play with my clit.

"I want you to come for me," he tells me. "Relax. Take your time."

And I want to please him, oh, so badly. So I think about the tawse and the whipping I've yet to endure. About the honey all over the place, and how he'll probably make me stand in the corner all sticky for a while before he lets me take a shower. I forget about the other man, except for that enormous cock of his that'll probably split me in two, and wish they were both fucking me right now at the exact same time.

Bruce grabs up a big handful of my hair and jerks my head to the side. He sinks his poor, unsharpened mortal teeth into my shoulder and suddenly I'm soaring. I wriggle around on his finger as much as I can as he pumps into me harder, harder, the way he's going to beat me.

And just like that, I'm there and I bring Bruce with me. He grabs my hips and clamps down harder with his teeth, filling my ass with sperm and honey.

Bruce lays his head on my back, panting softly to catch his breath.

"We'll have to change the sheets later," he tells me.

"I know."

He rubs my ass where he smacked it earlier, and slides out of me. My shoulder's still throbbing from his bite, and he stands, sliding the tawse out from under my head.

The heavy leather bites and surprises. I feel an instant welt form on my ass cheek, then another and another. It isn't Warren spanking me, because I can read his mind and he's shocked by how hard Bruce is hitting me.

"Stick your ass up, Antoinette, and arch your back," Bruce tells me, and then he does the thing I feared most, snapping me in the crotch with the tawse.

I howl in pain, but after a moment, I'm surprised to feel my clit throb with need. Bruce rubs it with the handle of the tawse, and I'm so horny I almost want to cry. He waits until I try to get down on it, then he pulls it away and slaps my calves with it.

I can feel Warren champing at the bit. My mind's eye sees him slathering honey all over his shaft already, and if Bruce doesn't hand me over soon, he's going to start a fight.

"Let me have my turn," he says.

Bruce doesn't say a word, but I know he's surrendering the tawse, because the next stroke is nothing like a Bruce stroke.

"Harder," he tells the man. "Really welt her up so she feels it later."

And feel it I do. When the man's hips are slapping against me a few minutes later, my ass is positively sizzling and my hole feels stretched out and enormous. Bruce stands by, calling me names and cheering the man on, so I fake a few orgasms to make him jealous again.

Finally, he tells Warren to get the fuck out.

"I need some alone time with my woman."

When Warren is gone, Bruce cuts me loose and makes me suck the honey off his dick, before he puts me over his lap for a nice, intimate spanking that goes on forever. When he's done, he throws me down on the bed and fucks the shit out of me. After, we take a shower together, but he *still* doesn't take off the blindfold.

"The Revolution Begins With . . ."

By Dirk Taylor

It scares people when I tell them I'm the leader of the Sons of Adam. We're an extremist group who actively hunts vampires. Nothing special, just a bunch of gutter punk guys and tattoo shop kids who guard towns against bloodsuckers and other demonic forces, hardly the stuff of legends. Yet we are compared to the KKK and told we will be ashamed of our actions. There's a big debate in our country right now about whether or not vampires are living or dead. Take a guess at where I stand on that debate. A couple of my radically left friends believe vampires are the next great frontier for the American Civil Rights movement. I think they're full of shit.

I'm proud to be alive and believe as long as you have a heartbeat, you deserve the same rights as everyone else on this God-given planet. If that makes me a human supremacist, then so be it. Fuck, I'm a gay man, and I have an open mind to just about everyone. The vampires are feeding on humans, it's been recorded and posted on You Tube. Yet there are still Americans who want to give them civil rights. We incarcerate murderers, put down rampant animals, and occupy hostile societies. But vampires? Vampires have a get out of jail free card because we don't know how to define them. Are they divine or natural? Are they man or animal? I say the answer is simple: kill them before they kill us. That's the basic law of the jungle.

I wasn't always this extreme. Radicalism isn't just born, it's either inherited or nourished throughout time. Since we just discovered the actual existence of vampires less than a decade ago, my radicalism was grown. The seed of my hate comes from the worse kind of pain, heartache from a vampire I once loved. See, I gave it a shot. I saw vampires as humans, but I got burnt and nearly killed.

I first met the vampire I fell in love with after the campus massacre. This was four years ago when Barack Obama's reelection campaign was barely on the horizon, and we were still debating the ethics of vampirism. I was a sophomore at Florida State College in Tallahassee, and had recently come out to my parents. I was waving the liberal flag high and they were angry, heck they were more angry at the fact I was a liberal than I was gay.

Tallahassee turned out to be a good city to be away for school in. Filled with people who were blissfully ignorant of the demonic forces that ran them, it was also a town absent of discrimination, which wasn't so unusual given the student population. I could finally be myself as a gay man.

I still don't understand how in an age of social media, vampires took so long to be exposed. The vampires grew stronger, and our small southern city saw a rise in murders. Some weeks it felt like there was a murder happening each night. It wasn't until the campus massacre that local officials begin to take serious action and involve the federal government. A vampire had slaughtered a late-night class on campus. The bodies of the students were drained of blood and left mangled below their desks. The massacre shook me at my core. I was supposed to be at that class, but missed it because I had taken a nap.

To say cheating death gave me a new lease on life is an understatement. I hate it when people tell me someone was watching over me that night. No one was watching over me. It was dumb luck.

There was some good that came out of this tragedy. The massacre motivated me to do something more. To go beyond the conventions of my simple campus life, and embrace my destiny as a leader.

I had nightmares the nights following the massacre. I envisioned the handsome frat boy I sat next to in that class, Jeff, with his sandy brown hair and freckles decomposing in the ground. Would Jeff's body rise again? How did that work? Would he still have his freckles and slender build or would he be wild and untamed?

I knew I had to do something about the murders. A week after the massacre, I went hunting for the vampire that slaughtered my class. The police had no leads, and I figured I could take justice into my own hands and be a vigilante. I felt a universal sense of justice pulling me towards this mission. I can't explain it, I would later see this pull as a divine intervention. A message from God himself, it was my destiny to fight vampires.

There were local legends of a chupacabra that lived

in Herald's Barn off the interstate. For years things just turned up dead there. I thought that would be a good place to begin. Maybe I would be a martyr, after all my parents hated me and my classmates were being killed, why not me? I wanted to show this country that gay men believed in safety and the American way.

I didn't go in half-cocked, I had trained as a gymnast in high school and was extremely skilled with a bow and arrow from growing up on a ranch.

The vampire was waiting for me when I entered the barnyard. I would later find out he had visions of my arrival and that our encounter wasn't serendipitous. Perched on one of the beams supporting the barn, he was built: his body was a perfect V-shape. I had never seen anyone so beautifully dark and macabre. His hair was the color of the night sky, and his eyes looked like drops of honey. I was hard the second I saw him: my cock throbbed and I hated myself for that. His very being disgusted me so why was I attracted to him? Wasn't it necrophilia to be attracted to vampires?

The vampire jumped down onto the floor. He was tall, taller than anyone I had ever met, and looked stronger than Hercules. He crept towards me and I shot a warning arrow, I should have just gone for the kill. He could ravage me in seconds, but I wasn't going for the kill. I wanted to tussle with him, grab those prideful locks of hair, and shove his handsome face into the ground.

"You just lurk in the dark waiting for young blond-haired boys to come stick you?" I asked with a smirk. "How desperate are you?"

He didn't say anything. His arms flexed as he walked towards me, and all I could do was stare at his muscles. I shot another arrow and got him in the calf. He screamed, yanked out the arrow with his strong arms and charged at me head on. He wasn't attacking me out of hate or bloodlust, he went after me because he was an animal fighting for survival. I was slammed onto the haystack, my bow flying out of my hand. My wrists were pinned to the ground, squashed by his boot.

"A vampire killer?" he asked. "An amateur, no doubt. You're taking on the duty of guarding this town?"

I struggled to move, but I couldn't wiggle free. His ass was on my hard crotch, so my wiggling was more like dry humping. Something told me he wasn't going to kill me, there was curiosity in his eyes as he caressed my cheek.

"This life isn't for scared little frat boys," he snarled. "You should run away. Go on. I'll give you a head start."

"Yup. That's me. A scared little frat boy like the ones you murdered last night," I said, freeing my leg and kicking him in the groin. "Fuck off, dead boy."

He let out a moan as I quickly got on my feet. He grabbed his crotch and knelt down before me, helpless and in pain. I pulled out my knife. Was this my life going forward? Getting off on humiliating vampires? I grew harder at his humiliation. I wanted to prolong this as long as I could, this was no longer a quest for vengeance. It was a sadistic situation in which I wanted to unleash the dark desires of my soul.

"No," he said, his hands still cupping his balls. "I'm not

the one doing the killings. I haven't fed on human blood in two centuries," he said.

"I'm pretty sure that's a lie," I said. "Or you've been watching a whole lot of melodramatic vampire movies."

"Then why haven't you killed me yet?" he asked. "You're strong and precise. You could have killed me with the first shot but you didn't. You know I'm not the one you're searching for. You claim to be on a quest for justice, but what you're really looking for is pleasure."

I froze, never having felt so transparent in my life. That was enough time for him to knock me off my feet, I landed on my back again and he straddled me.

"I like to be on top, handsome," he said.

He felt so warm, vampires are supposed to be cold, but he was warm. He sniffed me, taking in my scent as he unbuttoned my shirt. His touch seemed familiar, felt natural. I felt my cock getting wet, I succumbed to him.

"Oh," he said, moving his hand down to my crotch. "I knew you weren't going to kill me, but you were gonna try to stab me." He got off me and knelt by my side. "I'm not the one causing the murders," he said. "You have a growing revolution in this town. I'm here to help. Do you believe me?"

"I do," I said.

He looked more like a fallen human than a supernatural being, he was not pale nor did fangs protrude from his mouth. In fact, his fangs seemed as if they were tucked away, unable to reveal their true nature.

"What's your name?" I asked.

"Warren," he said.

"I'm Nicholas."

"I know," Warren said, sizing me up. "I saw you coming."

"What do you mean you saw me?"

"I see the future," he replied.

"How?"

"God sends me visions," he replied. "I knew you would be here."

"Do other vampires see the future?"

"Are all humans prophets?" he retaliated. "Vampires are God's next chosen people. God wants us all united, he's the divine hand making a revolution happen."

I had never given much thought about God, it never occurred to me that in a world of vampires the existence of God was possible. Up until now, I had considered myself agnostic. I reasoned if God existed, he operated at a level higher than any religious group can fathom. But when I founded the Sons of Adam, I believed that God touched down upon humanity in times of great peril. That the night I met Warren in the barnyard was the beginning of God's descent into the modern world.

"So why aren't you evil?" I joked. "Are you neutered?"

"Everything exists on a spectrum," Warren said. "Just because I'm a vampire doesn't mean I'm evil."

"Well your fellow vampires are slaughtering and murdering innocent people," I replied. "Don't you think that boils down to evil?"

"You don't call a shark that attacks evil, right?" he asked. "Sometimes there is a natural order to things. A hierarchy. It doesn't make it moral by your standards, it's just the laws of the jungle."

I knew he was trying to reason with me, to find some kind of middle ground so I didn't attack him again. I wouldn't attack him, I kept getting harder looking at him.

"What's happening to Tallahassee?" I asked. "What's this revolution?"

"The vampire revolution," he said. "It's beginning here. A vampire calling himself X is leading it. Vampires from all over the world are going to start campaigning for equality. It's drawing the good and bad of our society to this small Florida town."

"Sharks don't campaign for equal rights," I said. "So much for your law of the jungle theory."

Warren laughed.

"Well, we're different and have a higher understanding of the world, we are trying to implement a no feed on humans mandate."

"That's been attempted before," I sarcastically replied. "Isn't there a TV show about that?"

"I've seen the future. I've seen vampires and humans coexisting. It'll take years but it will happen."

"So you're St. Paul?" I teased. "A prophet blinded by the light of God?"

"What about you, Nicholas?" he asked. "When the revolution comes what kind of person will you be?"

I sat up and brushed the dirt off my hair, unable to answer that question, and we began to talk about our lives. How I had just come out and was an English major. I asked him who he was? He told me he was born before the

Louisiana Purchase, that he had been sipping Earl Gray tea when the allies invaded Normandy during World War II.

"That's when I had my first vision," he said. "On D-Day, I saw the Allies winning."

His life was so much bigger than mine, so much more defined. Warren was a missing piece in the personality I was still constructing, I could easily speak to him. He wasn't some filthy animal who needed to be put down, but a person with a backstory.

"You feel the connection we have?" he asked me, wrapping his arm around me. "It's like a magnetic pull."

"I can," I whispered. "Is this a trick?"

"No." He leaned in to kiss me. "I'm not a magician or witch."

We kissed and there was a spark so intense it felt like the whole universe had culminated to this moment. Were we the first vampire/human couple? It was surreal to think the one thing I was hunting had become the object of my affection. I believed Warren when he said he wasn't using sorcery or any kind of vampire voodoo on me. He lied about other things, but not about that. The feelings I had for him are still with me.

On the floor, I kissed his calf I had shot and made my way down to his boot. I removed the boot slowly, unraveling the laces like a gift and massaged his foot.

"Have you always had a foot fetish, love?" he asked. "That seems so pedestrian and boring."

I didn't remember having a foot fetish, but Warren awakened so much passion in me. Maybe I did and never noticed. I removed his black sock, stuck his toes in my mouth and bit down hard. He yelped.

Warren unbuckled his pants. He wasn't wearing underwear so when he unzipped his pants, his dick sprung out in the open. His cock was a good size, at least eight inches. It was my first time seeing an uncircumcised penis. Fuck, it was my first time seeing a penis that wasn't mine. I tried to make a joke of it so I didn't look inexperienced. But who was I kidding? Of course he could smell my inexperience, he had been around for centuries and I was just one of the many people he would sleep with.

"Victorian cock?" I joked nervously, sliding my blue briefs to my ankles.

He didn't react to my words; he just stroked my cock before he twirled it around in his mouth. His mouth was warm, as if all the lives he had ever lived were in there. He sucked my cock with skill, I had gotten a blowjob from a girl once, but it didn't compare. Something about a man's lips lubricated the cock better.

Warren began stroking himself. At that point he wasn't just sucking my cock, he was being mouth fucked by it. I wanted to pound that beautiful face of his. I had no idea why his pride turned me on, but I wanted to make sure I robbed him of it.

I slammed the back of his head onto the floor. I posed myself as if I were doing a push-up to really pound his mouth. He moaned as he stroked himself until he squirmed in bliss. He came first. I felt his come hit my bare ass. I came in his mouth a few seconds later, gripping his hair as I came. Warren continued to suck even after I was done, to make sure he had all of me.

As we lay on the ground of the barnyard, I told him, "I've never been with a man before."

Warren didn't reply, instead he grabbed my hand and held it to his heart. There was no beat, no rhythm, or life in his chest. What he lacked in a heartbeat he made up for with his eyes, his beautiful golden eyes. I saw proof of life in them, Warren had a soul.

He kissed my forehead, stood up, and slipped his pants back on while shaking hay out of his hair. Seeing him dress himself gave me a second wind, I began stroking myself.

"Where do you think you're going, handsome?" I asked. "I'm ready for round two."

Warren flashed me a mischievous smile. His teeth were so white I couldn't even make out where his fangs rested in his mouth. Maybe vampires weren't that different from us after all. I envisioned a life with Warren: of moving in together, adopting a stray dog, and introducing him to my parents. It could work because he looked so normal and human.

"Cute," he said, putting on his shirt. "But I have to get going. The sun is going to rise in a bit and I have some stuff to take care of."

"What about the vampire that killed my friends?" I asked.

"He was a rogue vampire," Warren said, matter of fact. "And X already dealt with him."

"I don't get to know who killed my friends?" I asked.

"It's been taken care of, Nicholas."

Warren walked towards the exit. I was frustrated, all my emotions hit me at once. I felt used, and I wasn't even getting the revenge I had sought. I had seen this mission as a call from the universe and yet here I was, sitting butt naked in a barnyard with nothing to show for my night. That is when it hit me. I had let a moment of passion blind-side me, vampires were the enemy. I would never have a life with Warren, society would never accept an interspecies gay couple. I had fought so much for gay rights already, and then I would have to add vampire rights to my agenda? I couldn't. It was better that Warren walked away, and we forgot about this night.

I put on my briefs and stood up. He was right: the sun hadn't risen yet, we had a good hour before it did. Warren stood at the door staring at me. I kept rationalizing why it wouldn't work between us, but the truth is I was coping with the fear that he was leaving so quickly because I didn't satisfy him properly.

Then to my surprise, Warren's mouth went agape. Was he upset about leaving? He began to shout. Was he angry with me? No. It wasn't a shout. It was a warning.

"Behind you," I heard him scream before I went unconscious.

I woke up with my hands tied to a chair in my blue briefs. It took me a few seconds to remember I was in the barn off the interstate. I could still smell freshly cut hay but the room I was in was different. I tried to take a deep breath but there was something in my mouth, something flavorless that broke apart each time I moved my tongue. Was it hay? I looked around the room in panic, trying to absorb as many details as I could, but I had a hard time focusing. My vision was cloudy but my hearing was coming back. Something . . . someone hit me. Warren had tried to warn me about something.

"So this is the boy?" I heard a man's voice question. "He's going to lead humanity against us?"

I turned to find a vampire staring right at me. I was able to focus now, and saw the wrinkles on his face like the lines of a highway on a map. He was an older vampire with thin salt-and-pepper hair. He had a giant scar in the shape of an X directly on his forehead.

"Good job, Warren," X said. "You delivered the boy right to me. Too bad you also double-crossed me."

Warren? Where was Warren? I quickly looked away from X and saw him, wrapped head to toe in twine in the chair next to me. His beautiful face was swollen, and blood dripped from his nose down his bare chest. He was naked and there was something different about him. He looked weird. I kept squinting my eyes until I realized his hair was lopsided, half of his hair had been sheared. What was in my mouth wasn't hay from the barn—it was Warren's dark hair.

I feverishly spit out his locks, the strands landed on my crotch as X laughed out loud.

"So Mister Nicholas Mendel," X said. "Look at you. You're a lot more lanky than what Warren described."

The room we were in had one small window, which was located all the way up by the door. It was light outside, the sun had finally risen and I took that as a sign that there was still hope I would get out of this alive.

"Oh that's right you don't know," X said to me. "Warren

told us about you. But did he tell you that you'd be the face of our oppression?"

"What do you mean?" I mustered out some of Warren's hair still in my mouth.

"That you're the son of a bitch who will enslave us," X said. "You'll champion America against us, you bigot fuck. We'll be second-class citizens because of you."

I couldn't understand what he was talking about, nor would I have ever guessed that I would lead a movement against a species. I was being punished for a sin I hadn't committed. Warren was right, vampires do operate on a different moral code.

"All of this was preordained," X continued. "I had an assassin kill those students to motivate you. While you were out hunting, Warren would meet up with you, gain your trust and bring you to me. Boom! Easy plan, and with you dead, generations of vampires and humans can coexist."

"There's good in him," Warren mumbled. "I saw it when he kissed me."

Warren then tried to make eye contact with me.

"That's why I had to leave . . . before he arrived . . ."

"What does he mean?" I wheezed, looking at Warren. "You were an assassin? You were gonna sacrifice me?"

X kicked Warren's chair over before he could answer so I couldn't see Warren's face anymore, only his helpless feet in the air.

"Yes, he was supposed to deliver you to me. But Warren just had to go screw the enemy, huh?" X ranted. "Well not exactly screw . . . you want to know what else he's keeping from you? Our little Warren here is a virgin. That's why he has those visions. He has never fucked another person in his life, he's our very own virgin vampire."

X pulled out a knife and held it to Warren's neck.

"An eye for an eye right? You double-crossed me and now I'll kill you."

I turned my head away, I didn't want to see Warren get murdered. Suddenly a burst of white light came from the small window and engulfed the room. I heard a voice shout out to me, "Deliver the world from evil, my son."

I opened my eyes to see who was talking, but the room looked exactly the same. Except one thing was different, I felt empowered. God had showered me with his holy light, and I had to cleanse the world of these vermin. I yanked the rope that bound my hands and jumped up with renewed purpose.

The light must have been only in my head because when I got onto my feet, X still had the knife on Warren's throat. I charged at X, grabbed him by the collar and wrestled him to the ground. But he was strong, and quickly overpowered me.

"You're not going to win," he said, punching my face. "We have God on our side."

My head became heavy and I could barely focus. This man wasn't a leader, he was a lunatic. But still . . . this lunatic was winning. Maybe the light wasn't a divine intervention, maybe this was how I was going to die and I was only kidding myself that I was a warrior of God.

Then Warren came up from behind him like an animal and got X in a headlock. Warren's fangs were pronounced, protruding from his mouth and it made his face demonic. He no longer looked human.

Warren dragged X out of the office and towards the exit of the barn. He made his way to the large wooden door and pushed it open with his leg.

I knew what he was going to do, it was the only penance Warren could offer. He would now have blood on his hands for killing X. I wanted to stop him—to tell him he didn't need to do this, but I felt desecrated.

"I'm sorry," Warren mouthed to me as he threw X into the sunlight.

There was a lot of screaming. X tried to open the door, but I held it shut. I heard his nails claw on the wood as he begged for us to open the door. In the end, there was nothing left of his revolution but a smoking skeleton and a small town full of wayward vampires.

Warren was weakly lying on the hay, holding his uncircumcised cock as he cried. His eyes no longer illuminated with a golden tone, they were glazed and void of life. Warren had been alive for over two centuries, but this was the first time he had ever been humiliated and defeated. It wasn't a role that suited him. As he wheezed I couldn't help but feel bad for him, he truly had believed in X's vision. He wanted a peaceful coexistence.

"I'm sorry," he cried as I approached him. "I couldn't foresee how I would feel about you."

"Is it true," I asked. "About the visions? You have them because you're a virgin?"

"I don't know," he sniffled. "It's one theory."

I stood over Warren like a dominatrix does over his sex slave. The sight of him defeated got me hard, but I was so angry. I wanted to kick the fallen revolutionist in the gut and drag him out to the sun. However, I could not bring myself to do that.

"I will never forgive you; my friends are dead 'cause of you. You used and exploited me."

"I know," he said. "I'm so sorry."

I sat down next to him, and ran my fingers through my hair. In the corner of the barn was my bow and arrow. I had forgotten about them. They seemed so important at the start of this mission, but now they felt inconsequential. I found out that I was the vampire community's antichrist, after I had fallen in love with one of their own. Love was a greater weapon, and it stung harder than any arrow I could shoot. I knew as I saw Warren wiping his tears that he too felt the sting and that both our hands were now dirty.

"Fuck me," Warren said.

"Uh, excuse me?' I asked. "I don't think this is . . ."

"You don't get it," Warren replied. "I want you to fuck me to take away my visions."

"I'm not going . . ." I began to say but then stopped myself, looking at Warren, and leaned in for a kiss.

The visions were all that Warren had left, this would be the ultimate form of humiliation—robbing him of everything he had. I spread his arms wide open and kissed his nipple, grabbed a hold of Warren's slender waist and shoved my cock into his ass. It was easy to get it in, we were both virgins but we had a natural chemistry. I still wonder till this day if I'll ever find that kind of magic with somebody else.

"Oh my God," he said. "I feel complete."

As I look back, I acknowledge the fact that Warren wanted to be dominated. He wanted to be free of the revolution and of the visions. Maybe that was his ultimate endgame, I don't know.

Warren wrapped his legs around me and brought me in deeper. I violently thrusted my cock into his ass as he grabbed his cock, as he jerked himself while I fucked him. He moaned out loud, begging for me to go harder. He wanted me to fuck his penance out of him.

"Come for me," I said squeezing his beautiful mouth. "I want you to come!"

Warren came all over himself, letting out a large sigh. I came a few minutes after. I had never come like that before, my penis felt like a ramped water hose spraying all over his ass.

We fell asleep after that, and woke up in the late afternoon as the sun was setting. It was a fitting end to our story.

"Do you feel different?" I asked as I reached for my blue briefs.

"I don't know," he said. "The visions come at their own will, I won't know until I don't get them anymore."

As I stood up, I heard police sirens outside. I hadn't called the police, but it didn't surprise me they showed up.

"You should go," I said. "Run. Get out of town. I never want to see you again."

I grabbed Warren by the remaining locks of hair he had, and escorted him to the backdoor. I didn't even let him get dressed.

"Go, get away, you filth," I said, tossing him out stark naked into the night.

I stood at the doorway for a few moments, watching Warren trip over himself as he ran into the woods. I hadn't noticed how perfectly sculpted his ass looked before. It bounced with such pride as he made his way through the field. Warren was liberated. Part of me was happy he had a fresh beginning, but it was a cold Florida night and I worried he would freeze in the woods.

"Jesus Christ, son." An officer asked, approaching me. "What the heck happened here?"

I pointed to Warren as he disappeared into the pine trees.

"That was vampire responsible for the campus massacre," I said.

I knew the coming storm was about to make landfall, that other vampires would come after me for revenge. The Sons of Adam was born that night, not out of prejudice or some dooming prophecy, but out of heartache.

The Manor

By Nicole Wilder

It was a beautiful day when I woke up, and I couldn't help thinking about what was going on in the house. I had heard whispers, and I knew something had been stirring for a little while but I wasn't quite sure what. I'd caught Master Justin whispering to Kyle many times. Each time I asked Master what was going on, he gave me that look and that look meant not to ask.

Master Justin took care of me, but there were also times when he loaned me to his friend, Kyle. Though I loved Master Justin, I was very attracted to Kyle, unnaturally so. He was my longhaired, motorcycle-riding guy. I was never sure what Kyle would have up his sleeve. He was always exciting, but he scared me.

"What's going on?" I asked Master Justin. I knew that I shouldn't come right out and ask him anything, but I couldn't help myself but ask.

"Aren't you the curious little one?" he answered, taking me into his arms and looking down at me. I loved the things he said to me, the way he made me feel safe, and his strength. He was firm, powerful, and what he said was law. I was drawn to everything about him, and would have done anything for him.

"Yes, Master Justin, I know it must be something concerning me by the look in your eyes," I said, pressing myself against him and smiling the way he liked me to.

"Today is Halloween, my dear," he said. "We want to surprise you."

Kyle was in the room. There was a hardness about him, but there was a softness too. Master Justin often let me or ordered me to be with Kyle, which was the best. He liked to watch, and sometimes he joined us.

"Surprise me?" I asked, looking between the two of them, feeling frightened. The combination of Halloween and Master Justin and Kyle's sense of humor made me nervous about what they had in mind.

"We would like to show you something. It's a manor that you have not seen. It's been hidden for a long time, and we think this is the best time to show you," Kyle said with a strange, semi-evil grin.

"What kind of manor, and why is Halloween the best time?" I asked suspiciously. The smirks on both their faces told me there was more to this than just some manor they wanted to show me. I had a bad feeling inside, I didn't want to be any part of whatever it was they were cooking up.

"You will see," Master Justin said. "Go and get into your slave gown."

I knew I was in for something odd, but I did as I was told. Moments later, I emerged with my pink slave dress on. It was low cut and only held on by one spaghetti strap. The bottom was cut high on the hip, and came down to the tops of my thighs. As soon as I came into the living room, I dropped to my knees before Master Justin and Kyle, who both eyed me. I was in perfect form with my back straight, my thighs spread wide for their pleasure.

"You are beautiful, my darling." Master Justin pulled me up into his arms. "No one has ever given me more pleasure than you do." The smile on my face must have brightened the room because he said, "Let's go, Sunshine."

It was nearly dark out. I often wondered why he never went out in the day. One time he told me he had a condition where the sun bothered him, and that I was the only sunshine he needed anyway.

I was sitting in the middle of the car with both wonderful men on either side of me. For a little while, I cuddled with Kyle: kissing his neck, biting his ear, and running my hands along his body. Then I did the same to Master Justin, which brought smiles to both men's faces. I sat with my legs spread so that they could both play with my soft shaven pussy, which was hopelessly wet. Kyle buried his fingers deep inside me, while Master Justin's fingertips ran over my thighs and legs. It was such an awesome feeling, I thrust my hips in response to Kyle's fingers, heard my wetness as I did so. I quivered, I was so close to orgasm, but Kyle squeezed my pussy lips to stop me from coming.

"Not yet, little one," he said.

My breathing raced like a heartbeat. I wanted and needed to come, but he wouldn't let me. It was so cruel and frustrating, yet so exciting.

By the time we arrived at Dungeon Manor, it was pitch black outside. There was an eerie glow around the entire castle, which is just what it was, a castle. In the next lot was a cemetery with old, dead trees, and a howling wolf inside the gate. The manor was huge with big pillars at the top. Bats flew around the lights at the top. It looked like a scene out of a horror movie or from *The Munsters*. I clung to Master Justin, my heart pounding so loudly in my chest that I thought I was going to be sick.

"What is this place?" I asked in sheer terror. I turned to Kyle begging him with my eyes not to make me go inside. I just felt whatever it was inside was not good. I don't know why I thought Master Justin or Kyle would have pity on me and not make me go in. They had been planning on this for a while, I was sure. Neither of them was going to drive me back home, but I felt I had to try.

"This is the surprise for you, my little one." Master Justin smiled.

"You will love it," Kyle said, with the same smile.

"Please don't make me go in there," I begged Master Justin. "There is something bad in there, I can feel it."

"Trust us," Kyle said. I had no real reason not to trust them, they had never hurt me, though they had made me often wonder . . . this was definitely one of those times.

They parked the car, and Kyle nearly had to pull me out of it.

"You have no choice, little one. You have to go in there, because it is my wish that you do so," Master Justin said.

"But, Master, please. I know you wish it, and I never

want to do anything to disappoint you, but I just don't have a good feeling," I whined.

"Stop that, you will do as I say," he said forcefully, letting me know I had no choice in the matter. He looked directly into my eyes, and for a moment I fell into something of a trance. Just the look he gave me made me do what he wanted me to do.

"Yes, Master Justin. Forgive me." I quivered.

As we walked up to the castle, I thought I saw shadows inside the windows. When I pointed them out to Master Justin and Kyle, they just laughed at me. I had never seen this side of either of them before, and didn't know why they were doing this to me. I understood it was Halloween and things should be frightening, but this was beyond frightening to me. I couldn't pin my feelings down, yet they were overwhelming. Tears ran down my cheeks, and I clung to the two strong men by my side, even though it was them who put me into this situation. Entering the castle made me quiver even more: cobwebs rested on everything, bats clung to the walls and lizards crawled all over. Two benches on either side of the room we were in invited someone to be chained to them. There were shackles and whips on the walls, and machines that I had no idea what they were used for. Spooky sounds and music poured from the walls, and I wanted to flee from this place of terror.

"What the hell is this?" I asked, horrified. "I don't want to be here, let me go! Take me back!" I begged, kneeling on the floor before Master Justin.

"Did you not say you trusted us?" he asked.

"Yes, Master Justin, I do, but this place is not right. I have never seen this side of you and Kyle before . . . please take me home."

Tears ran down my cheeks, and I could barely breathe. I didn't understand, nor did I want to, and I knew if this did not turn out to be a joyous thing to happen to me it would alter the way I thought about and loved them both.

"Kyle," Master Justin said. "Now."

Kyle came over and took off my slave gown, leaving me naked and open for them. He took me over to the wall and chained me to it, my arms above my head. He took a whip with a thick handle and many colorful tails from where it was on the wall and caressed me with it. The tails ran over my breasts, stomach, thighs, before he spread my legs wide and ran it over my pussy. I felt my clit twitch. *No, not here*, I wanted to say. *Please don't do this here.* But I didn't say it, I let him, though it was not a choice. He kept it up until I squirmed uncontrollably, then he turned the whip around and pressed the end of the handle to my pussy. I moved over against it even though I tried not to. He wiggled it against my clit, which really felt good and for a minute I forgot where I was. Suddenly he shoved the handle inside my pussy, moving it in and out of me. I fucked the handle for him.

Master Justin undressed and sat on one of the benches, watching what Kyle was doing to me. He seemed content just to watch, his hard cock telling me he approved of what was going on.

"You like it?" Kyle asked me, seeming utterly excited as well.

"Yes, Kyle, but please, sir, not here."

Though at that point it wasn't as big of a concern. I ached inside, needing and wanting more. I wanted to beg him to make me come, I just didn't want it with lizards and bats around.

"Yes, here." Kyle removed the handle from my pussy, unchained me from the wall, and tied me to the rack. I was spread wide open, helpless and wondering what would be in store for me. A tiny lizard crawled over me. I screamed, and Master Justin laughed.

"He won't hurt you. Let his tiny body excite you," he said.

I wouldn't have admitted it to him, but the ticklish nature of the creature roaming over my body was a bit exciting.

Kyle undressed. I stared, aching to please him and for him to please me. My clit was hard and needed release. I looked at Master Justin as he did nothing but stare at my body. His cock was hard and every so often, I saw him tickle his balls and stroke his cock a few times as he watched.

"Please let me pleasure you, Kyle. Please," I begged.

"No, you may not. Do you see this hard cock of mine?" I stared at him, his eyes captivating, mesmerizing, putting me into a trance. He took his cock into his hand and stroked it, I wanted it.

"Yes, Kyle."

He knew it was torture for me not to be able to touch him, and he loved to torture me. Yet I also loved watching him pleasure himself, it was a beautiful turn on. Every so often he dipped his cock into my mouth, let me suck him for a moment, and then back out again.

"Kyle, please let me pleasure you."

"Just watch," he told me as he played with his balls. He stood over me, moving his hand along the staff between his legs. "I'm going to come," he told me moments before his creamy thick come lurched from his body all over my breasts, tummy, and pussy. I ached inside to be able to come as he did, I wanted him so much.

"Please help me to come too, Kyle. Release me," I begged.

"Tell me it isn't so bad here," he requested, standing before me with his hard cock. "Tell me you want us no matter what we are."

"What do you mean what you are?"

"Just say it, or I won't release you," he said, his eyes catching mine again, making me do as he wanted.

"It isn't so bad here. I want you and Master Justin no matter what," I lied. I would have done anything at that point to be able to come.

Kyle slapped the whip over my pussy. I jumped, though it didn't hurt, just stung a bit. It actually made me more excited. He did it again before he began to lick all the way down my body: my breasts, belly button, and my pussy. When he licked my aching wet clit, I nearly came on contact. The end of the whip again pressed against the opening to the deep center of my wetness, I shifted to make him fuck me hard with it. All I wanted was to come, the manor had become less intimidating to me. Kyle sucked my clit and fucked the depth of me as hard as he could, I shivered as the strongest orgasm I had ever had escaped my body. Kyle removed the handle of the whip from my cunt and entered me with his cock.

"Yes, Kyle. Fuck me hard. Come inside of me."

As he slid inside, he grinned, then showed his canines. He brought his two sharp, pointed teeth down, biting my neck. I didn't care, I'd be anything he wanted. I wanted him, ached him for him. I would be theirs forever and ever, even as a vampire.

Kyle slid in and out of me, I felt him begin to stiffen, as my own orgasm approached quickly. I had more sensation in my body than I ever had in my life, nothing else mattered.

"Yes, Kyle, come in me," I yelled.

He slammed into me, moaning. I felt the warmth of his come flow deep inside me, making me go over the edge and come with him. He pinched my hard nipples one at a time, which felt so good.

When he let me go from the rack, I jumped down and went straight to Master Justin, who was now masterfully stroking his cock.

"Are you okay with us?" Master Justin asked.

"Yes, Master, I am yours forever."

Master Justin bared his own fangs, and I tilted the other side of my neck for him. "Bite me, Master."

His fangs came down onto my neck, and I knew I should have felt pain yet I didn't. I only felt pleasure, needing more of him than ever before.

"I need you, little one. Please me," he said. I climbed onto the bench and straddled him, slipping his cock inside me. I thrust my breasts upward, and he took them into his hands. "Yes, my lovely one, fuck me. Ride me hard."

I did as he told me to, riding him hard and fast, and reaching down to play with my clit. "Squeeze your pussy muscles hard. I'm coming, squeeze me," he moaned as his come burst inside me. As soon as the warmth hit my inner self, I came again. It never felt that strong, that good before. My body quivering, I screeched as I came. I barely noticed anything around me as I clung to Master Justin and continued to squeeze my pussy muscles around his hard shaft. Each time I squeezed my muscles, it was as if I was coming again.

"Oh, that's it, keep coming," Master Justin moaned. "You are so good."

I looked over at Kyle who was watching now as Master Justin had. He also loved to watch, and I loved being watched.

It took awhile to calm myself, to be able move from Master's lap. My nipples were so hard and my pussy was still so wet, and I believed that the creepy manor increased my excitement.

They knew that I would love being with them in the present world or the hereafter. It didn't matter, they knew that. I could tell by the smiles on their faces.

"This is good, isn't it?" Master Justin asked as he wrapped his arms around me.

"Oh, yes, Master."

I meant it. They had proven to me again that I could trust them to please me, as long as I did the same for them.

Love Bites in the Sin Room

By Kaysee Renee Robichaud

When Jenna first saw the tall, beautiful man with the golden mane, he was rushing across the National Coney Island dining room. He looked so grumpy and gorgeous at the same time, she just could not help herself—she stuck out her foot and tripped him.

His shin caught her ankle, his face transformed into a comical mask, and he fell forward. He hit the floor, rolled like a gymnast and then came up like a seasoned martial artist.

Jenna knew all about recovery. She had taken enough Kuk Sool Won to attain her black belt, after all. However, this guy moved with such grace, such poise, such determination, she was amazed.

And rather turned on too, despite herself.

People did not act like super-duper action heroes in the National. No way, nuh-uh. And yet there he was, hauling ass toward the front door and into the night.

"I can't believe you, Jenna!"

Her friend Eileen laughed despite herself, though the

night had been somewhat somber. Eileen's hubby was in hospital, and Eileen was supposed to be resting up for work tomorrow. Eileen did medical billing for the company where Jenna had worked while cruising through college. Now they were dinner pals—or midnight snack pals, in tonight's case.

Jenna played cool.

"It was just a hilarious accident."

The National was pretty dead, which was how Jenna liked it. The other patrons included a couple in the far corner sharing fries and lovey-dovey glances and five college kids plotting world domination in the rear. *If this place got any deader,* Jenna thought, *it'd trade places with the cemetery across the street.*

"Holy crap," Eileen said. Her gaze was locked on the National's front windows. "Check it out."

In the dark parking lot, Jenna spotted the man she had tripped. He'd hoisted a scrawny guy into the air by his jacket, a guy who looked kind of like her whiny ex-boyfriend Eioun. As the blond giant hoisted him high and shook, something fell from the little guy's hand. A cylinder.

Spray paint can. The Eioun lookalike was tagging something.

The two men started scuffling. The scrawny guy was flailed against the blond giant, who ignored his efforts. All of this was taking place right next to Jenna's car.

"Oh, hell no."

Jenna rose to her feet and hustled toward the door, cursing a blue streak while she hoped her suspicions were wrong. *Don't let him be tagging my car, please don't let him be—*

The door hinges squeaked protests as she emerged into the December night. Jenna felt the cold like a slap, realizing she had left both her threadbare black hoodie and leather jacket inside. Still, her combat boots carried her forward. Snow had been shoveled into piles around the lot, tire tracks drew crop-circle designs through the roadside slush.

When the runt in the golden giant's grip saw her, he wheezed and whined in an all too familiar way.

Jenna snapped.

"What the fuck, Eioun?"

Then, she saw the damage. UGLY FAT DY—. Her car door had bright yellow, drippy letters reading UGLY FAT DY—.

Her heart pounded triple time, and her chest felt empty enough to collapse on itself.

"You unbelievable shitbird."

"I was letting the world know," he whined, "you're an *ugly, fat d*—"

The giant with the golden mane shook Eioun silent.

"Let him finish," she said. "I want to hear this." Actually, she did not want to hear anything. The words had already stung too deeply. "I'm a fat, ugly what?"

"Dyke," Eioun said, but this last word was almost apologetic. He had been caught, and he was at a loss for what to do.

Near tears but refusing to back down, she demanded, "Why did you mess with my car?"

Even as she asked the question, she knew the reason. He messed with her car because he was a cowardly turd

who could never face her. Not after she confessed she
had never loved him, had never been *in love* with anyone
before and made him cry with her bravery in confessing
that. Jenna had not felt brave at the time, but now? Right
now she felt as brave as a fucking Valkyrie.

"Hey, Thor?" she said.

The blond man glanced her way. The parking lot's lamps
and shadows gave his long face enigmatic handsomeness.
If she'd had the time to get back into painting portraits,
she would ask him to pose for her.

"Yes?"

"You can drop him."

He opened his hands, letting Eioun fall to the asphalt.
He landed on his feet but hit black ice, ending on his duff.
She had the angry urge to kick him. Just once, just where
it would hurt the most. Instead, she said, "Go home,
Eioun." As he scrambled to his feet, she decided to add,
"I'm sending the bill to your folks."

He froze for a moment, then said, "They won't pay,
they won't believe you."

His own parents always apologized for him. She was
pretty sure they liked her just a teensy bit more than they
liked their own waste-of-space son.

"They're getting it anyway," she said. "And I'll let them
decide how to talk to you about it."

She had to admit it wasn't much of a threat to a socially
dysfunctional twenty-three-year-old. However, Eioun was
incapable of taking care of himself, so parental disapproval
was terrifying. His eyes bugged out in terror.

I can't believe I dated him, she thought to herself.

Eioun scuttled into the darkness.

To the blond, Jenna said,

"What did I expect? He's a Taurus. When they aren't bullying, they're such whiny bitches."

"We could've called the cops," Mr. Blond said.

"Too much trouble. Did you run out here to save my car?"

He considered the blue Ford with the rust spots around the front wheel wells.

"Didn't know it was your car."

"Would that knowledge have changed things?"

"You did trip me."

She cracked up. It felt so good to *laugh*.

"I suppose I should say thanks."

"I don't know about 'should'."

"Well, thanks."

"May I ask your name?"

"Jenna."

"I'm Aleph."

"Aleph?"

"It's short for Alephax."

"Wow. I never met one of those before."

"One might be enough."

"Maybe you're right." When another arctic wind blasted by, they both trembled. Jenna thought the blond looked hot in tight denim jeans and a loose shirt. He had the hair and physique to pull off a Renn Faire knight. "Are you cold? I'm cold. Are you?"

"It's brisk," he agreed. "Shall we?"

When Jenna shoved through the front door, she

realized the stranger's breath had not made plumes in the winter air. As though he wasn't breathing at all . . .

She shivered from something more than the cold. She had long been a fan of the bizarre, the unexpected, and the downright creepy. Being near a mystery was thrilling.

Maybe Alephax was more interesting than she first gave him credit for.

Eileen did not stay much longer, feigning sleepiness. Jenna knew though she would be up worrying a few more hours. so Jenna did what she could to raise Eileen's spirits.

"Eioun's so wrong," Eileen said, wrapping a Doctor Who-length scarf around her neck.

"What-what-what?"

"You're beautiful. And you're . . . you're not fat."

"I know," Jenna said, but sometimes she didn't. There were times when she would look in the mirror and hate the two-hundred-pound girl looking back at her. "Eioun is a douche canoe."

Eileen laughed again, pulling on her mittens.

They hugged and Jenna said, "Clyde's going to be fine," and Eileen thanked her.

"My old doofball's going to outlive us all," Eileen said and Jenna wished she had someone like him. A guy who knew how to laugh at himself, and didn't rankle when called a *doofball*.

Eileen trudged into the parking lot, her Fiat's headlights coming alive and guiding her to the road. Jenna waved through the window of the diner. The reflection in the window revealed someone approaching her: tallness, blondness, and freaking gorgeousness.

"Care for more company?" Alephax asked.

"If you can answer me one thing."

Alephax waited patiently, yet another surprise. In Jenna's experience, pretty people were uber-privileged and uber-pampered. Pretty people didn't like demands unless they were making them.

"What is a swallow's air speed velocity?"

When he failed her quiz, she would—

"African or European swallows?"

"You know Monty Python?"

"The movies and the Flying Circus," he said as he slid into the booth. He flashed her a wicked smile, revealing a set of very white choppers.

"Wow, you've got teeth made for biting." *Well, that sounds idiotic*, she thought. "I mean more than most people's. Yours are so—I'm going to shut up now."

He laughed.

"Do you like biting?"

"Biting is like kissing, but with a winner." She nodded sagely.

He nodded approval.

"So, tell me more."

"More?"

"About you," he said. "Tell me your story. I like smart perspectives and viciously intelligent women."

"Stop it."

He cocked a quizzical eyebrow.

"Stop what, exactly?"

"Stop . . ." She waved a hand before him, encompassing everything he was. "You're making me dizzy with disbelief."

He chuckled.

"This is serious. I'm not all that interested in 'good-looking men'." she said, using finger quotes like a pro, one set before her phrase and one set after. She could not get over the people who used them all through the phrase in question. They looked like hamsters weighing fluff. "They're usually so boring."

"I'm not boring?"

"Believe me when I tell you how much this surprises me."

"Why should it?"

"Because your kind just don't exist in the really-real world."

"What do you mean 'my kind'?" He also used finger quotes correctly.

Damn him.

"Now you're fishing for compliments." She rolled her eyes. "Buster, I'm not playing your game."

"At least I got one little tidbit from your tirade." He paused for effect. "You think I'm good-looking." Before she could protest, he asked, "So what brings a girl like you to a place like this? Tripping opportunities just too good to pass up?"

Jenna realized she had gone from simple amusement to full-on attraction.

"Much better than at Leo's on Main."

"Better cheese fries, too."

"How did you know I—" She glanced toward the

unbussed plate bearing the remnants of French fry and cheddary goodness. "Sassy, smart, *and* observant."

"Do you like walks?"

"Isn't it a bit cold?"

"*Au contraire*," he said. "It's perfect for a graveyard stroll."

Jenna's heart hammered like a military drummer transitioning from march to run. They were definitely flirting. She considered the man sitting across from her a little more.

He was older than her. Maybe late twenties? Possibly thirties . . . He had one of those difficult to gauge faces. And he had laugh lines, he was a real looker, as well as being strong, fast, and athletic. Why would he flirt with her? Shouldn't he go for athletic, pretty people?

Maybe, she thought with wry amusement, *he digs fat chicks*. There was a class of jerk who hit on anything overweight, the sort who preyed upon heavy girls' desperation. Those asshats always tried to pick up Jenna's friends at Hooka Joe's.

It was time to cut through the romantic bullshit.

"Are you trying to seduce me?"

If he answered maybe, then he was playing around. If he answered no, then he—

"Yes, I am."

"Why?" She shook her head to clear the cobwebs. "Why me?"

"Well, you called me Thor. And I like the way you didn't rise to that little shitbird's baiting."

"He was my boyfriend."

"'Was' being the operative word."

"Just another hit from my losers list," she said. She recalled the words on her car, the words Eioun launched like spears. "He's . . . He was right, you know."

"Right about what?"

"I'm . . ." *Ugly and fat.* Goddammit how could his words have penetrated into her head and heart so quickly? "I'm trouble." It was lame even as she said it, but she refused to give Eioun's hate speak the benefit of repetition.

"You're punk as fuck." He indicated her leather jacket with a nod. "I can see that plain as moonlight."

"Did you say punk as fuck?" She laughed to hide the warmth spreading across her cheeks. His use of *that word* made her blush, his using it so casually in relationship to her? "Who says that?"

"Obviously, I do."

"I think I'd like to walk."

They'd walked out without paying, she realized when she got across the parking lot.

"Oh crud."

"What?"

"I think I just ripped off National."

"Don't worry," he said. "I know the owners."

"But—"

"We'll be back."

No one came running after them. Alephax led her across the parking lot and then across the street. She was wearing her hoodie and jacket, but the wind cut across her exposed skin like an ice-edged knife. She edged closer to him, playing the subtlety card, and he put a protective arm around her shoulders.

"It's a hell of a night."

"I'm enjoying it."

"Well, my loser ex-boyfriend tagging my car was a downer," she said. "The rest has been good."

Headstones thrust up from the snowy earth beyond the iron fence. The iron bars circling the cemetery were solid but not continuous. Several good-sized gaps revealed places where kids had found weaknesses. Alephax eased through one such spot, holding out his hand to her.

"Careful," he said. "It's slippery."

"That's winter in a nutshell, huh? Wow, your hands are cold." Jenna squeezed his hand between her own, trying to rub it warm. It remained icy. "Well, I guess you know what they say: cold hands, warm heart. Hey, what's that?"

A dark shape shifted behind a nearby gravestone. Too small to be a person. Alephax glanced as a cloud swept past the gibbous moon. "A mutt, maybe." When wind gusted from that direction, he suddenly yanked his hand free and turned aside.

"You get something in your eye?"

"No, no." His voice was odd, muffled, though he was not wearing a scarf. "Just need a minute."

"Poor doggie," she said and trudged forward. "You don't want to go over there," he called, but it was too late. She had already gone too far to turn back.

With a low growl, a trembling, black dog emerged. A powerful mix, maybe shepherd or rottweiler. The moonlight returned to full strength, the clouds fast-tracking across the sky. She saw the mutt's muzzle was slick, its eyes wild.

She crouched, keeping her arms close by her sides. The animal braced itself for attack. When one did not come, it scampered into the night. She watched the dog depart, wishing there was something she could do for it. Behind the headstone, she expected to find whatever squirrel or critter the dog had been noshing on. The snow was red.

"I know how it is," she said to the departing shadow before it vanished among the headstones, "to be hungry, scared, and used to fending for yourself."

"I'll bet you do," Alephax said. He was right behind her, though still turned aside. She reached toward his cheek, and he finally faced her full. "Is this what you wanted to see?"

His bloodshot eyes gleamed in the moonlight, his teeth longer and sharper than before, but still perfectly white. She continued caressing his face.

"Did you bring me here to bite me?" she asked.

"You're not afraid?"

"This isn't my first rodeo," she said. She had known two vampires before. Wild buffoon kids who thought supernatural gifts and curses made them superheroes. They had been scary because they had been out of control. Alephax was different. "I knew you were too good to be true. You had to be harboring a big old dirty skeleton or two. So, did you?"

"No," he said. "The kill scent triggered . . . I only wanted to walk."

"So, let's walk," she said, and they did.

He told her about the trees and some of the headstones they passed. He was a history buff with a soothing manner and natural seductiveness. When he guided her back to the fence and across the street, she had decided she trusted him.

"I guess I should go pay my tab and maybe call it a night," she said, hoping he would catch the clue.

"Want to go some place quiet?"

"Yes."

Some place quiet turned out to be his house. A nice, nondescript colonial in a sleepy neighborhood. He invited her in and ushered her into a tastefully decorated sitting room. The plush chairs swallowed any discomforts.

When he offered tea, she said, "Only if you have honey."

He did.

While she sipped Russian Caravan, they talked awhile about movies, books, and music as well as the silly details strangers shared to become less strange. Before she was done with her tea, she decided she would like to go to bed with him.

"You are incredibly attractive," he eventually said. "Do you like to play?"

"What, gin rummy?"

"No," he said with a patient smile. "Play."

After a clueless moment, she realized what he was getting at.

"Oh, you mean *play*." The idea was rather inspiring. Instead of answering him, she asked, "Do I have an 'I Am Kinky' sticker on my forehead or something?"

"Well, anyone who likes Blue October *and* Depeche Mode must be open-minded. And you *are* punk as fuck."

Heat burned her cheeks, again.

"I like making you blush."

"You don't make me do anything."

"Would you like me to?"

Her embarrassed heat intensified.

"Maybe you would," he said. "What playtime activities do you favor?"

"You know the Depeche Mode song 'Master and Servant'?"

"Ahh. Which role do you prefer?"

I was hard to hold his eyes, embarrassment demanded she tear her gaze away. Damn it, she would not.

"Which do you think?" She fantasized about bottoming, too much of her life made her hold the reins. The jerks on her losers list had unanimously made her be strong. She longed to yield to someone, to find someone worth yielding to . . .

"I think you'd like to serve."

"Oh, you do, huh?"

"Your deepening blush tells me I'm not far off."

"Damn your heightened senses."

"Tell me, then."

"Tell you what?"

"Tell me you want to serve."

Her lips turned down in a playful frown. She couldn't just say it. No way!

"Yes, sir." She improvised and the way his eyes lit up, she discovered she had surprised him. Pleasure brought warmth to her heart. The way he looked at her brought heat elsewhere.

She glanced at the sitting room's bay window and

shivered. Though it was cool in the sitting room, it was far from the freeze settling outside.

"Can we go somewhere else?"

"How about my sin room?"

"Sin room?"

"Other people have sun rooms." He grinned. "What use would I have for that?"

"A place to sparkle?"

"I wish that was all sunlight did to me."

"What does it do?"

"Something a lot more debilitating, alas."

"You actually said alas. I think I might be falling in love with your vocabulary."

He chuckled.

"What sorts of things don't you like?"

Suddenly, he was all seriousness. Cataloging dos and don'ts, providing proper boundaries for playtime. She had heard of contracts being drawn up between players at passionate games, but her minor brushes with kinkiness had been "Whaddyathinkofthis?" conversations delivered with blushes, giggles, and nervousness. Alephax's straightforward, mature approach was appealing.

"Nothing gross, please. Don't pee or . . . I'm guessing that's not a problem."

"No," he agreed.

"Well, I want you to take charge."

"Good. I like to dominate." There it was. The second letter of BDSM tossed out of his mouth as casually as a comment about finches he had seen. *Dominate.* The word sent a thrilling shiver up her spine.

They exchanged a few more bits. He did not want too submissive a servant. Willfulness and the associated correction were part of the play.

"Would you like me to break you, Jenna?"

"You can try," she said.

"I'll take that as a maybe."

"What about safe words?"

"I like Sun and Canary, myself."

"Sun for stop, right? Why Canary?" Jenna grinned.

"I've always sympathized with Sylvester on Looney Tunes," he said. "Old Tweety Bird needs a time out."

She laughed. What a strange man this Alephax was.

"Sun and Canary it is."

He rose from his plush chair, offered her a hand, and led her upstairs. The house was a testament to antiquity, but with a lived-in feel. The rooms and hallways were decorated with acquisitions from numerous decades.

The sin room turned out to be a spacious, enclosed chamber upstairs. A former bedroom, it had been converted with liberal applications of brilliant paint and stained wood. The furnishings were Inquisition-fabulous: bondage crosses, titillating toys, and a gorgeous four-poster bed.

As soon as they crossed the threshold together, he turned his hungry gaze upon her. His lips curled into a delightful smirk.

"Strip."

"Yes, sir."

She dropped her jacket on the floor.

"Pick that up," he snapped. "Put your things in there."

He indicated the corner where there was a coat rack and an open cedar chest.

"Yes, sir."

As quickly as he had assumed the top role, she had become submissive. The character was more comfortable than she had expected. She hung her jacket on the rack, and placed her combat boots on the floor below it. Facing away, she pulled up her scoop-neck sweater.

"Stop." His commanding presence enfolded her like an embrace. "Face me."

She tugged her sweater back down and turned. His expression was stern, enhancing his handsomeness. He wanted to watch her, God help her but she wanted to perform for him. With exaggerated slowness, she removed her sweater, baring her sapphire blue, Cross My Heart bra.

Where his eyes roamed across her revealed flesh, goose pimples rose across every exposed inch. He could see her tummy and stretch marks. If he smiled wrong, it would destroy her.

"Show me more," he said sternly.

She folded her sweater in quick quarters and laid it on the chest. Facing him, she undid her pants. Her body felt like a furnace as she pulled her stretchy jeans down her thighs like uncorking a pheromone perfume bottle. His eyes roamed over her body, judging. Approving, she realized when she finally met his eyes.

Jenna's embarrassment did not evaporate, but it did diminish. She folded her pants, and placed them in the chest. Facing him, she unhooked her bra, letting the straps slide off. Only her white cotton panties and black socks remained on. She savored his scrutiny. Though she had only met him tonight, she felt safe. Complete in a way she had not realized she was incomplete.

"Socks, now."

"Yes, sir."

The socks joined her other clothes. She hooked her thumbs in the waistband of her panties, an invitation for more.

"Come to me."

She remained in place, shaking her head.

"Nuh-uh."

"Come to me, now."

"Yes, sir."

Every step closer to him made her heart pound faster. She was unprotected, her skin alive with gooseflesh, sensitive to every motion. When she was two paces away, his powerful hand snaked out, gripping the back of her neck. He dragged her closer to him, practically whisking her off her feet.

"Tell me you're beautiful."

"I . . ." She couldn't say it.

"Say it."

"I'm . . . beautiful?"

"Again."

The words became acidic, she spat them out to rid herself of them.

"I'm beautiful."

"We'll work on that one. Now, tell me you're not fat."

Tears blurred her vision. *Sun*, she thought. *Saying sun will end this.*

But she did not want to end it, she did not even want to *canary* it.

"I'm—" she swallowed and closed her eyes "—not fat."

"Open your eyes."

"Yes, sir."

"Now, say it. To me."

"Say it?"

"I'm not fat."

"No."

"Say it." His grip tightened behind her neck, reminding her who was in charge.

"I'm not."

"Not fat."

"I'm not fat."

"And you're not ugly. Say it."

"I'm not . . ."

"Not ugly."

The words clung to her throat, she had to force them out.

"Not ugly."

"Put it all together. 'I'm not . . .'"

"I'm not . . . fat."

"And?"

Had he smacked her in the face, it would not have stung any worse.

"I'm. Not. Ugly."

"And?" He nodded.

"And?"

"What are you?"

"I'm . . ."

"Say it. *Now*."

"I'm beautiful." She couldn't hold her tears back as she added. *"I'm beautiful."*

"You certainly are."

He pulled her into a kiss, his lips meeting hers and opening. His tongue met hers, and the sensation was magical. Her tears were so hot, she was burning up all over. His other arm went around her. She was caught now—no escape, no turning back.

This was the kind of kiss she could get lost in, far better than any losers list member had been capable of. It simultaneously soothed and stoked her. Her hands glided across his chest and then his hair, his scent strong in her nostrils.

Master me, she yearned. *Love me like no one ever has.*

The kiss ended, leaving her abuzz, yearning and fully aware the damned tears were falling faster. Soon, the sniffling would begin.

His voice penetrated the blurred veil of her tears, strong but compassionate.

"Do you want more?"

"Yes," she said, hating the choking from tears in her voice, "sir."

"I can smell your arousal," he said. "I hear the blood racing inside you. You're hot for this, aren't you?" He reached down, forcing his hand between her legs. She spread for him, gasping at his roughness. His fingertips teased through her panties, making stimulating circles around her clit. She thought she would collapse.

"Take it."

"Yes. *Sir.*"

She gasped when his fingers slid her panties aside and entered her. She leaned back into his strong grip behind her neck, spreading her legs more and whimpering while he fisted her.

"Take it, Jenna."

Pleasure made her regress to a primeval state. Animal grunts replaced language, as the internal pressure built. She bit her own cheek to keep from climaxing until he said she could.

His fingers stroked her G-spot, beckoning her excitement to new heights. Finally, he commanded her,

"Come for me." The release flooded her legs, intensifying her tears.

Moments later, he guided her to the floor. When she heard his clothes rustling, she blinked away her tears. Alephax was undressing, his body was pale but chiseled, his muscles toned and tight. His erection was powerful, slanted to his left she noticed as he rolled a condom down the shaft.

He leaned down over her, pinning her legs between his. His tongue caught her tears and his kisses caressed her, as his hands massaged her.

"Tell me you want me," he said.

"I want you."

"What will you do for me?"

"Anything."

"Anything?"

Oh, yes. Any-fucking-thing. "Anything."

"Tell me you want me inside you."

"I want you inside me."

"Tell me," he said, "that you're beautiful."

"I'm beautiful. You make me feel so beautiful."

"Tell me you're mine. For tonight."

"I'm yours." *For tonight. For longer, maybe.* "I'm yours."

"And you'll do anything for me?"

"Anything!"

He licked his lips as he pulled her panties down so he could eat her out. His mouth worked miracles, his tongue teased her clit and dipped inside her quim, turning, teasing, and tugging it in surprising ways. She squirmed at his attention, he clapped a hand atop her pelvis and shoved her against the floor, holding her down. Keeping her still as he licked, nibbled, and teased another climax from her. She wanted to squirm, but his hand pinned her in place.

Then an instantaneous painful prick followed by an incredible pleasure flow. Now, she screamed for him, wanted to touch his hair, but her arms . . . Where were they? How did they work?

He drank her come and blood, the intensity was maddening. It seemed to last forever, an endless string of orgasms. Afterward, she lay in a puddle, trying to reconnect her mind, spirit, and body.

He moved over her, his chest against hers.

"Open your eyes. Open them."

Eyes? What were eyes? Oh . . .

"Open your eyes. Do you want more?" His cock head tapped against her pussy.

"I want you."

"Tell me you're beautiful."

"Make me beautiful."

"Now, say my name."

"Alephax." He entered her, and she shouted, *"Alephax."* He pounded into her quim as she called his name over and over again, so it become a chant. Her hands moved over his chest and back, clutching him between pleasure spasms. He was warm now, *warmed by me, by my blood.*

"Take it."

"Yes! Sir!" She came, her body screamed with ecstasy, as she scratched her name into him. He rolled her over, spanking her ass and dragging her up onto her knees onto his engorged cock. She shrieked for him, her cheek against the floor, she clutched at air as though she might grasp it while he ravaged her.

Every stroke of his cock or paddling hand sent shivers through her body. He filled her so deeply, perfectly. How could she ever feel this way again? *Don't stop, don't stop, don't stop.*

When he climaxed, she was exhausted. Pleasantly fucked to oblivion's edge.

He picked her up as though she weighed no more than a doll, carried her to the bed, and laid her gently down, sitting beside her.

"You look done," he said.

She nodded, regretting she couldn't go longer. Regretting she'd let him down. She had given in too easy, too often.

"Me, too."

"What a night."

"Think about how our first real date will go." He winked.

She could have exploded with delight. Instead, she kissed him again.

"What did you think?"

"Different from what I expected."

"I'm guessing you had some fun?"

"A good time," she assured him, "was had."

"Would you like to try more things out? Some other night?"

"Yes, sir."

She snuggled against him. Outside, the winds blasted the walls, but in the sin room, she nestled in the warm, protective envelope of her master's arms.

Simple

By Giselle Renarde

I watch a lot of TV when Gall is away.

A program I saw not long ago featured a British couple that'd worked in the Secret Service during World War II. That's where they met, they both worked in the same building—she was a code-breaking mathematician, and he was a tactician of some sort. But because they were assigned to different missions, neither could discuss what they did all day. Under the Official Secrets Act, even after the war was over they couldn't disclose their assignments. The couple married and had children, but they were into their late seventies before they could finally discuss the roles they played in the war effort.

Most people wouldn't believe that anyone could keep such a big secret from their spouse for years upon years . . . but I believe it. I believe it because I live it.

It's not that I do anything important or militaristic in my career. The biggest secret I'm supposed to keep at work is that the produce manager is having an affair with the guy who delivers snack cakes. And, trust me, when the tomatoes are rubbing elbows with the Twinkies on the delivery dock, it's no secret. You can hear them halfway across the parking lot.

Gall's the one with a pocketful of secrets. I don't even know what he does for a living, to be honest. I tell people he works for the government, because, as far as I know, that's the truth. Doesn't matter that he's my husband, he can't tell me a thing. When he's away, I don't know where he's gone, who he's with or where he's sleeping. I don't even know if he's safe. He has a signal he uses at night, to show me he's thinking of me. At ten o'clock the phone rings once. Just once. That's how I know he's still alive. On nights when the phone doesn't ring, I tell you, I don't sleep.

I'm proud of my husband. Whatever he's out there doing, I know it's for the good of the public. He'd risk his life for any stranger off the street, and I'm sure he does, every day. I bet he's got hero medals squirreled away somewhere. When he's gone, sometimes I hunt behind the baseboards, in the back of the closet, anywhere he might have hidden something that would tell me more about him. The man I love is a mystery. Until he's home, I sometimes wonder if he's even real.

Tonight, the phone rings more than once. It's three in the morning and my heart rages. I'm not sure whether I was asleep before the ringing started, but I'm sure as hell awake now. When I pick up, there's helicopter noise in the background. It's so loud I hold the receiver away from my ear and shout, "Gall?"

"I'll be home in half an hour," he hollers over the roar of the chopper. "Be ready."

Gall makes it simple for me, and I love that about him.

He told me about a book he'd read. Either it was in Spanish or the writer was Spanish, I'm not really sure, but the character in the book is a doctor who's having an affair with a maid or a slave or someone like that. He doesn't have much time to fuck her, so he tells her to wait for him bent over the bed, no underwear, her skirts tossed up over her waist. Between home visits, he runs into her room, gets off on her wet pussy, and then zips up and leaves.

The idea makes my body pulse. I remember the way Gall looked at me when he first talked about it—like there was nothing hotter than a woman who was wet, ready, and waiting. That's what he wants from me, and his blatant sexual desire forged a blazing path through my want of tenderness. There was something in the sharpness of his teeth, the way his canines flashed when he told me he wanted me, that made me feel so necessary. He could see inside me, straight through my veins and into my soul.

My yearning for soft affection subsided the longer Gall was away. When he first left, I'd stand at my cash register, fantasizing about cuddling up with him in our big bed. As the days and nights went by, my daydreams grew more sordid, more hardcore. I wanted to give myself to him, unconditionally, and I wanted him to take, take, take.

Why did I always feel like he was holding out on me? Like there was something he wanted, something he needed, that he wasn't getting in our big bed? What a terrible, needling feeling. I pushed it away, buried it. Gone.

I thought incessantly about my husband's cock. I pictured it forcing its way inside of me, pummeling my pussy as his balls banged my clit. The friction took hold until my panties were slick with my juice. I'd writhe against the seam of my black pants as I pulled boxes of cereal across a barcode scanner, so distracted I'd ring bananas through as passion fruit. My work suffered in Gall's absence, but luckily, my work was not as important as his.

Now he's on his way home, half an hour until I get fucked. Hard. I could go back to sleep for a good twenty minutes. After a full day on my feet I need the rest, but anticipation gets the better of me.

Slipping out of bed, I plant both feet on the carpet. I pull up my nightie, bunching it under my belly so my ass is exposed. My nipples are hard already, I feel them poking into the rumpled duvet as my breath warms the fabric.

I stare at the digital clock—cruel red lines forming numbers that never seem to change. Closing my eyes, I tell myself that when I open them five minutes will have gone by.

I dream about Gall, the images unsettle my mind and leave me queasy. I try not to remember what I've seen, but how can I forget? I don't want to know what it means when I dream about his teeth becoming knives: he opens his mouth, and they emerge like weapons, seeking new flesh. They're horrific and fearsome, but I'm aroused beyond belief as he sinks them into an endless series of pale necks. When the gleaming knives retract, his tongue takes over, bathing his lips in the blood of other women. So much blood, it drizzles down his chin and out the sides of his mouth.

He's an animal, in my dreams. A predator, roaming the streets of whatever city he happened to be in. He always finds what he's looking for, because he always knows where to look. In dark alleyways and dilapidated rooms, he devours his prey. Everywhere he turns, he finds a willing victim, a willing neck. Hot blood, sweet, and metallic, pulsing with life. I can taste the blood on my tongue when I dream. Their essence lives on inside Gall, inside me. Whoever these girls are, they're *in me*.

He does it to protect me, I wake up thinking, but I don't understand. He does *what* to protect me?

I don't want to know. I don't want to know.

In my mind, I see him surrounded by buxom blonde Bond girls from the 60s. Their bouffant hairstyles are huge and their eyes are dead. I feel like I should be jealous— look how they're fawning over my husband! Instead, I pity them, I don't know why. He touches their bellies beneath the crass fabric of their baby doll nightgowns, strokes them, pulls them in close and kisses the swollen purple bruises on their necks. They're hideous, *those* girls. There's nothing inside of them, they're empty shells. When he tastes their necks, the salt is on my tongue. When he bites, their blood floods my mouth.

I must have fallen asleep waiting. The next thing I know the front door squeals open and bangs shut. There are footsteps downstairs, I bite my lip and twist the hem of my nightie. What if it's someone else, not Gall at all?

What if some strange man tears into our bedroom and ravaged me?

"Shelly?" Gall shouts. His boots pound up the stairs. "I hope you're ready."

"I am," I whisper to myself.

A smile paints itself across my lips, I want him so bad.

Gall throws open the bedroom door, I turn just enough to catch sight of his body in the moonlight. In his black pants and boots, he stands tall like a superhero. He's breathing hard, his white shirt open. There's a stain across the front, and it looks like blood, but I don't want to know. Even if he *could* tell me, I wouldn't want to know.

Gall isn't suave like James Bond. He's something else altogether.

"Good," he says.

The devil is in his eyes, and I want it.

I ask him to check my pussy, to see if I'm ready. I know the answer but I want him to find out for himself.

A smirk bleeds across his lips, like he's surprised that I've spoken. After a moment, he shakes his head and chuckles, tearing off his ripped and bloodied shirt. His shoulders are huge, I know this, but sometimes I forget. When Gall has been gone for a while, there are moments when I can't even summon his face to mind, let alone his firm chest or his washboard stomach.

He approaches the bed like a hurricane. I open my legs and arch my ass up to give him a good view of my cunt. I know I'm wet, but he needs to test the waters. He shoves not one but two fingers inside of me, and my heart rattles in my chest. I want his cock, God, I want it.

Gall slaps my ass and chuckles.

"I knew you'd be ready."

I bury my smile in the duvet, breathing in the heavy air until my lungs feel like cotton. His belt unbuckles, his zipper unzips, and my clit throbs. Everything turns me on, the moment Gall walks through that door, I am liquid arousal. All I want is to be a pool for him to play in. And, for the moment, that's all I am.

As his pants hit the floor, he grabs my ass cheeks and spreads them so wide I feel my asshole open up. He shoves his thumb in my pussy and drags my juice up to my ass. I gasp and tighten up as he traces the perimeter, but my hole is no match for Gall. He shoves his thick thumb in my ass, and once I'm finished expecting it to hurt, I remember how much I like this sort of thing.

Before my feathers have quite unruffled, Gall's cock head finds its way to the mouth of my pussy. I want him so badly my juice is slipping down my clit and spilling into my pubic hair, easing the impact of his rough thrusts. He streams into me like a battering ram, sparing no sweat. When his cock pounds that place deep inside of me, the pang bolts down my legs like lightning. I shriek, but he doesn't stop. My asshole clenches, milking his thumb. He pulls almost all the way out of my pussy, then bangs back inside.

My toes curl, grasping hold of carpet fibers. I've never felt quite this wide open before. Gall can see inside my gaping pussy and asshole as he fucks them both.

"How would you handle another cock?" Gall asks. I don't know what he means, but after a moment he clarifies. "What would you do if I brought a buddy home and he went at your cunt while I destroyed your tight little asshole?"

"Oh God . . ." My legs quiver against the side of the bed.

Gall fucks me in double time, his heavy balls whacking the mattress as he carves a path through my cunt. The night air is cool on my ass, but his body heat compensates, blazing against my skin. I buck back at his cock, pushing up from the mattress to meet him again and again. We thrust forward and back, moving in time with the other. I almost wish there was a second cock to fill my ass. Next time, will he bring home a friend? I imagine meeting one of his associates for the first time with my naked ass in the air, my wet pussy splayed for his eyes.

If I reach down with just one hand, I know I can push myself over the edge. Gall is close, I can tell by his ragged breath, and I want to come with him. But I need to ask permission.

"Sir?" My fingers stand at the ready, digging deep through my pubic hair, waiting for the perfect moment. "May I?"

He fucks me, but he doesn't answer my question.

I can smell us, the scent of pussy and cock combines with the faint aroma of ass to send a heady buzz through my pelvis and my thighs. His friction makes me whimper, he's so huge. I can feel his cock pulsing as he pounds me. I bet he's been thinking about this the whole time he's been away, doing whatever it is he does. I bet he went to bed each night with his cock in his hand, wishing his fist was my pulpy, wet pussy.

"May I?" I try again. "Please, Sir?"

"Fuck," he groans, low and reverberating. It's hardly even a word, but I take it as a signal.

When Gall digs his fingers into the swell of my ass cheek, I give my hand the go-ahead. My fingertips find my clit swollen and soaked, all it takes is the slightest stroke to start me coming.

My man bucks hard, filling me up as I scour my clit.

"Yes! Fuck, yeah! That's it! That's it!" We moan together.

"Stroke your clit," he instructs me. "Scour it hard. That's right. Harder!"

I'm working it as hard as I can—so hard my arm aches—but I build pleasure on pleasure. I'm getting there fast, and so is he. My pussy clamps down on his cock as we get there together.

We come at the same time, such things are not impossible. Gall gets off on the sweet swell of my pussy, and brings me along for the ride. My legs shake while he stands firm as a steel rod, his dick is lodged inside of me parting my pussy lips. The strain catches up with me, and I close my eyes to picture his cock head spewing hot cream inside my cunt. I groan against the duvet cover, feeling the heat of my breath spreading across the fabric.

He pulls out, slow as sin, and I feel every inch of him spreading me wide. When his still-engorged cock head pops out, I savor the sound but miss him already.

I remain folded over the bed, squinting against the bathroom light while Gall washes up. When he returns to me, he is naked, powerful, and all mine. He scoops me into his strong arms like I weigh nothing at all, then tosses me on the bed. Laughing, I scurry under the covers and he joins me.

"Your toes are freezing." He tugs at my nightie. "Here, get this off."

"Why?" I tease. "It's four in the morning and I don't know about you, but I've got to work in the morning."

"I don't care." He nuzzles my neck, his stubble pricks me, making me squeal. "Ouch! That hurts."

"Does it?"

In the moonlight, his eyes shine the strangest shade of silver. There's a flash, and for a moment I think I've seen the knives—the knives from my dreams. His teeth are not teeth, they gleam white as starlight, a pair of needling canines just dying for a bite. Then I blink, and they're gone. Just like that. Gone.

I stare and stare; there's something inside of him I just can't see. I know it's there, but it's not for me.

"Do you know how much I missed you?" he asks.

My heart surges, and so does my aching pussy.

"I missed you too."

"Do you know who else missed you?" Gall wraps his arms around me and presses his cock against my backside. I can't believe he's hard again already!

Rolling me onto my belly, Gall pins me under his weight. I'm his, completely. Trapped, I can kick my legs, but that's about it. As he rubs his cock slowly between my ass cheeks, he groans, and that sound tells me everything I need to know about his love for me and his commitment to our marriage. My husband promised to be true, but promises are just words and sometimes words only complicate matters.

Groans are simple, and simple never lies. There are gaps he never fills, but those gaps keep my life easy, and I appreciate that more than he'll ever know.

Cinderella in Hell

By Kimber Vale

"Rella, strike my backside with the birch. Leave a mark so his royal highness might take notice. He is sure to sample some of the ladies tonight, and I mean not to be ignored."

Drizella's voice trembled in time with her lip as she raised her ample skirts. The notion of Prince Dominic paying Driz his notoriously brutal attention had the lady agitated. The blemish she requested to go with her gown only added to her enthusiasm.

The switch sailed through the air, its whistle sweet, and the crack as it touched Driz's soft flesh sent a thrill through Rella. Giving the blows did not stir her, however. Her blue eyes stared, transfixed, as the angry red welt appeared against alabaster skin from the switch. She dreamt it was her own flesh that quivered with anticipation as she awaited certain punishment.

As long as she resided in this house, though, she was a slave. Serving as a reluctant dominatrix, she was forced to cater to the submissive desires of her two stepsisters and unloving stepmother. If she refused, she relinquished her claim to the family estate.

Rella's father had been a well-known master. His domineering streak had entranced Rella's mother. After Lady Tremaine's untimely death, his appetites had seduced the Widow Blakeslee. Their marriage ended when Rella's father died of apoplexy three years after their vows had been spoken. Eighteen-year-old Rella was left with her wretched stepfamily. Her new mother controlled the purse strings, and held Rella in a private perdition.

Rella's submissive family had expected her to continue where her father had left off. It did not matter that she had no taste for the role. Every crack of the whip, every slap of the crop against their bare skin left Rella hollow and blazing with a desire she could no longer satisfy on her own.

Another year catering to the desires of her family and surely she would go mad.

Rella had begun plotting her escape mere days before the invitation to the prince's ball had arrived. A life on her own would have hardships; she would have to work like a maid, scrubbing her knuckles raw for the tiniest scraps of food. But that, at least, would provide some of the humiliation she craved. Most importantly, she would be free, her sexual proclivities hers to nurture. Perhaps one day she would find the perfect mate to share her desires, and bend her, body and mind, to his will.

But news of the prince's reception had sparked new hope. The most eligible master in the kingdom, the future king and eternal prince of the night, was on the hunt for a sexual subservient. When he made his selection, one lucky woman would be given the gift of life without end, and become the vampire consort. The potential for pain-play with skin that healed remarkably fast left her body aching with sizzling need. The competition would be fierce, Rella had no doubt, but this was her one chance to finally break free of her invisible bonds. The butterfly would emerge from her chrysalis on this very eve, and one way or another she would fly far from this place.

She had to get the prince's attention.

Anastasia walked into the room, dressed in a flowing white gown. She was a picture of innocence, but her dark eyes rested on the switch in Rella's hand.

"Rella, I am afraid I broke your strand of pearls as I tried them on just now. You know; the necklace your mother left for you?" she added with a wicked gleam in her eye. "I deserve to be admonished."

Ana sank to all fours as she spoke, raising pristine folds of fabric to reveal a nearly unblemished ass. Subtle, fading bruises stained the creamy skin where last Rella had swung at her.

Rella swallowed a sob as she strove to imagine herself far beyond the walls of the crumbling manor. This was the final insult, and should be a happy occasion as such. But the destruction of something so precious to her was unpardonable. She placed a scuffed moccasin against the back of Ana's neck and forced her face to the stone floor.

A tear rolled down Rella's cheek as the thin branch sliced through the air, snapping against Ana's bottom again and again until the girl cried out her safe word, her voice thick with satisfied tears.

"You've soiled the back of her dress! Mother shall hear of it, Rella!" Drizella walked toward the door to tattle.

Rella let the branch slice through the air once more as she flung it across the room.

Starve me, as always, to correct my misdeeds, but tonight I shall feast at the royal table! And after that, I plan to never go hungry again, Sweet Sister. Say a prayer that my next meal isn't your lifeblood.

Rella waited in her room, door locked, until the sound of the departing carriage faded with the light of day. She crept into Drizella's room first. A draught sent goose bumps prickling down her arms. They added to the delicious sense of foreboding that had accompanied her into the chamber. She rifled through drawers until she found the objects of her desire. The butterfly nipple clips gleamed in the moonlight, jaws sparkled like precious stones. She placed the stolen jewelry on the bed and stripped. Moisture gathered between her legs as anticipation thrummed through her body.

A cool breeze billowed the sheer curtains at the window. They reached for her like ghosts that craved the touch of warm skin. Rella's nipples were erect from excitement from the chilly kiss. A shiver rippled through her as she pinched each of her stiff peaks with the jaws of the butterflies. She gave the chain on them a tug, sucking in her breath when the bite was amplified.

As she turned to leave, Rella noticed the wardrobe door hanging open. Driz had struggled to choose a gown that was both demure and beautiful, in the hope of catching the prince's eye. Rella imagined that most women in the kingdom would dress similarly. She prayed so. His highness was known to be a tyrannical dominant on the hunt for a bottom that could match his appetite, but it was still a royal ball. All the usual formalities would be respected.

But not by Rella; she planned to throw propriety out the window and relish the resulting punishment.

Ana's chamber was smaller, cozier. She kept a box under her bed with all of her implements. Rella chose the black leather cuffs and collar, and the chain that connected them. She locked the collar around her neck, and then a deflating thought struck her. She could not secure her own wrists.

"Damn it! It is no use!"

Helpless tears washed over her and she plopped down on her sister's bed. It was not fair! Her chance at happiness, foiled by a minor detail. Her makeup was running, but the knowledge did not staunch the flood of misery that streamed down her face.

"Oh, come now! Dry those eyes! You cannot go to the ball looking like that!"

Rella sucked in a hitching breath as her head swiveled toward the intruding voice.

A stunning woman with flaming red hair stood at the foot of the bed. Her dress was cut asymmetrically; the orange and red hues melded together like the licking tongues of flame devouring the curves of her body. Her eyes were black and seemed bottomless, which was disconcerting, but her tone and sympathetic smile reassured the stricken girl.

"Who are you?"

"Why, I'm Garnet, your Fetish Fairy, of course! Did your father never read you the old tales when you were a child? No? Never mind, you will know all you need to soon enough, my dear."

Rella stood, wiping her eyes.

It must be a dream.

"Fetish Fairy? You cannot be real." Rella reached out to touch the scalding hair. It slipped through her fingers like spun silk basked in summer sun.

"So hot." She looked wonderingly at the woman before her.

"Do I not feel real?" Garnet leaned forward, her body glowing and radiating heat. Her hand stroked Rella's cheek, and a wave of warmth wafted across her face. The fairy pulled her closer.

Face to face, Rella stared into two ebony pools. She wanted to jump into them and burn. Smoldering lips met hers, soft but demanding. They tasted of scorched leaves and warm cloves. Her tongue was almost unbearably hot, and so wet, as it stroked against Rella's. Rella felt her knees weaken and her core liquefy as she sat heavily on the bed. She touched her lips to be sure they had not burst into flame.

"I am indeed real, and your deepest desires have been granted." Garnet smiled down at her. A hand mirror had materialized in her grasp, ruby-crusted and incandescent. Rella took the proffered glass, the girl reflected back to her wore an intricate mask: scarlet and ebony feathers winged out from her temples and kohl-rimmed eyes were visible.

Shock consumed her. *When did this happen?* Rella skimmed quaking hands over her body as she gazed down at her attire. The clips held fast to her pink nipples, but the fine chain that connected them now bore a leather strap. The leash was hooked in the center and hung down between her breasts. Around her waist was a short skirt, formed from the same ebony and scarlet feathers. They were softer than the finest down, and floated around the curve of her ass as if a thousand whispering lips touched her flesh. She whirled to watch the fringe rise up like startled birds taking wing. Her naked skin beneath bathed in crisp night air.

"And a final touch . . ."

Lips of flame met hers once more, and Rella was drowning, melting. It ended too soon, and the sensation of her wrists locked between Ana's leather cuffs cut into her consciousness. She looked down in wonder, noting the chain that bridged the restraints. She tugged and felt the pull on the matching collar.

It was then that she noticed the marble floor under her bare feet. Rella looked up to see the grand foyer of the royal palace. A glittering chandelier the size of her family carriage twinkled with flickering flames against fine crystal. Matching sconces marched down a long hall, pointing the way toward the haunting strain of violins.

Rella followed.

The great hall was thronged with ladies in elaborate gowns. The men were dressed primly in the finest silken hose and lace-trimmed velvet coats. They came to watch the proceedings, and perhaps to choose their own submissive from the multitude of women who would be left after the prince made his selection. Many carried swords at their hips as fashion dictated, but a great number wore switches, cat-o'-nine tails, and paddles strapped to their belts.

Rella gazed across the expanse, shivering in delightful anticipation. As the musicians ended their tune, the dancers cleaved like a wanton woman opening her legs to a lover. In the center, she saw him.

Prince Dominic sat on his throne. His black hair was pulled back at his nape, and he rested his strong chin on a fist. Hooded eyes were glazed with obvious disinterest as they poured over the surrounding merriment. As if pulled by an invisible force, his gaze met hers.

Rella was on fire. Her fairy had kindled a conflagration within her. It felt as though the pyre was visible through flesh and bone, boiling her blood, and apparent to the man who possessed the matching spark. The prince stood, and stepped deliberately down from the dais, straight toward her.

"You dare arrive at a royal ball attired thusly?"

His eyes burned into hers, indomitable and hard. They were the color of pure emeralds, and equally unyielding.

"I mean no offense, Your Majesty." She curtsied, and black feathers fluttered around her. The entire congregation seemed to be similarly ruffled. Hushed whispers met her ears, snippets of speech rang clear in the low rumble. *Who is she? What impudence! Unmask her!*

"I would know who stands before me. You challenge the etiquette of my realm." The prince's hands pulled her mask away as he spoke.

"Rella, of House Tremaine, as it pleases Your Highness."

"*Please* me, indeed. My subjects never fail to *please* me, Rella of Tremaine. He leaned toward her and lowered his voice. "Why do you think I stage this travesty of a ball? All here are eager to please, but so few truly crave the role of submissive." His eyes raked her body. "Do you think I am blind to those that warm my hand and bed out of duty? Those affairs taste stale from the outset."

His voice was a dark whisper for only her ears, sharp teeth flashing between his lush lips as he spoke. A lustful tremor spiked through Rella.

"And yet, you throw my predilections in my face with your garb. It is a transgression worthy of punishment."

Fear and anticipation seized her with an intoxicating grip, and she gazed at the surrounding guests. A familiar one met her stare.

"Rella? I knew those clamps looked like my own!"

Drizella rushed out of the crowd, a blur of powder blue. A clawed hand reached for the leash. It yanked the butterfly clips tight and brought Rella to her knees, panting as white-hot pain obscured her vision.

"Women such as *this* pretend to be what they are not, simply to please a prince!" His majesty's voice rang out across the stunned silent hall as he speared Drizella with an accusing finger.

"No, your majesty! I swear, I am not false!" Driz squeaked in denial, but her delicate slippers padded out of Rella's view as she attempted to hide her embarrassment back into the crowd. The prince's fine leather boots were directly before Rella, she longed to press her lips against their hard tips.

"Arise, Rella of House Tremaine." His hand gripped her elbow steady as stone and he issued a final remark congregation.

"Stay! Enjoy! Perhaps some small number of you shall happen upon an equal match tonight. I have reason to believe my search is at an end."

The music swelled, bolstered by thunderous applause. Rella searched for sight of her stepfamily but saw only the obsequious smiles of strangers. Already, they treated her as a royal consort. Her knees weakened, like a steel blade left too long in the forge flame as she walked beside her prince.

Would she disappoint her master when the game was finally played? Had her life of servitude deceived her into believing she was something she was not?

Periodic torches lighted the shadowed hall, their flickers wavering against the gray stone as her conviction wavered in her breast.

This was the reckoning she'd coveted, and the long walk to the inevitable punishment was honeyed torture. She shook with trepidation, even as her nether lips slipped against each other with arousal.

Finally, they reached the prince's private sleeping quarters.

"Rella of Tremaine, you must be reprimanded for your insolent attire."

"Yes, Your Majesty." Her jellied knees were grateful to no longer bear weight as she sunk low in obeisance.

"Henceforth, you may call me Master in my bed-chamber. My formal royal address shall be used in public. What is your safe word?"

He circled her, his black lacquer cane swinging at his hip. One could argue whether the thick pole was for walking purposes, or fashion. It was intricate, with a diamond-eyed skull of silver that capped one end. A vicious pinwheel rested like a macabre hat on the head. Rella knew that such wheels were used for torture play. Her Master flouted decent society with the apparatus, but she would not speak of it. The unknown penalty she already faced was enough for now.

"Butterfly, Master."

"Very well. For your first lesson, I will have you on all fours."

Rella remained still, head bowed as she awaited his direct order.

The prince's hands reached her cuffs and worked the straps free.

"Another time, perhaps. You will be helpless enough with this device." He took hold of the leash and gave an experimental tug. Rella gasped from the exquisite pressure on her nipples, her feet inadvertently stepped toward him.

"Yes, this will do."

He pulled again, harder, wordlessly commanding her to follow. Her breath heaved from pain and pleasure, as Rella trailed him to the immense bed. Carved spindles branched upward from the four corners and held up thick, velvet curtains. The head was upholstered in matching finery. Iron links protruded from it in a highly unconventional design.

Prince Dominic pulled her leash up the length of the bed as he walked beside her, a stern countenance darkening his features. Rella crawled up the silken bedcovers until her face nearly touched the headboard. She watched her master lock her leather lead into an iron ring. The strap was taut, forcing her back to arch in compliance, and her nipples to strain forward.

"Do not move." She was blind to his actions and her heart sprinted in frenzied response. *Fumbling noises. Was that wood on wood? Metal?* He chose his instrument with pitiless languor, tormenting her with the unknown as her pussy grew wet with expectation.

Footsteps drew nearer until he stopped alongside her posterior. She knew that her moist slit was on display, her fringe of feathers too short to cover her. He expelled a breath that agitated the feathers, tossing them about her sensitive cheeks. The wait was worse torture than any spanking.

"How will you punish me, Your Highness?"

"Master," he growled. The shock of his granite hand on her bottom rocked her forward. It was unexpected; her elbows buckled with the blow, sending a shiver of sweet pain from each nipple. Rella swallowed back a sob, straightening her arms and arching to alleviate the pull on her burning breasts.

"In the future, I expect you will remember my rules." His palm cracked her other cheek, a blinding sting that forced a cry from her quivering lips. Tears welled in her eyes.

"That was for your verbal indiscretion. Now, for your brazen costume . . ."

The familiar whistle of a cane chirped in her ear before

the crack. A splinter of agony shot through the backs of her thighs as she jerked forward, away from the biting instrument. Her face was crushed against the soft bed frame. The warmth on her bottom bloomed like a spark fed dry tinder. Rella caught a sob and held it.

Breathe. Breathe.

She willed herself to exhale. *Inhale*. More might come. She needed to find a balance before the next blow.

Movement came from behind, but not the crisp pain she expected. Soft waves of warm air fanned her scalding backside. Rella reveled in the gentle breeze. Warm lips caressed her skin, undoubtedly brushing across a scarlet hand print, and tracing over a growing welt. She felt her pussy clench in response, her desire pushing her bottom toward him. The butterfly clamps bit, but she was so wet now, she needed it. The fine concoction of light and dark, pleasure and pain, spun together in a blur until they were one and the same.

She felt a cool, hard surface press against her lower lips. Smooth wood stroked across her exposed skin, and she wiggled further back into it.

"You crave a taste of my paddle, do you?"

Before she could answer, she felt the instrument draw back and spank her pussy in a rapid flick. Again and again. She bit her lower lip with the third slap, holding back a shout. The heat in her labia was a wildfire only he could quench. Once more, she felt his sting before she cried out for mercy.

"Please, Master!"

"Please, what, my lady?"

"I need . . . I want . . ." She struggled to put words to feelings. She had been driven to a precipice, and yearned to fly. But how?

She heard him discard his instruments with a clatter. The bed shifted behind her and then Rella felt the most magnificent balm soothing her aches. A warm tongue glided up her slit. He pulled her stinging labia into his mouth to suck away the burn. His strong tongue discovered her hole; it dove in and out while his fingers teased her clit. He worked the sensitive nub with circular strokes as he continued to lick away her wounds and his free hand tenderly massaged an aching cheek.

Rella smiled to know her prince could caress or castigate with equal mastery. She strained against her ties as he worked her to a fever pitch. The tide inside her rose, and crashed against her core in ever-stronger bursts.

His tongue skimmed up her backside, teeth scraping ominously.

"I need to taste all of you."

"Yes," she whispered, thirsting to feel him sink his sharp bite into her tender ass.

Pain stabbed from the spot where her right cheek met the back of her leg and Rella screamed. More than simple blood was pulled from her, part of her soul was drawn into his mouth. The more he took, the more she wanted to give.

Abruptly, his heavenly touch disappeared and Rella felt a drip of blood roll down the back of her thigh.

"Please, Master. I need to feel you."

The nudge of hard cock against her slit answered her

plea. He prodded her pussy slowly, leisurely entering her wet space with just his tip. She could not hasten his penetration with her breasts thrust forward, her chain pulled tight, she was completely at his mercy.

In and out he stroked with his wide head, moistening himself with her ample juice. Rella whimpered and squirmed.

"Please," Rella begged, her voice hitching with tears.

He froze in place before his hand reached around her to release first one, and then the other nipple. The rush of endorphins, as her swollen tips were freed, shook her entire body. She shivered uncontrollably while the tantalizing fingers of a climax brushed against her.

"Is this what you want?" His hands gripped her buttocks with fingers that bit into bruised tissue. Swiftly, he plunged into her, forcing her forward onto her elbows. Rella bit down on the rich bed covering as he slid in and out of her, more beast than man. She moaned, relishing the feel of his thick cock. Her fingers slid down her belly to her clit as he thrust into her again and again. Her master's balls slapped her stinging skin in a mockery of his paddle, the sensation threw her over the edge.

The orgasm rumbled fiercely through her, her slick walls clenched his rod and he pushed back, pounding her onward. As her climax abated, and the undulations of pleasure receded to a satisfied hum, he withdrew from her.

"I want your ass," he spoke in a harsh whisper. She felt him, slick and stiff, nuzzling her. Kneading her sore bottom, he squeezed her cheeks around his rod, slipping back and forth in the crack. His insistent cock head probed her clenched hole. She was so wet, he was covered with her own lubricant. He pushed against her resistance, and a groan ripped from his throat as his tip popped inside. Slowly, sweetly, the long length of him followed the initial sting, stole her breath as he filled her. The prince sighed, a harsh, grating sound. Wrapped completely inside her snug sheath, she felt his cock pulse rhythmically as he came in a warm flood.

He fell over her, spent, and they both sank deep into the mattress. Exhaustion settled in Rella's bones while a sublime sense of peace turned up the corners of her mouth. His arms wrapped around her from behind in a firm, but tender caress. She melted against his body.

"Have I pleased you, Master?"

"Completely, my love." He kissed her temple. "Like no other. Tonight I shall share my blood with you and make you mine forever. We will have eternity to discover our darkest desires together. Would you like that?"

"Yes, Master." Rella grinned broadly, knowing that sometimes wishes really did come true.

She leaned back and offered him her neck.

Also available from Black Lace:

THE BEAUTY OF SURRENDER

by Eden Bradley

Are you ready for the dark side of love…?

The moments when Ava Gregory feels her most beautiful
and complete are when she is tied up and bound.

Then she meets Desmond Hale, a master in the ancient
Japanese bondage art of Shibari. He takes her to the very
edge of ecstasy. But having learned the beauty of
surrender, dare Ava risk her heart?

The Beauty of Surrender is a hot erotic romance which
will delight fans of E L James, Sylvia Day and
Portia Da Costa.

BLACK
LACE